W9-BBA-942

SUNDOWN

Michael Zimmer

Walker and Company
New York

For my parents

First published in the United States of America in 1988 by the Walker Publishing Company, Inc.

Published simultaneously in Canada by Thomas Allen & Son Canada, Limited, Markham, Ontario.

Library of Congress Cataloging-in-Publication Data

Zimmer, Michael, 1955-
    Sundown / Michael Zimmer.
        p.   cm.
    ISBN 0-8027-4077-4
    I. Title.
[PS3576.I467S8 1988]
813'.54--dc19   87-33945
                                                        CIP

Printed in the United States of America

10 9 8 7 6 5 4 3 2 1

CHAPTER 1

LUKE Howard stood away from the others, his long, lanky frame lightly touching saddle leather, his right arm curled around the wide horn. He stood quiet, alert, with his head cocked slightly, listening for the first telltale sign of an approaching horse. The cool Nebraska night was clear but dark, freckled with a thousand tiny sparks of starlight, but moonless and deceiving. Below him, down the long, easy slope of the ridge, only the soft, nighttime lowing of the cattle convinced him that they had finally caught up with the rustlers.

Luke Howard was a slim man, with a slim man's sure, quick grace. He was thirty-one that summer of '76, with a lean, tanned face and light gray eyes the color of ash. He wore brown corduroy trousers over black boots, and small, plain spurs. His shirt was blue chambray, stained with sweat and trail dirt, and he wore a light, knee-length duster against the evening's chill. His hat was wide-brimmed and low-crowned, with a leather drawstring that hung against his throat. He carried a .44 Navy Colt snug against his right hip, and above the left was cocked the antler-slab grip of a short Bowie.

Behind and a little above him the others stood as he did, though grouped close, with their horses standing hipshot behind them like a stilled pinwheel. From time to time the erratic murmur of their voices would float down to him, as soft and indistinct as the shadows surrounding him, and only occasionally would Harper's bull-like voice rise enough for him to catch a word, and then never enough to grasp the drift of their conversation. It didn't matter. He could guess what they were talking about. The cattle, the soft glow of the

1

campfire ebbing into coals, and what they would likely face when they descended into the valley.

They had been on the trail nearly a week now, drawing gradually closer, and when they'd spotted the flickering light of the campfire from a distant ridge just after sunset, they'd decided to abandon the trail to chance. This far off the main road to Ogallala it seemed unlikely that the fire would belong to anyone but the men they followed. When they'd reined in half an hour before and heard the faint bellow of a steer, it seemed to clinch it. Still, to be sure, Sanchez had ridden on down alone to check the brands, humming softly as the darkness swallowed him and the paint mare he rode.

Saddle leather creaked behind Howard as the group broke apart. The near rider turned toward him, and he recognized Red's short, jaunty steps, the jingle of his spurs. Red halted nearby, mindful of the ill feelings that sometimes flared between his sorrel gelding and the short-coupled bay stud Howard rode, and careful to keep them apart.

"Wish that damn Mex would get back," Red said. "I need a smoke."

Howard smiled fleetingly but didn't reply.

After a moment, Red said, "You figure this is the bunch we're looking for?"

Howard shrugged in the dark. "Who else?"

Another short silence grew between them, and Howard was content to let it, but Red couldn't; he needed to talk, Howard knew, needed to relieve the tension building inside. "You don't figure he got himself caught, do you?"

Howard considered it a moment, then dismissed it. "Pete's too handy. Naw, he ain't caught. Just taking his time and doing it right."

Somewhere downslope a horses's shoe clipped a stone and they were all instantly alert. They fanned out just below the starlit rim, and the soft sounds of gun metal slipping free of leather and the gentle shifting of their horses were the only hints of their presence. They waited and watched until the faint image of a horse and rider took shape against the coal-colored sky and halted.

"What is this that I hear?" Sanchez called softly. "Five grown men quaking in their boots like the leaves on an aspen tree?"

Howard smiled then, seeing in his mind Pete Sanchez's dark face split in a wide, white grin; a short, wiry man in part Mexican, part American garb, forever playing with the ends of his reins.

"Goddamn." The word was as much a hiss as it was a whisper, and Howard's smile widened more as he holstered his Colt, the image of Barney Harper's churlishness against Sanchez's devil-may-care attitude washing away some of his nervousness.

Harper's shadow loomed out of the darkness, his hand going flat against the paint's shoulder. "Are they the ones we're looking for?" he asked in clipped tones. He was a big man, Harper was, and at fifty or thereabouts, he was starting to go heavy in the gut; he was surly as a spring bear most of the time, and just as quick to anger, but Howard knew that, like the others with their own quirks—his taut nerves, Red's need to talk and Sanchez's ill-timed humor—Harper would settle down when the time came. Like the others, he was a professional.

"*Si,*" Sanchez said, dismounting and leading his horse past Harper. "Mostly Bar-W stock, but I saw some Lazy-L and Broken Axle brands, too."

Luke Howard let his breath escape in a long, silent sigh, feeling the steady, hammering beat of his heart, and recognized it as normal. For a moment then, no one said anything, and he knew they were all experiencing the same emotions, each in his own way.

"What's the setup?" Harper asked suddenly.

"There are three of them, on the far side of the creek. They are all asleep. The horses are downstream, between the cattle and the camp. Four horses. One is a packhorse, I think."

"Okay," Harper grunted, and Howard watched his hat bob in the shadows as if he were approving his decisions as he made them. "Doc, get on down and keep an eye on the horses in case they slip past us somehow. Swede, you and Pete can take the far bank. Let Red and Luke handle the near side. I'll come in from upstream. Any questions?"

The silence was short; no one really expected any. "I'll give you thirty minutes to get into place, then I'll come in. Okay, let's go."

Howard drew away, looking down at what was left of the fire and knowing that by the time half an hour had passed, there wouldn't be much light left. "It's going to be dark," he said to no one in particular.

"Huh?" Red answered.

Howard looked around to find the others gone already. "Dark, I said. It's going to be dark down there."

Red shrugged, leaving the sorrel ground-tied and coming over next to Howard. "Be just as dark for them," he said casually. "Let's just do what we came for and go home."

Howard grunted, reaching across the saddle and sliding a brass-framed Henry rifle free of its scabbard. He started downslope on foot, alone, leaving Red to fetch his own rifle and catch up.

He walked rapidly over the rough ground, his spurs now and again snagging at the short growth of buffalo grass, but pulling free easily. Patches of prickly pear rose frequently, reflecting the faint starlight with a silvery sheen. He skirted them without notice, his attention riveted to the darkening embers of the campfire. He stopped finally, still several hundred feet from the near creek bank, sensing Red's hurried pace closing the gap behind him.

Red paused beside him, his gaze also on the coals. "You remember what Sanchez said? 'A packhorse, *I think.*' I hope to hell that cocky little sonofabitch didn't miss someone."

"Like a guard?"

"Seems likely."

It was something to consider, Howard thought. Sanchez was good, but only a cat could see in the dark. "They've been pushing pretty hard," he said doubtfully. "Could be they're just worn out."

"Maybe," Red grunted, but he cradled the stubby .56 Spencer close, as if he didn't believe it.

"Time's running out," Howard said. "Let's close in."

The prairie leveled out maybe sixty feet shy of the near bank, so their final approach was blind. They crawled the last few feet on their bellies, coming to the lip of the bank, about a dozen feet above a shallow pool of water. On their left the bank sloped steeply toward the creek bed. There was no real bank on the opposite side, the land just rose gradually toward the west, broken and rough. Scattered cottonwood and clumps of willow created some protection from the wind, and furnished fuel for the rustlers' fire as well. It was darker than Howard had anticipated, although the late-summer leaves of the cottonwood seemed to catch and reflect what light there was. A coffeepot sitting close to the coals still emitted a fresh aroma, and tack and gear were scattered haphazardly around it. The rustlers lay scattered around the fire, too, as if they'd spread their bedrolls wherever they'd dropped them. Canted out from one of the packs was the walnut sheen of a shotgun or rifle stock; it was the only weapon Howard saw. He thumbed the Henry's hammer back and aimed it loosely toward the man nearest the rifle.

Harper's appearance was sudden and surprising. Too soon, Howard thought, though he knew Barney wasn't the type to jump early. He had his Colt drawn and cocked, and his voice, breaking across the sleeping camp, seemed to shatter the night like an iron bar against fine crystal.

"Everybody to his feet," Harper shouted. "The first man to make a wrong move gets blown to hell and gone."

The figure on the far side of the fire rose and fired,

coming up as if he were spring-loaded and catching them all by surprise. White powder smoke blossomed with a roar from the rustler's revolver, and Harper spun away, clutching at his shoulder.

Howard swore and shouldered his rifle. The man on the far side of the fire, a kid, he saw, kicked free of his blankets and dropped to a crouch with a still-smoking muzzle of his revolver thrust before him. "Drop it, goddamnit," Howard yelled. The kid spun toward him and loosened a shot.

Howard swore and tipped his hat toward the spray of dirt from the kid's bullet, then swore again when the others dived for the cover of darkness, one of them dragging the rifle with him. Red's Spencer boomed beside him, deafening in its closeness, and Howard fired then, his bullet kicking up the coals of the fire, adding light to the confusion. The kid was still crouched above his blankets, and from the far darkness Howard heard the small, twin pops of revolvers, spitting out little bursts of muzzle flashes. The kid cried out hoarsely, twisting for a moment like a puppet caught in its own strings, then dropping limply into his bedroll.

Red's Spencer roared again, answered this time from behind a slanting cottonwood. Howard fired, tore bark from the cottonwood, heard the twin pop of revolvers again, and saw the rustler slump forward, the rifle slipping from his grasp, rattling down the trunk. From somewhere downstream they heard Doc's young voice, cracking shrilly in midsentence. Then silence settled over the campsite, and for the space of a minute, nobody moved.

"It's Doc," Red said then, nodding downstream with his chin. His voice seemed distant, muted, after the concussion of gunfire.

Howard watched Doc walk into camp, prodding a long-legged man in yellowed long johns ahead of him with his revolver.

"Let's go," Howard said, and scooted over the edge of the bank, sliding stiff-legged to the bottom and jumping the narrow pool. Red followed, and the others came into the light, converging on the old man held under Doc's gun. Harper was already by the fire, looking pallid and sheepish, the side of his shirt sodden with blood. He had his bandanna off, pressed tight against the wound.

Doc's prisoner stood on the opposite side of the fire from Harper, his eyes cast down to a spot of ground between his stockinged feet. He was an old man, on the far side of sixty, with thin gray hair and skin like burnt leather. His forehead, above the line of his hatbrim, was starkly white, in the manner of a man who seldom removed his hat.

They stood eyeing the old man silently, none of them liking what they saw, knowing what had to come. It was Howard who finally broke the silence, turning to Harper and saying, "You figure you'll live?"

Harper nodded, the arrogance suddenly taken out of him. Howard reached out and nudged the bandanna aside. A shallow trough of torn flesh was stretched across the meat of Harper's shoulder at the neck. The wound wasn't serious, but it was bleeding steadily and needed looking after.

"Doc?" Howard asked.

Doc nodded and holstered his revolver. He was an army brat, seventeen or so, the son of a widower surgeon, and had spent most of his few years knocking around the frontier from one post to another. Handy with medicine—his nickname was earned, not given—he carried a small, wooden case of medical supplies in his saddlebags.

Red added wood to the fire, building a blaze, while Sanchez wandered through the camp. He turned the kid in the blankets over and cursed softly. Moving to the other, he gave a muffled start of exclamation. "This one, he is alive," he said. Pulling his sombrero off, he leaned close, then frowned. "I think," he added then.

Keeping the Henry on the old man, Howard edged nearer. "You sure?" he asked sharply. "What do you mean, you think?"

Sanchez straightened slowly, letting his hand rest on the rustler's chest, and he shook his head. "He took a breath, this I saw, and moved his fingers. But now he is dead."

He looked bitter, Howard thought, and raising his eyes, his gaze locked with Swede's, dropped to the twin revolvers strapped around his waist, then rose again. Swede met his stare with a look of mild amusement, and a half-mocking smile tilted one corner of his mouth. "Fair shooting, I'd say," Swede offered. "Fifty yards or better, and poor light to boot."

Swede was a stranger among them yet, Howard thought; tall, cool and blonde, a killer, as mysterious now as when he had ridden in from nowhere two months before. No one knew his name, or where he hailed from, but they had learned quickly of his ruthlessness. Like an old, sore-with-age rattler, Swede was quick to lash out.

Howard looked away then, turning to the old man, demanding, "What's your name, old-timer? Where are you from?"

The old man ignored him, keeping his gaze on the ground. He had looked up, briefly, when Sanchez announced his partner still alive, but now seemed to have pulled into himself, shutting out those around him.

"His name doesn't matter," Swede said softly. "We won't take time to carve him a headstone."

"I reckon his name matters to someone," Doc said, looking up from his work on Harper's shoulder.

Swede ignored him, keeping his gaze on Howard. The antagonism had been growing between them for some time now, rootless in its source, and maybe nothing more than a natural dislike, yet growing toward a showdown, Howard knew. But not yet; it hadn't festered enough yet for that.

"Like Doc said, his name matters to someone," Howard said. "I'd like to give him a chance to speak."

The old rustler was looking up now, the meaning of their words finally penetrating. "Good Lord," he whispered, his eyes flitting from Howard to Swede and back again. "What are you talking about?"

"Hanging, old man," Swede replied, and his voice sounded hard, almost brittle. His eyes never left Howard's face, nor the smile his lips.

The rustler's eyes darted wildly, circling the men standing somberly around him. "You can't . . . you . . ." His voice broke, ceased.

Swede's smile was faint now, but mocking. "Tell him, Luke. Tell him what happens at sunup."

He brought his eyes open just as Swede's toe touched his ribs, coming awake to the predawn chill of the bottom ground, and Swede's silhouette against the growing light of the coming day.

"Come on, Howard. The show's about to begin," Swede said. There was an oddly anticipating lift to his words, as a child might use in describing a circus, and Howard wondered who he was trying to bait, him or the old rustler.

He pulled his hat and coat on, then kicked his blankets back and slipped into his boots. The rustler sat close to the fire, his legs pulled up to his chest and crossed at his ankles, his arms wrapped around his knees and his face tucked into them. Red hunkered farther out, bundled up in chaps and short sheepskin jacket, the Spencer cradled in his lap and a tin cup of coffee held in one gloved hand. The others were still wrapped in their blankets, though coming awake as Swede moved among them, prodding them with his boot.

Luke pulled his cup free of his saddlebags and helped himself to a cup from the pot set in the embers, then moved off to stand stiff-kneed and rigid, his back to the fire. From the sound, the others were doing the same, preferring the damp, chilly air of the creek to the comfort of the fire, where the presence of the old man seemed to dominate.

The sky was rosy in the east now, the sun only moments from cresting the rim of the prairie, and the dew-wet grass along the creek seemed to sparkle. The coffee was hot and just short of bitter, but it warmed him all the way down, radiating its heat like a healthy shot of whiskey. He finished the cup and threw the dregs on the ground, dreading the next few minutes as much as he had ever dreaded anything in his life, yet feeling compelled to see it through.

"Sun's up," Swede said.

They turned reluctantly back to the fire and ranged themselves in a half circle before the rustler. He looked up uncertainly, his old, sun-faded eyes red from lack of sleep. He looked tiny, sitting there before them, frail and frightened and whipped, too, the fight all taken out of him, and it struck Howard then that if they let him go he'd likely scamper on home and never rustle again, that hanging him now would be less a deterrent than it would be murder. Yet raising his eyes, he saw Swede watching him, and with something of a start, knew that Swede saw in the old man what he did. But Swede wanted to kill—or punish, and the difference was slight to him.

"What's your name, old-timer?" Harper asked. Given a night of rest, he was back in the saddle again, quick to take charge.

The old man sighed and shook his head. "Don't matter none," he said. "Don't matter to nobody no more."

"You have friends somewhere?" Harper persisted.

He snorted and looked at the open grave they had dug the night before. His two partners rested there now, wrapped in blankets. "Onliest friends there, 'cept . . ." He dropped his head and shook it again.

Gruffly then, Harper said, "Let's get this over with. Doc, string up a rope. Red, saddle the old man's horse."

Doc and Red turned quickly to their jobs, grateful, perhaps, for the opportunity to get away from the fire. Harper looked at Sanchez and said quietly, "Pete, go cut me a switch, will you? I guess I'll be doing that."

Sanchez nodded and headed for a clump of willows upstream, drawing a jackknife from a pocket of his jacket as he did. Only Howard and Harper and Swede were still at the fire when the old man began to talk.

"It was a mistake. It was all a mistake," he said in a low voice, staring into the fire. "But times are hard and we needed a stake."

"You don't make money off another man's sweat," Swede said.

"But I'm an old man," he said desperately, pleading for the first time. He looked up then, staring at Harper, then Howard. "I never broke a law in my life before this. I got . . . I . . ." He choked, looked at the fire, then up again. "I got an old woman waiting for me," he said, so quietly Howard had to lean forward to hear him. "Got an old woman, but no kids to care for her. Only me." He choked, or sobbed, and repeated, "Only me."

Howard looked at Harper, but the big man kept his gaze on a far ridge. Looking at Swede, he saw the contempt in his cold eyes, the light, mocking smile on his lips. "Rustling's a hanging offense out here, old man," Swede said. "You knew that."

"Everybody's rustling Sand Creek beef," the old man argued. "Mining camps in the Hills are full of it."

"Maybe it's time we let folks know what happens to cow thieves on the Sand Creek range," Harper replied gently.

"Take me back for a jury trial, then. God's sake, you can't just string me up like you was judge and jury rolled into one."

They were, though, Howard thought. Like it or not.

"We're ready," Doc called from beneath a cottonwood. The noose swung in a gentle breeze above his hat like some kind of a boyish prank, seeming almost obscene for it. Red held a long-legged gray gelding nearby, and Swede reached down suddenly and hauled the old man roughly to his feet. He pulled the old man's arms high behind his back and lashed them together with a piece of rawhide. The old man whimpered suddenly, his knees buckling, and Swede jerked him back with the rawhide.

"Shut up," Swede said harshly. "Don't make this any harder on yourself than you have to."

No chance to stop it now, Howard thought bitterly. The decision to start hanging rustlers had been reached some weeks before by the Sand Creek Cattlemen's Association. Any choice had been lifted from Howard's hands then.

The old man was jerking against the rawhide, his voice gone suddenly shrill. "Don't make this any harder on you is what you mean," he cried.

Swede brought his knee up sharply, driving it into the old man's buttocks, sending him tumbling into Howard's arms.

"Goddamnit, that's enough," Barney said angrily. "There's no call to manhandle him like that."

The old man twisted around to look at Swede, his eyes filled with terror. Howard could feel the hammering of the old man's heart through his coat. "Get him on his horse," Swede said flatly. Howard let the old man go, stepping back from the rustler, but Swede turned abruptly away. Harper came around the fire and took the old man's arm, guiding him to the gray. With the old rustler mounted, Red led the gray to the cottonwood.

Doc climbed up behind the old man and slipped the noose around his neck, then slid off. Sanchez handed Harper the switch, then stepped back, his usually cheerful look gone cold sober. Harper held the switch close to his leg and moved around to look up at the old man's face. "This is a goddamn hard country, old-timer," he said. "I'm sorry as hell about your woman, but we've got to do this. Give me her name and I'll see she gets your things."

The old rustler laughed softly and said, "Don't fret yourself, son. Just get about what you got to do. You'll toughen up to it by the time anybody stops this rustling."

Harper breathed deeply and stepped back. He looked around at the others, then slowly raised the switch. Howard flinched at the sharp *pop* of the old rustler's neck.

CHAPTER 2

RED reined his sorrel in at a point halfway up the side of the ridge and stood in his stirrups to ease the ache along his lean, sweaty shanks. He was a short man, broad in the chest and shoulders, clean-shaven and younger looking than his twenty-seven years. Quick and easygoing for the most part, he was steady enough when the need arose. He had short, curly red hair that would grow into a tight tangle if he didn't keep it cropped close, bright blue eyes, and a pug nose he hated. His nose and niggers were about all he really hated with a passion, and of the two, he figured his nose was something he couldn't do much about. Darkies were another matter though, and when on the subject he was adamant, almost radical. He had developed his hate early, in Virginia, had nurtured it punching cows around east Texas, had let it swell through the years since. A man who knew him usually avoided the matter altogether, and it was something Red never brought up himself. Like a reformed drunk, he was a man who knew his weaknesses.

Below him the cattle, eighty-plus head, moved sluggishly across a wide valley like a short, dusty stream, a patchwork of reds and grays and blacks floating below an upthrust of speckled snouts and needle-tipped horns. Those were Texas longhorns, mostly—though here and there he spotted the shorter, chunkier bodies of those crossbred with some of the new Eastern breeds. They'd been brought up the trail from Texas, most of them, brought up when free grass was opened in Nebraska. The ranchers had come up the trail together. Jim Young's Broken Axle; Ben Wyatt's giant Bar-W, which stretched in a forty mile crescent around the west side of

Sand Creek; Roscoe Plumb's Crooked Arrow; and the others.
Together, they'd settled the land around Sand Creek when it
had been no more than a wide spot in the road, a hide town
of crude huts and dugouts, clearing away the bones and
building their ranches. They'd been a ragtag group back
then, Red knew, coming up in ancient, patched wagons,
riding gaunt horses and pushing half-wild longhorns, standing mostly on pride. Those first years had been long and
lean, but the hard work gradually paid off. The shantytown
that was Sand Creek began to change too, as the buffalo
thinned out and finally disappeared. Plank buildings began
to replace the sod, and the riffraff that seemed to thrive in
the lawlessness of a hide town gave way to honest merchants.
Sand Creek grew with the ranches. Its very existence de-
pended upon the cattle business. When the ranches hurt,
Sand Creek hurt—and the ranches were hurting bad in 1876.

Custer's discovery of gold in the Black Hills had flooded
that land with people. Thousands of men and women had
swarmed into those cool, gold-rich valleys, raping the land
for its wealth. Lodging was primitive and usually hastily built.
Men worked around the clock, by sunlight and lantern light,
caught in the grip of gold fever. Food was more of a necessity
than a luxury; bear or venison was the usual fare, and if it
could be supplemented with withered vegetables or wrinkled
potatoes, it was considered a treat. Beef, lean and succulent,
brought premium prices.

Sand Creek lay south and east of the Hills, only a few days'
ride, and the temptation for men with long ropes and empty
bellies had proven too much. The rustling had been light at
first, and not particularly alarming. Yet as the months passed,
the rustling had increased. It wasn't a matter of a few head
taken to feed a camp anymore. It was bigger, hungrier,
almost as if it had taken on some kind of organization.
Eventually, the problem had grown large enough, desperate
enough, that the Cattlemen's Association had decided to
bring in professional help.

Word had spread quickly that guns were needed in Nebraska, and the response had been swift. Barney Harper was hired within a week, and the rest of them had joined him within the month.

Now, sitting his sorrel in the afternoon sunshine, Red thought they were still no closer to stopping the rustling than they had been when he had first ridden into Sand Creek early that spring. There was something of a rhythm to it, he thought, the way bunches would turn up missing, and sometimes seemingly from right beneath their noses. Fifty to a hundred head every few weeks, and if they recovered two herds out of three they were doing good. Still, it was a problem too big to get a loop around, and he shook his head, as if in doing so he could shake the problem from his mind. Below him, a rider broke from the herd to lope toward him, and he recognized Doc's roan, kicking up a swirl of grasshoppers as it passed through the dusty grass.

"Red," Doc greeted, reining in beside him. "Thought maybe you'd found yourself a piece of cool air and was hogging it to yourself."

"You'll get all the cool air you want after the sun drops."

"Ain't it the truth," Doc said, grinning.

"You're looking as pleased as a preacher with a full house," Red observed. "What's up?"

"Barney says we'll drop the herd on the other side of Twin Buttes, then head on into town."

"That," Red replied, "is something to grin about."

"Let's prod these cows on a little. Me and Howard want to stop off at the Tanks and scrape away a couple of layers of trail dirt."

This late in the summer, the Tanks were only a pair of shallow, muddy pools in the center of a wide basin, separated by the sun-bleached timbers of a slowly revolving windmill. Around the windmill the ground was churned into a thick, sucking goo from the hooves of cattle and the occasional bands of wild horses that drank there. Antelope tracks haunted the perimeter, as did those of smaller animals—badgers and prairie dogs and coyotes and such. Farther out, the earth was caked hard and white, cracked and curled up like an old shoe from the sun, and beyond, where the sparse growth of dusty buffalo grass rimmed the high-water mark, ankle-deep trails radiated outward like crooked spokes in a sun-warped wagon wheel.

There was a pair of gray-with-age wooden barrels beneath the windmill, planked off to keep the cattle away. The water was pumped here first, before running off into the Tanks. The barrels were always full, their insides slick with algae, but the water was fresh and cool and clear enough to see the bottom of the barrel when the sun was right.

Howard leaned back against his bedroll and hooked a knee around his saddlehorn. Pulling a crumpled cheroot from the breast pocket of his shirt, he smoothed it along his thigh and lit it with a grimace. Red peeled down with Doc and crawled into a barrel, sucking his breath in sharply at the cold. Doc went into his barrel fast, his eyes widening at the shock, hooting and swearing in the same breath. On top of his bay, Howard laughed.

Doc bathed quickly, using a slim bar of yellow lye soap someone had left on the windmill's lower brace and touching only the high spots. Climbing out, he balanced on a narrow board that tipped and swayed in the mud as he dressed, then jumped through the mud to his horse and vaulted into his saddle. Grinning at Howard, he said, "Slow as a mud turtle, ain't he?" and pointed with his chin toward Red.

"He don't mustard, for a fact," Howard agreed.

Doc whirled his roan, bringing his head up but holding him back. "I'll save you a place at Goff's," he called. "But I won't promise you anything to drink if you poke along too slow." With a yell then, he spurred his horse to a gallop.

Red stood, the water sluicing down his broad chest. The sun was down now, and dusk was spreading like smoke over the basin. In the silence they could hear the drumming of Doc's roan for some time after they lost sight of him.

"Everybody's in a hurry anymore," Howard said.

"Sign of the times," Red replied, thinking of the frenzy taking place in the Black Hills. Dressed, he settled onto a patch of dry earth beneath the windmill and hung his hat on his knee. With the sun down, the air had a sudden chill to it that felt pleasant after the hammering heat of the day. He dug the makings from a shirt pocket and began to shape a cigarette, his fingers slow but sure, and his eyes off elsewhere. From the water barrel, Howard was making small, splashing sounds, scrubbing with a slow deliberation that told Red his mind was elsewhere. With the old rustler, likely, he thought.

They had ridden together before, he and Luke, hunting shaggies down along the Canadian for a season and a half, until the Comanche had turned too troublesome to make the profit worth the risk. They'd had some good times back then, both of them being younger and more reckless, yet even then Howard had been some peculiar. He was the kind who could never let go completely, could never abandon it all to chance. He could look at a problem from both sides and see the other man's point of view as easily as his own, and sometimes was crazy enough to think the other man right and himself wrong. Like as not, if that was the case, he'd back off and give the other the go-on. It was an admirable trait in its way, Red admitted, but not always practical. Not living the way he did, with his gun. Like now, Red thought, knowing he was still thinking of the old man, and maybe the boys they'd caught and strung up on the Niobrara only a few weeks before, too. Red wondered how Howard could let it all eat at him like that, as if he could have done anything different from what he had. Cautiously then, he said, "How do you feel about the old man, Luke?"

Even in the shadows, he could see the pain on Howard's face, and knew that his guess had been correct. "A job's a job," Howard said harshly. "It could get a lot dirtier before it's over."

Red shrugged. "Might've been easier if he wasn't so old," he said. "Or the boys so young."

Howard didn't answer, and Red hid his irritation behind his cigarette. It was like Luke, he thought, bottling it in when another might need to talk it all out, so as to put it behind him. Not too far in the east a pack of coyotes set up a sudden, excited clamoring, and he figured they'd jumped a rabbit.

"I've been drifting more than twelve years," Howard said unexpectedly. "Hiring out to any man or company that needed a gun and never asking too many questions or making up my own mind as to what might be right or wrong. Hell, just passing through, it never seemed to matter." He hesitated, as if feeling his way along uncertain ground, but Red sensed that whatever he was thinking had been with him a while. "Seems like a man ought to settle down after a bit," Howard continued finally. "Seems like he ought to have his own place, someplace to hang his hat besides his saddle-horn." Quietly then, "He ought to know when to quit."

Howard's words didn't surprise Red, and thinking about it now, he wondered why he hadn't seen them coming. It wasn't a foreign thought, even to himself. "I've thought about it," he admitted quietly. "The others have, too, unless I miss my guess. All except Doc, maybe."

"Doc's young yet. Just a kid. Me, I'll be thirty-two come fall. That's too old to drift, Red."

"Barney's fifty, or thereabouts," Red said.

"Barney's got no more than I have right now. A horse, saddle, his weapons. Ought to be more in life than that."

"You want a place of your own," Red said softly. "Knowing you, you'll want a ranch. That takes money."

Howard ducked under, rinsing the soap off, then bobbed up and scrambled out. "I've got a few dollars tucked away in Denver. Plus what I'll make here. It'll be a start. More than the people around here had when they came up from Texas."

"They had each other," Red said. "A gunny doesn't always have those kind of friends." Quietly he added, "A gunny usually doesn't have any friends."

"A gunny ain't but a couple of steps short of a bush-whacker, Red, and I'm neither. I'm a troubleshooter. A problem solver."

They walked to their horses together, and Red tightened the sorrel's cinch, looking across the saddle at Howard. He said, "You're a steady hand, Luke, and I reckon I'd just as soon ride the river with you as any man I know, but we're both guns for hire, and out here folks figure any type of a gunfighter is a gunny. It's just something that comes with the territory."

Red swung into the saddle, and Howard into his, and they rode off at a walk toward Sand Creek. With the tanks behind them, Howard said, "A name's a name, I guess, and I've been branded with worse, but when this job's over . . ." He let the words trail off, and Red didn't push him further. He guessed he knew where Howard was headed.

It had been full dark for some time when they finally jogged their horses down the wide expanse of the business district, dodging a cluster of freight outfits camped in front of the Lone Oak Livery and reining up in the center of the street. Goff's Saloon was on their left, spilling yellow light and the tinny music of a piano onto the street. Farther down, the wide double doors of the Frontier House stood open, and even from half a block away Red could smell the enticing aroma of good home cooking. His stomach grumbled its emptiness.

"Looks like Clark is still open," Howard said, and Red spotted the flicker of lamplight toward the rear of the general store. "Let's see what kind of credit we've got coming before he closes for the night."

They tied up at the rail, and Howard knocked on the glass. Clark himself opened the door. "Been expecting you two," he said, stepping back to allow their entry.

"If you were expecting us, then Barney and the others must have already been in?"

"An hour ago," Clark said. He moved behind the counter and lit another lamp. "You boys have ten dollars worth of credit apiece for the gear they brought in."

Red frowned. "That gear was worth a hell of a lot more than sixty dollars."

Clark bristled and folded his arms above the heavy swell of his stomach. "That's all I'm allowing. I don't usually buy stolen merchandise."

Clark's words hit him hard, and Red swayed back as if the air next to the counter had become too thick to breathe. Then he leaned forward, blinking against the red haze of his anger. "I don't think I heard you right," he said tightly.

"You heard right," Clark whispered hoarsely. Perspiration beaded his forehead and he was blinking rapidly, but he didn't look away or change his words.

"It's all right," Howard said, his hand resting lightly on Red's shoulder. "Let's get what we need and forget it."

Red shook his hand away. "Like hell," he breathed. He stepped backed and brushed his coat back, his hand curling around the butt of the Peacemaker without actually touching it. Hunched, he felt hot but ready.

"Let it drop, Red," Howard said sharply. He lifted his hand, yet stopped short of touching him. He said, "Red, he doesn't even have a gun!"

The door swung open then, the bell above it jangling loudly in the charged air, and a sharp, authoritative voice broke the stalemate. "Back off, Red! Back off or face me."

Bronson.

Red let his arm go limp and turned slowly to face the Sand Creek Marshal. Sam Bronson was a large man, taller even than Harper, who stood something over six feet, but he was slimmer through the waist and hips. Something of a dandy, he was given to fancy suits of broadcloth or buckskins elaborately beaded and fringed. He wore his strawberry blond hair long and brushed back over his shoulders, and kept his mustache waxed and curled up toward his eyes. He was wearing his buckskins tonight, with a pair of ivory-handled revolvers jutting from a wide, red sash wrapped around his waist.

"This doesn't concern you, Bronson. Back on out and let it be."

Bronson's smile was thin, dangerous. Though a dandy in dress, he was fast, Red knew, and capable. Red straightened slowly, cautiously, and hooked his thumbs over the buckle of his gunbelt, forcing a cocky grin he didn't feel. Bronson's own smile disappeared then, and his face hardened. Looking to Clark, he said, "What's going on in here?"

"Man's trying to steal from us, Marshal," Red offered amiably. "Reckon you ought to haul him across the street and lock him up for us."

Bronson ignored him and kept his gaze on Clark. "Barney Harper and the Mex brought in a bunch of gear," Clark explained. "Saddles and blankets and rifles and such. A murdered man's outfit, I'd guess. I don't like to deal in that type of merchandise as a rule, but I went ahead and offered them sixty dollars for it all. Now this one wants more." He indicated Red with his chin.

Red said, "Your conscience going to bother you that much when you price it, Clark?"

The shopkeeper glared at him but held his tongue. Bronson looked at Luke and asked, "Was Harper acting for all of you when he brought this gear in?"

Howard nodded, and Red had to fight to keep his grin wide and in place. It was like Howard, he thought, to take another man's side against his own kind. Bronson looked at him and said, "Best back off, Red. Or deal with me first."

"Sure," Red said, nodding jerkily. "Sure." He looked at

Clark, the grin never fading, and said, "Give what credit I have coming to ol' Luke here, seeing as you two see the same on it." He nodded once to Bronson, then slipped outside, his smile disappearing as the door closed. Taken like a couple of rubes, he thought bitterly. He wished now they'd buried the damn gear rather than bringing it in to give to Clark.

The door opened behind him and Bronson stepped outside, followed by Howard. "Hold up, Red," Bronson called.

Bronson stepped to the edge of the boardwalk, Howard still following. After a brief pause Red joined them. "What happened out there?" Bronson asked abruptly.

"Reckon you know," Howard replied, and Red wished he could see Bronson's face, could penetrate the shadows of his beaver-felt Stetson and watch the slow flush of anger climb his face.

"I reckon I do. Some of the townspeople are already in an uproar about it. Hanging a man then bragging about it seems in bad taste. It's not the kind of reputation Sand Creek wants."

"Who's bragging about it?" Howard asked flaly.

"Harper."

Red snorted softly. Harper was the type, with a few drinks under his belt.

"The ranches around here are bleeding, Bronson," Howard retorted. "Your uproar is going to seem damn mild if the ranchers start to go under."

"Everyone is aware of the trouble on the range. It's the vigilante methods they are objecting to."

"We're doing the job we were hired to do," Red said. "We're stopping the rustling. Or at least we're trying."

"Your job?" Bronson tipped forward at the waist, and Red could feel the heat of his gaze. "Boy, I'm not even sure you have a job, legally speaking. I damn sure know you don't have the right to hang a man, whether you catch him rustling or not. There are laws to deal with that."

Red's anger swelled and he clenched his fists, then let them slowly unfurl. He had killed a man once for calling him boy.

"Whose laws?" Howard asked sharply. "Yours? The army's? Neither one of you seemed interested until we were hired."

"U.S. Marshal," Bronson replied. "We've had him up before. We can get him up again."

"He didn't stop it before," Howard said pointedly.

"Man can only be in one place at a time. This is a big country. The point you boys need to remember is that the law can work both ways. Next time you catch up with some rustlers, you bring them in and we'll ship them down to Ogallala and let the courts take care of it. You keep stringing up every man you find with someone else's cows, we might be shipping *you* down to Ogallala."

"You can always try," Red invited.

Bronson looked at him, and in the shadows Red saw the narrow glint of white teeth. "Yes, I can if I have to.'"

"Do something about the rustling, Bronson," Howard said. "Either handle it yourself or keep out of the way of those who will."

"My jurisdiction ends at city limits," Bronson replied calmly. "I'm not pulling you boys off the job. Let's just call it professional courtesy from someone who likes to see things roll smoothly."

Red wrinkled his nose. "Did someone fart?"

The glint of Bronson's smile disappeared. "Gentlemen, believe me, if I had the authority to do so I'd have you all packed in chains and on your way to Ogallala right now." He seemed on the verge of saying more, but spun abruptly instead, and plunged down the steps and across the street.

Howard laughed softly, stepping to the edge of the boardwalk to watch him. "That pompous sonofabitch," he said quietly, but with something like wonder in his voice, too.

"I hope he does," Red said in a low voice. "I hope the bastard tries to put us in chains." His hand swung back, brushed the hardwood butt of the Peacemaker holstered at his side.

CHAPTER 3

HOWARD sat on the top rail of the corral and studied the dozen or so horses that milled listlessly next to the hayrack. Solid colors mostly, bays and blacks and sorrels, and only a few lighter colors. His own bay had raised his head and nickered from a nearby corral when Howard had approached, but he opted for a Broken Axle mount instead. The bay had earned some time off.

He spotted the dun mare Jim Young had recommended as a rim rocker—muscled, surefooted, with good wind and endurance. She'd go a long way without raising a lather, and although he usually found mares to be somewhat flighty, he decided to trust the rancher's opinion of his own stock.

He dropped into the corral and shook out a loop, easing through the saddle band with his arm out and down, ready for the toss. The dun, sensing his approach, swung her rear end toward him, then broke to the left. Howard flipped his loop just as her front legs curled for a canter, dropping it neatly over her head. Like any good cow pony, she stopped at the touch of the rope.

Sanchez was waiting at the tack shed, his own mare already saddled. "You are tired of the bunkhouse already?"

Howard smiled. "Got a lot of thoughts running maverick in my mind, Pete. Thought a ride might let me sort a few out."

"I had saddled my own horse to do the same when I saw you in the corral, and I wondered if you might need some company."

"Not needed, but welcome."

Howard saddled the dun, shucking the Henry and hand-ing it to Sanchez while leading the mare clear of the buildings. Being a cow horse by breeding, she already had a kink in her back. He pulled his hat tighter and stepped into the saddle, letting the dun drop her head and take half a dozen easy bucks before pulling her up. It had been a while since he had topped a horse off, his bay being too gentle-natured for such foolishness.

It was past midmorning and already hot as they rode north, in the general direction of Sand Creek but angling east, away from town. The sky was a velvet blue, cluttered with tiny wisps of clouds that skimmed high overhead, and the wind, gusting now and again from the west, teased at the manes and tails of their horses.

They rode fast, pushing some, and shortly after noon came to the edge of the sandhill country, a broken region of low, dense hills and sandy draws, and covered with a coarse fur of buffalo grass and cactus. In the spring, when the grass was green and the wild flowers bloomed, the hills looked like something from an artist's brush. But now, in the waning days of summer, the tawny hills seemed to surround them like a wall, dry and hot and empty of life.

It was a deceiving impression, Howard knew. There was water enough, scattered about but easy to find, with stands of cottonwood and box elder for shelter. And wildlife in abundance—antelope and mule deer and a few small bands of mustangs, and coyotes enough to disturb the dead with their constant yipping through the long nights. Some said there were still a few buffalo deep within the sandhills, though Howard had never met a man who had seen any. It was good cattle country, though, even if most of the ranchers did try to keep their herds from penetrating too deeply. It was a bone-breaking job trying to haze a herd out come roundup. Still, it was impossible to keep small bunches from slipping through, scattering into a thousand twisting draws where they turned as wild as deer over the years.

Howard and Sanchez rode slowly, searching for nothing in

particular, each lost in his own thoughts. At midafternoon they rested in the scant shade of a cutbank and smoked a cigarette apiece in lieu of a noon meal. They had angled deep into the hills by now, well off the Sand Creek range, although they still spotted an occasional stray sporting one brand or another. "We have come far this day, and still I do not know what we are looking for," Sanchez said.

"Answers."

Sanchez smiled. "Always looking for the answers, eh? Myself, I have seen nothing all day, and it will be dark before we get back to the Broken Axle."

Howard picked up a handful of sand and let it run through his fingers. Locusts hummed in the grass, and nearby the jingle of the dun's bit made a small, merry melody as she grazed. They were the only sounds. He hadn't really expected to find anything today, but now that night was drawing close he found himself unwilling to give up the search. "What lies north of here, Pete? Do you know?"

"The badlands, I think. Maybe six hours away yet, maybe eight or ten, I do not know for sure. Very rough country. Nobody ranges cattle near there, and it is on the way to nowhere."

"Group of men wanted to hide out nearby without anyone knowing about it, that might be a good spot."

Sanchez shook his head. "Even without poking around as we have, they would be almost a day's ride from Sand Creek range. That is too far away to keep an eye on the ranches, and what part of the country they are working. If they are smart enough to always pick a herd that will not be missed for several days, they must be close. The badlands, they are too far away."

There was truth enough in his words, Howard thought, or at least about the uncanny way the rustlers had of always picking an unprotected herd. It was too big and too steady to be chance operations—owlhoots riding the night trails— yet he knew that a group of men couldn't just turn up missing for the time it would take to push a herd into the Hills either; Sand Creek was too small for that. There had to be someone behind it, someone local perhaps.

"What if they've got someone working with them?" Howard said slowly. "Someone right in Sand Creek, maybe, who doesn't go on the drives, but knows the ranges well enough?"

Sanchez chuckled. "I work with a detective. But I think not. The kind of man you are talking about would have to be important enough that he would not have to account for his time. A businessman, maybe, but what businessman would prosper from the collapse of the ranchers? And who would have this"—he tapped his forehead with his fingers—"the *inteligencia* to run such an operation?"

"Sam Bronson." Howard let the name drop like a stone in a quiet pool of water, and Sanchez's smile slipped, then disappeared.

Bronson's position as a lawman had always left him above suspicion. His actions, though often arrogant, had always been those of a dedicated Marshal. Yet there was much about the Sand Creek lawman that defied the office of a small-town Marshal. His clothing was just a little too fine for a fifty-dollar-a-month working man. His meals were usually taken at the Nebraska Hotel, slightly more elegant and considerably more expensive than the Frontier House. And although he wasn't conspicuous as a gambler, word around the bunk-house was that there were nights when he lost as much as twenty dollars at the tables. High stakes for any man on a salary.

"That is an interesting thought," Sanchez said. "Do you maybe have some reason to suspect him?"

Howard shook his head. In fact, apart from suspicions, he had nothing. Bronson's veiled threats of the night before might have been no more than a politician's efforts to soothe troubled waters. Yet they could easily serve the dual purpose of adding pressure to an already explosive situation, keeping the ranchers and the citizens of Sand Creek at each other's throats while the rustlers worked around the edges, snipping away at bits and pieces of everyone's livelihood.

"I think the man we should see is Ben Wyatt," Sanchez said suddenly, and Howard agreed. The Bar-W was easily the largest ranch on the Sand Creek range; Ben Wyatt's influence had spread even farther. He was known in Denver and Cheyenne, and his political weight was felt as far away as the state capital. If anyone would have access to Bronson's background, it would be Wyatt. In the meantime, he and Sanchez could poke around Sand Creek. If Bronson was spending more money than the town was paying him, Howard wanted to know where it was coming from.

Sanchez gathered his reins and tightened the cinch. "Will you be coming?" he asked.

"Uh, uh. You're probably right about the badlands being too far away for a hideout, but I want to ride up that way and look around a little anyway."

"You will not get back before late tomorrow, or the next day. Do you have food?"

"Hardtack and water from my canteen. I've made do with less."

Sanchez dug into his saddlebags and brought out a small bundle wrapped in brown waxed paper. "Jerky," he said. "It will help."

Howard took the meat and nodded his thanks. Sanchez mounted and turned away, lost from sight within minutes. After stowing the jerky away, Howard stepped into the saddle and turned the dun north. He didn't agree with Sanchez's opinion that the badlands were too far away. To him, it seemed a process of elimination. The sandhill country had been handy but less than promising once he had spent some time exploring it. The chance of accidental discovery by some far-riding cowhand was too great, the opportunity for concealment over any period of time too small. Shelter would be next to nonexistent, excepting those areas where timber and water were available, and those spots were too well known to the neighboring ranches.

But the badlands seemed to offer everything the sandhill country didn't. Although not as impregnable as those in the Dakotas, nor as far-flung, they did offer grass, timber and water. And perhaps as important as anything, it was the last place he could think of where a group of men could hide with any safety.

Howard didn't reach the badlands until shortly before noon the next day. He circled the perimeter to the east for a ways, until he found a likely-looking arroyo leading toward the interior. He followed this for a mile or so, climbing several hundred feet before finding a way out. From there he rode across an easy slope, angling upward to cross a narrow saddle between a pair of rocky peaks. He paused there, staring out across the unforgiving land, the sight taking his breath away.

Narrow, broken peaks rose around him, separated by a confusion of merging canyons, sheer bluffs, and steep, rock-studded hills. Scrawny pine, cedar and piñon clung to the flinty soil, adding color to the rugged landscape, highlighting the various hues of red and tan earth. The wind was stronger here than it had been in the lower country, and it bent the brim of his hat back and swept the dun's short tail away from her. He faced it, squinting his eyes and sniffing the air for any trace of wood smoke, but detected nothing. With the ever-changing currents of air shifting through the numerous canyons, that didn't surprise him.

He rode on, taking any trail that looked promising, keeping his eyes to the ground and searching for sign as much as he did the surrounding country. He camped that night next to a shallow pool scummed with the trash of wind and woke cold, hungry and stiff the next morning. He spotted antelope tracks in the soft soil on the far side of the pond, and later the broken hoofprint of a crippled mustang, but that was all.

He found his way out almost twenty-four hours after he had entered, only a dozen miles from the arroyo where he had begun, and realized sinkingly that he had only explored a small corner of that wild land. It would take several days to comb the interior thoroughly, yet it was a challenge he was willing to accept. But not now. Now, he turned his back wearily on the badlands and lifted the dun into a shuffling jog.

He topped the last low hill at sunset and put the mare into a lope while the sky in the west turned to vermilion. He slowed as he entered Sand Creek, walking the dun as far as the Lone Oak Livery. Anse wasn't around when he entered, so he led the horse back and put her in a stall, dropping his tack in a pile outside the door.

At the Frontier House he ordered steak and potatoes and stewed turnips, and afterward drank three cups of coffee laced with honey. He lit a cheroot with his second cup, and sat back and listened to the muted, homey rattle of pots and pans from the kitchen. Dusk settled in the street and faded swiftly into full dark. The great, overriding weariness he had felt since the hanging began to oddly ebb away, the way smoke did in a windless sky. It felt good to be back; Sand Creek, in the months he had been here, seemed almost like home now, something familiar if not entirely friendly. It was, he thought, as much as he had a right to ask for, and he was content to sit awhile, to relax and enjoy what he had.

He finished the cigar on the boardwalk, propped against a veranda post with his ankles crossed and watching traffic pass. A gunshot roared from down the street, echoing among the tall, false-fronted buildings, and the sharp bark of drunken laughter drew his attention toward Goff's. There were probably forty-some horses hitched to the rails along the front and side of the saloon; a small crowd of men stood on the boardwalk in front of the batwing doors, their voices loud and occasionally obscene. The off-tune thumping of the piano was almost drowned by their racket.

From a distance, away from the shouting and shoving, the

saloon looked alive and on the jump, inviting in its way, and Howard suddenly flicked the cheroot into the street, eager to be a part of a crowd again. It wasn't, he knew, the only reason he wanted to stop off at Goff's, but it would do for now.

He crossed the street and pushed his way through the crowd at the door. The place was packed, maybe forty or fifty men jammed around the poker and faro tables, and the press at the bar was elbow to hat brim. Smoke clung in ropy tatters to the ceiling above the big overhead lamps, and the sawdust under his boots felt gummy and in need of changing. The half-raw aroma of sweat, whiskey, and tobacco was something a man could almost get his hands around.

Howard took a spot at the bar, letting his gaze rake the crowd as he did. Disappointment crossed his face as he put his back to the room and propped his foot against the bar rail.

Isaac Goff came down the business side of the bar in his quick, rolling gait. He was a big man, not particularly tall, but broad throughout, and solid, the kind of man who carried his weight well. He usually dressed in fine tailored suits, and wore linen shirts with narrow string ties knotted loosely but neatly at his collar. He had his own table near the rear of the room, where he occasionally presided over various games of chance with stakes sometimes as high as a hundred dollars. Seeing him behind the bar tonight, an apron stretched across his wide girth and his face sheened with perspiration, gave Howard something of a start.

Goff stopped before him, his eyes showing no recognition. "What'll you have?" he asked.

"Where's Eddie?" Howard asked, meaning Goff's usual bartender.

"Black Hills, the sonofabitch. Left me shorthanded on the busiest night of the month. Today was payday on the ranches."

Howard nodded. There had been a noticeable drop in

Sand Creek's population over the summer. It seemed like everyone had gold fever anymore.

"It's a busy night," Goff said impatiently.

Howard laughed. "Give me rye."

Goff pulled a bottle and glass from the rear shelf and poured. Howard tossed a dime on the bar and took his drink in his hand, putting his back to the bar and hooking his elbows over it. There were a lot of punchers around the room, loud and mostly drunk, all of them dressed in their gaudy best. He nodded to a couple of Broken Axle hands and they looked away uncomfortably. He sighed then, turning back to the bar. The town's animosity was spreading, and while that didn't surprise him, it saddened him some. It would add new tension to the Broken Axle bunkhouse, and strain the enmity already felt between the townspeople and the six range riders. It wasn't a personal thing, Howard knew, but only a need to place blame . . . somewhere.

There was a small tug on his sleeve, and he turned then to find Charity standing beside him with a half-questioning smile on her lips, though her eyes for a moment looked uncertain.

"Charity." It was all he said, but it was enough.

Doubt faded from her eyes and her smile widened. "Hello, cowboy. Why the smile like the cat in an empty canary cage?"

He shrugged, embarrassed, and not sure why. "Because I'm happy, I guess." It sounded foolish even to his own ears, but she didn't seem to mind.

She shook her head. "Men and boys," she said. "What's the difference? Come on, Luke, buy a working girl a drink."

She snuggled in beside him, a short, full-figured woman with wavy auburn hair that just brushed the smooth creaminess of her bare shoulders. She was twenty, she had confessed to him once, although in the smoky haze of the saloon she often looked ten years older. Her eyes were as large and soft as a doe's, and just as dark, looking out of place against the powdered and rouged mask of her makeup. He had wondered from time to time where she came from, and what her life had been like before Goff's, but never had the courage to ask, and she had never offered.

"Been a long time," she said casually. "I heard you were in town the other night. I kept expecting you to show up."

He made a vague gesture with his hand and didn't reply. The other night he had still been battling with the ghost of the old rustler. He had felt almost tainted then, and unclean, but how could a man explain something like that to a woman he felt so much confusion over?

Charity didn't push it. She leaned forward on tiptoe and shouted down the bar for Goff to bring a bottle. He came eventually, setting the bottle and another shot glass down with a sharp slap. "Serve yourself," he grunted, moving off immediately, and Charity laughed after him.

They drank slowly, bantering back and forth in a reserved way, talking of the insignificant events of the past weeks—the sinking economy, the centennial celebration in Philadelphia, where A. G. Bell was fascinating visitors with his telephone machine, the deaths of Hickok and Custer, both of whom Charity dismissed as a pair of dandies, though hers was far from the common opinion. They talked of events closer to home, too. Of the four girls Goff had lost to the gold fields of the Hills, of local politics, and in a roundabout way, of the rustling.

He supposed they were something of an item around the bunkhouses of an evening, he and Charity, a bit of gossip to speculate on while whiling away a few quiet minutes before bunk time. He didn't blame them much, remembering his own amused feelings some months earlier, but things had changed since then. Getting to know her, he had discovered someone entirely different from the woman he had expected, and found himself drawn to that new stranger, and comfortable with her.

At times he thought she felt the same toward him, though as often as not he wasn't really sure. In fact, at times she downright baffled him. She was a hard woman, had to be in her trade, yet there was a softness about her too, and not in a physical sense, but in the way she sometimes acted toward him, the way she seemed to close out the world around them when they were together and give her attention fully to him. Still, there were other times when he thought her hide may as well be made of hammered iron, times when he thought she must surely despise him, and all men, and he would swear then that that would be the last time, that the next time he rode in needing a woman he would choose one of the others. But he never did; it was always Charity he came to, was drawn to, and she was always repentant. Sometimes he thought her evenings of indifference actually strengthened their relationship, though even with that thought for comfort it always left him confused and wondering.

They drank into the bottle for a ways, and the crowd had begun to thin, when Charity said, "You got your token?"

Howard nodded, suddenly tongue-tied. He had bought a token off Eddie some weeks back, and it was a slim weight in his pocket now.

She smiled a wry smile and nodded toward the stairs. "Let's go then."

He followed her across the room, the hoarse laughter and ribald shouting suddenly loud and unnatural to his ears. His eyes caught the back of her low-cut, knee-length dress, and for a while, the top hook seemed the only thing in the room in focus. A puncher shouted her name as she passed, reaching for her hand, but she pulled it away without looking at him and passed on by. The puncher's drunken gaze swung to Howard then, and he grinned a knowing grin that Howard wanted to bat away, but couldn't.

He sat on the edge of a small, cast-iron cot and allowed her to remove his boots. She made a production of it, pulling his foot up between her legs until her skirt was bunched above the black net of her stockings, and bending over more than she had to and stretching the thin fabric of her dress tight across her buttocks. She was all whore now, Howard thought bewilderedly.

The roar from downstairs had dulled somewhat, muted through the floor and closed door, and freeing the sounds of rustling lace and creaking bedsprings. The whaler's lamp on the far wall distorted their shadows, turning them short and squat and alien. Charity dropped his boots on the floor and stepped away, reaching behind her for the hooks that held her dress. She unfastened them slowly, but without the fanfare she had used removing his boots, sensing, perhaps, his disapproval. She was naked underneath, her skin startling white against the darkness of her dress.

"You're quiet all of a sudden," she said, and he shrugged and replied, "Been covering a lot of country lately."

He stood and removed his shirt, and as he did a brown bag fell from it, spilling hard candy across the thin carpet.

"What's that?" she asked, surprised.

He'd bought it at the Frontier House, knowing her weakness, and forgotten it completely since. He stooped to pick up the scattered pieces, missing entirely her swift display of emotions, from surprise to delight, then back to the indifferent flippancy of her mask. "Honey, that's going to satisfy my sweet tooth, but what's going to satisfy the rest of me?"

"Stop it!" Howard said harshly. He dropped the bag on the washstand and went to stand at the small, curtainless window, staring north toward an invisible horizon.

Charity came up behind him and slipped her arms around his waist, her palms flat against his bare stomach. "Luke, I'm sorry. The candy is sweet, it really is, but don't build something out of . . . this."

"This? There's nothing here to build from?"

She was silent for a moment, then said, "I like you. Maybe you like me. But I don't want anything more than that. Not right now."

He turned and took her into his arms, finding it easier

than trying to sift through the barrage of new emotions that moved like a whirlwind through his mind. His hands moved gently along her bare spine and the light evening dress she wore slid from her shoulders. Downstairs, the rumble of the crowd seemed to fade into memory.

He rode into the ranch yard at a jog, skirting patches of yellow lamplight beneath the bunkhouse windows and dismounting at the corral. The Youngs had no dog, and Howard thought his arrival had gone unnoticed until a door slammed at the ranch house and he spotted the short, burly silhouette of the rancher strolling purposefully toward him.

Howard lifted his saddle from the dun's back and turned her into the corral to roll. Young waited as he pulled the gate shut, his hands thrust into the pockets of a pair of faded blue denims. He was hatless, and his short, slightly wavy tufts of hair stood up at odd angles in the moonlight, in a manner of a man who ran his hand through it too often—a man worried, Howard thought.

In the corral, the dun rose and shook herself from front to back, raising a cloud of dust. "Good horse," Young said absently.

"Damn good," Howard agreed. "Maybe too good to be in a saddle band."

Young nodded. "Bred her to Wyatt's gray stud some years back and she threw a fine colt. Wish now I'd never put her back in the saddle band. Most of the boys won't ride a mare, and she isn't earning her keep the way she could." He looked at Howard and changed the subject. "The Mex said you was heading into the badlands. You have something definite to go on, or are you just playing a hunch?"

"Just playing a hunch," Howard replied.

Young sighed. "Well, at least somebody's doing something besides waiting for the bastards to strike again." There was bitterness in his words, a sense of hopelessness.

"We're doing what we can," Howard said. "We've brought the last two herds back. Maybe things will ease up for a spell."

Young laughed, a quick, harsh explosion of breath that sounded unnatural in the quiet yard. "You haven't noticed, then?"

Howard looked up sharply. "What's that?"

Young motioned toward the corral he and the others generally used; only his bay stood there now, his ears perked toward them. "Swede and one of my boys discovered them missing this morning," Young said. "More than a hundred head, all Broken Axle stock."

CHAPTER 4

JIM Young squatted against the outside wall of the Sand Creek Feed and Grain and packed his briarwood pipe carefully, taking enjoyment, or at least contentment, from a simple task that required no real thought and from which the results would be both predictable and pleasurable. It was a sorry state of affairs when a man was reduced to enjoying only the simple things, he thought. Like a smoke, or a good meal. There had been a time, not so long ago, when he had been able to derive the same satisfaction from his ranch. From the hard, honest work it took to manage a prosperous spread right. From watching the young beeves grow fat on good grass and the gangling colts grow sleek and sassy before joining the remuda.

Such days seemed past now, though. Today, when he rode the Broken Axle range, all he noticed was the good grass unused and dying under the hot fall wind. The empty miles where once cattle had grazed. In two long summers he had watched his herd shrink from an all-time high of more than a thousand head of breeding stock to something less than five hundred. Maybe even fewer than that, he thought, his fingers tightening around the bowl of his pipe. The last count had been during spring roundup, and he'd lost a sight of cattle since then. And with the fall roundup already started, he'd grudgingly come to realize he wouldn't be able to make a drive south to the markets this year. And no drive meant no money—money needed to keep the outfit going through the long winter months, buying food and supplies, meeting payrolls for the hands needed to keep what remained of his herds from bunching in the draws and freezing or starving, to move them onto the windswept hills or flats where they could find grass.

His options were few and desperate. Borrow from Aaron Mosby at the Cattleman's Bank, or sell some of his breeding stock, reducing the basic herd size to the bare minimum and starting over again. Yet reducing the herd would mean more than merely handling fewer cattle. It would mean trimming one of the best remudas on the range, as well as putting most of his crew on the grub line until they could find other work, a prospect that seemed unlikely this late in the season.

Still, reducing the herd seemed more appealing than borrowing the money he needed or, worse yet to his thinking, going on tick and buying his supplies on credit, owing damn near every businessman in Sand Creek. There was a deep streak of stubborn independence running through him. He had built a respectable ranch in Texas during the fifties, starting with a pair of saddle horses and two dozen cows, only to lose it all to the shifting politics of the postwar South. It had taken him ten years to repeat that in Nebraska, although this time he had started with eighty head of breeding stock, a couple of hands, and a new wife who cooked for the whole outfit. In all those years, no matter how lean or futile the situation seemed, he had never borrowed, never risked mortgaging what he already owned, to weather hard times. And he wouldn't start now.

He had already sold twenty head of his remuda to a horse trader from Cheyenne, sending two of his hands along with an extra month's pay as severance and a letter of recommendation. Come next payday, he'd have to let three more go, giving them a small bonus and the pick of the string as their personal horse. That would leave Goodnight Charlie, the cook, and just two hands. And as much as he dreaded putting the extra work on his wife, he knew Goodnight Charlie wasn't likely to stay with only two regular hands to feed. It didn't make a lot of sense to keep a cook anyway, without a full crew. Still, he'd always called it a poor outfit that couldn't keep a cook, and while it might be no more than an inconvenience to the management of the ranch, it would be a worse blow to his pride.

There was a rattle of a buggy from down the street, and he stood, fishing for a match as he watched it approach. A single rider followed at a respectful distance, pausing beside the buggy when it stopped in front of the Nebraska Hotel, then coming on alone. The rider reined in at the Feed and Grain and hitched his horse to a post. Young had recognized Wyatt's tall, skeleton-thin foreman as soon as he broke from the buggy's wake.

"Evening, Mr. Young," Jeff McKinley said.

"Jeff," Young greeted, hiding his face behind the flare of a match. "That Ben in the buggy?" he asked through a wreath of blue smoke.

McKinley glanced over his shoulder, as if to confirm the point of Young's question. "Yes sir. He and Mrs. Wyatt came in for a meal at the Nebraska. He saw your buckboard and saddle horse hitched down here and asked me to extend an invite for a drink later, at the Nebraska bar."

Young flipped the match into the street, his cheeks making shallow little pockets of shadows as he sucked on his pipe. "The Missus and I came in for the same reason. She's over to Clark's now, picking up some material she had ordered. We'll drop over later and let the women chat. It's been a spell since Edna's been off the ranch, and I reckon she'd appreciate a chance to talk about something besides cows and grass."

"I'll tell them that," Jeff said, gathering his reins. He stepped into the saddle, then paused, picking at the stitching on his horn uncertainly. "You hear anything from Harper and the boys yet?" he asked.

Young shook his head. They had been gone a week now, following a trail already several days old when they'd picked it up. He really didn't expect them back for another week.

Jeff nodded thoughtfully, digesting the information slowly, as if he was looking for something deeper than a simple shake of the head. "I'll tell Mr. Wyatt, then," he said finally, and turned away.

Young watched him go, standing with his arms folded, the briarwood cupped in one hand. The thought of Harper and the others and the missing herd was fixed in his mind now, meshing with all he had thought about before, the hands let go and the herd diminishing and the drive that wouldn't be made, everything banding together and taking away even the pleasure of his pipe, leaving him feeling betrayed and slightly angered.

The bar at the Nebraska Hotel was small and dark, but richly furnished; sequestered from the main lobby by a short hall just off the entrance to the dining room, it was off limits to all but the most elite of the hotel's guests and the handful of ranchers whose spreads extended onto the Sand Creek range. It was more of a private club than a drinking establishment, and its furnishings showed it. Chairs were padded and covered with a rich scarlet cloth, the two gaming tables were felt-topped, and there were four brass-studded leather arm-chairs against the rear wall. The mirror behind the bar was gilt-edged, and the walls were decorated with old, expensive rifles, Sioux and Cheyenne headdresses, war clubs, and short buffalo lances. There was a bookcase built into the wall next to the door, with a library of popular, leatherbound novels and the more practical volumes on cattle and horse breeding.

There were three men in the bar when Young entered something over two hours after Jeff McKinley had delivered Wyatt's invitation: the bartender, politely discreet and dressed in a knee-length white apron and a narrow string tie tight against the collar of a linen shirt; a short, slightly paunchy stranger in an expensive suit drinking at a rear table; and Ben Wyatt.

Wyatt was a man of average height, thick-set and hard, and although he had begun to spread through the girth in the last couple of years, it was a heaviness of age rather than easy living. There were some who called Wyatt a tyrant, Young knew, ruling the huge Bar-W as though it were a country separate from that around him, and there was enough truth in that observation to give it some merit. But those who knew him well knew he was fair, too, when he could afford it. Although not of Texas stock, he had left that state with the rest of them, coming to Nebraska with an outfit no larger than Young's. He had built it to its present size by driving himself, and those who worked for him, beyond what was required for a successful operation.

Wyatt was a gambler, willing to risk everything if the stakes were high enough, and he wasn't above hedging the odds when the opportunity offered, particularly in the early years, when they were all scratching for the best range. Early roundups and early drives sometimes netted him a better market on his beeves, and they had all run across a freshly branded Bar-W yearling they suspected had once suckled a cow carrying a different brand. It wasn't an uncommon practice; most of them were guilty of running an early brand at one time or another, and Wyatt's tolerance of others using the same practices stemmed any accusations.

Wyatt was standing at the far end of the short, polished bar, a blunt-fingered hand wrapped around a shot glass of Kentucky bourbon, a fat Havana cigar propped in the ashtray in front of him. His face lit up with honest pleasure when Young walked in. "Jim," he boomed. "I'm glad you could make it."

"Hello, Ben," Young returned. He acknowledged the bartender and the stranger with a nod, then hooked a heel over the brass footrail and put his elbows on the bar. "Brandy, Tom, if you would."

"Sure thing, Mr. Young," the bartender said, smiling. He poured a stiff shot into a glass and left the bottle.

"Jeff says Harper and his bunch aren't back yet." Wyatt shifted around to face Young.

"It's early yet. The trail was old when they found it." He

toyed with his glass a moment, then added, "I'll tell you, Ben, there's a hunger for beef up there that's scary. If that hunger wasn't in the bellies of men who couldn't afford honest beef and the damn market back East wasn't so good right now, a man could show a fair profit running a drive into the Hills."

"That day will come," Wyatt said. "Right now we're too close to the rails at Ogallala to risk a drive north without a bona fide buyer already up there."

Young took a healthy swig of his brandy and made no reply. He wasn't sure he agreed with Wyatt this time, and the thought worried him more than it should have. Wyatt wasn't the type to miss an opportunity, and right now the Hills were a golden one. He had, in fact, been somewhat surprised when Wyatt hadn't sent a herd north last year. But then, that was Wyatt's business. Future markets weren't the pressing problem right now. He said, "You don't generally offer an invitation without some reason behind it, Ben."

Wyatt chuckled. "I didn't know I was so easily read."

"We've been neighbors a long time now. We fought Indians and hide hunters and wolves together. I reckon a man gets to know his friends after that."

Wyatt stared at his drink for a long time without answering, and when he finally spoke the words came slowly, as if he had to drag them past other thoughts crowding his mind. "We've got some potential trouble brewing on the southern range, Jim, below you and Hutchinson's."

"Trouble?" Young's brows furrowed. Trouble had always seemed to come from the north. The wolves, down off the high plains, and the Sioux, when they still held a firm grip on the Hills and fought any encroachment toward them, or the hide hunters, who had given them trouble in '72, filling out their loads with hides from Sand Creek beef. The north and west had always been the frontier, the wild and untamed, while the south and east had represented civilization, with cities and laws basically unbroken; a wall, no matter how distant in actual miles, to put your back against.

"Word came in a couple of days ago by a freighter taking the Grant Creek cutoff," Wyatt continued. "So I had Jeff and a couple of the boys check it out. We've got grangers moving in along the big loop. Three or four German immigrants with a passel of kids, and a couple of ex-slaves with three or four young ones running around each soddy. Jeff gave them a warning to move on, but they haven't so far."

Young sighed hugely. He knew how most of the ranchers felt about nesters, how he felt about them. Let two or three move in, and the next summer you'd have a score of them, burrowing into the ground like prairie dogs, tearing the sod with wooden plows and fencing off the water holes. But right now, no matter the color or breed or number of barefooted, rags-clad youngsters they had running around, nesters were the least of his problems. Shorthanded as he was, he couldn't afford the time it would take to rout a bunch of grangers.

"They're crowding your range, Jim," Wyatt prodded.

"I've never used Grant Creek range," Young replied. "Not even with a full herd. Neither has Hutchinson, as far as I know."

Wyatt put two fingers inside his shot glass, spread them, and lifted the glass; he tapped it lightly, rhythmically, against the bar. It upset him some, Young knew, his lack of concern. Impatience was either a virtue or a curse of the successful, but he had never been able to decide which.

"I'm thinking of the future now," Wyatt pursued doggedly. "We've got to stop them now, before they start edging north, cutting into our southern range. One water hole will support a granger and maybe five acres of crop, or a dozen square miles of grazing land. We can't let them get a toehold on our range, Jim."

Young lifted his glass, emptying it with one swift swallow. He blinked and sucked at his lower lip, staring at his shadowed reflection in the mirror, then set the glass down with a slap. "All right, damnit. I know the problems nesters can cause. But they're crowding me and Hutchinson, so let us handle it."

Wyatt nodded, satisfied. "If you need help, I'll send Jeff and some of the boys."

"I said I'd handle it," Young repeated flatly. He was staring at his empty glass, his face suddenly dark. After a pause, he said, "I'll try to get over to Hutchinson's within the next few days. I want his input before I make any decisions."

"Fair enough," Wyatt said. He lifted the bottle and poured them both another drink. "I'm afraid I've got another touchy subject to bring up tonight."

"Christ, Ben. If you aren't the perfect way to top off an evening."

Wyatt's face remained sober, and Young felt something inside tighten a little. "I guess the best way to handle this is to introduce you to the gentleman and let him explain his purpose," Wyatt said reluctantly. He knocked the ashes from his cigar and clamped it between his teeth, then picked up the bottle and his glass and walked over to the stranger's table. Young looked from Wyatt to the stranger, then picked up his own glass and followed. "Jim, this is Bernie Jordache," Wyatt said, "a representative of the Dallas Land and Livestock Company."

Jordache stood, smoothing his vest and straightening his jacket, a wide smile dimpling each chubby cheek. He held his hand out and Young took it in a slow, almost disappointing grip, finding it soft and clammy and coated with a slight hint of the wax he used on the tiny mustache above his soft, feminine lips. "Mr. Young," Jordache greeted expansively. "I'm glad to meet you. I've heard many fine things about the Broken Axle and I've been looking forward to this."

Young nodded cautiously and resisted the urge to wipe his hand on his trousers.

"Won't you have a seat?" Jordache invited.

Young hooked a chair around and eased into it, keeping

his eyes on Jordache. "What can I do for you, sir?" Young asked reticently.

Jordache cleared his throat, leaning forward eagerly, Young thought, like a cat ready to pounce on a mouse, and folded his hands on the table. "Perhaps I'm being blunt here, but I'd like to get directly to the point. I realize these are difficult times, and my timing may be poor, but my company has been looking into the prospects of expanding its range onto some northern land for quite some time, and Sand Creek seems to offer everything we've been looking for. I'm here to investigate the possibilities of purchasing some of the ranches locally."

Young looked horrified. "My God, Ben! Did you invite him here?"

Wyatt's face turned red. "Mr. Jordache approached me about buying some of the ranches that might . . . if some of the ranchers wanted to sell because of the . . ." He sputtered a bit more, then shut up.

"So you introduced him to me?" Young asked softly. His voice was calm, but a flush of anger had returned to his face.

"Damnit, Jim, I just introduced you two. Where it goes from there is up to you."

"Mr. Young," Jordache interrupted. "My company is prepared to offer a sizable sum of cash, for such difficult times. The alternatives may not be as rewarding."

"Jordache, I'd rather freeze in hell than sell out to the likes of your company."

Jordache pulled back until he was sitting ramrod straight. "The DL&L is a fair and honorable firm," he said stiffly. "Perhaps bluntness is a failing of mine, but I'd urge you to reconsider allowing us to make you an offer. It may prove prudent in the future."

Young stood swiftly, pushing his chair back to slam into the other table. "Is that a threat, Jordache?"

Jordache refused to look at him, and Young turned to Wyatt, his anger complete now, encompassing them all.

"Ben, this man is a goddamn carpetbagger, the same kind that stole our land in Texas."

"Mr. Jordache is a representative of one of the largest and most respected companies in the South. I've dealt with the DL&L many times in the past and—"

"So have I," Young interrupted roughly. "When their kind ran us out of Texas." He whirled and headed for the door, bumping into the table as he did, jolting the bottle of brandy and tipping it over. It rolled toward the edge of the table, gurgling its contents over the felt, until Jordache caught it and righted it. Young slammed the door with enough force to rattle the glass doors of the bookcase.

Young paused on the boardwalk, his hand dipping without thought into his pocket and pulling out his pipe. He clenched it between his teeth, but didn't light it. He knew already that there would be no pleasure in its taste.

Doc's weariness was like a weight upon him, a giant's hand that wanted to tumble him from the saddle, and he shook his head irritably at the image, at his own wilting spirit. He raised his head to study Harper's broad back hunched, his head bobbing, and he felt some relief at that, at knowing Barney felt as he did, and likely the others, too. Behind him, Red and Pete sat limp on their plodding horses, half-asleep in the stifling heat of midday.

His roan strayed off the path to nip at a long blade of grass, and Doc pulled the horse's head around with a quick, aggravated motion. They rode single file, the four of them, strung out and silent, frustrated by their failure, the Hills three days behind them now, and Sand Creek just over the next ridge. Doc wondered if the others dreaded coming back empty-handed the same as he did.

They had made good time going north, for all the hard tracking, and by the time they spied the mountains, Sanchez announced them only half a day behind. Their optimism had soared for a while, and they'd pushed their flagging mounts on at a quicker pace. Sloping into the foothills, though, the ground had turned hard and rocky, unyielding. Soon enough then, the trail disappeared altogether. A hundred head of beeves swallowed by the mountains.

Even then, they hadn't given up. They had pushed on into the interior, poking around from one town to another, asking questions, searching, probing. All without luck. At the end of four days Harper had disgruntledly shaken his head and said, "We ain't gonna find 'em. Likely they're all in the bellies of miners by now."

Next morning, they'd reluctantly dropped out of the Hills and turned their horses south, toward home.

Now, at the top of the ridge, Harper halted his bay and the others crowded close around him. Far off, but sharp in the clean air, Sand Creek squatted like a child's miniature village, all pale gray from a distance, and clean-looking. On the eastern edge of town meandered the ribbon of creek that gave the town its name, its banks treeless here, though peppered with stumps enough to suggest that once a good-sized grove of cottonwood had stood there. Closer, angling in from the west and trailing its plume of roiling dust, was an Ogallala and Black Hills stage, looking small and defenseless from the ridge, but as clean-cut as the town. Doc could see the dark, liquid movement of the horses, and the passengers on top, clinging to the baggage there and looking like chicks in a nest.

"Still there," Red remarked dryly, and Harper choked up a hoarse bark of laughter.

They put their horses over the top then, and lifted them into a jog. Dust rose in tiny puffs beneath the hooves of their mounts, and swarms of grasshoppers whirled clicking out of their path. At the bottom of the ridge they spread out and went into a canter. Doc rode gracefully, the easy gait of the roan belying his own natural ability. From time to time he would cast a quick, sidelong glance at his shadow etched on the prairie, floating over knobs of dirt and cactus. In shadow, his size wasn't so obvious, and he liked that.

He was short and slim, willowy almost, a word he despised for its effeminate implications, smooth-cheeked yet, save for some fuzz beneath his chin and a mustache that looked more like a smudge of dirt than hair. Maybe some fuzz and a smudge was all a man could expect at seventeen, but sometimes he wished it would grow in a little faster; he hated all the jobbing it caused. The roan horse he rode was a good one, but most of everything else was worn in one way or another. Running away from home, putting the army finally behind him, he'd sworn he'd let it all go, becoming the opposite of what his old man and the others had been, and he supposed he'd done fair enough on everything but his niggardly ways. It was like he always had to hoard his money, always keep it tucked out of sight, as if his pa were still around and rummaging through his things in the middle of the night, looking for poker money. His pa had a powerful weakness for the game, and others of chance as well.

He was fourteen when he left Fort Davis, down in the dry mountains of Texas, and likely they still considered him a horse thief, though he'd left the animal with a hostler in El Paso who'd promised to get word back to old Colonel James that he was stabling a cavalry mount. Doc figured he would, figured he would make more on a padded feed bill to the government than he ever would trying to sell an army mount into Mexico. Not that Doc had hung around to find out. There was a freighter pulling out for Roswell the next morning, and he went with him, working his passage north.

That first year had been lean. He'd batted around a dozen towns, always drifting farther north, putting a few more miles between himself and his pa, whom he feared worse than Colonel James and a horse-stealing charge—the army being more or less limited only to hanging him—always half-starved and half-froze, it seemed, and always dirty. He was sweeping in a saloon in Fishhook, Colorado, for a dollar a week and two meals a day the first time he met Harper.

In those days he was just a nobody kid, wearing out-at-the-knee wool pants, a charcoal gray shirt that had once been white, and laceless shoes without socks. A bum at fifteen, with only his determination to keep him going, to keep him from sliding all the way down the chute to worthlessness. Anger fueled his determination, and gave it the strength needed to survive.

It was late that night, maybe three or four o'clock in the morning, but Fishhook was a mining town, open twenty-four hours a day serving the different shifts. Augie was there, drunk as usual and passing out union sheets to whomever would take one and trying to ignore the three hardcases at the bar. They worked for the mines and were touchy on the subject of unions. There was a lot of talk about unions that summer, Doc remembered, and it seemed the whole town was on edge about it. Augie didn't really care much for the unions, but he liked his whiskey well enough to risk a busted head passing out union information.

Some people said Augie used to be hell on wheels with a six-gun before the bottle bit him, but looking at him, old and bent, with long, dirty hair all streaked through with gray and tattered clothes, it was hard for Doc to imagine him as ever being anything but a rummy. Even at that, he liked the old drunk. Although Doc wasn't much of a drinker himself, never being able to afford the habit, they still had a lot in common.

On a normal evening the three hardcases would have run Augie out of the saloon and made a little fire of the union sheets, but word was that the mines had hired a new gun, due in on the four o'clock stage, and everyone figured the three hardcases were waiting for him. Everyone else was, and curiosity was rampant.

Nobody heard the stage coming in, but sometime around four the doors swung inward and a big man walked in and to the bar after the barest pause at the door. He was wearing a broadcloth suit and a black hat, and his boots gleamed richly under a reddish haze of dust.

Doc was near the rear of the saloon, leaning wearily against the wall and propped on his broom, yawning now and again. He had swept up a big pile of old sawdust and needed to cart that outside and spread some fresh from the burlap bag just inside the storeroom door. Seeing the big man enter, he thought he'd wait awhile and see what happened.

Hank, the barkeep, moved down the bar, exchanged a quick word with the big man, then poured him a shot of whiskey. They talked some more then, and Hank nodded toward the hardcases and moved off. After a while one of the hardcases pushed away from the bar and sauntered up to the big man as if he were bored. They talked a little, then the hardcase nodded to his buddies and picked up the bottle Hank had left and the four of them snaked their way through the crowd to a table in back, not ten feet away from where Doc stood propped against his broom. The big man's eyes passed quickly over him, dismissing him, Doc thought, and his anger flared briefly.

They talked for a bit, knocking off a few rounds, and directly one of the hardcases, a wiry little fellow wearing a beaded and quilled buckskin shirt with long fringe and a Colt Baby Dragoon at his waist, started getting loud. It was Augie who was bothering him, though by this time Augie had ditched his fliers and was standing at the bar, nursing a whiskey.

"Third time," Buckskin said loudly enough that Augie could hear, though he didn't turn around or acknowledge it in any fashion. "Maybe it's time we explained it to him so he'll remember."

One of the other hardcases said something, and they laughed, all except the big man. The big man was staring at Augie with a quiet intensity, his eyes hooded beneath his furrowed brows.

Buckskin scraped his chair back and stood awkwardly, balancing himself with his fingertips on the table. He'd been drinking all night, Doc remembered, not fast but steady, and it looked like it was finally catching up with him. He said, "Who's giving you those lies to pass out, old man?"

Augie looked around, his face showing brief surprise, then a quick fear. Doc could feel the muscles in his stomach drawing up. The big man stood then, and took a couple of steps toward Augie, and one of the hardcases still seated said, "Now we'll see what grit he's made of," but the big man stopped a dozen feet away from the bar. Augie looked like he wanted to run, but wouldn't. At first Doc had thought they were talking about the big man's grit, but now he wondered if they were really talking about Augie. The big man said, "August Skinner?"

Augie looked puzzled, then something changed in his face, and he said, "My God. Barney?"

Barney laughed and crossed to the bar and he and Augie shook and slapped one another on the shoulder like they were brothers.

Buckskin got a funny look on his face then, and glanced down quickly at his two hardcase friends, then took a slow step toward the pair at the bar. "Back off there, Harper," he called. "That's a goddamn union man you're talking to."

"Naw," Harper said. "This is an old friend. He's all right." He looked at Augie then, and invited him over to the table for a drink, but Augie quickly shook his head.

"I said to back off, Harper," Buckskin said in a threatening tone. He stood loosely, ready, his flat, black eyes glinting. Doc put his back to the wall and tried to spread it there. Harper turned, smiling, and said he didn't believe he would. He looked ready, too, and Doc wanted to drop to the floor and crawl away, but was afraid it would draw too much attention to him. The other hardcases stood up then.

At the bar, Augie turned and said, "Hank, give me a gun," but Hank had backed off to the far end of the bar, and he just mutely shook his head. "Barney, I ain't carrying," Augie said desperately.

Harper's smile never changed. "That's all right, pard," he said. "I can handle these girls." His eyes were on Buckskin, unwavering. He stood with his back to the bar, and Augie beside him, both of them so calm and assured that Doc felt his own fears easing some. He had never felt so expectant, so charged.

Buckskin drew first, but Harper's revolver tipped from the holster and belched a cloud of gray smoke, and Buckskin cried out and jerked sharply upright, all the way to tiptoe, his Dragoon spilling from his fingers. The other two had drawn almost as quickly, their revolvers sounding as one, deafening in the closed confines of the saloon, then Harper's Colt exploded again, from lower and several paces off, and the hardcase nearest Doc spun away, his face gone chalky. He sagged against the wall, sliding slowly toward the floor. A bottle crashed against the back wall after glancing off the third hardcase's head, and Doc saw Augie reaching for a second bottle, but Harper's Colt roared a third time, and the last hardcase tipped over backward and fell with his arms spread. Doc had never seen so much action crammed into a single second of time.

The smoke began to drift toward the ceiling, and Doc saw Augie bent over Harper, helping him to his feet. Harper's face was pale, his left arm held at a peculiar angle, as if it might be broken, although Doc didn't see any blood that might indicate a bullet wound. He did see Harper's eyes widen, though, saw him staring at a spot just to Doc's side, then glance around wildly for the revolver he must have dropped. Doc looked around just as the second hardcase rose to his knees, the front of his shirt cherry with blood and his revolver thrust before him in both hands; Doc swung his broom without thought, catching the revolver just as the hammer dropped and lifting the muzzle toward the ceiling. It boomed in Doc's face and he flinched back, slamming against the wall, hearing as if from a long way off the hardcase's sobbing curses, and Harper's fourth shot. The hardcase flopped back, and Doc looked only once at the mess that was the side of his head.

For a while, then, everything seemed to blur, and he squeezed his eyes shut and leaned weakly into the wall. After half a dozen deep breaths, he opened them, seeing Harper seated at a table close to the bar, and somebody had put a bottle and glass in front of him, next to where his hand was resting on his Colt. Augie had helped him slip his coat off, and they had his shirt half off, too. Harper's face was white now, with little beads of perspiration rolling off his forehead and down his nose. His arm wasn't broken, Doc noticed, but pulled out of its joint.

Doc approached the table on leaden feet, Harper's gaze hard on him with a mixture of gratitude and wariness. He nodded as Doc approached the table, and said, "I'm obliged to you for what you did."

Doc didn't know what to say to that, and so blurted out what had brought him to the table to begin with, and likely seemed a simpleton for it. "I can fix that shoulder, if you're of a mind."

Harper looked suspicious, and Augie said, "You know about doctoring, Matty?" His eyes said he had doubts too.

Doc didn't trust himself to speak, so he took Harper's arm and prodded at his shoulder with experienced fingers, finding the spot and snapping the arm quickly. Harper squawked, like they all did, but the anger faded swiftly, replaced with a look of awe as the pain abated. Harper studied him curiously for a moment, then nodded and said, "Thanks, Doc," with something of a twinkle in his eyes.

At the bar, Hank said, "Matty, drag those bodies out back and throw a tarp over them, then go get the sheriff."

Harper and Augie were gone by the time he got all that Hank had ordered him to do finished, so he stood outside in the chill mountain dawn shivering in his coat until the undertaker showed up, his eyes still gummy with sleep. The undertaker eyed the trio of lumps under the frost-covered tarp, then looked at Doc. "I'll give you four bits to dig the graves for me," he offered.

Doc just laughed. He figured his days of four bits a job were over.

Harper had given him a sense of worth, no doubt about that, Doc thought, and cut off to the side a little, the roan turning suddenly frisky, sensing the way horses sometimes did that the end of the trail was coming up. Harper's big rangy bay was setting a brisk pace, too, and Red and Pete were slowly falling behind.

Off to the side, Doc studied Harper surreptitiously from the shade of his hat, and thought it funny the way a thing could stand out vividly in one man's mind and be nothing but a fuzzy memory in another's. His last night in Fishhook had changed his life, but he doubted now that Harper even remembered it; certainly, he never mentioned it. Or Doc, either, though it was Buckskin's Dragoon he carried now, and his shirt, cleaned and patched.

He hadn't seen himself as following Harper, yet he was honest enough with himself to admit the possibility. He had drifted east after Colorado, and taken a job for a spell riding shotgun for a decrepit little stage line down in the Nations. One rainy spring day he had been sitting at a rough-hewn plank table wolfing down a meal of sowbelly and beans, when a group of men had come riding in fast, reining their lathered and muddy mounts to a sliding stop at the stables. He'd gone to stand at the door to watch them, and the hunchbacked little stationkeeper had joined him there. The riders were stripping gear from their mounts and throwing it on fresh horses in the corral.

"Who are they?" Doc asked.

"Rangers," the hunchback snorted.

"*Texas* rangers?" Doc asked incredulously.

"No. Just rangers. They look for horse thieves, I think."

"But they're stealing your horses."

The hunchback shrugged indifferently. "Not my horses," he said. "Company horses." He turned his back on them then, and went inside, and after a bit Doc heard the lid lifted on the stove and the clink of coal added to the fire.

They rode out as fast as they came in, Harper among them, and Doc remembered thinking, "Well, it's true," meaning that Harper was working down in the Nations now.

Remembering that, he wondered if his coming to Sand Creek had been as much chance as it had seemed at the time.

They slowed coming into town, bunching close again and dropping to a walk. Down at the stage office holsters were backing a fresh pair of wheelers into the traces, and there was a knot of men standing on the boardwalk in front of it, passengers with bushy beards and old, floppy hats stained with sweat, and probably shovel-calloused hands, Doc thought. They had the look of miners, abandoning their claims for one reason or another.

There were a couple of wagons in front of the Feed and Grain, dilapidated things, with warped sideboards and splintering spokes, each with a single span of ribby mules standing hipshot in the heat; there was a shovel and a pick and a posthole digger in the bed of one of the wagons, but nothing else that Doc could see, and staring into the interior of the Feed and Grain as they passed, he saw only shadows. More miners, he figured, either coming or going, but the others, Harper and Red and Pete, were eyeing the wagons in quiet study. Past them then, he twisted in the saddle for another look, but all he saw was the off-mule on the near wagon stomp its hoof irritably at a fly.

He was about to turn away when a shift in the shadows at the door caught his attention, and he pulled the roan up. A kid appeared there, black as a chunk of coal, and Doc's mouth gaped a little in surprise.

"I'll be goddamned," Red said, and stopped his sorrel next to Doc.

The kid wasn't any more than seven or eight years old, a boy wearing oversized bibs and nothing else Doc could see. He stood in the entry of the Feed and Grain and drew a circle in the dirt with his big toe, oblivious to the four men watching him.

Harper's laugh was without humor. "As if they ain't got enough troubles," he said, and turned away.

Pete rode after Harper, and Red's sorrel wanted to follow, but Red jerked his head around roughly and sat watching the kid. Doc's instinct was to go with Barney and Pete, but Red was mad for some reason, maybe madder than Doc had ever seen him, and his curiosity won out. "Know him?" he asked, just to say something.

Red didn't even look at him. His gaze was on the kid, and after a minute, as if feeling its heat, the kid looked up and his eyes widened. His fear was easily read, even from here, and Doc winced, seeing it. The kid backed up a few paces, then turned and went inside as if he wasn't bothered, but the jerky way his legs were working called him a liar.

"What is it?" Doc asked, thoroughly puzzled now.

"Nothing," Red replied shortly. "Why don't you go get a drink with Harper and Sanchez?"

He was wishing then that he had, but he'd stayed, and now he felt committed, though he couldn't say why.

Red nudged his sorrel forward, bringing his hand back to slip the leather thong off the hammer of his big Peacemaker, then letting it rest close by on his thigh. There was a stirring in the entry, and a towheaded man of twenty or so stepped out, dressed in worn brogans and overalls and a floppy hat pushed back on his head, looking enough like a miner that for a moment Doc thought he was. Then it all came together, and Harper's remark suddenly made sense.

Red pushed his horse so close to the towheaded farmer that he had to step back or risk getting his feet trampled.

"You're a long way from Ohio, ain't you, plow-pusher?" Red asked in a derisive tone.

The granger's eyes clouded in question, and he repeated, "O-ai-o?" like he'd never heard it before.

"Christ in a bucket," Red muttered. "A goddamn Bavarian."

"*Ja!*" the granger said, his face suddenly lightening. "Regensburg."

Red made a small sound of disgust and gigged his horse past the granger, on up the small dirt incline to the entry of the Feed and Grain. "McCall," he called into the darkness.

"What do you want?" McCall's voice came muffled from the interior. Red didn't reply, but just sat his horse, waiting.

Presently McCall appeared, a brawny man wearing old, dusty work clothes and a bandanna around his forehead to catch his sweat. He was fifty or so, and as sour as week-old milk those few times Doc had been around him. He looked sour now too, Doc thought, and impatient.

"Since when are you doing business with grangers?" Red asked.

"Since when do I have to ask a gunfighter who to do business with?" McCall returned.

Red, already mad, bristled even more. "You hiding niggers in there, McCall?"

"Niggers," Doc breathed, and suddenly it all made sense. He remembered some of the Broken Axle hands talking about some of the darkies they'd wrangled with down Texasway, and the way Red's face would always flush with an unexplained anger, and like as not he'd leave the bunkhouse. He hadn't put it together then, but he saw it clearly now.

McCall looked suddenly amused; it was the first time Doc ever remembered seeing him smile. He said, "Who I got in my business is no business of yours."

"Best not get too cozy with their money," Red said. "The Cattlemen's Association won't cotton to their being here."

"I ain't worried about gunfighters or cattlemen," McCall said. "They can take their business to Ogallala if they want."

Bold talk for a man in the feed and grain business, Doc thought, and had it been anyone but McCall, he would have figured it to be all bluff.

A second figure appeared at the door, a black man, thirty or so, tall and well built. He was hatless, and Doc noticed that baldness had made deep inroads above each ear. "It be all right, Mr. McCall," he said gravely. "Reckons these gentlemen be lookin' fer me." His accent was deeply southern, thickened with the inflection of slavery, so that Doc found himself leaning forward to follow his words.

"You're not wanted here, nigger," Red said tightly. His face looked pale, Doc thought, as if all the color had drained from it to feed his anger.

"I reckon I's here, though," the black man replied evenly. If he was frightened he was hiding it well, Doc thought, and felt a quick rush of admiration at the granger's pluck. He felt a sudden urge to tell Red to back off and let it drop, but when he looked at Red and saw the rigid way he sat his saddle, the words deserted him. He didn't think Red was in the mood to listen to anyone unless they could back their words up with a gun, and Doc knew he wasn't any match for Red.

"Red, this is Simon Washington," McCall said, grinning. He dropped a friendly hand over the black man's shoulder. "And this is Lafe Gutzweiler." He indicated the towheaded German with a nod of his head. "The Gutzweilers are just over from Germany on a promise of homestead from the Nebraska Immigration Association."

McCall seemed to be enjoying Red's anger immensely, Doc noted, and was reminded once again of Bronson's warning some weeks back that the population of Sand Creek was generally against them. Bronson had searched each one of them out individually to pass along that information. Remembering that, he wondered if McCall wasn't siding with the grangers just to rile Red. Of course, it wasn't the grangers that were riling Red.

For a moment Red didn't reply, and it dawned on Doc then that Red had plateaued, that the time for talking was past, and that he was either going to have to draw his pistol or back off. For one quick, crazy moment then, Doc felt the sinking fear that Red was going to draw, that his hatred, no matter what its cause, would make him draw against three unarmed men, and Doc felt panicked that he might. Then the moment passed and Red whirled his horse, making the three men on the ground skip back out of the way.

"You made a bad choice here today," Red said to McCall.

"I make my own choices," McCall countered.

Red touched his spurs to the sorrel and set off down the street at a gallop.

"What about you, sonny?" McCall said. "You got anything to say?"

Doc studied him for a minute, then grinned suddenly and winked. Reining around, he set off after Red, pondering. Though it had been a confusing exchange, he had the uneasy feeling that it was far from finished.

CHAPTER 5

TOWARD dusk the crowd picked up a little, lifting the gloomy spirits of the room. Johnny, Goff's new barkeep, made the rounds lighting the big overhead kerosene lamps, and the skinny little man with the waxy mustache who called himself the Professor came downstairs to play the piano, and all that helped, too, Sanchez thought.

They had been a moody bunch all afternoon, growling and snapping like pups weaned from the tit, until they'd finally just all drifted apart, sitting as far from one another as the saloon would allow. Had someone else gone on ahead of him, Sanchez would have ridden back to the Broken Axle hours ago. But no one had, of course, since the first man back would naturally be obligated to tell the *patron* that they hadn't recovered his herd.

It was odd, the way they all took it so personal anymore, as if they had a stake in every herd that got away from them and weren't just hands hired on, and temporary, to boot. It was because the job had stretched on so long, Sanchez knew. As a rule, he liked his work to be quick and efficient. He didn't like getting to know the men he worked for, or worse, seeing the second side of an affair. In his line of work, he thought a man was better off not seeing the whole picture. There was a basic right and wrong, and looking any deeper than that would only lead a man into confusion, the confusion into melancholy. And Pete Sanchez wasn't a man given to melancholy.

He had never been able to take life too seriously, something he viewed as a fault but was unwilling to change. It seemed he could find humor in damn near anything, then either had to point it out or bust trying to hold it back. It was a ruthless thing at times, and more than once he thought he'd let it range too far, but nobody'd shot him yet, and close didn't count.

Nobody'd fired him yet, either, though on occasion he had some difficulty in being hired. It was the damn Mex reputation, he knew, that of being lazy and worthless and only able to grow beans and children with any success. It was a lie, of course; most of the big spreads in the southwest had Mex hands, some of them top hands, but it seemed to Sanchez that if you didn't have some kind of reputation already, someone would go ahead and tag you with *lazy* and *worthless*. Even Harper had shown some white at hiring him, saying he'd never heard of a Mexican being handy with a six-shooter. Sanchez had fast-drawed then, slapping his pistol out and fanning off a quick shot from the hip, his bullet *pinging* off a blade of Ben Wyatt's windmill, a shot he knew to be about half luck. It had impressed Harper, though, and he'd been hired on the spot. In time Harper grew to respect his tracking even more, as Sanchez knew he would. He had the knack, and there weren't many who were better.

Pete Sanchez was a slim man, not much taller than Doc, bowlegged as any waddie and twice as good, by his own admission. He didn't know how old he was, but suspected forty wasn't so far off anymore. He was Mexican through and through, and there wouldn't have been any doubt of that even if his last name had been Jones or Edwards or some such. He had a rough, swarthy complexion, a huge walrus mustache, and coarse black hair that curled thickly past his collar. A whore had once told him that if it wasn't for the twinkle in his eyes he would have looked like a *bandido*. With the twinkle, she said, he looked more like a good-natured grandfather. That was in San Antonio, the whore. There weren't so many he couldn't keep track of them, and this one had a big wart on the lid of her eye that always made it droop. He liked them well enough, or at least enjoyed the feminine companionship, but he didn't frequent them much, for reasons of his own. He was thinking about the whore from San Antonio—Sad-eyed Sally, they'd called her—when Luke Howard walked in.

Sanchez liked Luke, for all his morose ways, and was glad to see him. It was the whore, Charity, that made him that way, Sanchez knew. Luke was studding after her, or maybe wanting more by now, but Charity was holding him off, keeping him at a distance, and Pete smiled, thinking about it. He thought Luke could have her soon enough if he just wouldn't try so hard. Turn his back for a while and she'd likely come running. But he wouldn't, and Sanchez wanted to laugh, thinking about that and seeing the hangdog expression on his face as he searched the crowd for her. She wasn't around, though she had been earlier, which meant she was probably upstairs, and he studied the crowd himself then, wondering who she was with.

Harper wasn't in sight, and he felt something like a twitch pull at him. Although he hadn't actually seen Harper go upstairs with Charity, it was something he would do. Sanchez knew Harper would see it as a sort of retribution for losing the herd, as if Howard's not being along had made a difference.

Sanchez returned a small wave as Luke stepped up to the bar beside Red, then swore softly. He hoped he was wrong about Harper, hoped he had only stepped out back to the privy or something, and that Charity was upstairs with some fat drummer. There was enough bad blood between them all already.

Doc joined them at the bar, and after a few minutes all three turned away, looking for a table. It seemed only natural that they should choose his.

"Pete," Luke greeted, hooking a chair around and sitting. He looked tired, but was maybe only disappointed. "Red says you lost them."

"It is not the first time," he replied nonchalantly. "Too bad."

"Yeah," Luke agreed.

"We trailed them all the way into the Hills before losing them," Doc said. "The ground up there is as hard as hammered hell. Like trying to track a bug across hard rock."

Red pulled a bag of Lone Jack from the breast pocket of his shirt and began to roll a cigarette. "Lot more people up there than the last time we were there," he said. "Little camps of miners on damn near every bend of every creek up there. Tent cities where there wasn't anything a month ago, and empty bottles and dead grass where there used to be a hundred people."

"Hill City and Custer were booming last spring," Doc added. "Now there aren't more than a couple of hundred people in each. Everybody's going north to the Deadwood Gulch."

"Anybody serving beef?" Luke asked.

"Not that we saw," Doc replied. "But Swede stayed behind to poke around some more."

Howard nodded approvingly, and Sanchez wondered if it wasn't Swede's staying behind, as much as the reasoning behind it, that he liked. "What about here?" Sanchez asked then. "What is new on the Sand Creek?"

Howard shook his head. "No trouble. With all the hands working roundup, I don't think anybody's had a chance to take a herd."

"After roundup there will be trouble again. This is what I think."

"Maybe," Red said. He finished rolling his cigarette, lit it. "What else?" he asked Howard.

"Nesters on the Grant. A land speculator up from Texas rubbing some of the ranchers the wrong way. Young let three more of his hands go."

"Nesters," Red snorted. "Goddamn gophers is more like it."

"Which three hands?" Sanchez asked.

"Hogan, Slaughter and Tyson. Leaves Jess and Jory. Come spring Young's going to find himself with a handful of work and only a fingerful of crew."

"By next spring he won't have the rustlers chewing at his herd," Doc said. "He can build up again. A cook like Goodnight Charlie will bring hands in."

"Charlie's not here," Howard said gently. "Young sent him along on roundup to rep for the Broken Axle. Said he was going down the trail with the herd and wouldn't be back."

"What?" Doc exclaimed.

"Claims he doesn't have the recipes for just two hands, or the talent to waste on such a small outfit."

"We make seven," Red grunted.

Howard just shrugged, and Sanchez thought, So, Goodnight Charlie would not cook for an outfit of gunnies.

"Goddamn cooks," Red muttered. "Ain't seen one yet that didn't think he was prince of the prairie."

There was a small commotion at the head of the stairs, and Sanchez looked up, his heart sinking a little. Harper stood there, as Pete knew he eventually would, with Charity looking worried beside him. Harper's face had a sullen set to it yet, and Sanchez wondered if it wasn't suddenly seeing Luke that brought it back. Sanchez glanced quickly at Luke and saw that he hadn't noticed them yet. He had a glass of beer in his hands and was twirling it slowly on top of the scarred table. If Harper came down without any more noise . . .

At Sanchez's elbow, Doc chuckled. "Doesn't look like Charity's drawn much steam off after all, does it?" he said.

Luke looked at Doc, then to the head of the stairs, and his eyes went suddenly hard. He rose abruptly and went to the bar, and Sanchez heard him order a whiskey.

Doc lowered his head and slowly wagged it. "Goddamn me," he said quietly, and Sanchez, whose anger had started to swell, felt it melt swiftly away. Sometimes it was easy to forget Doc was just a kid.

Harper's boots sounded loud on the stairs, and he bulled himself a spot at the bar not far from Luke and ordered a whiskey from Johnny. Three townsmen between quickly finished their drinks and left as a silence settled over the big room. Charity, Sanchez noted, still stood at the head of the stairs, clutching a bannister with both hands. Twice Harper looked at Luke as if he wanted to say something, but he never did, and Luke faced the bar stiffly, looking neither right nor left. When Johnny brought him his drink, Harper knocked it off in three quick swallows, then dropped a coin on the bar and walked from the room.

Watching the doors swing behind him, Sanchez felt strangely confused. He felt as if he had dozed briefly, and in doing so missed something crucial between the two men. A ripple of conversation ran through the room and swiftly grew. Harper was gone and Charity had disappeared and everyone in the room was throwing quick, puzzled glances at Luke's back, and Sanchez wondered how many really knew what had happened here, and how many only sensed trouble. Still confused himself, he rose and took his beer and Luke's and joined him at the bar.

"You look like a dogie calf, amigo," he said. "As down as a dead mule." He smiled a little, but Luke didn't reply or look around, and Sanchez noticed that his knuckles were white around his shot glass.

Sanchez sighed and took a sip of his beer. Then he began to talk. "In the San Juans I once saw two bull elk fighting over a cow. She was pretty, for an elk. She was fat and her hide was slick. The bulls, they fought for most of an afternoon, but when they finally tried to pull away, they couldn't. Their racks were locked as tight as an Apache's heart. In the end I had to shoot them both, for they would have starved had I not, fighting each other until their deaths and neither winning. The cow, she wandered off to find another bull, and they say that today Colorado is full with her offspring. Why did I think of that now, amigo?"

"Go to hell, Pete," Luke said grudgingly.

Sanchez smiled sadly. "Sometimes, my friend, I think I have already been there. But tonight I will go back to the Broken Axle. It is time someone told the *patron* of his cattle."

Charity looked at the big wag-on-the-wall clock behind the bar and sighed, wondering, fleetingly, just who her enemy really was, the steady troop of men who flocked into the saloon every night to squander their money on whiskey and chance, or the creeping hands of the open-works clock that ticked away the months and years.

She paused at the top of the stairs, one hand on the rail, and her gaze flicked quickly toward Luke, then away. He stood at the bar leaning wearily, or drunkenly, against it with his ankles crossed and a drink in his hand. He smiled as her gaze touched him, and raised his drink in a salute. She let her gaze rake the rest of the throng as if that had been her intention all along.

There was a good-sized crowd for it being the middle of the week, with a lot of strangers drifting down from the Hills as summer ebbed, but there were a lot of familiar faces, too. Meg was there, of course, sitting on the bar near the far end with her dress hiked up well past her knees. A red-faced miner in a broken-down stained hat stood beside her, his hands on the tight flesh of her shin encased in fish-net stockings, rubbing slowly, and climbing toward her knee. Meg held a mug of beer in one hand and was trying to drink and slap at the miner's hand at the same time, laughing and choking on the beer as she did. It was a game, Charity knew, and one they had likely been playing for a while, with a dozen or so men at the nearby tables whooping and cheering him on.

Nearer, Belle sat at the faro table. She also had a prospect in tow, a curly-haired puncher with a shy grin and a black-

and-white cowhide vest with the hair still on. He was letting Belle handle the chips; his own interest was focused on the shadowy vee of her cleavage, and the way the freckled swell of her breasts would shift and jiggle as she placed his bets. She wasn't unaware of the direction of the young puncher's gaze, Charity knew. Belle was a professional, and she took her work seriously.

They all had their little tricks, she thought wryly; the way they would look at a man in a certain way, or swing their hips when the eyes of the crowd were on them. It became, after a while, their trademark, something the regular customers came to recognize and expect. Like Meg, with her bawdiness, or Belle's exhibitionism. Or, for that matter, her own little ways of flirting, the way she would look at a man over a bare shoulder and throw him a special smile, or bump into a likely-looking customer as if by accident. Tricks of the trade, those and a dozen others she had learned since leaving the train at Ogallala, all of seventeen, and broke to boot.

Those who knew her well knew it was a gambit, a role she played. Repeat customers found her polite but distant, sometimes bordering on cool. In a larger city she would have suffered as a prostitute, but here, perched on the edge of the frontier where a man might go for weeks without seeing a woman, she enjoyed a certain popularity.

Her indifference was her defense, the wall she hid behind when the crowds grew large and ribald. Few knew what she was like behind the mask of her makeup, and she preferred it that way, afraid that any little break in her wall could eventually send it tumbling down. She had seen too many women give up on the future, turning bitter or alcoholic, to allow the same to happen to her. She would stay with the game as long as she could, save her money; then, when the time seemed right, leave without a backward glance. Leave it all, she thought, and irritably pulled her gaze away from the bar, where it had started to drift.

She squared her shoulders and took a deep breath, looking

once more at the big wag-on-the-wall, where the hands stood at a quarter past nine, then started down the stairs with her hands on her hips and an enticing smile playing at her lips. There were seven or eight cowhands crowded around a table near the foot of the stairs, and she recognized the tall young puncher with the head full of hair tonic who had scooted bashfully out of her crib only moments before. Now, surrounded by his friends, an already-empty shot glass almost lost in the curl of his hand, he was riding high on false bravado.

The other hands cheered loudly when they spotted her, slapping the puncher on the back and offering to buy her a drink. The young puncher looked up, his face flushed with whiskey or embarrassment. Their eyes met and he looked away, the blush deepening to an almost scarlet color, and Charity fought the impulse to laugh. They were all the same, she thought, loud and bold among their friends, yet turning as clumsy and insecure as schoolboys when they got upstairs.

"Hey, honey," one of the hands called. "Why don't you let ol' Lance here buy you a drink. One good turn deserves another, don't you think?" They laughed and hooted, all except Lance, who stared into his empty shot glass as though he had found something interesting in it.

"Who got the good turn upstairs?" Charity shot back. "Oh, you mean ol' quick draw there?"

The cowhands howled and a couple of teamsters at the next table smiled. Lance's ears were red now, but he wouldn't look up. "Try me," another puncher shouted. "I'll stay the full round."

"Honey, a full round is only ten seconds," Charity deadpanned. "I'm looking for a man who can last the whole show."

"That's me," the puncher yelped boyishly amid laughter. He was younger than Lance, maybe no more than seventeen or eighteen, but he was screwed up with whiskey courage, randy and ready.

Charity paused at their table, studying the puncher, but speaking loudly enough for them all to hear. "Honey, you still look fresh cut to me. Why don't you come back after weaning?"

This brought whoops from several nearby tables, but the kid suddenly got a funny, provoked look on his face, and for a moment she thought he was going to come up from the table, though she wasn't really sure whether he would be bawling when he did, or swinging. Then a puncher standing behind him clamped a hand on his shoulder and splashed some whiskey in his glass. "Ol' Charlie here gets his heels dusted every once in a while," he laughed. "But I'll wager a dollar he can outride this filly."

"I'll match that wager," Charity smiled. She looked at Charlie and said, "You hunt me up later, honey. Right now I see a friend at the bar I want to say howdy to."

She left them to their laughter and made her way to the bar. The time had come to get it settled, she decided. To have it out in the open, and over, if that's what it came to, although the thought seemed to leave her short of breath.

He was facing the bar again, hunched over it and staring at his drink when she stepped up beside him. "I swear, you're the most down-in-the-mouth customer we get in here anymore," she said. "What's got you by the shank line tonight?"

He looked at her, his eyes blazing momentarily, but the fire died quickly, and he shook his head. "Is the show over?"

"That?" She lifted the drink from his hand and threw it against the back of her throat, grimacing at its bite. Shuddering, she slapped the glass down on the bar in front of her. "It's what I do for a living, remember," she said, her voice suddenly harsh, maybe from the whiskey, but maybe not.

"I haven't forgotten," he replied stiffly. "But do you have to act like . . . like . . ." His words trailed off.

"A whore?" she asked quietly. She stared at him a moment, then shut her eyes and tipped her head back. "God, the last thing I need tonight is another lovesick pup." She looked at him and there was a spark of anger in her eyes. "Do you know how many men tell me they love me every night? Do you know how many propose to me?"

Luke just looked at her, his eyes big and solemn, and said, "I'm different."

"Yeah, I hear that one quite a bit, too," she said, but felt a hitch at her heart just the same. In many ways, she knew, he was.

"I don't want to argue," he said. "Can't we go somewhere and talk? Privately."

"Sure. You got your token?"

He shook his head. "Not that way. I don't even want to go upstairs. What time do you get off tonight?"

She looked at the clock and scowled. "I'll get off when the last customer leaves. Some nights that can be two or three o'clock."

"Tomorrow, then?"

"I won't get up until noon," she replied stubbornly.

"Then I'll pick you up at one. We'll get some food from the Frontier House and take a buggy ride out on the prairie."

She was about to argue more, but the words faded from her lips. She hadn't been outside Sand Creek in more than a year. "Oh, Luke, I'd like that."

He smiled, tried to bite it back, and she let her own come. Then an overweight drummer in striped pants and a silk-edged derby leaned against the bar beside her. He had a large, florid face, a bulbous nose, and thin, watery eyes that flicked nervously from one spot to the next. Clearing his throat, he smiled broadly. "My name is Chester Nelson," he said. "Medical and veterinary supplies. I'd like to buy you a drink, if I may?" He leaned past her and nodded at Luke. "How do."

"The lady doesn't need another drink," Luke replied irritably. "And she's full up on any veterinary supplies she might need."

Nelson's smile faded, and he looked again at Charity. "I

was told that you would be happy to have a drink with me. Then . . . well . . ." He fished a brass token from his vest and put it on the bar, nudging it toward her with pudgy fingers. Her name was stamped across the top, arched above the embossed image of a longhorn.

"She's busy," Luke said flatly. "Move on." His words barely came to her. She was looking past the drummer to where Goff stood at the foot of the stairs, an elbow resting on the lowest banister and a taunting, half-smile fixed on his face. Over the summer four of the girls had slipped off to the Hills, and she knew he was watching the others closely. "Luke, maybe I'd better," she said uncertainly.

"Hold on now," Luke protested.

"No, Luke, please." She flashed him a quick look and saw that he had noticed Goff, too. His brows were furrowed in a scowl. "Tomorrow," she said, smiling and took the drummer's arm and led him away. Tomorrow.

He watched them go, biting back the raw taste of his anger. Goff, still smiling, was already threading through the crowd toward him, and as he got close, Howard said, "You were behind that."

"Lot of men here tonight," Goff offered. "Can't have the girls cozying up to just one man. You have to spread that kind of pleasure around."

"You don't have a brand on her."

Goff shrugged slightly. "I could argue that, but I won't. As long as she works here, she'll do as I want. And from here on, I want her off limits to you. You feel the need for a woman, go see one of the other girls."

"Don't push it too far," Howard replied. "I'll see the woman I want."

Goff met his gaze, silent for a moment, then nodded. "Okay, we've both had our say, we'll let it go at that."

He nodded, feeling his anger boiling all the more; he suddenly wanted to take a swing at Goff but wasn't sure he had reason enough to, so instead he turned abruptly and left the saloon.

On the boardwalk he stopped and lit a cheroot, the image of Charity and the overweight drummer sharp in his mind. It left him feeling sick and helpless, as he had felt earlier, seeing Harper at the top of the stairs with Charity looking stricken beside him. Behind and above him, a lantern creaked rustily from an iron spike on the evening's breeze. On the street a pair of riders jogged in from the north, paused at the intersection, then turned down Second toward the Colorado Lady. Suddenly, the urge for another drink came strong. He had been slipping toward drunk earlier, and now he wanted to take it all the way.

He stepped down off the boardwalk and loosened the bay's reins, swinging up and following the riders. His anger had settled like a lump of clay in the pit of his stomach, not hot the way it normally did, but cold as a winter wind. He felt cold all over now.

There were a dozen horses hitched at the rails outside the Lady, standing patiently with their heads hanging. A bearded hide hunter in a ripped shirt sat in the dirt against the Lady's front wall, humming a nameless tune and punctuating it now and again with short nips from a bottle. He looked up as Howard reined the bay in at the rail and dismounted, then turned back to his bottle, uninterested. The flesh under the rip in his shirt was gapping, slicked with blood that glistened in the faint light of a lantern.

The Colorado Lady, for all its grand name, was little more than a hole in the wall, a long, narrow building of twisted cottonwood logs and a sod roof put up during hide town days. The bar was rough lumber nailed to the rear wall and extending the length of the building. There were seven or eight tables scattered haphazardly throughout the room, and half a dozen smoky lamps mounted to the walls that threw out only about half the light needed. The floor was still dirt—the only one left in Sand Creek—slick in spots, and sour-smelling.

The Lady took its name, and kept its business, from a dark oil canvas of a woman's face and torso hanging behind the bar. It was a young woman there, though just how young was hard to tell. She had a round, full face with black hair parted in the middle and flowing like a river down over each shoulder. Her dress was green, unbuttoned in an innocent way to expose a shoulder and the rounded, pink-tipped swell of a breast.

Against the dark, heavy strokes of oil and in the dim interior of the saloon, the one golden breast seemed to dominate, grabbing a man's attention as he entered and stopping him in his tracks for a space of a heartbeat.

Howard had paused the first time he'd entered the Lady, his eyes drawn to the painting then, but that had been months ago, and tonight he paused again, as if seeing it for the first time. There was, he thought, something more compelling than the mildly erotic exposure of the breast. There was the expression of her face, the haunting, half-promising sparkle in her eyes, and the slightest hint of a smile, as if maybe she was telling a man that the exposed breast wasn't totally innocent, but the secret was only hers and his.

Howard made his way to the bar and ordered a beer. There were a couple of freighters on his right, sweaty and smelling of mules, and a teenage cowhand on his left, standing straight, stiffly, with both hands on the bar and staring with unfocused eyes at the gilt-framed painting, romping together, maybe, along the hazy passages of the whiskey.

Behind him, four men in dirty buckskins were playing a shell game with a handful of pennies. A Mexican woman sat in the lap of one of the players, watching the game with bored patience while the player absently stroked the side of her leg. A second woman moved through the crowd in a tired manner, holding a tray of empty glasses against her hip. At the end of the bar a third woman sat alone. She was a large woman, buxom and wide–hipped, in a tight-fitting red gown. Her name was Kate, and she owned the Colorado Lady.

The beer was lukewarm and weak, but it tasted good in the wake of his anger, soothing the ruffled feathers of his pride. The press at the bar was tight but not uncomfortable, and the single swinging door fanned the thick air every time a man entered or left. From time to time the hoarse, grating bark of drunken laughter would split the low hum of conversation like an axe, leaving a momentary cleft of taut silence. For all the sounds of joviality, the shouting and laughter and clinking of glasses, there was an undercurrent of tension that ran the length of the room. Here there was none of the pranks so common at Goff's, no back slapping or good-natured insults or rough horseplay. These were mostly strangers, freighters passing through, hide hunters down from the buffalo ranges of Montana and Dakota territories; drifters who kept their guns handy. There was a honed wariness in their pinched faces, a long-tended cautiousness that even whiskey couldn't erase.

Howard finished his beer and ordered a second. The action at the shell game was picking up as the men became drunker and freer with their money. The Mexican woman who had been with them earlier was weaving through the crowd now, pausing to talk or share a joke here and there. After a while she slipped into a space beside him and smiled an invitation, but he shook his head, content to drink alone. She looked at the stiff-kneed cowboy at her elbow, then shrugged and moved off. The door banged open then, and three men entered noisily, trooping in a group to the bar and ordering whiskey in loud voices. Broken Axle hands, Howard saw, Hogan, Tyson and Slaughter—the three hands Young had let go. They were all drunk, and seeing them that way cooled his own need for it.

"There was a time when I thought the wild days were over. Guess I was wrong."

Howard turned, finding Kate at his elbow, smiling up at him from beneath a pile of sequined blond hair. Up close, he saw that her face was heavily powdered, stiff with it, and that her smile didn't reach her eyes, which looked cold and calculating to him, though he couldn't guess what she'd be calculating on.

"I'm Kate Muldoon," Kate said. "I guess you'd be Luke Howard, the gunfighter?"

He had begun to nod, a polite greeting forming at his lips, when her last words struck him like a lash, leaving him feeling embarassed and confused. "Yes," he said then, "I'm Luke Howard." He extended a hand and she took it and shook.

"Grab your beer, Luke, I want to palaver a bit." She turned and started for the rear of the saloon, and after a brief hesitation, Howard followed.

There was a small table set back in one dark corner, and Kate sat on the far side, facing most of the saloon, and motioned toward a second chair with a wave of her hand. Howard sat and put his beer on the table and scooted around until he had his back to the wall. Kate smiled again, seeing that, and Howard wondered idly why her makeup didn't crack and flake off; it looked that thick.

"Curious as a cat, ain't cha?" Kate asked, but then didn't wait for a reply. "Did you know you were sitting in the oldest establishment in Sand Creek? The Lady was sitting here when this place was called Hide Town. There were six saloons here then. Course, most were just flint buildings, made from stiff buffalo hides. Left 'em to rot when they cleared the range hereabouts."

"What made you stay?" he asked, suddenly wanting to know.

Kate shrugged, arched her eyebrows, and a piece of her powder did fall off then, landing on the table beside her drink; she flicked it away absently, saying, "Wyatt came in that summer, and the others. Buffalo wasn't hardly gone by then and the hide market wasn't what it is today, so I thought I'd stay around awhile and see what happened."

A loud whoop came from the bar, and Hogan stepped back and kicked at the rail, laughing. "That's the way to do it, goddamnit," he shouted. He seemed impervious to the edged silence from the rest of the room.

Kate sighed. "There was a time when I dreamed of owning a place like Goff's. Someplace fun. But the Lady always did seem to attract the hardcases."

Howard sipped his beer and waited patiently. He figured a woman like Kate seldom invoked idle conversation without reason.

"Do you remember Tishner?" Kate asked. "The little guy with the ivory-handled pistols?"

Tishner was a ferret-faced man with mean eyes and a worse reputation. He was a tiny man, slight of build and not even five feet in his boots, and he seemed to hate the world for it. "He worked for you, right?"

"Kept the peace," Kate said. "He was a sight, too, going up against some of the big men we've had in here. He knew how to work 'em. Tish was a lot of bluff, and not much with his fists, but, oh, he was handy with his pistols."

"What about him?" Howard asked.

Kate laughed. "Tried to run Barney Harper out of the Lady some weeks back."

Harper. He kept popping up like a bad smell, Luke thought. In his belly, his anger turned over like a piece of spoiled meat.

"He told Tish to be out of town the next time he came in. Well, he walked in the door tonight, and Tish just stood up and walked out the back. I followed him and he was saddling his horse. Didn't even ask for his pay, just rode out." She laughed again, but it was a small thing this time, without humor, and she shook her head slowly at the memory. "I never would have believed it. Not of Tish."

"What's this got to do with me?" Howard asked bluntly. He was tired of hearing about Harper tonight.

"I need another peacekeeper. Interested?"

"Why not Harper?" Howard asked. "He was tough enough to scare Tishner off."

"I offered him the job," Kate said simply. "But he didn't want it. So I asked around and they say the best hand with a gun is Luke Howard. If you hadn't wandered in tonight, I was going to send someone out to the Broken Axle tomorrow."

Surprise stayed Howard's tongue. He had heard of Harper and Red before coming to Sand Creek, had heard of Red even before they hunted together down south. They both carried a reputation as gunhands, gunfighters, as Kate had said, and although he hadn't been unaware of that, he had never really seen them in that light, either. That others did, and ranked him among them, proved unsettling. It wasn't a reputation he wanted.

"The pay ain't as good as what you're making now, but it's steady," Kate said. "Fifty a month and found, and that includes whiskey and women, unless you start swilling them. Then I'll put a limit on you."

Howard shook his head. "I haven't finished the job I'm on now."

"Think they're going to miss one hand?"

Howard shrugged, drained his beer, and rose. "I guess I wouldn't be interested, Kate. But I'll keep my eyes open and if I see anybody that looks promising, I'll send him over to talk to you."

"Don't bother," Kate replied curtly. "I'll find someone before the night's over."

She was mad now, Howard saw. In her position she was probably used to getting her way, and now he and Harper both had turned her down within hours of each other. It didn't matter, he thought, and nodded and left. He was feeling closed in of a sudden, cramped, as if the walls had drawn in some, and he knew then that even had he wanted to, he would never be able to work in a saloon—any saloon. He wasn't cut out for inside work, though sometimes he wasn't sure he'd ever see his ranch, either. Now, though, he needed fresh air. He had drunk too much tonight, trying to get drunk and never really succeeding, and he wished now that he had never tried. He thought if he didn't get air soon he might be sick. Feeling that way, he was in no mood to be grabbed by Hogan.

"Well hell, boys, if it ain't ol' Luke Howard, come to buy us a drink after taking our jobs away from us."

It was coming from all sides tonight, Howard thought, and jerked free of Hogan's grip. He was aware of an expectant silence over the room but ignored it as he started for the door.

"Hey!" Hogan cried, dropping his glass on the bar and spilling his drink over it. He lunged and grabbed Howard by the shoulder, spinning him around.

Luke came around fast, and his fist slammed into Hogan's jaw, sending him stumbling backward with his arms flailing. Then Hogan's spurs tangled and he went down hard, his breath escaping with a guttural sound. He sat there then, his mouth agape, and put one hand comically to his jaw. When he didn't get up immediately, Howard turned and left.

On the street, he paused for a deep breath, letting the cool night air soothe his anger and ease the distant rumblings of his stomach. It seemed a long time back now when he had ridden into town, but he remembered vaguely that he had been looking forward to it all day. Coming hadn't turned out the way he had hoped, but then, he hadn't known the others were back. That made the difference, he thought. The news that they hadn't brought the herd back; finding Charity upstairs with Harper, which rankled even deeper than the drummer; and even Hogan, he thought, could be blamed on finding the others back, for it had all led to his coming to the Colorado Lady.

His bay whickered softly from the rail and he went to him and rubbed the broad forehead under his forelock. The bay whickered again and pushed at him with his nose, nuzzling Howard's breast pocket. Howard laughed and patted the side of the bay's neck. "Sorry, boy, no sugar tonight."

They had been through a lot together, he and the bay. Every since that *paseo* he had taken into New Mexico Territory in '68, delivering a string of harness mules for a breeder from the Nations. He had spotted him in an adobe corral behind the cantina in Las Cruces, his ribs scarred from the rowels of a half-drunk little *pistolero* from below the border. The bay had set him back close to a hundred dollars, three times what a good cow pony would cost, yet over the years he often thought he had gotten him at a bargain.

He was an Arabian, Howard judged, pure-blooded from his lines, with big, intelligent eyes and a proud way of moving, as if the world was his for the taking, his and his partner's. He was spoiled some, playful and teasing at times, and sometimes, as if preferring the company of men to other horses, would slip up to a fire at night and stand with his head over Howard's shoulder. But a man alone came to depend on his horse, not just for transportation but for company, someone to talk to when the trail grew long and lonely. Considering that, Howard didn't figure a little spoiling hurt much. Not when you had a horse like the bay.

Caught up thinking of the bay, Howard at first didn't hear the scuff of boots coming up quick behind him. He turned into a fist, looping from the shadows like lead on the end of an axe handle. With a grunt, he fell back against the bay, and the bay snorted and backed off, spilling him onto the street. A pair of hands descended from nowhere and grabbed him by the front of the shirt, pulling him around, slamming again into his jaw. The lights from the Colorado Lady seemed to spin in different directions, fading in and out of focus. He blinked, his eyes tearing, and in a moment realized he was down again, lying in the dust in the middle of the street.

"He don't look so tough, does he?" The voice seemed to come from a long way off, muffled through the roaring in his ears, yet he recognized it easily enough. It was Hogan, towering above him with his fist cradled in his arm. He laughed as Howard's gaze finally focused on him, flexing his hand. "Goddamn, if you ain't the hard-headedest sonofabitch I've ever hit. Bet you're mule stubborn, too." He looked over his shoulder and smiled. Tyson stood behind him, a bottle of whiskey dangling from his hand, and Slaughter stood close by.

Howard gritted his teeth against the receding pain and came off the ground in a sudden lunge, catching Hogan flat-footed and driving him back against the building with a hard right. He turned on Tyson before Hogan slid to the ground, slipping a fist through Tyson's quickly-raised defense and catching the ex-puncher full in the face. He never saw Slaughter's swing, only felt the sudden jolt of pain below his ear. He lost his sight for a moment, and most of his other senses, hearing only the dull thud of his own body striking the earth, followed by a sharp stab in his ribs.

He rolled to his back, blinking against the dust, his senses stilling reeling. Hogan's voice seemed to float somewhere just out of his reach, the words jumbled and meaningless. Another sharp stab of pain in his ribs brought some clarity. "Kick him again, Charlie." Tyson, he thought, or Hogan. It meant Slaughter was the man kicking him.

Luke rolled quickly and grabbed Slaughter's boot as it sliced the air close to his ribs, twisting then, and spilling him to the ground. He rose to meet Hogan's rush and they fell together, slapping and punching from the ground, too close to do much damage until Luke managed to bring an elbow around and drive it into Hogan's face. He rolled free and gained his feet, leaving Hogan blinking and snorting blood. Tyson waded in before he was all the way up, driving a hard fist into Howard's forehead, then another to his cheek, knocking him back into Slaughter's arms.

Slaughter pinned him from behind while Tyson lashed at Howard's face and stomach, putting everything he had into his swings. Howard choked against a mouthful of blood, hacking and spitting past a loose tooth, swallowing enough to make him gag. A cut above one eye closed it with blood and he could feel the sour taste of vomit against the back of his throat. He sagged into Slaughter's arms, but the puncher wouldn't let him go down; he jerked him back and around to face another blow. Howard kicked out before it came, catching Tyson's unprotected knee and forcing his leg out from under him, then brought his foot back, driving the rowel of his spur into the thin flesh of Slaughter's shin.

Slaughter screamed and fell back, and Howard brought his fist around in a long, looping swing, catching Slaughter above the ear and dropping him. He was still turning, coming back around to Tyson again, when the cold steel of a gun barrel rapped sharply at his skull.

He came to for a second maybe halfway to the ground and tried to push his arms out to break his fall, but the rushing ground faded once more into blackness, and the blackness lasted a long time.

Howard woke cold and weak, stretched out on a narrow iron bunk chained to the wall. The taste of vomit was strong now, the smell of it rising from his shirt. His face felt stiff and unyielding, flushed with a slight fever, and he had to pry the lid of his left eye open with his fingers; the lashes felt thick and gummy, threatening to stick every time he blinked. His head throbbed with a dull ache that kept time to the beat of his heart.

It was still dark outside, but chilled, the way it was just before dawn. He rose stiffly and stood swaying, one hand braced against the cold brick wall, then shuffled slowly across the room, stopping abruptly at the thin straps of horizontal and vertical iron that formed the inside wall. He leaned weakly against the cell door and called out in a rasping voice, but if anyone heard, he didn't answer. There was a lamp sitting on a small shelf just inside the door that led to the outer office, its wick turned low so that its light was feeble.

There had been a humming in his head since he had awakened, a low, monotonous reverberation that he had thought was only a part of the pain at first. But now, slowly gathering his strength, he became aware that the sound was separate from the throbbing, coming from the cell opposite him. He stared into the shadows there until his eyes ached and watered, the shadows slowly shaping themselves into something recognizable. He made out the white glow of a bandage first, the rest of the features taking form around it. With something of a start then, he recognized the hide hunter from the Colorado Lady, the one with the gaping wound, sitting out front as he'd entered. He was sitting on his bunk with his arms hanging slack at his sides, staring with glassy eyes at a spot on the floor. Howard stared too, and at first saw nothing, until a spot there moved, scurrying across the floor toward the hunter. It was a roach, nothing more, but in the drunken stupor of the hunter, it must have been much more. He screamed suddenly, drawing his legs high and falling back against the wall, then screamed again, the roach gone from sight now. But whatever it had evoked in the hunter was still there, still on the attack.

Howard clutched at the bars, swaying, the screams raking at his wounds. He thought his head might explode with the sound. He turned and stumbled toward his bunk, falling into it and pulling the scratchy wool blanket over his head.

CHAPTER 6

THEY called it Sonofabitch Creek when they called it anything at all. It started somewhere near the thick-pined flank of Harney's Peak and flowed in a roundabout way to the southeast, where it joined the French. It was a small creek, fast and tumbling, though no more than a couple of long jumps at its widest. There had been some fish when they arrived, small rainbow trout and such, easy to catch and good eating. But the trout had disappeared when they started digging. Still, there was venison and bear and a few elk left, plus rabbit for stews, and if a man was lucky or good at birding, he could find grouse in the grassy meadows. There were still buffalo, too, along the edge of the Hills. Maybe not as many as there had been even a year ago, but enough that a man wouldn't starve if he had a good rifle and a few wits about him.

If they had given their camp a name, they would have likely called it Sonofabitch Camp, but they were drifters, ex-gandy dancers, and they didn't talk of the camp at all, except of what they hoped to find there. They had come up from North Platte in the spring and there had been snow on the ground when they arrived, patches here and there among the shady valleys, speckled with pine needles and bark and bits of dirt, like pepper over flour. They'd come up with a wagon load of ex's like themselves, farmers and carpenters and soldiers, and even a few shop owners, willing to risk family and business on the chance of gold.

The papers back East were screaming gold. Gold dust in the grass, nuggets the size of a man's thumb gleaming in the stream beds, gold as easy to pick as fruit from an orchard.

But they'd been at it for five months now, and so far the only gold they'd seen was somebody else's.

Their camp was in a twisting little east-west valley, set back in a stand of white-barked aspen under a rocky ledge that rose probably two hundred feet above them. There were a couple of tents and a brush and canvas shelter over a dwindling supply of firewood. The space in front of the tents was littered with drying wash, discarded pieces of leather, an axe and several shovels. Farther out, almost hidden in the tall grass, broken bottles and rusting tins lay scattered.

There was a deerhide hanging from a nearby limb, and thin strips of venison drying over racks above a low fire. Closer to the flames and dripping fat that hissed and popped among the coals was a slice of deer haunch skewered with a green branch.

There was a road of sorts snaking along the far side of the valley, and a rider jogging up from the east at an easy gait.

The placer was idle today. Two of the miners had ridden up to Easy Street for supplies, leaving the third to guard their camp and watch after the drying jerky. He was a short man, stocky in build, somewhere in his fifties. He had a full, gray beard that rode high on his cheeks, patched overalls, and broken down brogans. He watched the stranger on the horse surreptitiously from beneath wooly brows. When the rider turned off the road to pick his way through the scattering aspen, he stood up, bringing an old Sharps percussion rifle into the crook of his arm.

Swede halted his buckskin at the edge of the stream, resting his eyes on the miner, then letting them shift carefully through the forest surrounding the camp. Satisfied, he gigged the horse and splashed across the creek, skirting the dried-mud cones of earth dug from the gravel bars, and halted again at the edge of the camp.

"Afternoon, stranger. What can I do for you?" the miner said.

Swede ignored him, studying the camp. His gaze stopped

briefly on the deerhide and the venison, then came back to the miner. "There's three bedrolls in that far tent," he said quietly. "Where are the others?"

The miner bristled, letting the Sharps slide down to his hands, then swinging the barrel up. Swede smiled coolly, and the miner stopped the muzzle before it climbed to Swede's chest. "You're awful nosy for just riding in out of nowhere, ain't cha?"

"Been doing a lot of riding the last couple of weeks. My patience is wearing out."

"Stranger, when you ride into my camp, you'll abide by the rules of my camp, which are the same rules you'd abide to in any man's camp. Good old-fashioned manners."

Swede straightened in the saddle, his eyes going cold, flinty. He moved his right hand from the saddle horn to his thigh, and for the first time the miner noticed there was no leather thong over the revolver's hammer. The miner's gaze flitted back to the stranger's face, and he licked his lips. "There's three here, most days," he said finally. "My partners went into town to pick up some flour and a new pick."

"I'm looking for beeves. Somebody buying or selling."

The miner shook his head. "Ain't no beef here. We been eating deer or bear all summer."

"Heard of any beef in this area?"

The miner glanced again at the revolver on Swede's thigh, and the hand that almost seemed to twitch in its eagerness to draw it. "Maybe. There's a little town eight, ten miles up the valley. Easy Street, they call it. Heard there's a place there that sells beef sometimes. Heard it goes for two dollars a plate."

Swede nodded, satisfied. He looked the camp over a final time, taking in the patched clothes, the sagging canvas of the tents, and the litter of trash lying where it had been tossed. "Tell me, dirt puncher, you strike it rich yet?"

The miner's grip tightened on his rifle and his lip quivered, but he held his tongue. Swede laughed and turned his horse, putting his back contemptuously to the miner. The miner's finger twitched on the Sharp's trigger, but he didn't raise the rifle. He watched until the stranger was out of sight, then sank back to his seat and leaned the Sharps against a tent line. His hands were shaking as he brought them back, and the sight of them shamed him deeply.

Sam Bronson leaned back in the wooden swivel chair and raised his heels to the desk top, crossing one ankle above the other. He looked sleepy, almost indolent, but there was a sharpness in his hooded eyes that commanded attention. He was dressed in his suit clothes today, but he had his coat off and his shirt sleeves rolled up.

"Your head hurt?" Bronson asked mildly.

"Don't let it bother you," Howard replied. His voice was hoarse, raspy, unfamiliar to his ears. He sat casually in a chair opposite Bronson and masked the throbbing in his head behind indifference.

Bronson chuckled. "It doesn't bother me. I enjoyed doing it."

Howard studied him quietly for a moment, then said, "You hit me?"

Bronson spread his hands in admission. "Seemed the easiest way to stop the fight."

"You son of a bitch."

Bronson's smile turned tight. "You know, in St. Louis they pay men to go around and sweep the streets of garbage. It's what I do every morning, picking your kind out of the dirt and mud and throwing them in a cell to puke and piss over everything." He took a deep breath, let it out through his nose. Howard shut his eyes. He felt dizzy yet, weak and nauseous and disjointed, half smothered under a blanket of . . . what? Pain? Fever?

"I've warned you before about taking the law into your own hands," Bronson continued. "I won't tolerate this."

Howard sighed. "Give me my things, Bronson. I've got things to do."

"You still don't understand, do you? You think because you work for the God Almighty Cattlemen's Association you have a free rein in this town. You're wrong, Howard, damn wrong. This is my town, not yours. I brought the peace . . . goddamnit, I brought civilization here. I made it safe for women to walk the streets without some hardcase bothering them. I made it safe for men to bring their families here. I'll not let your kind of lawlessness come back to Sand Creek."

Anger flashed in Howard's eyes, bringing with it a fresh throbbing in his temples. He stood and braced himself against the mule-kicking bolts of pain that racked his body, glaring down at the startled marshal. "We didn't bring trouble to Sand Creek. It was here when we arrived. We came to stop it, but every time we turn around we have one of your damn family men standing there trying to cut us down. If we pulled out now Sand Creek would turn to dust. Just another little dirt-water town that didn't make it.

"So you pass the word, Bronson. You keep Goff and Hogan and Clark off our backs, or we'll pull out of here and turn this town over to the rustlers."

Bronson didn't like it, Howard knew, didn't like anyone challenging his authority, but he didn't say anything. No matter how much Bronson resented the Sand Creek Cattlemen's Association, Howard knew he was bound to respect its power. Yet he wouldn't back down either, and he rose now, facing Howard across the desk.

"I won't let this town blow up, Howard. It's come too far from what it was. I ran Hogan and Tyson and Slaughter out of town last night, and when this job is finished I'll run you and your friends out, too." He reached into a drawer and tossed Howard's gunbelt on the desk. "I'll pass the word around town to stay off your back, and I'll make damn sure Goff and Clark get it. But my warning still holds. When this job is finished I'll want all of you out of Sand Creek."

The point didn't seem worth arguing. Howard buckled the belt on and settled the Colt at his hip. His hat was on a rack, and he put it over his head and let it fall against his back, the drawstring pulling tight against his throat; the raw flesh along his scalp was still too tender to take the tightness of his sweatband. He glanced at Bronson a final time, then left without speaking.

Stepping onto the boardwalk, he winced at the sudden stab of sunlight striking his eyes. There was a warm breath of air stirring the dust along the street, coming in sharp and clean from the prairie. Wasps buzzed lazily at a corner rafter, and down the street a dozen or so chickens pecked in the dirt next to the Feed and Grain. The sun was like a warm hand laid across the town, and its strength felt good against Howard's bruised flesh. He walked slowly down First, letting the sun and exercise limber his stiffened muscles. The wounds he had taken in his fight with the three punchers were sore, stinging in places, but nothing he couldn't shrug away. It was the crack Bronson had given him above the ear that gave him trouble. His vision was still fuzzy around the edges, and there was a far-off whistle muffling his hearing, like a teapot in the next room letting off steam. He was dizzy, too, and by the time he reached the dappled shade of the Lone Oak Livery, sweat was sheening his face and creating a dark crescent beneath his arms.

Old Anse was stretched out in a cot in the cluttered office when Howard entered, but he came awake quickly and swung his skinny legs out of bed, rubbing at the back of his head until his stringy gray hair looked as tangled as a bird's nest. He grunted when he saw Howard, and his eyes widened. "Jehoshaphat, boy, you step in front of the Black Hills stagecoach?"

Howard sank gratefully to a bench against one wall. "You have the bay?" he asked.

"Sure, sure. Marshal brought him in last night." Anse skinned into a pair of worn wool trousers, shiny at the knees, slipped his feet barefoot into a pair of shoes, then hooked his suspenders over his bony shoulders. "Fightin', huh?" he said, studying Howard from the corner of his eye as he bent over a little potbellied stove and stirred the coals there into flame. "Coffee'll help," he said, sliding a pot over the lid.

Anse went back to his cot and sat, grinning. "You young bucks come waltzing into town like you own the world, drinking and whoring and like as not waking up to the staggers." He laughed and shook his head. "I, God, boy, do it while you can, and don't let anyone tell you different, cause once you get to be my age all you can do is watch the younger ones go after it and wish to hell you'd've known better back when." He rubbed at his rheumy eyes, wiping the tears away and still chuckling.

Howard leaned back, resting his head gently against the wall and shutting his eyes. "I got a jug," Anse offered. "Little hair of the dog?"

"Thanks, old-timer, but I'll just wait for that coffee."

There was movement outside the office, the rustle of material, and a tentative voice calling his name. Anse grinned and winked, pulling a light jacket on over the bare contours of his age-sunken chest. He leaned close as he passed and whispered, "Was a time when they wouldn't leave me alone, either." Then he was gone, and Howard heard him saying, "He's inside, missy. Had him a hard night, I reckon."

Charity appeared in the door, clutching the skirt of a lime green dress out of the dust with one hand. Her hair was done up high, clasped on top with a turtle-shell clip, and she held a small, cloth purse in her free hand. "Luke?" she said uncertainly. She let her skirt drop then and hurried to his side, raising a hand as if to touch his face, then pausing, holding her hand close. "Oh, Luke, your face. Are you okay?"

He pulled away and stood, suddenly embarrassed at being caught as he was, bruised and swollen, with traces of blood and vomit still lingering on his clothes. She followed him though, touching him this time, tracing the puffed line of his jaw. Her touch was gentle, the fingers floating along like feathers, and her lips made a small "o" when she came to the bloody mat of hair below the scalp wound. He thought her eyes looked sorrowful in the dim light, as if she could feel the throbbing through her fingers.

"I just heard. Oh, Luke, what were you doing at the Colorado Lady? That place attracts trouble like a dog attracts fleas."

In his embarrassment and pain he lashed out, wanting to cut. "You were busy, remember? Quite a night."

She drew back, her lips pursing into a thin, tight line, but there was hurt in her eyes, and although it pained him to see it there, he couldn't stop, couldn't pull back. "How much did you make last night, Charity? Between the drummer and Harper and the cowhands you were flirting with? Did you take them all?" The words came as if torn, and just as painful; he had to bite his lip to keep from saying more.

Tears welled in her eyes, and she fought them back with anger. Her cheeks were red with it. He thought she was going to shout at first; her throat worked convulsively, as if the words, the energy, were there, but when she finally spoke her voice was low, though shaky, as if with anger. "I am a whore," she said slowly. "And that was good enough for you at first."

She spun and stalked from the room, leaving in her wake a wagonful of words left unspoken. Howard sank slowly to the bench and swore. He had done wrong, he knew, the wrong prompted by pain, yet even knowing that, he felt something like relief, too. It was over, he supposed, and while that hurt in a way, he couldn't help but wonder if it wouldn't be for the best in the long run.

The rails were full, so Swede reined the buckskin through the crowd and into a vacant lot between a pair of saloons and dropped the reins, knowing the horse wouldn't stray unless someone led him off. He paused at the corner of a saloon, free from the press of traffic, and studied the town with a critical eye.

Easy Street was new, wild and raw, bigger than most, for being so new. There was a boardwalk along a big chunk on the opposite side of the single street, and a few plank buildings looking new and oddly inferior to the squat log structures that most of the businesses were housed in— maybe fifty buildings, all told, strung out across a wide meadow that sloped gently up into the surrounding mountains. He counted twenty-three saloons, two houses of prostitution, and a billiards hall, all open and doing a steady business. The rest were drygoods stores, mining outfitters, stables, a couple of blacksmith shops, plus several restaurants.

The street was lined with wagons of every description, from converted army ambulances and sagging farm wagons to heavy freight outfits with twenty-mule jerk-line hitches. The rails were lined with pack animals and saddle horses, and for every animal on the street there seemed to be three men on the boardwalk or the dirt path that substituted as a boardwalk on the near side of the street. From time to time he heard the high-pitched laugh of a woman from one of the saloons, sounding as shrill as a jay's scold above the deep-throated rumble of men, but the only woman in sight was a slat-thin farm wife in a muddy gingham dress and full bonnet, perched on the seat of a covered wagon with two dirty-faced youngsters on either side of her.

Swede joined the flow of the crowd, dropping out at the doorless entrance of a log saloon with a simple sign nailed above the entrance that advertised, simply, "Whiskey," in crude script.

It was dark and crowded inside, with a hard-packed and lumpy dirt floor and half a dozen tree stumps cut off at knee level as seats. Swede forced a place near the center of the bar, and a sweating, bald man in a dirty shirt set a glass and jug before him.

"Forty-rod?" the barkeep asked.

"What have you got?"

"I can call it whatever you want, but it all comes from the same still."

Swede shrugged and nodded toward the glass.

"Fifty cents," the barkeep smiled apologetically. "Rules of the house, money first."

Swede dropped half a dollar—boom town prices—on the bar and took his drink. He took it easy on the first sip, expecting a bite, and grimaced anyway. The whiskey burned all the way down, like coals shoveled straight from the fire into his belly. His eyes watered and he tried to blink them clear.

On his right a heavyset man in beard and suspenders chuckled. "Tastes a little like rattlesnake piss, don't it?"

Swede looked at him and blinked owlishly, and the bearded man laughed again. "It isn't snakehead, is it?" Swede asked hoarsely.

"Naw, I don't think so. I'd take this place apart log by log if it was. Snakehead's only fit for Injuns, and then only the tame ones."

"I'm called Swede. I'm new in town."

"Mister, everybody's new in Easy Street. Six months ago there wasn't but a couple of tents down at the far end of the meadow. I'm Harry Anders."

"Been here long, Harry?"

"In this saloon? Maybe twenty minutes. In Easy Street, a couple of months. You might say I'm an old-timer here. Had a diggings on the Blue Bell for a while, but decided there was more money in carpentering."

Swede took another sip, barely touching it to his lips. The bite was just as harsh as the first, like touching his tongue to a match, and he pushed the glass away with disgust. "Harry," he said, "I'm from cow country and I'm thinking of running some beef up here to market. Who do I need to see?"

"Mister, beef is about as scarce as virgins up here, and I wouldn't know who to see about either one. Sometimes we get beef in town, sometimes some of the other towns get it. There's maybe two or three places around Easy Street that sells it from time to time."

"I didn't know anybody was making drives up here yet," Swede said casually.

Harry chuckled again, to himself this time.

"Something funny, Harry?" Swede was leaning against the bar, his thumb hooked in his gunbelt above a revolver.

Harry looked uncertainly toward him, noticing for the first time the twin revolvers strapped around Swede's waist. "No," he grunted. "Nothing's funny. People bring cattle into the Hills all the time."

"Enough to supply a restaurant?"

"Cows drift. Who knows where they come from."

"Harry, I lied to you," Swede said softly. "I didn't come up here to scout a market. Somebody's rustling cattle off the range I work for. I came up here to kill them."

Harry sidled away, his gaze dropping once more to the revolvers strapped around Swede's slim waist. "Mister, I don't know anything."

"Who sells beef around here?"

"I don't know. I can't afford beef at mining town prices."

"Harry, I'm going to ask you one more time. If you don't give me an answer I like, I'm going to pull my right hand gun and shoot you in the stomach. Who sells beef, Harry?"

Harry licked his lips, his eyes roving the crowd as if in search of a friendly face, then settled again on Swede. "Mister, you can't just shoot a man for not answering a question."

"Sure I can," Swede said, smiling. His hands drifted back, rested lightly on the revolver's grips, while his thumb curled around the hammer.

"The Placer, damnit. Sandy's Placer, up the hill. They've got beef on the menu today."

Swede nodded and his smile never flickered. "Go ahead and finish my snakehead, Harry. It's on me." He stepped away from the bar and walked through the door without looking back, knowing Harry wouldn't do anything, though he kept his ears tuned just in case.

Outside, Swede leaned back against the logs of the saloon and hooked a heel into them, waiting. He brought a toothpick from his pocket and chewed it absently, watching the bustle of the crowd, thinking that except for the buildings it wasn't a lot different from New York City.

The thought surprised him, coming when it did, although there was always a little surprise, thinking back that far. It was a long time ago now, and seemed it. Remembering the skinny, towheaded kid he'd been was like remembering a stranger, somebody you'd seen once maybe, and heard about. He remembered Barnes, too, the man he had killed, his face sharp and dark, with black hair and a black mustache, both always combed and slicked, and fancy suits to turn a woman's eye, as they had his sister's. It was something he had never been able to figure out; they had both known what Barnes was, had shunned him for it, yet when Janice had turned sixteen, when Barnes had turned his attention toward her, she seemed to forget it all. She was different, she had told him once, and Barnes would change because of her. He didn't think either of them was ever surprised that he didn't.

So Barnes pimped for his sister and a dozen others and eventually his sister died, and so did Barnes, but Barnes had friends and Swede was only an immigrant's son, friendless and without family by this time. If not for the war he might have been lost, but the Army took him and taught him how to kill; he had already learned how to hate with Barnes.

A long time ago now. . . .

Down the street the farm wife still waited with her children. In the opposite direction, backed up against the black backdrop of forest, was a wide, squat building of logs. There was a sign out front, hanging from a chain above the door, reading: "Sandy's Placer," and below that the crude painting of a miner and his burro. There was a slate menu board next to the door, dusted with blue chalk but unreadable at this distance. Swede rolled the toothpick from one side of his mouth to the other, waiting for Harry. He didn't have to wait long.

Harry paused at the edge of the street, looked toward Sandy's Placer, then hitched at his trousers and hurried across the street. Swede waited until he'd entered a plank building with real glass in the front windows, then sauntered after him.

It was another saloon, larger than the one he had just exited, with gaming tables near the rear of the room and painted and powdered girls wandering among the tables with tight, artificial smiles. The crowd was heavy, but the room was large enough to handle it without a closed-in feeling. Almost immediately, Swede spotted Harry, leaning across the table near the back of the room and whispering into the ear of a man in a broadcloth suit with one arm pinned up at the shoulder.

The one-armed man was watching the door when Swede walked in, and his eyes opened slightly in recognition. Harry looked toward the door at the same time, and his face turned white. He backed away from the table, bumping into a woman in a skimpy black dress who shoved back and cursed. The man with one arm stood and finished his drink, then walked slowly toward a rear door, exiting quietly and with little notice. Swede followed, ignoring Harry.

He expected a back room and was surprised to find himself outside again, the ground sloping down to the banks of a muddy little creek hardly a good jump across. The one-armed man was standing next to a lightning-struck pine at the creek's edge, a short-barreled revolver clenched tightly in his fist. Swede's eyes widened some at that. It had been a long time since anyone had gotten a drop on him, but this stranger had, sure enough. Swede stepped outside and pulled the door shut behind him. He studied the stranger, remembering the look of recognition on his face in the saloon, but if they had met before, Swede didn't remember it. He took a step toward the one-armed man, whose revolver tipped toward Swede's chest. Swede's own hand moved back, a casual thing, as if by accident, and the one-armed man's revolver spat flame and smoke.

Swede felt a numbing jolt to his chest and looked down at the frayed hole just below the third button of his shirt, surrounded by a small crimson stain. A second hole appeared as he watched, accompanied this time by a roaring that drowned out the merry sound of rushing water. He wasn't sure where the roaring came from; it just seemed to surround him, while the air thickened and became hard to breath. The ground was rising toward his face, whirling, and he tried to draw his own revolver, feeling a powerful need to do just that much, but he couldn't seem to find it.

He didn't feel the fall. He didn't feel anything at all. He closed his eyes as the roaring faded, grateful for the soundless darkness.

Red held the sorrel to a fast lope, following a twisting trail south along the Sand Creek. Willow brush and scrub oak popped his chaps like buggy whips, and the tall grass that always grew close to water flashed backward beneath his stirrups. He had no destination in mind, only a need to ride, to be alone while he sorted through the jumbled confusion of his feelings.

The easy gait of the sorrel and the warm touch of the afternoon sun flickering through the trees had a lulling effect on him; he felt lethargic, sleepy beyond what his sleeplessness of the night before could account for, and he knew it was more than all that. It was his feelings, hate and anger combined, the two like a pair of heavy logging chains around his neck, weighing him down and wearing him out. It wasn't a new feeling, of course, but it had lain dormant for so long it could have been. It seemed fresher and stronger now than he could ever remember it.

His thoughts kept skipping erratically through the past, picking out odd bits of memory, some he thought he'd forgotten. He remembered Texas some, and the war, but mostly his thoughts drifted deeper, all the way back to Virginia. He remembered the big houses along the Roanoke, the green fields stretching back from the river with the black, black soil. Then, as if mocking, he saw his father's swampy patch of ground, and the damn uppity niggers turned free like cattle out of a pasture, and the looting and raping and burning, and the hangings, soon enough. Men a-horseback with dirty flour sacks pulled over their heads and round holes cut out for the eyes. His father's face confused, and Reba's, her eyes wide and frightened, the torchlight glowing on her black skin. The shot, the one loud shot out of so many, and seeing the red muzzle blast and showering sparks, hearing Reba's scream as his father fell. . . .

The sorrel shied suddenly, and even with his mind wandering, Red stayed with him. A big jackrabbit bounded off toward the prairie and the sorrel, snorting and blowing, crow-hopped off the trail. Scolding in a gentle voice, Red brought him back, and in doing so lost the memory of that evening.

He came up out of the creek bottom and was startled by his shadow, stretched long from the westering sun, and by the lather along the cinch. Maybe a hundred yards off he could see the Sand Creek road, and that surprised him too. Lost in the past, he had let time slip away, had ridden like a pilgrim or a blind man through hostile country. Keeping the sorrel to a walk then, he rode on.

He was a long way south of the cattle range here, in country he had passed through only once, but he had a good memory for land, and thought he wasn't so far from the Grant Creek cutoff. On down the road he spotted a thin cloud of dust, and a bull train taking shape beneath it. He saw three big outfits with their low, canvas-covered loads boomed tight, each pulled by a twelve-yoke team of oxen. The whackers plodded along upwind, out of the dust, and there was a swamper perched on each wagon, where he could handle the brakes on the grades. Ahead of the wagons rode a solitary horseman, a rifle canted across his saddlebow. He was a scout, Red knew, though with a trail so plain it was likely he was only along for whatever protection his rifle could offer. Although he hadn't been here then, talk in Goff's was that only the year before six freighters had lost their scalps along this road, and a man didn't really know whether it was safe yet, or if the Sioux were just raiding elsewhere for a while.

The scout spurred his horse forward, and Red reined up to let him approach. He was a lean old codger, with an easy, loose-jointed way of riding that told Red he was a man used to the saddle. Closer, he saw that the rifle was a Remington buffalo gun, and that he carried a couple of shell belts around his middle, above his gunbelt. His hair was long, flowing down his back, streaked with gray, and his beardless face had a gaunt look of age. He pulled his horse down to a trot as he came closer, then a walk, turning his head and arching a golden stream of tobacco into the dust. Pulling up, he nodded his howdy, and Red saw humor in his old, sun-faded eyes. "How," the old scout said finally.

"How," Red returned.

"Ain't seen no screaming horde of redskins, have ye?" he asked, his eyes crinkling.

"Nary a one," Red replied. "Been looking for some?"

The scout laughed. "Figured these yahoos coming up must know something I don't, the way they been expectin' redskins to pop up over every ridge. Hate to see 'em get all the way to Deadwood without seein' a one."

"Freight going into Deadwood already?"

"Oh, mister, everything's going into Deadwood. Big city new. Ain't you heard about Hickok?"

"Man doesn't need a big city to get shot in the back in."

The scout chuckled. "Right enough at that, but Deadwood's still big enough. Maybe the biggest up there now, if they ain't discovered a new strike somewhere else."

Red shrugged, thinking it really didn't matter anyway. Nodding his head toward the back trail, he said, "You come up the Grant Creek cutoff?"

"Naw, straight up from Ogallala. It ain't so far back, though. Maybe a mile or two. She cuts over yonder ridge, and the Grant be right on the other side." He studied Red curiously for a moment, then said, "People say there's farmers settled on the Grant Creek. Said the Sand Creek ranchers are some ruffled by it, that they've got some hired guns to roust 'em out."

"Saloon talk," Red said. "I just come from Sand Creek, and I haven't heard anything about hired guns to roust nesters."

"Aye," the scout said. "Hear a lot in a saloon, ye do that." He grinned suddenly. "Almost enough to make a man give up his drinkin', but only almost."

The train was getting close now; Red could hear the rattle of rope and canvas, the clinking of chains and the dull plodding of hooves. The oxen moved in a laggardly fashion, their heads drooped low under the weight of the yokes, but they moved steadily, too, and Red knew they were likely the best animal for freighting there was, if a man could only stand the pace.

"I God, best get out of the road," the scout said. "Go hard on my conscience if you was to get run over in the stampede, it would."

Red grinned and touched the brim of his hat. "Obliged for the information, old timer. Drink a shot of red-eye to stampeding ox for me when you get to Deadwood."

The scout laughed. "I'll do that, and a few others, besides."

The scout rode ahead and Red went wide around the bull train, lifting the sorrel into a jog now. He came to the cutoff sooner than he expected, and halted there, studying the twin wagon tracks on the prairie.

The Grant Creek road was misleading, Red remembered. Coming north out of Ogallala and not long after passing the first Ogallala and Black Hills stage station, a man was offered a choice: the main road cutting straight across the prairie, or the Grant Creek cutoff, looping down along the Grant. Most took the main road, trusting the judgment of those before them, but from time to time some freighter or lone rider would follow the rutted trail leading down to the Grant, trading a night of firewood and sure water for maybe a dozen extra miles the next day.

Red sat the sorrel awhile, just watching the road, trying briefly to recapture the memory of that night his father died, but it wouldn't come now, nor would it usually, and he wondered what had summoned it as he loped along the creek. Finally, on his own accord, the sorrel stepped out, down the cutoff, and Red let him go, gave him his head. After a while, he tickled the sorrel's ribs with his spurs, lifting him into a trot, then a canter. From time to time he would slow, but soon enough then, they'd be back in a canter. An hour later he came to the Grant and pulled off the cutoff and into the trees, slowing finally to a walk. He had no idea where the nesters had built their soddies, but reasoned that it wouldn't be far or else the men would have driven into Ogallala for grain and supplies.

Close to the creek, the shadows were gathering, and he knew that full darkness wasn't far off anymore. Without reason for being here, a smart man would have headed on back, yet he felt compelled to go on, without knowing what was compelling him. Apparently the sorrel felt it too, through the rein, for he pushed on without urging now, stepping high and lively. Seeing the woman, Red jerked back suddenly on the reins, his mouth gaping a little, his eyes wide and startled.

It was the flash of white that caught his attention at first, just a brief, quick movement he thought at first was the rump of an antelope, then knew immediately that he was wrong. That's when he jerked the sorrel up.

It was one of the darkies, he saw, crouched down at the edge of a pool with her blouse off, though she was still wearing a chemise; it was the chemise that had caught his attention. She hadn't seen him yet, busy with her work; she had a willow basket piled high with washed clothes on the bank beside her, and was wringing yellow suds from a dark blouse even as he watched. In the fading light her hands seemed to dart like a pair of birds, but he noticed they were deft too, without wasted motion. Stopped, he could hear the low sound of her humming, the tune one he didn't know, but the deep, throaty, businesslike sound of it brought back a memory as sharp as a skinning knife: Reba again, humming the way this woman hummed, the little shack where they lived rich with the smells of canning, and he thought then that it had been a happy home, for all the poverty. Maybe that was what brought this one incident so vividly back. Reba's dark face fearful suddenly, the sound of her humming stopped abruptly, his own question dying on his lips . . . "Reba, did you know my ma?" . . . and his own fear as Reba burst into tears. He didn't understand then, and blindly perhaps, wouldn't until after his father had died. Reba had taken him in her arms that day and buried his face into the warm swell of her bosom until he thought he would suffocate, her words muffled by her arms, "Yes, chile, I knowed yore mammy. She loved you, chile. Like Reba loves you. 'Member that, hear. 'Member she loved you like Reba loves you. . . ."

It seemed like he was the last to know, and eventually he came to hate his father for what he had done. Though the hate had never died completely, he usually kept it in check.

"You again."

The voice came from behind him, and Red swore, viciously this time. Across the creek, the woman looked up, her eyes wide and frightened, and then she bolted, ducking into the willow brush but not stopping there.

"What you want wid us, huh? Why you keep bothin' us?" There was a desperate note to his voice, a sound of weary fear. Turning slowly to look over his shoulder, Red saw that the man had a shotgun, and his face was ducked behind it, his eyes as wide as the twin bores of the gun. There was fear in his face, but determination, too, and Red turned the sorrel slowly, keeping his hands in sight.

"It's a free country," Red said. "I saw no fence to keep me out."

"You spyin' on my woman. Peepin' like some dirty little boy."

Red laughed, saw the anger flare in the nester's face, and let his laugh die. But he could feel his own anger rising, and his face hardening to it. "Best let that scattergun drop, boy, before it accidentally goes off and buys you a hang rope."

"No," he said angrily. "No, you go on. You get outta here, let us be." He made a quick motion with the shotgun, without really taking it off Red. "Go on now, git."

On Red's hip, the solid feel of the Peacemaker seemed to be throwing off a heat he could feel through the holster. He held the reins in his left hand, with his right resting on his leg below the holster. Maybe eight or ten inches from the butt of the big revolver.

As if reading his mind, the nester said, "Don't you go tryin' that now. You jus' let it be and go on. Go."

Red's breath came out in a long sigh. Still he didn't move, didn't seem able. His eyes were locked with the black man's, down the long length of the shotgun, seeing, down deep, past the weariness and the fear, a hatred that matched his own; and seeing that, he felt the deadlock break. His brows furrowed and he said with something like wonder, "You'd like to, wouldn't you? You'd like nothing better than to pull that trigger?"

"Lord, forgive me, please, but I would," he whispered.

Red had known the black man would shoot, of course, would pull the trigger without hesitation, but he had thought it would be the act of a desperate man, one pushed to it. Seeing then the naked lust on the farmer's face put a fear in Red he hadn't known before. The man wanted to kill him, not for any one incident, but for a hundred different ones, most committed by someone else. The irony of it wasn't lost on him, but it didn't change his feelings any either. If anything, he thought it strengthened them.

"Maybe I'll be back, nigger. Maybe me and some friends."

"Mighty big talk for a scared white boy, that be."

Red could feel his face flushing, and he might have drawn then rather than let a black man see that, but it struck him that the light had gone, dusk had settled, and all he could see of the nester was the dark silhouette of his body, the faint white spots of his eyes, and the gleam of the shotgun's barrels. The man would see no more of him, he knew, and he smiled suddenly, showing his teeth. Red reined the sorrel and put him into the creek, splashing across and up the far bank, putting him into a run across the dark prairie, risking a broken leg in a prairie dog hole or a badger's hole, but spurring on just the same, spurring on until the wind whipped tears from his eyes and pushed them back across his cheeks. God, how he hated them.

CHAPTER 7

THEY split the riders on Monday. It was Wyatt's idea and nobody cared for it much, but only Harper and Doc really complained.

"Half-assed idea," Harper grumbled, rolling his bedroll into a tight bundle. "They was supposed to give us free rein, and now they're bossing us around like a bunch of waddies."

"Like the army," Doc said. "Orders coming from someone you never see, then just the opposite of what you ought to do." His complaint seemed more of an escort to Harper's criticism than a product of his own feelings, and Howard noticed Harper's quick flinch, and knew he was aware of it. Lately, Doc had taken after Harper more than usual, mimicking the way he talked or gestured, like a boy would sometimes, uncertain and looking for an identity.

"We could all just ride out," Sanchez suggested. "That will show them who is the ramrod."

Harper looked up uncertainly, as if he wasn't sure whether Sanchez was serious or not. "Naw," he said. "When I start a job I see it through." He looked down just before Sanchez's smile flashed across his face.

"Splitting us up will just drag it out longer," Doc said, picking up Harper's old trail of conversation.

"The big man is paying us," Red shrugged. "At a hundred dollars a month I wouldn't care if it drug out all winter."

It was about as much as Red had said in one sitting since his ride south three nights previous. He'd been moody and withdrawn, quick to anger, and even Harper had checked his rough ways some. Red seemed like a keg of powder all primed and ready to blow, and Howard figured it was easy enough to know what was bothering him, if not the why.

"The big man can afford to pay us," Sanchez was saying. "But the money comes from everyone. The little ranches, these will hurt if the rustling is not stopped."

"They all had their say," Harper grunted. "It's their headache now." He hefted his saddlebags and bedroll and headed for the door. The others followed at their own pace, Howard bringing up the rear, empty-handed. He would be staying on at the Broken Axle.

Harper was already saddled and waiting in the yard, sitting his big bay gelding with a tight rein. A horse fly was buzzing the bay's legs, causing him to dance in the dust and stomp his feet nervously. Harper swung at the fly and missed, spooking the bay even more. Red and Doc sat their own horses nearby, watching Harper, but Sanchez stood with Howard, his paint saddled but loosely cinched.

The fly lit on the bay's rump and the bay tucked its tail under him and scooted across the yard. "Goddamn," Harper swore, pulling his hat off and slapping at the bay's tail. The bay squealed and buck-jumped halfway across the yard.

Sanchez grinned a wicked little grin and leaned close to Howard. "I will bet one dollar that friend Harper will not keep his seat."

Howard smiled and nodded. Harper was a fair rider but no bronc buster. Still, it would be worth a dollar to see what Sanchez had in mind.

Harper jerked the gelding's head up and sawed him around, using more spur than was needed to bring him back to the bunkhouse. The horse fly was a thumb-sized black bullet around the bay's legs. "Come on, Sanchez," Harper shouted. "Let's get out of here before this screw brain gets eat up."

"It is the fly," Sanchez said innocently. "I have seen them raise a welt on a man the size of your palm." He walked toward the bay with a nonchalant gait, his face as guiltless as a babe's.

The bay blew hard and backed up a step, tossing his head. The saddle rose above the kink in the bay's back, tipping Harper slightly forward. The horse was wired as tight as a banjo string, Luke thought, and it wouldn't take much to set him off. The fly took off at Sanchez's approach and for a minute Howard thought it was all over. Then suddenly the fly was back, landing on the inside of the bay's front leg, just above the knee. There had been a keen disappointment on Sanchez's face when the fly disappeared, and a sort of elation when it returned. Looking up, Luke saw Harper watching Sanchez, saw understanding come with a rush, and heard the squawk of his protest, cut off as Sanchez made his move. "I will get him," Sanchez shouted suddenly, lunging forward and sweeping his sombrero off to flap it beneath the bay's nose with a loud *whoosh*.

The bay exploded, coming straight up like a cork out of a bottle and landing in the same spot, though facing in the opposite direction. Harper landed on his bedroll with a grunt audible across the yard, his face drained of color and a surprised look twisting his face. His reins had slipped through his fingers until he held only the useless ends. The bay stood as though frozen, almost crouched.

"I have him now," Sanchez shouted, laughing and swinging his sombrero at the bay's rear legs. The bay lashed out, his iron-shod hooves fanning the air close to Sanchez's head, but the wiry little Mexican dodged nimbly to one side and swung again, beyond caring. He stumbled backward, laughing until the tears flowed, while the bay took off toward the main house pitching crazily. Harper lasted a full six jumps by the grace of luck, then flipped out of the saddle in a slow spin and landed belly first in the dust.

He came up fast, sucking for wind, weaving, clawing at his holster, and Sanchez's laughter began to die. "You little greasy-haired sonofabitch," Harper wheezed, bringing his

Colt up and leveling it on Sanchez. "I ought to plug you where you stand." His face was chalky with dust and he kept blinking to clear his eyes and trying to sneeze as he talked and none of it working too well, but the Colt never wavered.

Sanchez raised his hands slowly, the smile still on his face, but stretched now. His throat bobbed a couple of times as if he wanted to speak, but no words came. He seemed frozen there.

"Barney," Red said helplessly, leaning over his saddle horn.

Harper cocked the Colt, the sound sharp and ominous. His knuckles were white on the revolver, and his eyes, rimmed in dust and still tearing, seemed to blaze with a fury barely contained.

"Barney," Red pleaded, his voice taut.

'Let it go, Barney," Howard said, and even to his own ears he thought there was a note of begging.

Harper straightened slowly, uncocked the Colt, but didn't lower it. He kept his gaze hard on Sanchez.

"Go get his horse," Red said quietly to Doc, and Doc jogged over to where the bay stood at the edge of the prairie, quietly grazing. In the corrals, one of Young's draft horses squealed and nipped at the fly.

No one moved or spoke until Doc returned with the bay. Only then did Harper holster the Colt. He took the reins from Doc and stepped into the saddle, sitting hunched a little to the left as if something was still paining him. The bay sidled some, spooked yet, but Harper yanked savagely on the reins and brought him around. To Sanchez, he said, "You ever try something like that again and I'll kill you. Understand?"

Sanchez didn't reply, nor did his smile fade, but a tic pulled suddenly at his left eye, and sweat ran freely down his face. Harper pulled the bay around then and touched him with his spurs; the bay lunged against the bit, then settled into a fast lope, out of the yard and across the prairie, toward the Bar-W.

Sanchez lowered his arms and his smile widened. "Whewee," he laughed. "That Barney, he is no man to prod, I think."

"Your sense of humor is going to get somebody killed one of these days," Red said shortly.

"Probably," Sanchez agreed. "Most likely myself."

Red turned his horse away without answering, riding out at a lope. Doc followed silently, his lips pulled tight and the flesh around them white. "Red was right," Howard said, and his voice sounded shaky in his ears. He was thinking that this was probably the most hair-trigger outfit he had ever ridden with, although in some ways it was the best bunch, too. To a man they were all quick and capable, and there was none of the bulliness toward the townsfolk a man sometimes saw with a bunch of hired guns, excepting maybe Harper some, and with Harper it seemed more natural than petty, and nothing that couldn't be lived with.

"Probably," Sanchez said again. He tightened his cinch and stepped into the saddle. "But you still owe me a dollar, amigo."

Howard dug the silver from his poke and tossed it to Sanchez. "Was I you, I'd shy clear of Harper until he's cooled off," he offered.

Sanchez slapped absently at his thighs with the loose ends of his reins. "Barney I will not worry so much about. It is Bronson I think of often."

"Have you heard from Wyatt?"

Sanchez shook his head. "He said he would look into it, but such a thing takes time, and for some reason I feel we are running out of that. I had thought maybe one of us could always stay near town, but now that seems unlikely."

"This won't last long. Harper was right about that, it's a half-assed idea. We're doing the work the regular hands could be doing, and if somebody does discover a herd gone now, it'll take a day to round all of us up. Man can cover a lot of miles in a day, even pushing beef."

Sanchez looked north across the low rolling hills, and sighed. "I think you are right. Bronson is the man we need to watch, and instead we are wet-nursing cows while he is free to ride where he pleases. But perhaps Wyatt is right, also. It will be harder for the rustlers to take a herd with us spread out." He looked at Howard and cocked an eyebrow. "As the trappers say, we will see which way the stick floats, eh? Adios, *compadre.*"

Howard stood with his arms folded and watched Sanchez ride off toward the Circle-R. Red would bunk at the Lazy-L, and Doc would ride for Roscoe Plumb's Crooked Arrow. With Harper at the Bar-W and him staying on the Broken Axle, they would have all the ranches covered except the Wagon Wheel, lying between the Bar-W and the Broken Axle; he and Harper would cover that range together, or what was left of it. The Wagon Wheel had been a small outfit in the beginning, and the rustling had hit it hardest of them all; rumor had it that there wasn't much Wagon Wheel stock left.

Howard went back inside and straddled a chair in the kitchen. The Navy lay scattered on the table before him, broken down as far as he could take it. Outside the perimeter of revolver parts was a small basin of water, a can of lubricating oil, and two piles of rags, one clean and the other blackened with powder residue.

He worked without haste, the simple routine and early morning coolness easing the ache of stiffened muscles. For the most part he felt healed of the bruises and lumps inflicted in the brawl outside the Colorado Lady—the cuts on his face were scabbed and shrinking, itching now, and the bruises fading. Only the long laceration along his scalp put there by the barrel of Bronson's pistol still gave him any fits, and even that was easing. Still, he found himself waking during the night, his head stuffy and full, or stopping

suddenly during the day, wincing and squeezing his eyes
shut against the bright stab of sunlight, or fighting a wave of
dizziness that would disappear as quickly as it came, though
at other times it would linger for as long as a quarter of an
hour.

Doc had taken a look at the wound the afternoon he
returned, and through the hazy blur of his memory he
remembered the words "concussion," and "possible frac-
ture." The cure was rest, Doc had said, and sleep if he could
manage it, and stay out of the sun and saddle. Yet he
wouldn't, and they had both known it. A man with strength
enough to climb into a saddle had no business a-bed, Howard
had argued, and Doc had merely shrugged.

He saddled the bay that afternoon and rode south toward
the Tanks, then made a long sweep past Twin Buttes to check
on the bunch they had brought back after the hanging. The
prairie undulated before him like frozen waves of a tawny
ocean, stretching to the horizon and beyond. Above, the sun
slid through a cloudless sky, touching him with a gentle
warmth that lacked the punch it had held only a few days
before.

Fall was in the air now, as plain to see as the rise of the
next ridge if a man just took the time to look. Plainer even
than the leaves starting to yellow along the creek banks, or
the crisp morning breeze that made men and animals feel
alive and full of energy. Dawn came later now, and its chill
lasted further into the morning, while the coats on the horses
were turning shaggy, full and soft to the touch.

The bay jogged along at a fair pace, swinging his rear
around playfully from time to time. Around them grasshoppers flew up with a clattering whirl, settling in the short grass
ahead, then rising again before the bay's hooves. They were
everywhere a man looked anymore, as much a part of the
land as the grass and dust.

It was twilight when he finally rode into the Broken Axle,
past the flatbed wagon parked near the house, its load of

wood roped down; firewood, likely, waiting to be sawed down to stove length. He smiled sympathetically. Someone would be courting blisters on the morrow, he figured.

He unsaddled the bay and turned him into the corral to roll, then lugged his gear to the tack shed. Young was waiting for him at the wash bench, tipped back on a three-legged stool and leaning against the bunkhouse when Howard returned. He had his legs crossed, his hands laced around one knee with a pipe clamped between thumb and forefinger, empty and unlit.

"Ever feel like an old man, Luke?" Young asked amiably.

"Sometimes," Howard smiled, rolling his sleeves up. "Depends on the day, usually." He dipped his hands into the basin and splashed water over his face. From inside the bunkhouse came the muted rumble of talk between the two remaining hands, accompanied by the hesitant chords of a guitar. Jess had ordered the instrument from St. Louis several months back and was making a half-hearted attempt at learning to play it.

"I don't know where they find their energy," Young said, indicating the bunkhouse with a nod of his head. "They worked with me all day and took the time to clown around on the way back. Now I've been sitting here for an hour listening to them cutup in there." He shook his head sadly at the injustice of age as Howard toweled his face dry.

"I guess you know I didn't make my own drive to market this year," Young continued. "I sent a few head along with Wyatt to buy the basics for winter. Goodnight Charlie repped for me." He paused and Howard said nothing, and soon enough he went on then, as if musing. "Always liked to buy the wife a little something extra for Christmas, some foofaraw she didn't really need but wanted anyway. It kind of made up for all the years when I couldn't buy her anything. She won't complain, mind you—but still, a man doesn't like to think he's sliding backward, even when he is."

"Outfit like yours, your credit will be good."

Young smiled into the shadows of his hat. "You sound like Ben Wyatt. But I won't go on tick. Long as I've got one cow and a horse to move her with, the Broken Axle will get along."

Howard patted his pockets for a cheroot, then scratched a match alight against the bunkhouse wall, realizing in the sudden flare of flame that full darkness had come unnoticed. Just another sign of fall, he thought.

"Goodnight Charlie won't be coming back," Young said. "I'd kind of hoped he'd change his mind, though I guess I really ain't all surprised. But that leaves me with just Jess and Jory to handle all the work, and the wife to cook for us all. I sold part of my remuda to a horse trader in Cheyenne, and he sent word that he'd be interested in another fifteen or twenty head of young stuff. Trouble is, I've got a winter's worth of firewood to bring in and cut up, and I need to get into the meadow grass for hay for the saddle band. I'm just too damn shorthanded to handle it all."

"What are you getting at, Mr. Young?"

"Luke, it isn't your job by a long shot, but if you're of a mind and think your head can take the beating, I'm needing somebody to bring in the saddle stock that's still on grass and top them off. They're four and five year olds. Most of them have been ridden before, but they'll still be a rambunctious group."

"I'm not a bronc buster, Mr. Young."

"You've got a way with horses, Luke. I saw the way you handled the dun a couple of weeks ago. You can set your own pace and break them as you see fit. I can't give you any pay, but I'd be willing to give you a bill of sale on five good mares. That includes the dun, if you want her."

Young's proposal hit Howard like a jolt of raw whiskey. He walked slowly to the corral where the bay chewed hay and folded his arms over the second rail.

"He's small for cow work," Young said, coming up beside him. "But he's got the blood of a king's breed in him. You can see that. Match him with the right mares and he'll throw you some of the best colts this country will have to offer."

As if sensing the attention, the bay raised his head and nickered questioningly.

"Sometimes I think he's got more sense than most men," Howard said. "I've never put him to stud because I didn't want him turning mare-crazy. I didn't want to have to geld him."

"Don't geld him, Luke. At his age he'd still likely be mare-crazy."

Howard wasn't listening though. Instead, he was seeing the ranch he'd put together in his mind. The pines and a stream and a little bay colt running through belly-deep grass at the dun's side, and maybe mountains growing purple not far off.

"You don't have to make up your mind tonight," Young said. "Sleep on it. If you decide to do it, I'll cut Jory loose from the cutting to help you bring them in."

"Do it," Howard said suddenly. He could feel his heart hammering at his ribs with unexpected vitality. How many years had he promised himself such a place, only to drift on without making an attempt at it? Now, finally, it was beginning to take shape, and the mares would be the cornerstone.

The band had scattered widely over the summer months, breaking into scores of small bunches, hidden in draws or narrow valleys, some as wild as mustangs. Ordinarily they would have been brought in that spring, part of the summer cavvy for a dozen hands, but Young had started the season shorthanded and the situation had steadily worsened. The horses, most of them only green-broke to begin with, would be crazy-mean, fighting the gather now as much as they would the rope and saddle later.

They rode in a southerly direction from the ranch, Luke, Jory and Jim Young, then spread into a three-pointed fan that would converge on the ranch yard sometime late in the afternoon. Howard took the eastern tip of the fan, crossing

Sand Creek several miles north of the cutoff and working the draws that opened into it. The going was easy at first, the morning cool and the ride pleasant, but by noon he had close to forty head gathered on the flat ground west of the creek, moseying north under a hot sun. The dust rose in a choking cloud that settled over the bay's coat like a gray blanket, coating his throat the same way. He moved them easily, keeping them at a steady walk while he rode back across the creek from time to time to comb another draw or check a twisting meadow, and time and again he'd come back to find part of the bunch broken from the main gather. Still, they moved easily, and those that did break off did so at a walk, so they weren't hard to find or haze back, only a nuisance.

The sun was still a couple of hours above the horizon when he and Young brought their gathers together, the horses turning suddenly skittish as the herd merged. Together, Howard figured they had maybe a hundred and fifty head, and Young's face was puzzled as he watched the approaching dust of Jory's band.

"He's got fifty, maybe sixty head, judging from the dust," Young observed. The bandanna he wore over his mouth puffed in and out as he spoke. "That's maybe sixty-five or seventy head more than there ought to be."

Howard took a swig from his canteen and ran a moistened tongue over his chapped lips, studying the approaching herd speculatively. Jory was bringing them in easy, and Howard and Young rode off toward a small rise to await his arrival out of the dust.

He was all smiles riding up, with puffs of dust rising off his clothing like little clouds and his horse streaked with mud from the dust and sweat. "Beats hell out of cutting firewood," he grinned, taking his hat off and slapping it out against his chaps. He was a freckle-faced kid of twenty or so, as gangling as a fourteen year old on the ground, though he rode as if he were born mounted. He was Texas-born and proud of that, and sometimes said that things would have been different had he been old enough to tag after his brother going off to war. Sometimes it seemed the war bothered him more than it did some of those who fought; as though, when he was feeling down, he was the only one who ever lost a brother to it.

"You been raiding someone else's pasture?" Young asked casually, leaning back to rest an elbow against his mount's hip.

Jory's face turned suddenly serious. "About half my gather is wearing the Wagon Wheel brand," he said. "I figured we could cut them out at the ranch and haze them back later."

Young pinched his lower lip between thumb and forefinger and a frown creased his forehead. "What's Hutchinson's stock doing on my range? It ain't like Mack to let his band drift so far. And it ain't like horses to drift through cattle the way these had to to get this far."

"Ain't so many cattle between us anymore," Jory said soberly.

Young scowled at the puncher, who shrugged apologetically and looked away. Young turned to Howard and said, "It still isn't like him to let his band drift this far. I'm going to ride over to the Wagon Wheel and see what's up. Jory can ease this bunch in alone if you want to come along."

Howard nodded, and Young looked at Jory. "I'll stop by the ranch and see if I can't persuade Jess to quit cutting firewood and give you a hand. He ought to be here in about twenty minutes," he finished dryly.

The Wagon Wheel was a knocked-together outfit of mud-chinked log buildings squatting in the dappled shade of a fair-sized cottonwood grove, maybe two hours from the Broken Axle. The sun was down but there was still some daylight left when Young and Howard rode under the crossbar that marked the ranch yard's entrance. They paused just inside the bar and let their gaze rove the place. The corrals were empty, the windows in the main house and bunkhouse dark and vacant-looking. There was a tumbleweed caught at the bottom step of the porch on the main house; on all the place the only things that moved were the turning leaves of the cottonwood.

"Looks like a graveyard," Young said thickly.

Howard pulled his Colt and let it rest against his thigh. "There's a paper tacked to the front door," he said. "Might be an answer there."

They rode up and Young leaned under the porch and caught the paper, pulling it free with just his finger tips. Grunting as he straightened, he began to read slowly, his lips moving as he struggled over the words, his face gradually darkening. "Sons of bitches," he swore then, the tone venomous. He handed the notice to Howard, his gaze going back to the empty corral, as if that said as much as the notice pulled from the porch shadows.

"So Hutchinson sold out to the Dallas Land and Livestock Company," Howard mused. He folded the notice once and handed it back to Young. "I guess that explains the drifting saddle bands."

"Must have sold out lock, stock and barrel," Young said bitterly. "And to a goddamn carpetbagger at that. I guess I can understand why he didn't let anyone know before pulling out."

"This Bernard Jordache the notice mentions the same speculator they're talking about in Sand Creek?"

"The same. A little slick-backed sonofabitch with hands like a woman's."

They were walking their horses back toward the prairie now, and Howard thought Young seemed anxious to put the Wagon Wheel behind him. Young's vehemence surprised him some; he wasn't a man often given to cursing, yet the words came sharp and quick now, tinged with bitterness.

"I've got half a notion to torch the place," Young said suddenly. "A damn carpetbagger is worse than a thief, worse

than the damn rustlers. You can hang a rustler if you catch
him. A carpetbagger stays in the finest hotel in town, just
waiting for a man to go under. Vultures are what they are.
Damn vultures. Sometimes they don't even wait for you to
die, they just swoop down and pluck your eyes out of your
head as soon as you're too damn weak to swat at 'em." He
swore again, then added in a softer voice, "A carpetbagger's
the same, only he wants more than a meal. He wants everything you've got, everything you've worked for all these
years . . ."

He went on like that for a long time, while dusk settled,
then full dark, and Howard began to wonder how much of
his anger was fear. Fear of the vulture.

For a long time there was nothing, no feeling nor thought
nor need, just a drifting blackness that might have flowed
into eternity. Then the light came, and the pain, and he
reacted as a child might, with screams and pleading and a
wild terror of the unknown that never left his mind except
through the deep-chested groans and occasional thrashings.
For a while then he would alternate between darkness and
light, peace and pain, loving one, cursing the other, but
finding, with the harsh unjustness that was life, that he
couldn't keep what he longed for, nor could he halt what he
dreaded.

When he finally regained consciousness, he was cursing
the light, and what it brought.

Tod Jessup stood hunched in the entrance of the old wall
tent and stared past the glistening bark of the scarred aspen
and rain-bent grass to the shrouded outline of their diggings,
maybe fifty yards away. Above him, the rain drummed gently
against canvas, leaking some along the seams and turning
the air inside misty with condensation that beaded over
blankets and gear. From time to time a stray gust of wind
would slip past him and swell the sagging walls and ceiling,

shaking loose little droplets of moisture that rained on the dirt floor, turning it damp and slick. Thunder rumbled low and drawn out in the distance—that and the slap of rain being all that broke the stillness of the meadow.

Jessup was tall for his age, man-sized really, broad-shouldered and strong. His curly blond hair was cropped short above his ears but kinked into a tangle on top of his head, kinked even tighter now with the dampness. He had a splattering of freckles across the bridge of his button nose, and deep-set eyes that could match the sadness of a hound's when his mood was low, or the twinkle of a circus clown when it wasn't, which was most of the time. His hands, large-knuckled and vein-ridged, were huge, made for shovel or plow, and familiar with each.

From time to time he would look over his shoulder at the mound of blankets where the stranger muttered and kicked, sometimes slapping feebly at the air, as if caught in some nightmare he could not awaken from. The time was close at hand now, he could sense it, when the stranger would finally come around; although he was glad to see it happen, he was nervous about it too. He'd had him better than a week now, nursing him along like some orphaned pup, and not really expecting him to live. Still, he'd kept stubbornly after it, spooning warm broth down his throat, keeping the bandages changed and cleaned—keeping him clean, too, which had been a gut-wrenching chore. The others—his pa and Old Tom and Hawk—had moved into the supply tent after the second night, complaining of the stench and the flies it drew. They'd complained some at the time he devoted to the stranger too, time better spent at his work, what with winter coming and all.

He'd stuck with it though, and now it looked like it might pan out, that the tall, lean stranger might actually pull through. But now, with a better than even chance of his making it, Tod wasn't sure he wasn't bringing more trouble into the camp than it could handle. Trouble they didn't need, with a showdown already brewing.

The stranger stirred and opened his eyes, his gaze wandering jerkingly over the tent's interior, coming to rest on Jessup. Tod waited until the stranger was finished with his looking, then ducked through the tent flap and squatted flat-footed beside him, letting his elbows rest across his knees and his hands dangle above the stranger's chest. He nodded, unsure of himself now, everything he had planned to say sounding inappropriate to his mind.

"You got water?" the stranger rasped, his face wreathed in pain from the simple act of just speaking.

"Sure," Tod said. He fetched a canteen and poured some water into a tin cup, then tipped the stranger's head up to drink.

He sucked noisily at the water, spilling some into the coarse stubble of his beard. After several swallows, Tod took the cup away and set it aside. "Reckon that'll be enough for now," he said. Then, somewhat shyly he said, "I'm Tod Jessup. I'm the one who's been caring for you."

The stranger nodded and closed his eyes, as if he wasn't interested, and Tod swayed back and rose. He heard voices through the rain—angry, arguing voices, and knew his pa and the others were at it again. They went on like that almost every night now, and days like today when they couldn't work. It would bring trouble in the end, he knew, and his pa was beginning to see it also. Tod was young but he hadn't been born with blinders on. He had sensed the wildness in Old Tom and Hawk the day they rode in, maybe even knowing then that if they stayed there would be trouble.

He ought to be there now, he thought, though he knew it wouldn't do any good. His pa would dismiss him because of his age, and likely, because he still saw him as a shavetailed kid, and Old Tom and Hawk would dismiss him simply because his pa had, and in doing so were shifting the odds more to their favor.

Below him, the stranger groaned and stirred, his eyes flickering open.

"Thought you were going back to sleep," Tod said. He hunkered down beside him again, feeling more at ease now than he had earlier, though knowing there were still a number of touchy subjects yet to cover.

"Could use some more water," the stranger said, his throat raspy still.

"Well, maybe a little," Tod conceded. He poured half a cup and helped the stranger drink again. "Now I reckon that is enough," he said. "You need something solid inside."

"Could use it. Could eat a skunk raw."

Tod laughed. "We're fresh out of skunk, but there's rabbit on the spit. Think you could chew a tough jack?"

The stranger nodded, and Tod wrapped a rubber poncho over his shoulders and ducked into the rain. He was gone a long time, his pa and Old Tom plying him with questions when they found out the stranger had finally come around. When he got back, the stranger was asleep again. Tod shrugged the poncho aside and pulled the rear legs from the rabbit, setting them to the side to cool. Steam rose in wispy clouds from the meat and drifted toward the stranger; he opened his eyes.

"Thought you was sleeping again," Tod said around a mouthful. He was picking meat from the forequarters and making a meal for himself.

"Was, for a while. Smell woke me."

Tod handed him a rear leg and the stranger pulled at it with yellowing teeth. The meat was tough and stringy, an old snowshoe well past its prime, but it was fresh and solid and would go a long way after nearly a week of fasting, Tod thought. But the stranger was a long time in cleaning the bone, and when Tod offered him the second leg, he declined.

Tod wiped his greasy hands on a piece of old sacking and hitched around closer to the stranger. He said, "Pa says it ain't right to ask a man his name out here, but I reckon I'll have to call you something."

The stranger didn't reply, his eyes fixed on the rain-sagged ceiling as though his mind was far away now. He lay motionless for a long time, not even blinking, then said, "Where's my guns, boy? And my horse?"

Tod started, then coughed and looked guiltily toward the old grass that was the floor. His ears burned and his voice thickened. "Ain't got 'em," he said then.

The stranger's face looked cold, emotionless. "What's that mean?" he asked gruffly.

"It was part of the deal," Tod said defensively. "It was . . . I was to look after you, till you died, then give you a proper burial. They give me your guns to sell. Never was no horse."

"Who gave you my guns?"

"The doctor, the one who patched you up."

"And he was so damn sure I was going to die?"

"Seemed pretty likely," Tod admitted.

"So you sold my guns?"

"Yeah," Tod said, ducking his head again. "Got thirty-five dollars for the both of them."

The stranger laughed, a short, harsh sound, cut short then as his eyes widened and his face paled.

Tod leaned forward and put his hand on the stranger's shoulder. "Hey, take it easy," he said. "You ain't healed yet."

"So I feel." He shut his eyes and his breathing deepened. After a bit, Tod picked up the second leg of the rabbit and bit into it, his face smoothed in thought. When the stranger spoke again, his voice was faint, almost lost in the patter of rain. "Swede," he said. "Call me Swede."

CHAPTER 8

THEY cut the Wagon Wheel horses out first, and Jess hazed them back to their own range. Then Young began the painful process of picking the string he wanted to sell. He wanted to keep the best for himself, yet wanted to be fair with the Cheyenne trader, too. In the end, he chose eighteen head, running them into a separate corral. After that he had Howard make his pick.

Howard took the dun without hesitation, then spent the better part of an hour easing one of Young's roping horses through the gather, picking out a couple of bays, because he was partial to the color, then a black filly that looked promising, and finally a strawberry roan with long, clean limbs that had a look of speed.

Afterward, while Young took what was left back onto his southern range, Jory roped out a mouse-colored gelding and dragged him into the breaking pen, making a hitch at the snubbing post. He shook out a second loop and heeled him, backing his roping horse off until the gelding was stretched out and unable to move.

"Your dance now, Yank," Jory called, grinning. "He's stretched out as pretty as a whore on a feather mattress."

Howard ignored him, moving in close to the grulla and keeping up a steady patter of meaningless words, meant to soothe rather than make sense, He carried Young's single-rigged breaking saddle—deep-seated and hornless—on his hip, shielding it from the grulla with his body.

The grulla snorted and rolled his eyes. Howard ran a hand along his neck and back over his withers, rubbing gently, scratching, keeping up a constant, low monologue of sweet nothings. The gelding trembled under his touch, blowing a frothy spray of slaver as Howard slid his arm over the far side of the grulla's barrel and leaned his weight against the horse's back.

He brought the saddle around and settled it lightly over the grulla. The gelding snorted again, then suddenly lunged back, away from the post, twisting his head frantically in an effort to shake loose of the rope circling his neck. Howard skipped back, bringing the saddle with him, while the grulla fought the rope. Finally Jory backed his horse off and the gelding fell, still squealing with his head stretched above the ground. He lay immobile after that, exhaling in rapid bursts.

"Give him some slack," Howard called, and the grulla rose shakily. Howard bit at his lower lip. There were other ways, he knew, slower but easier on the horses. Ways that would bring out the best in an animal rather than just conquering him, but on a cow outfit time was money and a horse got his formal training on the roundup. If an animal wasn't handling well enough for the range in a week or two, it was branded an outlaw and cut loose, or shot; grass was for the production of beef, not food for unusable animals.

Sensing his feelings, perhaps, Jory called, "He's gonna try to bust your insides loose when you get in the saddle. Better let him know who's boss now, before he's got his freedom."

Howard eased up to the gelding again, moving with the same gentle delicacy as before. The grulla's muscles rippled like spring grass under a breeze as Howard lifted the saddle to his back and drew the cinch tight. Pressure against the grulla's ribs was something new, and the horse sucked his gut in, yet remained quiet. Howard, breathing shallowly, moving with slow caution, slipped a hackamore over the grulla's head, then gathered the reins above his neck.

Howard looked at Jory and cocked an eyebrow in a here-we-go gesture and slipped the rope off the gelding's neck while Jory flipped his rope a few times, until the loop slipped free of the grulla's legs and fell in the dust. Howard grabbed a handful of mane in one hand and the grulla's ear in the other, twisting the ear until the horse bowed his neck in pain. He didn't let go until he was in the saddle.

It took the grulla a moment to realize he was free, then the horse came unscrewed, exploding in a ball of fear and rage. Howard didn't have a cowhand's flair for riding, and what he did have had been softened by the bay's gentle nature. He grabbed the swell on the first jump and held on all the way through, giving the grulla just enough rein to buck, but keeping his head away from his knees, too. The lower the head, the rougher the ride, and he saw no point in giving the grulla an advantage.

The grulla tore up the ground close to the snubbing post for a while, then widened his territory, hitting the ground with stiff-legged jars that rocked Howard's head. The grulla was squealing his fury with every buck, kicking out at the corral or his shadow, burning himself out in ten minutes. He stopped suddenly, without warning, puffing and sweating, and Howard dismounted before the horse caught its wind.

He walked across the corral to where Jory sat his own horse, the coil of his rope drapped over the saddle horn. His knees were weak and he was belching his breakfast, the taste sour against the back of his throat. His head rang with a dull hammering and he touched his fingers to the flaky scab of his scalp wound, then looked at them expectantly for blood.

"Shake something loose?" Jory asked blandly. He had his leg cocked around the saddle horn, a cigarette protruding from the dimpled corner of his mouth.

Howard wished silently that Jory would tangle his spurs in his rope, then poked his head through the corral poles and lost his breakfast.

"You know he was just mad this time, don't you?" Jory asked, after Howard had finished. "He spent as much time squealing as he did pitching. Next time he'll be more calculating. Next time you'll fan the grass, I'm betting."

As if to punctuate Jory's words, the grulla exploded once

more, riderless, tearing around the far side of the corral until the empty stirrups were flapping like the leathery wings of a huge bat.

They topped off four more head that day, and eight the next. Jory rode a few. He was good, knew it, and wasn't above showing off a little, raising his hat above his head and raking the broncs to bring out their worst. Yet as the days wore on, Howard thought the young puncher began to find a new respect for his riding. He wasn't a bronc buster, would likely never be as good as Jory was right now, but he kept after it, sticking out most of his rides and climbing back on those he didn't as soon as Jory snubbed them up again. He suffered some in those early days, though he never mentioned it or let it slow him down any. Still, he could see it in the mirror at nights, the pale, drawn cast of his face, the somber eyes. Busting horses was a young man's game, and it brought to the surface his own years; not so old yet, he thought, but not so young anymore, either.

By the end of the week they had gone through most of the string three times, and had a few starting to respond to the reins. Three more weeks, given the size of the bunch, and they'd be ready for Cheyenne.

On Saturday, after running through half a dozen head, Jory and Jess dressed in their gaudy Sunday best for a ride into town. There wouldn't be much work the next day, just the everyday chores Young usually handled himself anyway, and they planned to spend the night. Before leaving Jory offered Luke an invitation to ride along, but he declined, thinking of Charity, as he often did of late. He had thought it was over with her there in Anse's that day, yet found the memory of her still painful. He was, he sometimes thought, as confused now as he had ever been.

He stretched out on a bunk after they left and thumbed through a dog-eared copy of Mark Twain's *Roughing It*, but found the words too much of a struggle. He put the book aside and sat on the edge of his bunk, staring at the shadowy tintype of a New Orleans whore clad only in a spotted loincloth that Jess kept on a shelf above his bunk.

Howard was a loner by nature, a man who tired quickly of cities and crowds, yet tonight his solitude was a burden. The walls seemed to close in on him, the bunks and blankets and clutter of gear pressing on his spirit. He got up and wandered outside, slipping into the corral with the bay. The bay came to him without bidding, blowing softly and pressing his forelock into Howard's chest. He smiled and scratched the bay behind the ears, grateful for the company, more satisfied, in truth, than he would have been with a bunkhouse full of riders.

He killed an hour brushing the bay down, and another sitting on the top rail of the corral watching his mares pick grass under the lower rail. His mind skipped and wandered, and from time to time Charity would slip into it, and each time she did he would shake his head with a quick, angry motion and force his thoughts elsewhere, back to the mares, or his ranch, the one he wanted so badly anymore.

He heard a distant clatter of hooves from the north and knew without looking that it was a rider on the Sand Creek road, coming at a hard gallop. He turned to see the rider etched sharply against the moonlit prairie, slapping his mount with the loose ends of his reins, and Howard slid from the top rail then, and drifted toward the bunkhouse and his revolver. He stopped then, recognizing, if not the person, then at least the way he was riding. It was Jory, and even from a distance Howard could hear the gut-grunting pound of his horse.

Jory didn't haul up until the last minute, bringing his lathered mount to a sliding stop, jumping clear before the horse could get his feet back under him. "Luke, there's trouble brewing down on the Grant tonight. Big trouble." He was breathing hard, his words coming quick but choked.

"Be big trouble here if Young catches you jamming a horse like that."

"You don't understand," Jory pleaded desperately. "There's going to be a hanging."

"What are you talking about, boy?"

"Bunch of riders are gathering where the Ogallala road crosses Sand Creek. There's talk of burning the grangers out and hanging some of the menfolk."

"You tell Bronson?"

"Bronson says what happens on the Grant ain't his concern. Says to go up to Fort Robinson for the army, or wire a U.S. Marshal."

Howard snorted, then said, "So what makes you think it's my concern?"

"Hell's bells, Luke, those are family men." His young face looked twisted in the moonlight, pained.

"They're nesters," Howard said roughly. "Chances are, when he can afford the time, Young will send you and Jess down there to run them out himself."

"Running them out is one thing. Lynching's another. Besides, Mr. Young has a right. They're crowding his range. These men are just saddle bums and drifters. Most of them are drunk, too."

Howard scowled. Nesters were no concern of his, and he resented Jory's riding out here hell-for-leather as if it were. They were, in a way, as much a threat to the range as the rustlers. He felt the way most of the ranchers felt, he thought; nesters needed to be routed and sent back to where they came from. The prairie was cattle country, and no place for a plow. Still, even as he thought that, he knew he would go. In his mind he saw the face of the old rustler they had hung, his fear so vivid on his face and his knees buckling as they led him toward his horse. And he remembered, too, the kids they had caught earlier on the Niobrara, wide-eyed and pleading, begging for one more chance. To his mind now came the sickeningly audible *pop* of their necks snapping, the sound so sharp in his mind he sometimes wanted to scream.

So Jory had been right. Lynching was another matter. It was much more. "Okay, boy. You got a gun?"

"I have that old Remington revolver in a box under my bunk."

"Get it," Howard said flatly. "I'll saddle my horse."

The moon was like a thin, cold wafer hanging above the western horizon when they dropped down among the cottonwoods and halted their sweating mounts. The breeze at their backs was cool, shifting the dry leaves over their heads with a quiet rattle that filtered the pale light of the moon until the shadowed ground around them seemed to writhe under its touch.

"Spooky as a goddamn graveyard at midnight, ain't it?" Jory whispered. He stood in his stirrups to peer downstream, as if his eyes could penetrate the dusky veil of shadows. His voice seemed a notch higher when he spoke, his excitement only thinly concealed. "According to what I've heard, the niggers will be first, then the Germans three or four miles beyond that." He looked dubiously toward Howard, saying, "I hear the old German's got seventeen children. Couple of them homesteading close by, but most of them still at home."

Howard shrugged. "Man needs a lot of help if he wants a big farm. Which do you think they'll hit first?"

Jory laughed softly. "These are white men, Luke. Who do you think they'll hit first?"

"You're a white man," Howard said thoughtfully. "Why aren't you with them?"

Jory eased back in his saddle and adjusted the huge Remington in its holster. "Mr. Young says to come down here and shoot every nigger in sight, I'll come down and do it. Until then, I'll just give them a wide berth, like I would a badger."

"You didn't answer my question, son."

Jory looked at Howard as if he were just then considering

the question. "I don't know. I don't guess I've ever really known any darkies, so I don't know why everybody hates 'em. I guess it just seems that every man should get a fair shake."

Howard shook his head, smiling slightly. "There are men in Sand Creek who would want you horsewhipped for those feelings."

"More that wouldn't," Jory countered.

True enough, Howard thought, lifting the bay's reins. It was something easy to forget, sometimes.

"What about you?" Jory called softly after him. "Why are you down here?"

"Because I'm a damn fool," Howard replied. He said it brittlely, thinking of the old man and the boys on the Niobrara.

They rode without speaking for a ways, the wind teasing among the branches, slipping down around their necks and chilling the flesh. The horses felt their tension through the reins and reacted accordingly, tossing their heads and wanting to jog. The moon was dipping into the horizon with just a small arch of gauzy light left when they heard the scream.

They froze, and even the horses halted at the sudden and unexpected sound, throwing their heads up with their ears perked forward.

"No! Please, Lord, no!" High-pitched and womanly, it came from around the next bend, so wild and desperate it raised the flesh across the back of Howard's neck like a chill.

"Oh, Lord," Jory whispered, his eyes wide and white in the shadows of his hat.

Howard reached down and jerked the Henry from its scabbard, levering a round into the chamber. "Stay behind me and back whatever move I make," he said tersely. "And get that damn hogleg out of your holster."

They rode forward at a fast walk, keeping a tight rein on their horses as they rounded the bend and watched the scene unfold before them. There were several men—a dozen or more—all mounted and spread out in front of a sod-bricked wall in the side of a low hill, maybe fifty yards back from the creek. Torches bobbed among falling sparks that blinked out before reaching the ground, the dancing light painting the soddy yard with an eerie, flickering glow.

The mounted men all wore white flour sacks over their heads, tied loosely around their necks, with gaping holes cut away for their eyes; from a distance and under the crackling light of the torches they looked almost ghostly.

The granger was on his hands and knees, his head hanging between his arms, and even from the bend, Howard could see the dark, glistening drops of blood from his head. A tall, thin man sat a chestnut horse above him, a long-barreled Winchester extened down to the granger's head, with the muzzle buried in the black, kinky hair.

The woman was standing in the doorway, hunched as if in pain. She was crying, her cheeks glistening wetly in the light, though with a lighter sheen than her husband's blood. She had a hand pressed tight against her mouth, as if physically trying to block the sobs from tearing loose.

Closer to the creek, Howard could see two men working with a rope under the limb of a thick cottonwood. Howard and Jory rode out of the darkness together, coming in so silently that the man holding the business end of the rope dropped it with a short, sharp yelp. It created a ripple of movement through the crowd in front of the soddy, a subtle shifting of horses. Howard kept the Henry cradled in his left arm, his right hand curled around the stock, his thumb on the hammer, finger on the trigger. Jory had the butt of his Remington resting on his saddle horn.

For a moment, nobody spoke. Then an angry voice called, "What's your business here, Howard?"

The granger looked up, his face suddenly hopeful. He was wearing a white, collarless shirt arched with a misty spray of blood across the front, and his eyes looked wide, desperate.

Howard stopped just inside the pulsating circle of light

and Jory reined in beside him, though staying fifteen or twenty feet to the side. Close in, he saw that there were fewer men here than he had at first thought, counting only seven mounted men and the two down under the cottonwood. Beside him, he could hear Jory muttering incoherently, blinking and licking at his lips and looking like he might come apart at any minute. Looking, in fact, like he was already starting to fray around the edges.

A rider came up beside the man on the chestnut and leaned in close to whisper something to him. The man on the chestnut looked at Jory then, the empty sockets of his eyes like something inhuman. A torch popped in the hands of one of the riders, sounding strangely like the far-off echo of a gunshot, and the horses shuffled nervously at the sound.

The man on the chestnut rode toward them, forcing his horse over the nearly prone figure of the granger, The animal lifted its hooves delicately over him, yet still clipped a shoulder, rolling the granger to his back. The rider who had done the whispering drew his revolver and lazily pointed it toward the granger.

"I ought to shoot the both of you right here," the man on the chestnut said. "But you've both got work to do come Monday morning, so I'm going to figure this was some kind of a mistake on your part. I'm going to figure you rode in here by accident, and that now you're going to turn around and ride out of here and forget you ever saw anything."

"It was no mistake," Howard said. He recognized the voice of the man on the chestnut but couldn't put a face to it. He knew the next time he heard it he would place it instantly, tying it automatically to the shuffling horses and flickering torches and the empty-socketed gaze of the gunnies.

The man on the chestnut looked behind him, twisting in the saddle, and the others shifted and moved, facing Howard and Jory full on now, the granger forgotten. In the move, Howard spotted a clean-limbed sorrel near the far side of the light, the rider dressed in batwing chaps and a sheepskin jacket and holding his horse back, as if afraid to come too close, maybe fearing that the light of the torches might penetrate the thick material of the sacking.

Howard felt revulsion touch at his stomach, then quickly pass on, leaving him feeling hollow inside, but angry, too, so that all the doubts he had felt toward butting into something that didn't really involve him vanished under its weight.

"You're fixing to step into a lot of trouble, Howard," the man on the chestnut said bluntly. "More than you can handle. I've got close to a dozen rifles backing me. Ride on out now and we'll forget the whole thing. Otherwise I'll have to let them cut you down. You and the boy.

"I'll give you just one minute to ride out of here," Howard said quietly, though with enough strength to reach them all. He felt like ice inside, noncaring. His eyes kept flitting back to the rider on the sorrel and then quickly away, as if he couldn't believe it at first, and then didn't want to.

"I don't believe you know what you're getting yourself into here, Howard," the man on the chestnut said. "We're protecting the range, and I don't care how good a gun you are, we won't let you stand in the way of that."

Howard nodded. "A man has a right to fight for what he believes in. If you're willing to pay the price, let 'er rip."

The man on the chestnut leaned forward, over his horn. "You *can't* win. You'll die for something that doesn't concern you."

Howard pulled the Henry's hammer back, the sound crisp, final.

The man on the chestnut didn't move, yet Howard could feel the heat of his rage, could see it in the tensed, forward set of his shoulders. His thumb stroked the hammer of the Winchester, and the chestnut stirred uneasily. Howard's finger tightened almost imperceptibly on the Henry's trigger, but the barrel never wavered. From the corner of his eye he saw the granger slowly backing out from under the revolver of the gunny who was supposed to be watching him.

It passed then, the man on the chestnut easing back in his saddle, and a sudden gust of wind suddenly swirled through the yard, lowering the light of the torches but seeming to cleanse the air, too, so that they all sensed the change. "Let's go," the man on the chestnut said abruptly, reining his horse roughly toward the creek, The others followed slowly, but without question, their torches blinking like fireflies through the cottonwood and brush, doused out one by one as they splashed across the creek.

Howard slipped the Henry back into its scabbard and dismounted. "Keep your eyes open," he said to Jory. "And your ears. If they come back, you'll probably hear them before you see them."

Jory nodded, his face still white and strained. He swung down from the saddle and walked toward the creek, keeping the Remington unholstered. Howard walked over to the granger, cradled now in his wife's arms.

"Mister, I owes you my life tonight." His accent was Southern, slurred now with pain but growing stronger even as he spoke.

"Are you hurt bad?" Howard asked, squatting and reaching out to touch the granger's shoulder. The woman rocked him swiftly back, away from Howard's hand.

"Woman, this man saved my life tonight. I reckon he is a friend."

"Ain't no man ever be a friend to us, long as his face be white."

The granger smiled apologetically. "She be a bit upset, but she don't mean no harm by it."

Howard looked at the woman, his voice harsher than it had to be, and said, "Just because they're out of sight doesn't mean they've left."

Her breath caught in her throat, and they lifted him together, carrying him toward the soddy where she kicked the door open with a bare foot. It was as black as pitch inside, a total lack of light that surprised him after being able to study the granger's face in just the starlight outside, and he felt a quick, unreasonable panic stirring in his breast until the woman struck a match and touched it to a coal-oil lamp. She hurried to a pine-framed bed then and pulled the quilts back as Howard helped the granger to it. They laid him down, protesting, on a straw mattress. Against the rear wall four small faces stared at him with curious eyes; the oldest a girl of eight or so, while the youngest was still wrapped in blankets. Howard shut the door and dropped the bar in place.

"I bar that door when you leaves," the woman said hotly.

"Woman, I ain't gonna tell you agin. This man saved my life tonight. He be our friend."

"Friend or no, I wants him out."

The granger sat up, his face contorting uncontrollably under the effort. "Woman," he said. "I am the man of this house, and I say this man stays till he wants to leave or I wants him to leave. You just go heat me some water, so's I can tend this cut."

She flashed Howard a dark look but went to a squat little three-burner stove and opened the firebox without further argument. There was a bank of coals still glowing inside, he saw, dimmed by a film of white ashes but still casting a warm, red glow over the room. She added kindling with quick, angry jabs, her face set in a scowl.

Howard looked from the woman to the soddy's walls. The furnishings were sparse, mostly handbuilt but solid and well made. There was a mirrorless dresser next to the bed, and against the far wall a tall chest of drawers. The kitchen table was made of planks, unstained and pocked with old nail holes. There were benches around it, and in the corner, next to an ox hide-bound trunk, was a fruit crate stacked with dirty laundry. The children were still huddled in their blankets against the rear wall, likely on a pallet of some kind.

The granger watched his slow inspection with tired eyes,

then said, "It ain't no fancy mansion like they had on the old place, but I built it with my own hands. This home is *mine*."

Howard grunted a noncommittal reply and moved the lamp closer to the granger.

"Set it on the dresser there," the granger said. He swung his legs out of bed and leaned his elbows against his knees. A drop of blood furrowed on his brow, then dripped to the floor. "Give me a rag, woman, fores I splatter over something can't be washed clean."

The woman brought him a piece of washed sacking and he pressed it lightly to his wound. "Name's George Shatner," he said. "This be my wife, Isabel. I heared them call you Howard. That be a first name, or a last?"

"Last. I'm Luke Howard, Sand Creek way."

"We from Omaha. We come west . . ." His words trailed off, then he said, "We come out here 'cause we was looking for a place to settle. Somewhere where a body could live without nobody else to bother them. Reckons we didn't go far 'nough."

"They ain't no place that far," Isabel said.

Howard looked around the soddy a second time. "You got a gun?"

"They is a shotgun behind that chest o' drawers there."

Howard brought the weapon into the light. It was an old, nondescript twelve-gauge with a single barrel and a scarred stock, a muzzle loader, yet. It was cared for, though, even with the rough treatment it had suffered at some earlier time. The bluing was fresh, and it shone richly under an even coat of oil. The curly maple stock had been waxed. It had a heavy, well-balanced feel.

"Loaded?" Howard asked.

Shatner shook his head. His wife, sitting beside him now and helping him strip off his shirt, made a small clucking noise as she studied the wound. Howard found shot and patch and powder on top of the chest of drawers and loaded the shotgun, ramming it tight. He spilled a handful of caps

over the top of the chest and slipped one over the nipple,
squeezing it between thumb and forefinger for a tight fit.
"Keep this loaded all the time now," he said. "And keep it
handy. Nobody's forgot that you're down here."

"I don't want no loaded gun in my house," Isabel snapped.

"Woman," Shatner spoke sharply. He looked at Howard.
"We be obliged to you, mister," he said quietly. "More than
you knows, most like."

"You ain't stayin' now?" Isabel's stare was accusing, angry
yet. "You just gonna ride out and let them come back?"

"He didn't come to wet-nurse no bunch of ol' niggers,"
George soothed. "Jus' be thankful he come when he did."

"If you're dead set on staying, you'd better get yourself
something faster than a single-shot muzzle loader," Howard
said. "You need a repeating rifle, or at least a revolver. You
aren't just niggers, you're farmers, too, and that isn't setting
too well with anyone."

"I reckon once they cools off some, they won't be botherin'
us agin. Sand Creek to here be a long way to stay mad."

Howard shrugged. They had come once, likely they would
come again, but Shatner was warned now; he knew what to
expect if they did. Luke wouldn't come back a second time,
and now that it was over he felt some skepticism at his
interference. There was more at stake here than a single
farm, a single family. More at stake than single issue of race,
really. Shatner's color was only a springboard used to stir up
old feelings that had never died, yet he thought that had
never really flared all that brightly out here, either. It wasn't
color that burned like live coals in the bellies of the ranchers,
he knew, but the vocation of the Grant Creek settlers. For all
the sport and banter thrown at them, for all the feigned
indifference, there was a threat in the grangers' presence as
serious as any they had ever faced.

The grangers represented more than just crowded range
and fenced-off water holes, or even the annoying inconvenience of having to drive their herds around the settlers' farms

on their way to market. It meant, eventually, the end of free range, and all that went with it—the sprawling ranches a man couldn't cross in two days, the feudal-styled system of government the Cattlemen's Association fostered so carefully, and the deep-rooted satisfaction a man felt at the end of a good year, when he could sit back in his favorite rocker and let the snow drift high against the outside walls, or maybe take his wife to New York or Philadelphia and spend the winter like royalty.

It meant the end of the ranchers themselves, and any man with half his sight could see that coming. To an extent, Howard could share the feelings of the ranchers; he knew the panicky terror that clawed at their guts. The prairie wasn't meant to be turned back and broken by a plow, defaced like a schoolyard privy. It was meant to remain open and free, home to those who could accept it for what it was, and not try to bend it to their own wills.

He held no respect for Shatner, nor any nester for that matter. Living in a hole in the ground that wasn't much better than a badger's den, scratching out a living that would never be quite enough. There was no pride in farming, or none that he could see, only back-breaking work with no promise of a better future. Yet there was no denying the pride in Shatner's voice when he described these crumbling dirt walls as a home, nor was there any knowing of what he had come from, of what his life had been like in Omaha, or before. Howard had seen a few slave rows during the war, the absolute hopelessness and poverty that seemed infectious there. It could be, Howard thought, that what Shatner had here was beyond anything he had ever dreamed of as a boy. Seen in that light, and held against the thousands of acres a rancher might claim, the justice in running Shatner from his small piece of land seemed somehow corrupt.

Yet even seeing it as corrupt, Howard could no more change his feelings about the land than Young could, or Wyatt, or any of the ranchers. He was a stockman at heart, and what Shatner represented was just as corrupt in its own fashion. He wasn't siding with Shatner's dreams when he faced the gunnies in the yellow light from the torches, but the methods they used. There were other ways to handle nesters, ways that were just as effective and a lot less violent. Could be, once the rustling was settled, they'd be hired to handle Shatner and the other nesters. It wouldn't be a job he would be opposed to, he thought.

A sound like that of a slamming door in the distance came muffled through the thick soddy walls. Shatner looked up, puzzled, as Howard drew his revolver and went to the door. He lifted the bar and pulled the door back a few inches, putting his face to the crack and listening to the night. There was a breeze on his face, its caress like ice after the warm stuffiness of the closed soddy, but no sound for a while.

"What was it?" Shatner asked. He sounded worried.

It came again then, louder with the door cracked, deep-throated and echoing—a shotgun, maybe, and then a flurry of shots, eight or ten all together, all coming from downstream.

Howard looked at Shatner, who was staring at the wall with unfocused eyes, perhaps seeing in his mind the country beyond, and what lay there. Isabel dropped the wet cloth she held and her hand flew to her mouth. "Oh, dear Lord," she cried. "George, those shots coming from Gracie and Simon's farm."

Howard looked back at Shatner questioningly.

"Simon Washington. He come with us from Omaha. He's got hisself a farm 'bout a mile down the crik, on the old buff'lo waller, where all the bones be."

Howard swore and slipped outside, leaving the door swinging. Jory was rushing up from the creek, his voice high-pitched and excited. "Shooting downstream, Luke. There's another family of niggers down there."

"I know. Get the horses."

"I'm coming," Shatner said. He stood in the door, leaning

weakly against the frame with Isabel at his side, supporting him but not holding him back.

"Get back inside before you fall down," Howard grunted.

"I am coming," Shatner repeated doggedly. "I am coming if I gots to tie myself to my mule to do it."

"Isabel, get him back in bed. They could come back."

"The Washingtons our friends. They need our help. Any white man show up here anymore tonight, I shoot his lily-whites off. I can handle that goose gun well 'nough for that."

Jory came up mounted and leading the bay. "He's coming," Howard said shortly, jerking his head toward Shatner. "Let's get him up behind you."

Jory kicked a stirrup free, and Howard and Isabel helped Shatner mount. Howard swung atop the bay and frowned down at the woman. "Bar that door and don't open it for anyone, not even your neighbors. Nobody's your friend tonight."

"I knows that," she said, backing toward the soddy. "You get on to Gracie's. Hurry now." She stood at the door until they rode off. Howard heard the slam of the door and, dimly, the bar dropping into place.

With Shatner groaning and swaying behind Jory, they were forced to hold their horses to a fast walk. The delay rankled Howard, yet he knew that whatever happened at the Washington farm had likely already ended. The best they would be able to do was maybe pick up the pieces. Still, there was no telling what they had in mind, what could be happening right now, while they poked along at a snail's pace, and the thought was like a rough bastard file across Howard's nerves.

The moon had been gone for a long time, and now the brilliant starlight was beginning to fade under the promise of dawn. It was cold, too, and damp along the creek. Howard's fingers felt stiff around the Henry, and he kept working them one at a time and wishing he had brought his gloves. Beside him, Jory's horse was wanting to dance under the unfamiliar weight of a second rider, and it was keeping the young puncher busy to prevent his mount from pitching. One little crow-hop would drop Shatner to the grass, Howard thought.

There was an ebbing grayness in the eastern sky as they approached the 'Washington soddy, a false brightness that seemed to flow across the land, pushing the shadows back. Yet for all the light, the land refused to take shape, remaining vague and indistinct, with earth and sky blending into one solid, leaden color; only the thinning pattern of trees and brush along the creek had any real shape.

They pulled up on the lip of a wide wash, the dull silhouette of the Washington soddy rising above the ground on the far side. They faced the rear of the house, with the Grant forming a rough L a couple of hundred yards beyond, cradling the farm in its curve. There were no trees, no brush closer than the Grant, and as far as they could tell, no one around the soddy.

They crossed the wash with their weapons ready, nerves stretched taut. Both horses were skittish at the litter of sun-bleached buffalo bones; some hide hunter's old stand, Howard thought, missed by the bone pickers. There were twenty or thirty fleshless skeletons scattered through the wash, mostly grown over with grass and pulled apart by the wolves. Some looked half buried already, though here and there a skull sat out in full view, the short, up-curving horns looking black against the white skulls and the gray grass.

The bank was steeper on the far side of the wash, and the horses kicked away little avalanches of loose dirt as they buck-jumped their way to the rim. Shatner slid off the rear of Jory's horse about halfway up, but clambered after them on his hands and knees. He'd regained some of his strength on the ride, and although the bandage around his head was moist with fresh blood, he was walking under his own power.

They found Grace Washington on the far side of the house, kneeling over the prone body of her husband, silent, trembling. Between her and the house four children stood coatless and barefoot in the morning cold, their breath puffing in frosty little clouds. The oldest, a boy about the size of Shatner's oldest girl, held an old Army Springfield at his side, butt to the dirt.

The woman looked up when she heard the horses. Then, screaming, she ran for the rifle. The boy stepped back as she jerked it from his hand. She swung it toward them, clawing at the hammer. Then Shatner was at her side, pulling the rifle away, voicing the same soothing nothings Howard had used on the grulla. She let him take it without a struggle, huddling in his arms, crying openly now, the sound harsh in the gray world. Shatner led her into the soddy, and one by one the youngest children peeled off to follow. Only the oldest remained, staring at Howard and Jory with unmasked hatred until Shatner's voice finally pulled him away.

Howard dismounted and let his reins trail. Simon Washington had been a tall man, broad-shouldered and balding. His fingers were long but blunt-tipped, and his palms, curled skyward, were calloused, His chest seemed sunken, caved in under the impact of half a dozen bullets. He was barefoot, and his trousers were only half buttoned. Looking toward the door, Howard saw where the top hinge had given away under a battering. Dragged from his bed, Howard thought, waking to find a rabid mob at his door, as thirsty for his blood as a half-starved coyote after a rabbit, and he wondered crazily then if Washington had felt like a rabbit, trapped and without hope.

He walked back to the bay and hooked a toe in the stirrup, pausing there, at Jory's words.

"There's a shovel against the wall there," Jory said in a choked voice. "I guess the least we could do is dig a grave."

"Why?" Howard asked, keeping his toe in the stirrup and his back to Jory.

"To make up for what happened here," Jory said. "Show them we're not all like that."

"Aren't we?" Howard asked bitterly. He took a gather on the reins and swung aboard. "Nothing here was our doing," he said then. "Best we can do is just ride out and leave them to their grief." He felt suddenly tired, weak in muscle and mind and half sick from lack of sleep. Yet it was more mental than physical, he knew, an aftermath to the violence that seemed to drain him of stength and will.

They left Simon Washington face up in his yard while the morning dew began to settle on his face. Down on the Grant a meadowlark began to trill, and the grayness of dawn seemed to float away before the rosy pinkness of first light. They stopped again on the west side of the wash, and Howard turned the collar of his duster up against the chill. He patted his pockets for a cheroot, then rolled it smooth against his thigh and struck a match.

"What do we do now?" Jory asked.

"Go home and get some sleep, if we can."

"But what about what happened here?"

"Ain't nothing going to change what happened here."

"I recognized some of them," Jory said quietly, staring at the stitching around his horn. "Couple of the Crooked Arrow boys, the Circle-R waddy." He looked at Howard. "The one on the chestnut was Jeff McKinley, Ben Wyatt's foreman."

Howard nodded, the face coming to him now, meshing with the voice. Still, he said, "Hard to recognize any man with a sack over his head. Particulary in that kind of light."

"A man can hide his face, but he can't hide his horse or chaps or the way he sits a saddle."

He can't hide a Spencer .56 or a long-legged sorrel, either, Howard thought, but all he said was, "You go to making accusations and somebody's going to slip a knife into your ribs some night. Best you just forget tonight."

"I don't reckon I'll ever forget tonight," Jory said soberly.

Nor me, boy, Howard thought, nor me. George Shatner

and Simon Washington would be packed away with the old rustler and the young hands they had caught on the Niobrara, and a dozen other faces through the years. A trunk full of memories that could be closed, but never really locked.

CHAPTER 9

IT seemed the rain had set in to stay. Not steady, the way it did back home sometimes, the clouds low and gray and spitting rain for days on end, but regular enough to count on after a while. Days would dawn bright and sunny, with big, puffy clouds rising above the rim of mountains, but by noon the clouds would turn dark and merge into a solid ceiling, with lightning glowing deep within. The rain usually lasted the rest of the day then, only now and again clearing just before sunset to leave the world sparkling. It was cold too, with frost some mornings, and the cold and dampness working on a man, turning him stiff and old.

It was hell on a man trying to work, Orin Jessup thought, especially with winter coming on so fast now. Seemed like everywhere you looked anymore, you saw the signs of it. Best they could do, though, was to get down to the box early and be ready as soon as there was light enough to spot color.

Orin Jessup was an elder version of his son, though darker in hair, and thicker now, and shorter, as if he had settled some over the years. He was a slow-moving, stoop-shouldered man, work-simple in some ways, he supposed. But hard, gut-busting labor was all he'd ever known through his life, and he'd come to expect no more from the rest of it.

Like Old Tom and Hawk, he had opposed Tod's bringing the wounded man into their camp, though for different reasons. He wasn't worried about Tod not keeping up with his share of the work. Even nursing the stranger, Tod would handle all his work, and likely some of the others' too. It was more the kind of man Swede was, and what he represented. Even wrapped in blankets and strapped to a crude travois

145

Tod had rigged to the blue ox, his eyes gummy and his face flushed with fever, there was an air of deadliness about him, a sense of danger that hung over him like the stink of something dead. It was something he didn't want Tod exposed to, though he knew he wouldn't be able to shield him forever.

Orin let the bit of his long-handled shovel settle into the creek gravel, and straightened the kinks from his back. Tod was manhandling a pair of deep oak buckets filled with gravel through the spongy ground at the base of the sluice. The thin fabric of his shirt was stretched tight across the ridged muscles of his back. Farther, where the slim, white-barked aspen met the high meadow grass, he saw Swede, staring upstream, unconsciously humping his shoulders to favor his wounds.

Orin pushed the shovel deeper and waded from the shallow waters that riffled like ice around his shoes. He passed his son at the head of the box and patted his shoulder clumsily. "You dig alone awhile, huh, Toddy? I want to talk to your friend a bit."

"Swede? Sure, Pa," Tod answered curiously.

Orin followed the summer-worn path to the edge of the aspen, marveling at the way Swede was letting himself go. Even as bad off as he was when Tod had brought him in, there was no mistaking that Swede was the kind of man to take some pride in his appearance, keeping his hair trimmed and combed and the neat little mustache of his even and in place. Even his clothes, though nothing fancy and soiled with trail dirt, had a look of tailored quality about them. Now though, he looked little better than any saloon bum. His hair was growing long and dirty and tangled, and the blond stubble that sprouted over his chin and jaw had thickened into a full beard. He never washed, not even his hands before a meal, and his clothes were slick with dirt. He wore a crude pair of moccasins he had stitched himself and a cloth cap Tod had given him.

Orin stopped half a dozen paces away and pulled a long-stemmed spear of grass loose from the wet soil, tucking it in the corner of his mouth, where it bobbed and swayed with his words. "I'm wanting to talk with you, Swede, you got a minute?"

Swede didn't bother to look around. "What do you want?"

Orin folded his arms and cleared his throat. " 'Pears like we haven't talked much. Seems like maybe we should, you sharing our camp and all." When Swede didn't reply, he pushed on determinedly. "I ain't begrudging you the meat you eat, or the time Toddy spent looking after you, but it 'pears like your holes are 'bout healed and I was thinkin' maybe you could start helpin' with some of the chores. Nothing heavy, mind you, but maybe the cookin' and keeping after the fire and the like. If'n you're still weak or sickish, I won't be holdin' you to it, you understand."

Swede turned slowly, staring without answering for a long time, then he laughed. "You've got more nerve than I would have thought," he said.

Orin bit his lip, his eyes flashing, but careful. "It ain't the time you spent sick I'm thinkin' of, man. The boy's been paid well for that. But that's been a spell back now, and your appetite is as big as a bear's, it is now."

Swede grunted. "I didn't ask him to bring me in. And I didn't tell the little fool to sell custom revolvers for a third of what they were worth. He got my revolvers for his work; that's all he'll get from me."

Orin looked surprised. "He didn't do it for the money. If he'd of left you there, you'd be dead now, sure, and not likely buried." Orin paused, waited, then went on. "You can't be blaming the boy for the other, your poke and your boots. It was the doctor what took them, and nobody even knew there was a horse somewheres."

"Seems like everyone was pretty sure I was going to die."

"You were shot up pretty bad. Had yourself two holes, right here." He tapped his chest.

"I know where they are," Swede replied curtly. "I can still feel them."

"Aye, I reckon you can." Orin toed an exposed root, moving the wet dirt back from it. He took the stem from his mouth and studied the tassled end. "I reckon you feel that, and that the boy's something of a thief to boot," he said quietly. "But he did only what he thought right and best. He wouldn't have sold the pistols if he'd a thought you were gonna live. He wouldn't."

Swede's eyes flashed. "The revolvers aren't enough, is that it? All right, old man, I'll see that my debt is paid before I leave. In aces, if that's what it'll take to satisfy you."

Orin's face reddened and he spit a piece of grass from his mouth. When he spoke, his voice was shaky. "By God, you're not much in the way of manners, are you?"

Swede's face was hard, his eyes emotionless now, and his lips pulled into a tight, thin line. Orin swallowed, choked, and stepped back suddenly, unaccountably. Swede said, "Is that all you came to say?"

Orin nodded, blinked, and his shoulders drooped suddenly. "Aye," he said softly. "I reckon it is."

His anger faded quickly, and thinking about it, Swede knew it wasn't Orin's request for help with the camp chores that had pricked his anger, nor was it a question of the boy's honor. It went deeper than that somehow, touching something in him that was new and unfamiliar, something just uncovered, maybe. Was this what gratitude felt like, he wondered? Did he, after all, owe the boy still more? Maybe, he thought; he wasn't sure. But if there was a debt yet to be paid, he would do it in his own fashion and in his own time.

Thinking of that, he thought then of Old Tom and Hawk, partners of a sort with the elder Jessup, though it seemed neither Tod nor his pa remembered exactly how the partnership had been formed.

They had ridden in together a month or so before, Tod

had told him, settling into camp like old friends. They'd helped with the hard work at first, both around camp and on the placer. Then Hawk had taken to hunting, claiming fresh meat was a fair share, what with mining town prices being what they were. Tod said neither of them had been all that surprised when Hawk claimed he couldn't manage alone, that all the digging and activity had scared the game off, and Old Tom had given up the shovel to help. It was then they had started using the word partnership, and talking as if they held more than a passing interest in the claim.

Tod had told him of Old Tom and Hawk in a voice without shame or surprise, adding that they would have to come to a reckoning soon. Tod had figured there'd likely be trouble then, and thinking about it now, Swede was inclined to agree. Old Tom and Hawk would likely claim a quarter-share each, and use the meat they had brought in as their ticket. Tod had hinted at it in telling the story, though Swede had seen it all along. It wasn't that uncommon a practice, he knew.

Swede smiled, watching Tod lunge stiff-backed up the creek bank with his buckets. Maybe Old Tom and Hawk held the answer to his debt to the kid.

Swede shifted, his hind end almost numb from holding the same spot for so long. He held a blue enamel cup in his fingers, the bottom freckled with chunky coffee grounds. A ratty old bearskin cape was draped over his shoulders, held together with his free hand, and Tod's old cap-and-ball Walker Colt was a heavy, solid weight against his belly, tucked into his belt; a small leather shooting bag hung from his shoulder, the strap crossing his chest. A brass buckle, tarnished with age, winked dully through a gap in the bearskin from the bag's strap.

Across the fire, Orin Jessup worked over a shirt, adding buttons that had popped off during the summer that he hadn't taken time to replace before. His face was pale and tight, and he kept glancing beyond the flickering circle of firelight, as if trying to probe the shadows there. Tod sat on a crate between them, cracking his knuckles and staring into the flame. When the splash of horses crossing the creek finally came to them, he almost fell off the crate.

"I could use some more coffee, boy," Swede said calmly.

Tod leaned close. "They're coming," he whispered.

"I can hear them. Just stay calm and fetch me some coffee."

Tod nodded and wrapped the brim of his cap around the pot's handle and tipped the spout over Swede's cup. Orin was bent almost double over his sewing now, though missing and poking a finger or his thigh about every other stitch.

Swede listened without turning as Old Tom and Hawk led their horses into the aspen and stripped the gear from them, then came forward, slow and careful, as if sensing something out of kilter. Old Tom came into the firelight first, cradling a Sharps over one arm and carrying a bloody piece of hide in the other hand. He dropped it next to the fire, where it kicked up a breeze that stirred the ashes and flame; a corner fell open to reveal chunks of raw, bloody meat.

Old Tom was a man shorter than average, standing only an inch or so above five feet, with a bow-legged, rolling gait and narrow shoulders. His nose was long and thin and beaked, the tip curving down to a point above his mouth, which was shrunken with a lack of teeth. His face was almost as black as old leather, wrinkled and lined, with everything seeming to curl inward, giving him a curious, punched-in look in the right kind of light. He said he had been a mountain man, and claimed to have known them all, old Gabe and Carson and Meek, and to have had fourteen Indian wives from as many tribes.

"Antelope," Tom said, indicating the hide. "Coarse, but fresh. Game's getting hard to find . . ." He let the words trail off, and his eyes traveled the trio sitting by the fire, settling finally on Swede.

Swede tipped his head toward the pot and smiled disarmingly. "Coffee's hot. Ought to go down good after a long day of hunting."

Old Tom studied him a moment, then nodded and squatted. He carried a battered old tin cup at his belt, and he loosened it now and brought it around, keeping the Sharps close at hand.

Hawk came in from the darkness, though standing back where the light barely reached him. Hawk was younger than Tom by quite a few years, and taller. His hair was cropped short, for a breed, and combed, white man's fashion, to the side. Hawk carried himself like a caged lion Swede had once seen, with a quick, impatient savageness only thinly veiled behind a show of lazy indifference. A man would likely never notice Hawk unless he happened to look into his eyes. He'd notice him then, all right, and remember him, too. Hawk carried a new-looking Winchester like it was a part of him and a Green River skinner on his hip. He carried another knife, Tod had told him, a long, slim dirk Tod had seen only once, and that by accident. Likely, he was good with it, Swede thought. A dirk wasn't much good for anything but fighting, and a man didn't usually carry a fighting knife without knowing how to use it.

Hawk stood in the shifting shadows without speaking; Swede could feel Hawk's eyes drilling him from behind, so he made no effort to include the breed at the fire. Hawk was suspicious enough at the unnatural way Tod and his pa were acting.

Old Tom sipped noisily at his coffee, his eyes coming around after a while to rest on Orin. "Good day?" he asked, as if just passing the time.

Orin looked up, startled, still poking blindly with his needle. "Good enough, yeah. Maybe three or four dollars. Not like earlier this summer."

Old Tom nodded as if he had expected as much. "Me and Hawk, we been noticing that. Seems like you're coming up with a little less each day."

"Maybe we could use a little more help on digging from our partners," Tod said, leaning heavily on the last word.

Old Tom graced him with a quick, irritated glance, then turned back to the elder Jessup. "A diggings plays out after a while, 'less you've got the money to bring in big equipment. Me and Hawk, we been thinking the time might be ripe to sell this claim to one of the big outfits and push on. Winter ain't much more than a fart away anymore. We need to start thinking about that. I ain't hankering to winter here."

Swede breathed a silent sigh. Old Tom and Hawk were forcing it now, and that was unexpected, but good. It made it look as if they had caught the Jessups unprepared, which nudged the odds slightly to Swede's advantage. The Jessups' nervousness could be put down as surprise, now. Everything seemed to be rolling smoothly, save for the boy.

"Thought you was an old mountain man?" Tod said. "Thought you said you've been wintering out here for forty years?"

Tom started to look his way, then caught himself. From the shadows Hawk said, "The pup howls like the wolf." He said it softly, but they all heard the laughter in his voice.

Tod looked down swiftly, clenching his fists but not replying. Swede sipped his coffee. He wanted to shift around until he could see Hawk better, but didn't dare.

"We figure the claim ought to be worth a thousand dollars, dust, even worked all summer like it has been," Old Tom said. "With what we've dug so far, that figures to near two thousand, total, or five hundred dollars apiece." Old Tom spoke with the oily smoothness of a man trying to coax a horse into water, like the words were just talk, but there was a pack full of meaning behind them, Swede knew—behind the words and the way Old Tom kept his rifle handy.

Orin's lips were parted, his reply caught somewhere in his throat. Tod said, "You're loon-crazy. This claim ain't worth no thousand dollars, and we ain't panned no thousand dollars this summer, either. You're asking for more than we made as just your share!"

Hawk threatened, "Sometimes the pup don't quit his yapping, you knock it in the head with an axe handle."

"He's speaking the truth, God's sake," Orin said. "Even sellin' the claim, if'n we could find a buyer, we wouldn't see a thousand dollars. And you're asking for equal shares? Hell, man, me and Toddy's worked this claim near 'bout three months 'fore you and Hawk ever showed up."

Old Tom lowered his cup and sighed elaborately. "Hawk said you'd try to do us out of our rightful share. I'd hoped maybe you'd be more Christian than that." He stood, and Orin with him, letting his sewing fall in the dirt. Only Swede and Tod remained seated. Tod swung a wild, desperate look at Swede.

"Tell you what," Tom said. "You just fork over what dust you have in camp and we'll let you keep the rest, what you have notes for and what you get for the claim."

Hawk moved closer, his boots like a whisper of wind stirring the grass. Behind him yet, Swede thought, but edging closer and around to the side. Swede sipped his coffee without tasting it, the conversation muted now, the words without meaning.

"Got no notes," Orin protested. "And the claim will be worth no more than a couple of hundred dollars. By God, man, you're trying to rob us!"

Old Tom let the Sharps slide down his arm, coming to rest in his hands, ready to cock and swing around. Swede risked a slow, casual glance over his shoulder and was relieved to see Hawk's Winchester resting butt first against the ground. But Hawk's right hand was hidden just inside the flap of his wool coat, and Swede wondered if that was where he carried the dirk.

Swede turned back. Tod was light on the crate now, looking like he was ready to jump but maybe not knowing which way to go. Old Tom had swung the Sharps around a little so that the muzzle was toward Tod, perhaps sensing the youth's eagerness to fight.

"That's enough talk," Hawk said impatiently. "It's time we go."

Old Tom said to Orin, "Why don't you have the whelp fetch the dust so's we can leave peaceful?"

"You can go to hell," Tod shouted, the words echoing back from some far-off cliff.

Hawk moved closer to the fire, edging into the corner of Swede's vision. "You go fetch the dust, pup, or I'll skin you slow." His hand came from his coat, the firelight glinting off polished steel. Old Tom's thumb curled around the Sharps' hammer.

"Hell, boys, no call for that," Swede said, standing easy and letting the bearskin drop. Other than looking suddenly his way, Old Tom and Hawk seemed frozen. Swede grinned and let the contents of his cup spill into the fire, sending a great ball of white steam and smoke puffing up like a small, hissing explosion. He had the old Walker almost free before Old Tom or Hawk really knew what was about.

Hawk was close and dangerous and likely as good with a knife as most men were with a rifle, but it was Old Tom who scared Swede. Old Tom and his Sharps rifle that could mangle flesh and bone like paper and twigs. So when he brought the old Walker up he leveled it on Tom first, cocking and firing even as he moved. The revolver belched a cloud of gray smoke center-punched with rosy sparks, bucking against his palm and jolting his arm to the elbow. The Sharps roared in Old Tom's hands, but the muzzle was pointed skyward by then, as Old Tom fell backward. Swede was already spinning toward Hawk, fanning off a second shot just as Hawk launched his knife.

The slim dirk buried itself in the flesh of Swede's chest and he gasped at the white-hot searing of steel slicing into his rib bones. He took a step back, stumbled, and fell hard to his buttocks, gasping again at the jolt of pain along his spine. He felt blood, warm and wet, and looked down to see the rosewood handle of the dirk jutting upward from his breast. Then he lay back and shut his eyes as the darkness swirled in once more to claim him.

Tod backed Blue into place and tipped the cart up until he could run the hook through the yoke over the ox's neck. He worked with a quick, quiet determination, looking neither left nor right nor even ahead, beyond the next chore. Orin watched from a distance, his lips pursed, a stem of dried grass caught between his teeth, then turned away. "You could go speak with him," he said quietly.

Swede lifted the mule's tail and pulled the breeching up and cinched it to the pack saddle's rigging. He moved stiffly, the old wounds sore with the dampness, and the fresh one, the knife wound, still breaking open to spill a little blood when he stretched too far or too fast. He was lucky, he knew. Were it not for the thick, heavy strap of the shoulder bag, the knife might have gone all the way in to his heart—Hawk's aim had been true.

"The boy saved your life," Orin went on doggedly, the way he had the past week. "Figured you for some kind of a hero, he did, doing what you did there. There's no call to treat him like he was dirt."

Swede ran the mule's lead rope to the saddle horn on Hawk's blood bay, then took the bay's lead rope and gathered the reins on Old Tom's gray. He'd taken it all, weapons and stock and clothes, figuring they would bring a fair price in Deadwood. He'd hunt up the gunsmith Tod had sold his revolvers to and buy them back. Time enough then to head back to Easy Street and pick up a trail grown cold.

"Treating him like this, then leavin', he'll be thinkin' you did what you did just to outfit yourself," Orin said. "My God, man, you're turning yourself into a murderer in the boy's eyes. Is that what you're after?"

Swede stepped into the saddle, the leather creaking under

his weight. It was a cloudy day, damp and cool, and he was wearing Hawk's wool coat against the chill. It had rained a little already that morning and looked like it could do it again any time. He looked down to the camp where Tod was wedging the last of the gear into the cart. The place had a deserted air about it, the old diggings and litter of cans and bottles adding to the sense of desolation. Swede breathed deeply of the air, then said, "I didn't figure you'd mind the boy thinking hard of me, considering how you feel about me."

"I know what you are, true enough, and I can understand that, at least as well as any man can ever understand a killer. But Toddy's still a boy, even if he is bigger than his pa, and I'd like him to think there's a bit of good in the worst of men."

Swede watched the boy a moment, then looked down at the old man, and a grin spread slowly across his face. "You're a card, all right. More nerve than a fool." He laughed and turned the gray into the timber, putting his back to the Jessups. After a while it began to rain again, and he pulled the collar of Hawk's old coat up tight around his neck.

CHAPTER 10

THE sky had dropped almost to the tops of the hills overnight, slate gray and streaked with black, damp-cold. Occasionally, thin wisps of whirling clouds would drop lower, brushing the crests of the ridges and leaving everything they touched slick with mist. The rain came intermittently, slapping against slicker and chaps with an angry, popping force. Only yesterday the sun had shone with enough warmth to raise a sweat on a working man.

Doc came along the high ridge at a slow jog, the black gelding he rode pulling up little hoof-shaped chunks of mud and flinging them behind. The ridge sloped steeply on either side, flowing down into wide valleys that rose again into rolling hills. The ridge was dotted with sage and greasewood and little clumps of cactus that glistened from the rain. The world seemed barren from up here, the land as colorless as the sky, empty of bird or animal.

He was riding north, long since leaving the Crooked Arrow range in a wide sweep of the country above Sand Creek. His hat was pulled low, leaving only an inch or so of the horizon below the brim, and his coat, beneath the yellow folds of his slicker, was buttoned tight against the cold. The wind buffeted him from face-on, slipping through the tiniest crack in his clothing with an uncanny ease. Moisture clung to the fuzz along his cheeks and beaded the brim of his hat.

He was cold and miserable and getting hungry now, with no bite of food in his saddlebags and noon already past. His nose had been running earlier, but it had closed now, and the area around his nose and under his eyes was aching from the pressure. He thought again of returning to the bunkhouse and kicking up a fire in the potbellied stove, but shook the thought from his mind. He'd be damned if he'd be sitting with his boots propped to the heat when the Crooked Arrow hands came in.

The ridge started to break up after a while, dropping down into a broken jumble of smaller hills with little pockets of bare earth between. In the spring those pockets would hold water for a few weeks, but now the ground was cracked from the summer sun, though slick with mud from the rain.

He swung to the east, coming down into the valley bordering the ridge. There was a stand of box elder at the head of the valley, swaying in the wind above a cutbank creek, and now and again showering it with yellow leaves. He rode toward it on impulse, thinking of building a fire and thawing out for an hour or so. He didn't notice the tracks until he was almost past them.

He reined up sharply, feeling a moment of puzzlement at finding cattle sign where there shouldn't have been any. Then, gradually, the puzzlement gave way to excitement. He crisscrossed the trail a number of times, angling north with the sign. It was only a few hours old, judging from the droppings, likely made that morning or late the night before. He stopped once, and swung out of the saddle after spotting horse prints flanking the trail, and whispered to himself, "Rustlers." He remounted and pulled the black around, pausing, undecided, then struck out along the trail alone.

It crossed the ridge he had been following about a mile above where he had left it and dropped into the next valley, angling west now as much as north. He didn't have Sanchez's knack for reading sign, but he thought it was a large herd, with maybe four or five men pushing them along at a good clip. From time to time he thought about riding back to the Crooked Arrow for help, knowing he should, yet the trail seemed to beckon him along, and he would push on a little farther.

The clouds lifted some as the afternoon waned, and the

mist that had clung to the higher ridges cleared away, but it was still cold. Riding through the valley at a lope with his slicker flapping around him, he thought how odd it seemed that winter was so close now.

The black held the lope easily, without strain. Doc pushed the brim of his hat back against the crown and rode straight in the saddle, ignoring the cold now that he had the heady rush of anticipation to warm his blood. He paid scant attention to the trail, only glancing at it from time to time as if to reassure himself that he was still following it. The miles ticked past and the trail grew fresher. He was a long way from Sand Creek range now, passing through a country that was unfamiliar to him. Other than the trail, he saw no sign of cattle, hadn't in a long time, though he occasionally saw antelope and once spotted a band of mustangs, tiny in the distance and disappearing through a gap in the hills.

He spotted the herd finally late in the afternoon, passing snakelike over a far ridge, and he spurred his horse on with a fresh determination. The black was blowing now, with a dirty lather working up around his breastband and the cinch, and when the country became rougher, Doc pulled him back to a jog. He rode that way for an hour, jogging a bit, then pulling back to a walk, then jogging again, winding through a maze of broken hills and sandy draws that seemed to have no set pattern of direction. He'd lost all sight of the herd, but the ground was still fresh-torn from their hooves, and the patties were steaming on the ground. The sharp, unmistakable smell of wet hide hung in the air, yet he knew that as long as he didn't hear them, he wasn't too close. Cattle on the move always complained.

He spotted them again, coming out of the hills into another valley, narrow and long—a black river of beef flowing toward the center of the valley. He reined the black in and pulled his hand back under his slicker, over the Dragoon. The sound of protesting cattle reached him faintly now, over the wind and the blowing of his horse. There were four riders flanking the herd, pushing hard and swinging their ropes or quirts over the backs of the stragglers.

Doc sucked his breath in sharply and pulled the black back off the ridge. He turned into a wide draw that seemed to parallel the valley and followed its winding path until it veered back to the east. There he crossed a low ridge and dropped into another draw, keeping the sound of the drive always on his left.

The black spooked once at some sound Doc didn't hear, but he pulled him down with an impatient jerk and continued on, conscious only of the cattle. He wasn't aware of the rider flanking him on his right until the rider's horse nickered, and his own answered.

Doc swung around swiftly, his eyes going wide at the sight of the Winchester resting across the pommel of the rider's saddle, the muzzle leaning toward him. He reined the black around carefully, his hand tight on the Dragoon, yet bitterly aware that it was still trapped in its holster, the holster buried beneath the heavy weight of the slicker.

"You looking for someone in particular?" the stranger asked. He sat his horse calmly atop the bank of the draw, a skinny little whip of a man, not much bigger than himself, with a dark face and a hawked nose peaking over a thick mustache and a week's growth of beard. He wore an Arizona-styled stetson pulled low and a gaudily-colored poncho, the kind Doc had seen the Mexicans wear the year his father was stationed at Fort Davis.

Doc's thumb curled over the Dragoon's hammer, his mind whirling in a quiet panic. Behind him, the faint bellow of an angry steer came sharp on the wind. He didn't know what to do or how to react, so for a moment he didn't react at all. He sat on the black and licked at his lips.

"Lose your way?" the stranger prompted. "Or maybe you're looking for your friends?"

Now or never, Doc thought then. Cock the piece and pull, fire through the slicker while the stranger was still engrossed with his questions. Doc's grip tightened on the Dragoon, but the revolver had barely broken the leather's grip when the stranger fired.

The Winchester puffed a blue-gray cloud of smoke, bucking in the stranger's hand. The bullet hit Doc high on the right side of his chest, tumbling him from the saddle in a tangle of color, the bright yellow slicker dropping like a canary from the sky.

Doc fell hard, face first against the hard, wet ground, the blow driving the wind from his lungs. He lay without moving, his breathing coming in slow, deep draughts, conscious but dazed. His chest felt numb, tight, as if he were caught in a bear hug. He'd broken his nose in the fall, the pain sharp on his clogged sinuses. He only dully heard the stranger sliding his horse down into the draw and dismounting. Doc thought of the Dragoon still holstered at his hip, but he couldn't seem to move. He felt numbed in body, sleepy and lethargic, removed from what was happening, as if it was all only a dream, and dimly remembered at that.

He felt the rustler's hand under his slicker and knew he didn't carry the Dragoon or his Bowie anymore. A toe under his stomach flipped him over and the sky whirled dizzily over him, the stranger towering treelike now, and the bright reds and blues of his poncho stinging his eyes. He felt as helpless as a turtle flipped to its back.

The rustler brought his rifle down to Doc's head, resting it against his forehead, the muzzle hard and cold. The rustler kept it there for a long time, pressed lightly into the thin flesh, his eyes cloudy with thought. "Hell," he said finally, his voice floating disjointedly above Doc. "You ain't much more than a kid." He sounded surprised, Doc thought.

There was a rapid drumming of a running horse, the beat ringing hollowly through the ground under Doc's head, and he saw the rustler look up expectantly past the rim of the draw.

"Was he alone?" This new voice sounded wild and a little frightened.

The rustler in the poncho nodded.

"You sure?"

"I'm sure. I've followed him for an hour."

Doc thought there was relief in the new voice now. It said, "Well, get his money and whatever else is worth taking and let's go. When he ain't back by dark, somebody's gonna start wondering." He turned and spurred off, the hooves fading into silence.

Above him, the rustler in the poncho frowned. "You should be dead," he said. "If you live you'll just cause more trouble."

Doc didn't answer; he wasn't sure he could. His whole body felt dull, detached from his shifting thoughts. All he could do was stare at the stranger and await his decision. The rustler finally pulled the Winchester away from Doc's forehead; the muzzle left a small, white imprint on the flesh. He looked up the draw where Doc's black had disappeared and said, "Your horse is probably halfway to Dakota Territory by now, and I ain't so sure Ace-High was speaking the truth when he said you'd be missed by dark. Anyway, I ain't killing no kid. If you live, then you will have earned it. If you die, well, that'll be the fall of the dice." He kicked the Dragoon and Bowie closer to Doc's side. "Maybe these will help. Good luck, kid."

Doc waited until the rustler had mounted and climbed his horse from the draw, then closed his eyes. The wind picked at his slicker, rustling it around his ears, but he was too tired to care.

Charity walked down the hall on tired feet, her shoes whispering quietly on the thin carpet. It was late, past midnight, and the crowd downstairs had thinned to only a dozen or so, more intent on faro than women. Goff had come over to the table where she and Belle had been resting and told them to give it up for the night, that he'd be shutting the place down in an hour or so anyway. Charity hadn't argued.

She had felt an unexplainable weariness since the day of her argument with Luke, a gnawing depression that left her wrung out and dragging by quitting time. Looking back, it all seemed so unreal, so like a dream. She had searched for him with an honest concern, and a need that was new and unfamiliar, but pleasant, too. She had felt in herself a willingness to give what she had never experienced before, and so she had searched with an eagerness to match her worry.

She could laugh about it now, and call herself a fool for believing any man was different from the next, and say she got what she deserved for letting one persuade her otherwise. But beneath it all she knew that his betrayal had cut her deeply. She felt like a vase shattered and picked up and put back together with weak glue; fragile, she felt, and on precarious footing to boot. She was tired of her life here, tired of the long hours and the smoke and noise and smell and the same men every night, the same men whose faces were the only thing that changed. She was tired of the heat and cold and the jokes and food, too, and of everything that was her life, until she felt a dread of each new day that sometimes made her want to scream.

She opened the door to her room and lit a lamp. It was her private room, not the crib at the head of the stairs where she took her customers, but the sanctuary she retreated to each night. There was pale blue paper on the walls, patterned with flowers of a darker blue, a whitewashed ceiling and on the floor an Oriental rug of large peacocks standing in front of a blue-tinged fan of feathers, the design of each bird blending so well into the overall pattern of the rug that at times it was hard to pick each one out individually.

There was a wardrobe closet and a dresser with a mirror and a washstand with a painted pitcher and bowl beneath. The bed was large and dark, cut from the same heavy wood as the closet and dresser, with a thick feather mattress, two pillows, and a wedding ring quilt. There was a straight-backed wooden chair against the far wall, a padded easy chair against the near wall, and a dressing table in the corner.

It was something to see, she knew, a rare luxury on the frontier, and a gesture of faith and friendship on Goff's part. Yet lately she had come to view this room as more of a prison than a sanctuary, a trap, for all its frills.

She walked to the window, pulling the straight-backed chair with her, and sat down. But it was dark outside, without even the moon or stars for light, and all she saw was her own reflection in the glass, backed by the distorted image of her room. The cold wind seeping in around the sill raised the flesh along her bare arms, and she went back to the bed, falling across it fully clothed, staring at the ceiling. The wind rattled at the panes, as if angry with her for pulling back, and the rain slashed at the glass with a sudden, powerful force.

She sat up after a while and looked at the room, wondering how it would change in ten years, and with a kind of dull terror, if she would be here that long to see it happen.

She felt like crying at the thought, but didn't have the energy. Then she thought of herself in ten years, the image bringing a wretched gasp; she leaned forward, clutching little bundles of the quilt, seeing in her mind herself, wrinkled and graying and puffy-faced, the hopelessness etched solidly on her by then.

She rolled quickly from the bed and pulled a cloth valise from the top shelf of the closet and began stuffing it with clothing, shoving it in without thought to wrinkles or tears.

"Charity?" There was a quick tap at the door. Charity whirled, trying to hide the valise behind the flare of her skirt, a panic coming into her eyes. "Charity, it's me, Meg." The door swung slowly open, and Meg came in with a questioning frown. "I heard noises, thumpings and bangings."

"I was getting into my closet," Charity said in a small, breathless voice.

Charity pointed toward the closet, but Meg had already spotted the corner of her valise, and she came farther into the room, her gaze traveling from the valise to Charity's face. "What's going on?" Meg asked. "Are you going to Ogallala? Are you going to the doctor? Do you feel bad?"

There was genuine concern on Meg's face, but Charity seemed to shrink before the barrage of her questions. It was her out if she wanted it, she knew, her ticket south, but stubbornly, she refused it. "I'm leaving for good, Meg. I'm going crazy here."

"Girl, if you need some time off, talk to Isaac. He gave me a week off last year, remember?"

"A week wouldn't be enough anymore." She made a faint gesture with her hands, as if to say more, then let them drop to her side.

"Is it Luke?" Meg asked. "What happened in the livery?"

"Maybe," she admitted. "But it's more than that. It's my whole life here, what I've become."

"Girl, don't come down with morality now. What you're doing is a service. Without you and me the frontier would still be back on the other side of the Mississippi."

Charity laughed in spite of herself. "Morality has nothing to do with it," she said. "I'm not ashamed of what I do, I'm just tired of it."

"All you need is a night or two off. Talk to Isaac."

Charity sighed and sat on the edge of the bed. Meg didn't understand, and she wasn't sure she did herself. It went so much deeper than the surface questions of morality or weariness, she knew. It was almost a weariness of life, of past and present—and likely the future, if she didn't change it somehow.

After a while she stood and resumed her packing, pulling what she had already shoved into the valise out and repacking it with care. She said, "There's a stage due tomorrow or the next day. I intend to be on it."

"Isaac's not going to like that, Charity. Half his girls have already slipped off to the Hills. Your leaving will be like a slap to his face."

Charity nodded. She knew Goff, knew what he was capable of when provoked, but she had to leave now. Or go mad, staying.

He was waiting for her when she descended the stairs the next morning, sitting at a felt-topped poker table with his sleeves rolled above his elbows and his eyes puffed and red-veined. Not so far away, a stove radiated its warmth. There was a bottle of whiskey and a glass on the table beside him, the bottle half empty. Meg stood behind his chair, her hands on his shoulders, and that surprised Charity at first, until she thought about it some. Although Goff had never slept with her, or even attempted it, she knew he occasionally did with some of the others.

Charity stopped at the foot of the stairs and set her valise and a heavy, ankle-length cloak on a nearby table. She clutched a simple, black cloth purse banded with a pair of dove gray strips of cloth that matched the high-buttoned gray dress she wore. Her hair was piled high and pinned for travel, and a gray bonnet hung over her shoulders.

Goff's eyes traveled her up and down and he grunted, pouring himself some more whiskey. "So you're leaving," he said, without looking up.

"I've got to go," Charity said. Her voice sounded small in the large room, and weak.

Goff smiled and set the bottle down and took a sip, still without looking at her. Setting his glass aside, he said, "Have a drink, Charity. Meg, get Charity a glass."

Meg didn't move and Charity shook her head. He was mocking her, she knew, playing with her. "I thank you for the time I've been here, Isaac. You've been good to me, and more than fair. I'm grateful for that."

"Funny way of showing gratitude," Goff said. "Slipping out early, and me four girls short already."

"Winter's coming on. Business is always slow then, and you'll find plenty of girls in the spring."

It was the wrong thing to say, Charity saw. Under the hood of his brows, Goff's eyes flashed dangerously. Still, he kept his voice low and nearly calm. "I don't figure business will slack off that much this year. Be a lot of people down from the mountains that won't want to get too far from their claims. Sand Creek is about the closest they can get to the Hills without staying in them."

"I'm going, Isaac. You can't stop me."

He looked at her then, studying her with a lazy patience. Finally, he said, "Go upstairs, Meg. Charity and I want to talk alone for a minute."

For a moment Meg looked as if she was going to refuse, but then she flounced past and upstairs, passing Charity without looking at her. They waited until they heard the sound of her door closing, then Goff stood and motioned to the chair opposite him. "Please, Charity, sit down."

Charity shook her head, and Goff sighed. "I can't let you go," he said quietly. "Not now, not this way. A year ago I would have, but I've lost four already, and if you go I'm not sure I'll be able to keep any. I've got to have whores, Charity. Without, there's no reason for a man to stop over in Sand Creek."

"I'm not going to the Hills, Isaac. I won't be your competition."

"No, you can't. I can't allow that at all." He was speaking slowly, coming around the table, coming closer.

"Isaac, no."

Close enough then, he grabbed her arm, his fingers digging.

"Isaac, you're drunk. Let me go."

He leaned close and now she could smell the whiskey on him, but not strong, and she knew he wasn't drunk, either. Not really. "Don't walk out on me, Charity," he said. "Don't."

"You can't stop me!"

"I'll send word to Ogallala, tell them you robbed me. They'll throw you in a cell with soldiers or hide hunters, or worse. You know what they'd do. You know what kind of hell that would be."

A sudden panic rose in her face, smothering her in its grip. She felt trapped, caught in a hell worse than anything Goff threatened, and she struck out blindly, the panic adding strength to her swing.

Goff stepped back, his eyes wide with surprise, his nose sprouting a cherry flow of blood over his chin. Charity grabbed the valise in both her hands and swung it. Goff fell back, tripping himself in the legs of a chair and sprawling with a force that rattled the bottles behind the bar. A second spurt of blood arched from his lower lip and puddled on the floor.

Charity grabbed her cloak and leaped wide over Goff's inert form, slamming into tables and tripping over chairs and coming so close to making it . . . so close. . . .

Goff grabbed her by the hair, jerking her back, throwing her against the bar. His eyes were wild, his face twisted in a wrath worse than any she had ever seen. "You bitch," he hissed through bloody lips. "You bitch, you bitch, you bitch." He kept repeating it over and over, grabbing her above her elbow and dragging her toward the stairs.

She tripped on the lower step, crying out at the *pop* of her shoulder as Goff pulled her up. She dropped the valise and cloak and pelted him with her fist, but it was like striking a sack of grain. He kicked her door open and spun her into the room, where she fell against the bed.

"Now, you little whore, you just sit there and think about it for a while. And tonight you'd better have your ass downstairs, and I want to see you shake it a little. I'm getting tired of your snotty attitude. You start earning your keep around here or I'll take a quirt to you."

His voice was thick, ragged, raw as a fresh wound, but Charity's own anger was fired now, and she wouldn't let it drop. "You go to hell," she shouted. "I'm getting out of here and if you try to stop me I'll claw your goddamn eyes out!" She came off the bed and took another swing, rocking Goff's head back.

Goff blinked and snorted blood, and Charity backed off. She flexed her fist and cocked her arm. "Get out of the door, you damn big ox," she breathed.

Goff blinked against his tearing eyes and ran a tongue out to taste his blood, as if not quite believing it was there. He looked at Charity, blinked, then suddenly backhanded her. She backed off a step, her hand to her cheek, and a little cry of pain and surprise escaped her. Goff swung a second time, using his fist now, and she fell over the mattress in a flurry of skirts, thudding to the floor on the other side. When she got up, Goff was on her again, grabbing her around her throat and swinging her into the wall, driving a fist into her stomach as she bounced back. She gasped, gagging, her eyes bugging. Goff hooked his fingers inside the neck of her dress and twisted it into his fist.

Charity felt his blows only faintly by then, through a red haze of pain. She could feel her body jerking like a rag doll, and her head rocking, and wondered if it would ever end, or if she would dangle from his fist forever. It ended, finally, when her bodice ripped and she dropped to the floor in a swirl of skirt. Through the red haze of her vision she saw Goff backing off, his eyes wide with a kind of horror, and heard him mutter, *"Christ,"* in a choked voice.

Goff was gone then and she was staring at the floor, where the blue peacock seemed to swell and roll in front of her, disappearing finally into an obscene whirlpool of colors. She coughed and gagged on her own blood, and whimpered, childlike.

Hands then, soft and gentle, helping, lifting, guiding. A warm quilt over her naked body and darkness for a while, then Belle floating near the ceiling, and warm water and bandages and a cool salve.

Belle finished soon enough and left her alone. Charity didn't move, or want to. Her strength was gone, her will broken, and all that was left was a dull weariness of the mind and body, with sleep the only escape left open now.

CHAPTER 11

ROSCOE Plumb was the first to take any real notice of Doc's absence. He walked into the Crooked Arrow bunkhouse while dawn was just a cold promise on the horizon. The hands were scattered throughout the bunkhouse, stomping into their boots or coats, and moving with the lazy stiffness of early morning. It was dark inside, with only a single lamp casting its feeble light from a blackened chimney. The air was stale with the odor of horses and sweat and leather and tobacco. Bachelor smells, Plumb thought, wrinkling his nose. He passed through the sleeping quarters, acknowledging them all with a general greeting, pausing once to kick a bunk where a hand still burrowed under his blankets, then on into the kitchen and warmth. A few of the hands were already there, sitting at the long plank table and smoking and drinking coffee. The cook paused in his work long enough to set a cup at the end of the table, and Plumb took it gratefully, savoring the rich aroma of Arbuckle.

"Gonna have johnnycakes and sidepork to go with that in a minute," the cook said.

"I've eaten already, John," Plumb said. "This coffee'll do fine."

The rest of the hands began to troop in and take their places at the table. There was some good-natured banter and some small horseplay, but nothing any bunkhouse didn't see. Plumb nodded to a former Wagon Wheel hand who was riding the grub line, waiting until they were all in and seated before assigning their various chores for the day. The hands nodded without much comment as John slid platters of food on the table, then dug in with a quiet determination. John ate his meal standing, keeping an eye on the pot of beans and ham simmering for the midday meal. Plumb counted heads and frowned. "Where's the kid?" he asked.

"Didn't come in last night," Snappy replied around a mouthful of food. He was a randy little cowboy with bowed legs and yellow hair. He was taken with showy outfits, pin-striped pants, or plaids, and fancily-stitched shirts, double-breasted and yoked. He wore gauntlets studded with silver and big Mexican spurs that jingled when he walked or rode. A snappy dresser, he was fond of saying, and the name stuck.

"It ain't our place to question a gun shark," Delmonico said. "Might shoot us." He laughed and some of the others joined him. Delmonico was skinny and dark and quick with a rope or cutting remark. He didn't like Doc, and the fact that Doc didn't really give a damn whether he did or didn't increased his dislike all the more. "He's probably sleeping off a drunk with one of Goff's whores," he added.

"Maybe," Plumb grunted, but he didn't like the idea of not knowing where one of his hands was, gun shark or not. He finished his coffee and went outside for a cigarette while dawn crept slowly over the ranch. The men began to file out after a while, tracking off to the privies or to the corrals to rope their mounts for the day. Plumb caught Snappy and Delmonico as they headed for the corrals and pulled them aside. "I still don't like that empty bunk in there," he said. "I want you to saddle your rim rockers today and see if you can find him. If he's in town, buy yourself a drink on my tab and get on back to your jobs, but if he's not, he might be needing help. Either way, I want to know."

They bitched until Plumb was out of hearing, then roped and saddled their mounts, whistling. They both figured Doc was in town, and the prospect of a free drink on top of what they would buy themselves was pleasing.

It was cold yet, and damp, with a cutting wind, but the clouds had pulled up high, easing the wet, closed-in feel of the day before. They rode north at a good clip, along the general path Doc had taken the day before, picking up his trail without too much trouble. The tracks were plain in the soft soil, and they swapped jokes as they rode. The day didn't turn serious until Doc's trail merged with that of the rustlers. After that they rode with their guns loose, though the trail was better than a day old already, and the men who made it probably fifty miles away by now.

They found Doc in the middle of the afternoon. Delmonico's horse spotted him first and spooked at the sudden flash of the yellow slicker. They drew their guns and rode forward at a walk, their eyes on the rim of the draw. Delmonico stepped from his saddle and handed his reins to Snappy, then kneeled in the sticky mud beside Doc.

There was a lot of blood across Doc's shirt, not all of it old. His naturally curly hair was kinked tight and pasted flat on his forehead. His breathing was low and raspy and his face, even under the mud and blackened eyes, looked pale and lifeless, like raw dough waiting for the oven. His nose was angled off to one side, swollen and bloody.

"He looks like hell warmed over," Delmonico said.

"He alive?"

"He's breathing, but he's making a funny noise in his chest, like Ma did the time she caught pneumonia." He looked up, and his voice quivered. "Snappy, he's hurt bad, real bad. Maybe even bad enough to die."

"We've got to get a buckboard out here," Snappy said. "But first we ought to start a fire and draw some of the chill off him." He dismounted and crawled up the side of the draw and looked around. Below him the narrow valley lay nestled against rolling hills, barren of wood. He turned a slow circle, his eyes darting in desperation, but he saw nothing but cactus and buffalo grass. He slid back down beside Delmonico and shook his head. "Cow chips are too fresh and buffalo chips are too old."

"We passed a stand of trees back where we picked up the rustler's trail."

Snappy slipped out of his coat. "Too far back," he said. "We'll just have to cover him with what we've got and make do."

They wrapped Doc in their coats and slickers and propped his head on his hat. Other than the slow, raspy draw of his breath, Doc made no sound. They stood afterward and faced each other in their shirt sleeves, shivering some, with the cold. "Who's going back for help?" Delmonico asked.

"Reckon I will."

"Uh, uh. I'm not going to stay here alone while he dies. We'll flip to see who goes." He dug a silver dollar from his pocket, the same silver dollar he'd planned to spend on whiskey that afternoon after they'd found Doc, and flipped it, letting Snappy make the call in the air. The coin dropped in the mud between Doc's boots with a wet plop. Snappy won the toss.

Snappy rode hell for leather, pushing through the afternoon and into the evening, coming finally into the Crooked Arrow ranch yard shortly before full dark. It was well past midnight before he got back, with Plumb and three others riding with him, and John, the cook, handling a team of mules and a rattling old buckboard. They lifted Doc into the buckboard, wrapped in a bunch of blankets, and cushioned on a bed of hay. John climbed in beside him and pulled the blankets back far enough to look at his wounds, pursing his lips in the thin light of a lantern.

"Is he going to live?" Plumb asked.

"Don't look too likely," John replied shortly. He sat back and shook his head. "I've seen men pull through with worse," he said, then added, "But not by much."

It was midmorning when they got back. Plumb drove the team, while John and Delmonico sat in back with Doc and tried to keep him from bouncing around too much. The others rode ahead, scouting for easy crossings through the draws or over the ridges until dawn broke. Then they came in close, smoking and talking quiet and now and again glancing back to see if Doc was still alive.

They took him to the main house, where Plumb's wife took over. His breathing had worsened through the night, and now the rattle of his breath filled the tiny room where he lay like the sound of distant sabers clashing in battle, Plumb thought. But sometimes the rattling would stop for long, drawnout stretches of time, so long he would wonder if it had stopped for good; then it would start again, seeming louder and more startling than it had before. When Plumb looked at his wife's face he saw helplessness etched there, drawing her brows into a tight furrow. "We need a doctor," she said.

"Doctor couldn't get here inside of a week, if he'd come at all."

"Then we need to pray," she said softly.

Howard recognized Harper by the bulldog way he sat his saddle long before he got close enough to make out any other features. Harper was coming from Sand Creek at a gallop, a pace above what a man would ride without something important on his mind. Howard reined the grulla back to the snubbing post and dismounted slowly, taking a short grip on the reins to ease the grulla's confusion.

The grulla was coming along now, as they all were. Still as green as spring grass, but not fighting the rope and saddle as they had those first few times, and picking up a little on reining and handling, most of them doing all right with it if a man didn't rush them.

Howard stripped the saddle and hackamore from the grulla and stepped clear as the horse went pitching toward the far side of the corral. Harper pulled his big bay down to a walk as he entered the ranch yard, stopping close to the corral while Howard slung his gear over the top rail.

"Find yourself new work?" Harper asked gruffly. He looked cold atop the bay, bundled up in a heavy mackinaw and shotgun chaps, with his hat pulled down over the top of his ears.

"You didn't ride all the way out here to ask me that," Howard said. "What's up?"

"The Crooked Arrow has a herd missing. I'll fill you in while you saddle your horse."

Howard whistled the bay in and led him to the tack shed by his forelock. Harper followed without dismounting, and from time to time while saddling Luke would shy a glance toward him. He seemed distracted, Harper did, and downcast, though angry, too, and he kept fidgeting with his reins in an absent way, pulling them here and there until his horse was throwing his head with short, quick passes. There was more to this than a herd missing, Luke thought; there was something digging at Harper's craw like a pup after a bone. Though curious, all he said was, "How much of a start do they have?"

"I haven't seen the trail yet, but from what I could gather, maybe two or three days." He paused, then added bluntly, "Doc's been hit."

Howard pulled his cinch tight, mulling that over. "Bad?" he asked.

"Shoulder wound and a broken nose, they say. Maybe pneumonia."

"What happened?" He could feel his stomach drawing into a knot.

"Sounds like he cut their trail while it was still fresh and followed. They ambushed him about twenty-five miles north of the Crooked Arrow range, way the hell and gone to the middle of nowhere." He leaned from the saddle and spat, the gesture one of frustration. "The goddamn little greenhorn tried to take them by himself. He was wearing that bright yellow slicker when Plumb's boys found him. Sonofabitching rustlers probably spotted him five miles back."

Howard looked across the saddle at Harper, his face tight. "Will he live?"

"Doesn't look too promising," Harper replied glumly. "But hell, you can't tell. He's young and tough. I'm just glad it was Roscoe Plumb he was riding for. Some of these other bastards might not have even sent a man looking for him."

Howard led the bay to the bunkhouse and fetched his bedroll and saddlebags. Booting the Henry, he swung into the saddle and reined around, forcing Barney to back his mount away. "We have a lot of miles to cover," Howard said grimly. "We'd better ride."

Sanchez was waiting for them in Sand Creek, his mare tied to the rail outside the Frontier House while he waited on a bench out front. Red rode in before they had a chance to dismount, and by the time he reached them Sanchez was already mounted and ready to ride.

The Black Hills road ran due north for several miles, then angled to the west in a long curve. They stayed with it that far and a little beyond before cutting back to the north. They rode in a tight bunch, loping their horses for a while, then pulling down to jog a ways. The wind had died some from earlier, and with the air still, it seemed almost warm again. The sky looked big and distant, pale and free of clouds save for a few tattered rags far to the north. The land was low and rolling here, stretching north and west into the indefinite distance like a shaggy brown carpet, empty of tree or bush or building to give it size or perspective. To the east the broken ridge of hills came down to Sand Creek in a tumbled mass, tawny in color, though striped dark in the draws and washes by berry bushes; sometimes, when the hills on this side of the creek broke just right, Howard could see the dark line of trees bordering the creek, quite some distance off now.

They picked up the rustlers' trail just before sunset, stopping to let the horses blow, dismounting and walking the kinks out of their legs. Sand Creek lay thirty miles behind them now, and the horses showed it.

They mounted soon enough and set off at a lope again,

but pulling apart this time, stretching out over a quarter of a mile or more. They made camp in the open that night, rolling up in their blankets without a fire and eating jerky and hardtack, capped with a pull from their canteens. Daylight found them in the saddle and half a dozen miles from where they'd spent the night, following the same line they'd followed the night before and finding the trail still beneath them at sunrise.

The morning held a promise of warmth, the sun rising big and golden and the sky bluer than it had been for a week, but it was a faithless promise; by noon the wind had picked up again, coming from the north and bringing with it a low, surging bank of black clouds. The pace dropped at the first scattered drops of rain, slowing even more when the wind picked up, the horses fighting the weather and the men fighting the horses and time and everyone short-tempered and snapping, men and animals alike.

The rain struck with a needlelike intensity, slashing at their faces, but hurrying before the wind and leaving in its wake a land drab and lifeless again, and a low covering of gray clouds that dropped a fine, cold mist.

The country became rougher as the afternoon waned. The hills rose steeper and dropped off sharper, with stands of timber in the low land between them, and sometimes a creek cutting through the timber, the water rolling and muddy.

They camped among the cottonwood that night, building a fire against the cold and brewing coffee they laced from a bottle Harper kept stowed in his saddlebags. Howard slept in his chaps and coat, rolled tight in his blankets with only a small pocket around his face free to the wind. Harper prodded him awake sometime after midnight, squatting close and talking in a low voice, though the others were already awake and standing. "Clouds are breaking up and there's a full moon. Sanchez thinks he can follow the trail as long as it's as clear-cut as it has been. Looks like maybe this rain will be to our advantage after all. A blind man could follow their trail by feel."

It was plain, all right, the veed prints of the cattle cut sharp in the prairie, though it wasn't like tracking in daylight. They stayed at a walk with their eyes on the trail, having to stop every time the moon ducked behind a sheaf of clouds. Still, they probably made a dozen miles before the moon slid below the horizon, and Howard figured that was twelve more than the rustlers made that night.

They stopped at the top of a tall rise, bleary-eyed and saddle-weary, their horses standing hipshot, and making no attempt to pull at the short grass. "This I think is as far as I go," Sanchez said, straightening and arching his back. He had been riding the last half mile or so leaning so far from the saddle he had been forced to hang onto the horn.

"There's timber down there," Harper said, looking into the wide, slow-curving valley below them. "We can catch a couple of hours sleep there and hit the trail again at sunup." His voice sounded worn out, Howard thought, the words forced. They were all like that now, caught in the first wave of surface weariness that was worse now than it would be later, when they had settled into the grind.

They rode down single file, the horses picking up to a stiff-legged jog on their own, as if sensing the timber would be the end of the trail for the night. Howard didn't see the wagon until the first shot rang out, sounding flat and distant, though the hard slap of the bullet hitting the sod to his left sounded close enough.

Howard shucked the Henry and whipped the bay to the right in one motion. Harper drew and fired, and this time Howard spotted the tiny spit of muzzle flash from the wagon box. "Sonofabitch," Red howled, jerking his sorrel around and spurring upslope.

"Hold on," Howard called. "We're sitting ducks out here."

"By God, no man fires on me without my firing back," Harper shouted angrily, though he didn't shoot again.

"Go away." The voice drifted up from the timber like an apparition and died on the wind.

"We look for a place to camp," Sanchez responded. Howard could see the men now, shapeless forms moving among the shadows next to a big Conestoga wagon, its naked hoops making an odd geometric shape against the shadows of the trees and the bleached prairie beyond.

There was a long silence stretching into minutes, then the same voice, "Put your guns away and come down easy."

"We won't put our guns away," Harper shouted back. "But we're coming down." They rode down slowly then, spread out and riding light in the saddle.

They entered the timber at four separate points, the sound of their horses muffled by a layer of fallen leaves, and it struck Howard suddenly that the trees here were almost bare, their limbs curving overhead in a delicate weave of spidery shadows. Likely the leaves around Sand Creek were down now, too, he thought, stripped in yesterday's wind and rain.

Up close, he could see the burned-down coals of their fire, orange and almost dead. He could see the mules now, too, four of them tied to the far side of the Conestoga, and only half of what was needed, some would say. The harness lay in a dark jumble against the tongue. One of the men came forward as they approached, cradling a long rifle across his chest, and in the shifting shadows around the wagon, Howard realized that there were more men here than he had at first thought.

The man cradling the rifle said, "What's your business here?" like he had a right to know.

Harper laughed. "That's kind of personal, ain't it?"

"You was the one to come riding down that hill single file like a bunch of damn redskins, uninvited into our camp."

"We didn't see the wagon," Howard offered.

"Why are you so worried abut the redskin?" Sanchez asked. "They do not raid so far south no more, eh?"

"Huh? I reckon. You ain't but a long spit from the Hills right now. Party of Sioux hit some panners up on the Bear Butte River just last week. Scalped 'em and hacked their arms and legs off. Peckers, too, I hear."

Could be, Howard thought, getting the lay of the land straight in his mind. A man pushing could make the Bear Butte in a day, and another would see him on the Slim Buttes, where Sitting Bull got his tail whipped by Crook just a month or so back. They'd pretty well lost their hold on the Hills after that, but it was likely there were a lot of little bunches out yet, hotheads raising hell all up and down the Hills. The Black Hills had been big medicine with them, he knew.

"We're looking for a place to camp the rest of the night," Harper said. He didn't sound like he believed their tale of being Indian-spooked, but he was showing more restraint than normal for it.

The man tipped his rifle upstream. "There's some down timber up there for a fire. I reckon you're welcome to use it. We're just stopping for the night ourselves."

"Obliged," Luke said, turning the bay away. The others fell into line behind him, though keeping their weapons out and their eyes over their shoulders.

Later, dropping his bedroll on the ground, Sanchez said, "They have a hunted look. I think tonight I will sit up for a while, just to see that they find their blankets."

"Think I'll sit up a spell myself," Harper said. "There's a couple of hours of darkness left. We'll wake you two in an hour."

Howard wasn't really sure he'd closed his eyes when Barney nudged him with the butt of his rifle. He rose, his hand closing automatically over the Henry, but there was no urgency in Harper's voice. "Not a peep out of them, but I'd lay odds they have a man or two sitting up, just like us."

Howard kicked his blankets back and struggled into his boots, the leather stiff and cold. They hadn't built a fire, and the dampness from a stream lay over everything. Farther out, in the meadow, the grass glistened dully with frost. Howard pulled his blanket over his shoulder and stood at the edge of their camp, staring through the timber, unable to see even the vague outline of the wagon now. Behind him, Red settled on a fallen log, the Spencer resting across his lap. Howard could feel his stare on him, and turned slowly, reluctantly. "I figure we got some talking to do," Red said finally.

"Time's past for talking, I guess," Howard said. They spoke quietly, below the sounds of Harper's and Sanchez's snores.

"I know you recognized me down there on the Grant," Red said. "I could see it in your eyes."

Red could see it now, too, Howard thought, if it weren't for the darkness. He had avoided Red in the weeks since the night on the Grant, feeling a sickness in his stomach every time he thought of the mob, and Simon Washington lying in front of his soddy with his family numb over him. Luke was a Northerner, a Yankee, and no matter how Red explained it, he knew he wouldn't ever comprehend the hate Red felt toward blacks.

"They've got to go," Red said. "You know nesters, they're a herd animal. They ain't happy unless they've got a whole troupe of others around them. You've got to roust them out quick, before they dig in too deep."

"What happened on the Grant that night had nothing to do with nesters," Howard said in a tight voice. "It was just a bunch of Southern boys who couldn't let the past lie." He turned away, the argument already old between them. Red had been poisoned with a hate that was far older than he, and he would likely take it to his grave with him. Yet it had soured their friendship, standing between them now like the putrid odor of rotten meat.

"You think you're any better?" Red suddenly called after

him, his voice soft yet, but edged with a steel meant to cut. "How many men have you killed? Or hung?"

Howard flinched, turning slowly. "Seven," he said tonelessly. "Seven I've killed, and hung a few more. But I never had to put a sack over my head to do it."

The Conestoga pulled out at dawn, the mules straining on the grade. Two men sat on the seat, handling the team together while the rest crowded down among the barrels and boxes, with shovels and picks and rifles poking out at odd angles. They were a silent bunch, breaking camp and harnessing the mules without conversation, and pulling out then without taking time for breakfast. Saddled and dressed differently, they would have had the look of outlaws, but in their brogan shoes and floppy hats nicked and punctured, they just looked curious and out of place.

Howard stood with the others in the spreading light and watched them go, the bay saddled and waiting. Red held his hat in his hands, idly running a finger through the hole the man with the rifle had punched in it on his second shot.

Watching him finger the thumb-sized hole, Sanchez said, "I think you were almost scalped last night and did not know it."

"I knew it," Red answered shortly. He put his hat on then, settling it with a quick little forward and backward twist of his wrist. "Time we pushed on," he said. "They ain't who we're after, not unless they got the whole damn herd boxed up in crates."

They mounted and rode out in a scattered bunch, twisting in the saddle from time to time to watch the wagon's progress until it disappeared over the hill, leaving only the dark trail of its wheels through the crushed frost.

The sun rose amber through a low bank of clouds, then broke clear with an intensity they hadn't seen in more than a week. The wind shifted and came from the west, and in the draws the meadowlarks and finches tuned up. They saw antelope everywhere, white rumps flashing as they drew close, though the day before they had seen none. They had their coats off by noon, the sun warm and penetrating on their shoulders.

The country became rougher, the swells of land gradually steeper, patchy with jackpine and slashed here and there with cliffs that looked white in the sun. The trail remained plain though, and as the afternoon wore on it became fresher, as if the cattle had turned balky after hitting rougher country. By noon Howard had spotted the bluish gray line of the mountains rising from the prairie like a jagged spine. By nightfall the ridges were thick with pine, and the creeks had a power that they lacked on the plains, pulled swiftly down from the Hills by the pitch of the land, and the bare limbs of the brush that grew along them rattled in the wind, as if they also felt the rush of the water, and a need to be moving.

Howard's bay felt it, the song of wind and water, and arched his neck to it, blowing softly with his big eyes moving here and there, like a colt fresh to the world.

They camped at the edge of the Hills that night, putting in early and building a fire for a meal and coffee. Later, rolling a cigarette, Sanchez said, "I think maybe this time we will catch up." His face glowed copper in the dancing light, as lined and aged as any Indian's.

"How far ahead?" Harper asked.

"Maybe two hours. The ground is too broken to track tonight, but maybe if we rode on we could find them before dawn."

"Or stumble on past them," Harper replied. "I say we go on like we have been, steady and sure."

"*Si*, it is best," Sanchez agreed. "Then tomorrow, we fight. By noon, maybe. Or before."

CHAPTER 12

THEY had the cattle stretched into a long, slim line, hugging the timber while a big, twenty-mule jerk-line outfit passed on the opposite side of the road. Red slid the Spencer from the scabbard and rested its butt against his thigh. His heart was hammering at his ribs and his throat felt dry and scratchy. Beside him, Barney pulled his Colt and checked the loads, and behind him he could hear Howard and Sanchez doing the same. The protesting bawl of cattle floated past them on the breeze.

"Anybody ever see that Arizona poncho before?" Harper asked quietly, though the drag riders were still a hundred yards away.

"Nope," Red said. "And that's something a man would remember."

Harper nodded grimly, glanced over his shoulder at the others, then said, "Okay, we ride along slow and easy, maybe get close enough to get the drop on 'em." There was a tautness to Harper's voice, a sense of stubborn determination that Red knew stemmed from Doc's ambush. He'd been that way leaving Sand Creek, then eased off some on the trail, but he'd changed again last night after Sanchez announced they were close this time. It was odd, Red thought, and funny in a way, after the big show of irritation Harper was always making toward the kid, that he should feel so vengeful now. Before Plumb's hand had come pounding in with the news, he had always half imagined Harper was ready to plug the kid himself.

Well, there was no knowing a man, he reasoned, Harper or Howard, either. He couldn't understand Howard, never had for that matter, but to let something like what happened on the Grant come between friends seemed foolish, womanish almost. They had only been nesters, after all, and niggers at that, so what was there to kindle the fire that heated Howard's anger? Where was the point in it?

At Red's side Harper swore loudly, and he looked up to see the rustlers breaking for cover. Red swore too, then, knowing a thief or wanted man always rode with one eye cocked over his shoulder, and cursing himself for letting his thoughts stray.

Red whipped the Spencer to his shoulder and let fly, though the distance was too great for a man on horseback. The rustlers were abandoning the cattle, lossening a couple of shots with their revolvers. Red could see the little spurts of dust kicked up far ahead by the rustlers' bullets.

Pulling to the side, he swung from the saddle and dropped to one knee, trying a long shot and cursing at the little explosion of bark from a pine twenty feet or so shy of the nearest rustler.

They were gone then, the cattle scattering in confusion and panic, spreading across the road and blocking traffic. The teamster hauled up on his jerk-line, his mules braying and plunging against the traces as the needle-tipped horns of the cattle scratched their flanks, kicking out in defense and tangling themselves all the worse in their harness, while the teamster turned the air around him blue with obscenities.

The sorrel had run off a little ways and now, with all the gunfire popping around and the pandemonium breaking loose with the cattle, he was shying back away from Red's reaching hand. He caught him soon enough, but by the time he mounted and got up to the cattle, the rustlers were long gone. Barney and Luke were riding slow along the edge of the timber, peering up the steep slope, and Harper was swearing in frustration. Sanchez was riding into the cattle, toward the tangled mules, with a grin wide on his face, and seeing it, the teamster broke out a new batch of curses.

"The dirty sonofabitches," Harper gritted, coming close. "They did it again, they did it again."

"You figure this is the same bunch we followed last time?" Red asked.

"Seems like it," Harper said. "At least they followed the same route, more or less." He holstered his Colt. "Well, I ain't riding into the timber after 'em."

"No," Red agreed. "Be easy to ride into an ambush that way."

Sanchez was moving the cattle away from the mules, flicking them with his quirt in a way that would likely raise a welt, and cursing some himself now, though with his back to the teamster, Red could see the quick, devilish flash of his grin. The teamster was on foot now, moving along the line of his mules with a length of chain in one hand and a long bullwhip in the other, and he was using both freely. Red slid the Spencer into the scabbard and rode in to help. With the cattle spooked and scattered, it took a while to gather them and bunch them in a nearby side valley where there was tall grass and water.

Coming back to the mouth of the valley, they dismounted and built up a small fire and put some coffee on. On hobbles, the horses grazed greedily, the sound of tearing grass loud, with only the popping of the fire and the far-off scolding of a jay to break the silence. Nobody moved much or spoke at all until the coffee was brewed, and Red knew they were all feeling the same keen disappointment he felt. It made them feel incompetent, so many failures stacking up one atop the other.

With the coffee done, Harper seemed to have lost his thirst. He leaned forward, clearing a space in the dirt next to the fire and tracing out a pattern with his knife. "Well, we know we can't track 'em separate," he said. "We've tried that before. They head into town and lose their trail in the traffic, or split up. Ground's too damn rocky up here anyway. But this is twice now they've come this same route."

"Three times," Sanchez interrupted. "The very first time I rode with you we came this way."

Harper looked excited now. "Okay, three times, even better." He stabbed the ground. "See, here's the Ogallala road running up this way, and over here's a little mining town called Easy Street. It's off the Ogallala road some, but it's the closest I know of, and I figure maybe that's where these yahoos will head. Be a place to regroup.

"Now, we ain't never spotted any before, so we didn't know who we was looking for, but I figure I can recognize a couple of them, and I can damn sure recognize that poncho. I say me and . . ." his voice trailed off and his eyes circled the group, settling finally on Red, "Red here take a ride into Easy Street and see what we can see."

"I'm thinking that could put you in a tight spot," Howard said. "I counted five men pushing those cows."

"You worried about us or yourself?" Red said. The words were out before he knew it, regretted immediately.

"Luke and I, we will handle our end," Sanchez said, his questioning gaze on Red. "Luke is thinking, and so am I, that they will recognize you before you can recognize them. Five against two is not good odds."

"Maybe so," Harper conceded, and his eyes, too, were on Red, and puzzled. "But we can't ride back without giving it a shot, and I don't want just one man staying with the cattle."

Sanchez shrugged, and Barney stood, Red with him, feeling Howard's gaze on him without looking Luke's way. To busy himself, Red went to the sorrel and pulled the hobbles, tightened the cinch and put the bridle on. By the time he was finished, Harper was readying his bay.

"We'll start them on back, come morning," Howard said. He and Sanchez had followed Harper to the horses and stood there with their cups of coffee in their hands.

Harper nodded and swung up, and he and Red started out of the valley, but Howard's voice stopped them, coming hesitant. "Keep an eye peeled for Sand Creek people, huh?" he said.

"Why?" Harper asked. "Who?"

"Bronson, maybe, or someone close to Bronson."

"Ain't nobody close to that long-haired dandy. And what would he be doing up here?"

"Somebody's behind this rustling. It's too well organized not to be."

Harper laughed. "And you figure Bronson? Naw. It's just a bunch of owlhoots. Maybe it's one bunch, but it ain't no organization."

"All the same, keep an eye peeled."

Harper shrugged and touched his hat brim. He whirled his bay around and rode out of the valley at a lope. Red followed, feeling small and mean. Turning just before the road took them out of sight, Red saw the both of them still standing with the horses, watching them ride out. He thought it was funny, the way he had to force his hand into a wave. Funny, but sad, too, the way it all turned out.

Easy Street seemed caught in an exodus, a mass migration from the Hills back to the settlements. The irregular stages leaving town were always filled, and even the big freighting rigs, hauling in heavy mining equipment and general supplies, left crammed with men perching anywhere they could find space and clinging to boxes or ropes as the great, lumbering wagons lurched southward. There were no horses for sale any more, and the men who couldn't find or afford passage by stage or freight were walking, some of them carrying awkward packs on their backs, and others pushing everything they owned in wheelbarrows. When possible, they traveled in groups, and tales of long, deep freezes and belly-deep snows seemed to spur them on.

Yet for all the desertion, the single street still teemed with a bustle of permanence, a continuity; for every man leaving there was another buying flour and salt and dried fruit and cartridges for his rifle, preferring to sit out the winter in a crude shack rather than return to the settlements and lose a month traveling in the spring.

Businessmen nailed green lumber or stretched stiff rawhide over their windows, and drifters without money could earn a meal or passage south cutting firewood for those who were staying. At some places the firewood was stacked so high and so deep in front of the buildings that a man had to pass through an aisle head high and twenty feet long to enter a business. Come winter, Red knew it would serve a dual purpose, acting as insulation until it was burned.

Red and Harper rode side-by-side, close enough that their stirrups clattered against each other occasionally, hugging the side of the street away from the heavy traffic toward its center. Mud was hock-deep, almost liquid, and it churned and rolled and flowed back under hooves and wheels. Across the way a freighter was lining out a team of oxen with a sense of urgency that had been absent earlier.

"Kind of like watching a kicked-over anthill, ain't it," Harper commented. They reined up behind a parked rig to watch the scurry of activity along the street. From the saloon behind them an accordian wheezed out an off-tune version of "Old Joe Clark," the musician missing about every third or fourth note.

"For all the people leaving and all the empty land we've been trailing through, it makes a man wonder where everybody came from," Red said.

"Cherry Creek all over again," Harper remarked, but didn't expand further. Instead, he said, "I guess the thing to do is start at one end of town and work our way around through the saloons."

"We'll be drunk before we get down one side," Red said critically. He twisted in the saddle, counting the saloons.

"It's a thought," Harper said, smiling. He turned his bay in to a rail and dismounted. Red followed, shaking his head, but smiling, too.

They shouldered their way into the smoky recesses of the saloon where the accordian still wheezed and choked, and up to the bar. The musician was lost in the press of customers—miners, mostly, hard-bodied and bearded; here and there a cowboy up to try his luck; hide hunters, smelling of blood and green hides; and freighters, smelling of mules. And as common to boom towns as the talk of gold, gamblers and prostitutes, a curious blend of flash and color against the grubbiness of the miners.

They took their drinks to a counter at the rear of the room where cold slices of deer roast were laid out with coarse-grained breads and jars of tart buffalo berry preserves. They wandered through the crowd with their sandwiches and drinks then, watching the games, studying the faces of the men who entered or left, watching until they were sure all the prostitutes were accounted for, and the men they led back from their cribs were miners or hunters or freighters. They worked their way through one saloon after another in such a manner, always keeping their eyes open for the man in the gaudy Arizona poncho.

It was clouding up toward a rain—big, black-bellied clouds rolling in from the northwest and kicking up a chill wind—when they entered the plank saloon with the glass windows and a long bar down its side. They took a table near a front window without ordering, feeling the whiskey by then, and still half the length of the street to cover.

Harper pulled his hat off and dropped it on the table, smiling sickly. "I ain't drunk," he said. "But I reckon I ain't a whole long way from it, either."

Red laughed and leaned back. He was tired and sleepy from the drink, with his mind turning inward, though shying away from the past now. With drink in his belly, the past wasn't something he wanted on his mind.

The stranger seemed to appear from nowhere, a well-dressed man, clean-shaven, somewhere in his late forties or early fifties, Red thought. He wore a narrow-brimmed black

hat pushed back on his forehead and a black coat with the
tail pushed back over a short-barreled revolver snugged up
in a quick-draw holster of tooled leather. The left sleeve of
his coat was pinned up tight, empty from the shoulder on
down. He stood before them with a bottle in his hand, smiling
cordially. "Evening, gents. Mind if I buy you a drink?" He
hooked a chair out without waiting for an invitation and set
the bottle on the table. From the pocket of his coat he pulled
three glasses, bringing them out one at a time and lining
them up in a neat row and pouring from the bottle, sliding
two across afterward. Red cut Harper a quick, expressionless
glance, then looked back to the stranger. "Your health," the
stranger toasted, and raised his glass.

Red drank and wiped his mouth with his sleeve and looked
at the stranger. "Man doesn't get many free drinks anymore," he said. "Or are you the official welcoming committee
to Easy Street?"

The stranger laughed and leaned back, his movements
slow, graceful as a cat's. "My name is Matt Hollis," he said. "I
saw you boys sitting here without a drink and thought maybe
you were short of dust. Man don't drink in here, they'll
generally kick him out." His hand made a quick motion.
"Something about profit, they say."

"Last man that tried to kick me out of a saloon left town
the next time I came in," Harper said. He grinned suddenly.
"Something about keeping his teeth in his head and not in
his pocket, they say."

Hollis smiled accommodatingly, but his eyes turned
thoughtful, almost hard. "No, you don't look like a man who
could be pushed easy."

Outside, thunder rumbled in the distance and rolled down
the street. The first big, scattered splashes were striking the
windows, plopping into the muddy puddles in the street.
There was a sudden scurry outside, with everyone ducking
for shelter, and as if on cue, the sun abruptly slid behind the
bank of clouds, plunging the street into shadow.

Hollis watched the rain thicken, his face somber, reflective, and Red and Harper exchanged glances again. He was a puzzle, Hollis was, and a danger, though Red was not yet sure how. It was just something he could feel, like the chill of the storm, or its dampness. He said then, impatiently, "I don't guess there's much left that's free. Including drinks."

Hollis nodded, turning his glass between his fingers, as if choosing his next words with care. Then he looked up, catching them, holding them, in his stare. "You're Barney Harper," he said. "You worked for several of the mining companies above Denver and south toward Cripple Creek as a strike breaker. You sheriffed for a while in Central City. Last year you worked recovering stolen stock for some of the bigger ranches down in Kansas." He looked at Red then. "And you're Red Wheatherford, first name Tom, a sometime buffalo hunter, mustanger and gunfighter. You're both working for the Sand Creek Cattlemen's Association. Right so far?"

Red remembered the Mississippi in flood near New Orleans, the slow, heavy roll of it, thick with silt; the whiskey in his belly felt suddenly like that. Without looking around, he heard Harper say, "Why don't you cut to the bone, Hollis?" He thought there was a hitch to Harper's voice, and knew that this stranger knowing so much about them bothered him, too.

"I want to hire you both," Hollis said. "I can match what Sand Creek is paying you and top it by fifty dollars a month."

"Nobody knows what we're making at Sand Creek except the men that hired us," Red said in a low, tense voice. He was thinking of Howard and Sanchez then, and the way they were both so sure there was somebody in Sand Creek behind the rustling.

Hollis laughed. "Everybody in Sand Creek knows what you're making. You can't keep that kind of information quiet."

"You haven't said what kind of work we'd be doing," Harper said.

"Haven't you guessed?" Hollis asked softly. "I'm rustling the Sand Creek cattle."

Red's hands had been on the table, curled around his glass, but at Hollis's words he straightened, his hands going palm flat on the table and edging backward. Hollis smiled a tight little smile empty of humor, and his eyes flicked up, past Red's shoulder. Red stopped his hands and turned slowly, twisting around at his waist. The man in the poncho leaned against the rear wall only twenty feet or so away with a cocked Winchester held loosely in his hands. Closer, sitting alone at the table directly behind them, was another man, holding a long-barreled Smith and Wesson beside a glass of whiskey. He smiled when Red's eyes met his, and raised the muzzle of the S&W in a kind of salute.

"There's another at the bar," Hollis said. "Though not as conspicuous as these two. Plus one at the front door and another at the back."

Red's eyes flashed, but rocklike, he didn't move. Harper said, "You're a careful man Hollis."

Hollis shrugged, regarding them thoughtfully. "You boys have given me a lot of trouble over the summer. You've cost me money. Under different circumstances I'd have had you shot on the way into town, or taken care of you myself. But I'm finding myself in a difficult situation. Winter is nearly upon us, and that means an end to my business before I've reached the goal I set for myself last spring. Unless I can make one more drive, the biggest ever. But I can't do that and fight you two at the same time." A faint smile touched his face. "Besides, handling more cattle, I'm going to need more men. If you two were to throw in with me I could solve two problems with the same solution. Clever, huh?"

And you figure we'll just throw right in?' Harper's voice sounded incredulous.

Hollis leaned forward, his voice lifting some. 'I know you

will. We're cut from the same mold, Barney. You and me and
Red here, all hiring out to the highest bidder. Well, I'm
outbidding the Cattlemen's Association. And to top that, I'll
add a two hundred dollar bonus at the end of the drive if it's
successful.

"Gentlemen, I have a ready market for two hundred and
fifty head of beef. That's mining camp markets, twice what
you'd get shipping them east. Think of it, boys. Three
hundred and fifty dollars for only a month's work! Have you
ever made that kind of money before?"

Harper looked at Red, and Red saw the same disbelief on
his face that Red felt on his. Yet looking at Hollis, he knew
the rustler was blind to it, that he really believed they could
be bought, turning on their partners and the Cattlemen's
Association the way a pack of dogs would turn on one of
their own when weakened or injured. And maybe as unsettling as anything, Hollis seemed to think that they thought
as he did, that loyalty and pride meant nothing without a
price tag to it. A man just listening, not seeing the cut of his
clothes and the groomed hair with the faint smell of tonic
still on it, might imagine an old skinflint crying over lost
rent, Red thought, or a harpy with her eye fastened on a
copper penny wedged in the crack on a cobblestoned street.
It left a distaste in a man's mouth, Red thought, like a cheap
cigar.

Still, they were in a tight spot, no doubting that. Letting
Hollis know how they felt wouldn't be a whole lot different
than turning their revolvers on themselves, what with all the
men Hollis had scattered around the saloon. There was no
way out that he could see, except to tag along for a while and
hope for the best.

"And you're just taking us in on faith?" Harper asked
doubtfully.

"Not quite," Hollis said, leaning back again, and smiling
some, confident, maybe, that they were going to throw in
with him now and that his plans were once more rolling

smoothly. "I've got a little job I want the two of you to do first."

"What's that?" Red asked. He felt the whiskey rolling slowly in his belly like muddy water.

"I've got about seventy head of beef your partners are holding for me. I want them back, and I want the two of you to get them for me. And I want you to kill Luke Howard and Pete Sanchez while you do it. My boys will ride along to see that the job's done right."

Isaac Goff's office was at the rear of the saloon, under the stairs and extending back partway into the storage room. The inside door to the office was located under the stairs, so that a man seeing it and not knowing better would likely think it was only a closet of some kind. There was a second door to Goff's office, this one opening into the alley separating the saloon from the Sand Creek law offices of Johnson, Firch and Meyers—Johnson being Frosty Johnson, Sand Creek's part time mayor and justice of the peace.

Goff's office was long and narrow, sparse of furnishings, with only a rolltop desk, a couple of straight-back chairs and a spittoon; as a rule he spent most of his time in the saloon and as little as possible in the office.

Lately, though, it had been just the opposite. It seemed like the close, dark confines of the tiny, low-ceilinged room offered a security he hadn't felt or needed before. It was Charity bothering him, he knew, that and what he'd done, losing all control the way he had. It hadn't been the first time, of course, but it had been a long time back now—St. Louis, in '71, and the whores had sicced the law on him then, forcing him to flee in the middle of the night like a common criminal. He'd been two years recovering from that, convincing himself that it wasn't his fault, that he wasn't the animal. Two long years forgetting, and now this, a whore beat and not working, friendly with a damn gun hand, too, which was almost enough to make a man laugh.

He had been a respectable man for a while there, quick and confident and sure of himself, but that had changed now. He knew what the West thought of a woman beater, and that likely he would have to leave Sand Creek now, but he didn't want to. Didn't want one little mistake to wipe out all he had built—not again. Thinking about it alone in the small, dark room, he had about half convinced himself that it didn't have to be that way this time. Thinking about it, he thought maybe there was a way out, if he played his hand right.

He waited with the quiet patience of a hunter, a revolver resting on the desk next to his elbow, the wick turned low in the lamp. The crowd in the saloon was light, it being late and the middle of the week, too; a dozen or so at the bar, fewer yet at the tables. The music from the piano seemed unnaturally loud above the small hum of conversation, seeping in around the door like a winter breeze. Now and then he heard the clink of glasses at the bar, or the crowlike laughter of Sue, already well into her bottle. Sometimes, when the low din from the big room faded into a short stretch of silence, he thought he could almost hear the ticking of the wag-on-the-wall.

When the tap came at the alley door, he reached calmly for the revolver and brought it down into the shadows below the edge of the desk. "Come in," he said softly.

The door swung inward on protesting hinges, coming all the way back and framing the dark silhouette of the puncher. "Mr. Goff?"

"Come in, Hogan. Shut the door."

Hogan stepped inside and elbowed the door shut, pausing nervously and squinting. Goff cocked the revolver with a slow, deliberate movement, the sound loud even above the thumping of the piano. He saw Hogan's startled, backward step, saw his hand go to the butt of his own revolver and stop there. Goff shifted his revolver to his left hand and reached up and turned the wick high, flooding the room with a warm, yellow glow. Hogan's hand tightened on his revolver, but still he didn't draw it, and Goff nodded, satisfied. "Come on in, Hogan, and have a seat."

Hogan sidled over, feeling for the chair with his hand, his eyes hard on Goff's revolver. "No need for that pistol, Mr. Goff. You and me always got along well."

"I know that, Hogan. There's nothing personal in it. I just wanted to prove something to myself." He uncocked the revolver and laid it aside.

Hogan looked up then, and met his eyes. "What's that, Mr. Goff?"

Goff smiled and shook his head vaguely, dismissing the subject. "How are things, Hogan? You and your friends making out all right?"

"Sure, we're doing okay." He took his hat off, then looked like he didn't know what to do with it, whether to drop it on the floor or put it back; in the end he kept it in his hands, curling the brim up and letting it fall back. "Got us a camp in the badlands," he said. "Tyson's got himself an old Ballard rifle and he gets a deer sometimes. We're making out."

"Jess says you're gathering cattle," Goff said mildly.

Hogan's head snapped up. "We ain't rustling, if that's what you're getting at. We just been gathering a few mavericks from the sandhill country, cattle the ranchers wouldn't waste time chasing out. Ain't a rancher on the range ain't done the same, one time or another."

"They might feel a little different now, times being what they are."

Hogan shook his head. "No, sir, those are strays, by God, free to any man that puts his brand on them. Me and Tyson and Slaughter have worked up a brand we'll register right here in Sand Creek when the time comes."

"If Bronson lets you come into town, you mean?" Goff said derisively. "What was it he said? That he'd lock you up for six months if he ever caught you in Sand Creek again?"

"Bronson's hot air wrapped in fancy."

Maybe, but I've seen him pistol-whip a man until his own mother wouldn't recognize him. Big man, too, and Bronson took a knife away from him first. You know he can do it.' Goff smiled, mockingly. "You would have been back before now if you didn't."

Hogan's mouth opened, then closed, and he looked away.

"Jess says you're living in an old Sibley tent," Goff went on, unrelenting now. "Says it's coming apart at the seams and leaking in the rain and that you built a fire inside and like to smoked yourself out. He says you're living on antelope and jackrabbits, neither fit for an Indian, and not enough cattle yet to warrant a brand. What was it, nine head? You'd be better off butchering them."

Hogan's face was red with anger, and he stood, putting his hat on. "We'll make out," he said flatly. "We ain't so green."

"If you could've handled Luke Howard in the first place, you wouldn't be in this fix." Goff threw the words out quick, venomously, and saw Hogan flinch, feeling a small smile come to his face then.

"We handled Howard," Hogan said hotly. "We would've taken care of him good if Bronson hadn't horned in."

There was honest hatred in Hogan's voice, born, Goff knew, on the day Jim Young had let them go, and it had grown a little every miserable day since. "Do you still want him?" Goff asked.

"Yeah," Hogan said. He sat back down. "I still want him."

"Enough to kill him?"

Hogan didn't answer, didn't say yes but didn't say no, either, and Goff said, "I'm going to give you a reason. All of you. It's worth five hundred dollars to me to see Luke Howard dead. I don't care how it happens. I don't care if he's bushwhacked or his horse throws him or if he starves to death. I just want him dead."

"Why?" Hogan asked suspiciously.

"That's my business," Goff replied, and saw the doubt come suddenly to Hogan's face, the confusion. "Are you afraid?" Goff asked bluntly. "Was all your talk a coward's bluff?"

"No," Hogan said sharply, his eyes bright, but doubtful yet. "I don't know."

"You want to," Goff said softly, nodding as if to himself. "You want to, all right, but you're afraid—"

"I ain't!" Hogan's voice was still sharp, and he stood then, the doubt gone. "Okay, Goff. You got your reasons and I have mine. Good enough." He nodded and put his hand on his revolver.

Goff sighed silently.

"Jess says they're in the Hills, though. You want me to go after him?"

"No. Be too easy to miss him that way. They'll come to town first. They always do. Take care of him here. But right away, understand. It won't do me any good if you wait until the next day. I want him dead immediately."

Hogan nodded slowly. "Okay, Luke Howard is as good as dead right now. Only thing, I ain't so sure Tyson and Slaughter will feel the same about it. I'll need something to convince them."

"A hundred dollars up front. Enough for flour and salt and coffee. But I don't want you buying it. I don't want you seen at all. I'll get your stuff together and send it out with Jess tomorrow."

"Put a couple of bottles of rye in with it," Hogan said. "It gets cold at night."

Goff smiled thinly but nodded. He reached into the inner pocket of his coat and pulled out a long, yellow envelope, wagging it slowly before Hogan's face. "The supplies will be on me this time. I'm going to send a couple of Winchesters along, too. Howard is no man to go up against close range. Those will come out of your pay. But hear me good, Hogan. Listen damn good. Don't double-cross me. You do and I'll put that five hundred dollars on your head and that'll attract every bounty hunter and back-shooter east of the Rocky Mountains. Do we understand each other?"

Hogan was looking at him uncertainly, wishing maybe he hadn't acted so hastily. "I understand, Mr. Goff. Ain't nobody going to double-cross you. Like I said, Luke Howard is as good as dead right now."

Silence then in the big room, and the little scratch of cloth at the door, and Goff's heart rose and choked him. He stood and crossed swiftly yet silently to the door and jerked it open just as the noise started again, as the Professor started "Buffalo Gals" and Sue cawed hoarse laughter from the bar and the jumbled sound of a dozen voices talking at once rose from the room like a flock of starlings from a tree. There was no one near or anyone even looking his way, but there had been, and he wondered with a kind of dread who it had been, and what had been heard.

CHAPTER 13

SWEDE sat the gray mare in the thick timber and chewed reflectively on the frayed end of a toothpick, from time to time absently spitting out little splinters worked loose with his teeth. The gray heaved a heavy sigh and shifted restlessly under him like a swell beneath a dinghy, stretching her nose for grass that wasn't there.

It was cold, as mountains were at night, and damp after the evening's rain. The thick carpet of fallen pine needles was spongy and the limbs above him still dripped. The storm had passed on after a while and the moon rose silver and nearly full, filtered through the shifting, whispering boughs like a fine spray of frost.

Below him, tiny in the distance, the black shadows of riders moved across the moonlit meadow, shifting and pulling apart and merging again, heading more or less toward an old Indian trail that paralleled the Ogallala and Black Hills road, keeping to the shadows when they could, and off the main trails, like owlhoots.

Swede nodded, satisfied, and spat what remained of the toothpick into the shadows. He'd been dogging them since they'd left O'Hanaran's saloon in Easy Street almost two hours before, always keeping back and out of sight, or sometimes, like now, riding on ahead when he was pretty sure he knew where they were heading.

He waited now until the last rider had turned onto the old trail, then brought the gray to life with his heels, surprising a grunt out of her after so long a halt. He knew the Indian trail, had traveled it once in his wanderings around Easy Street, and knew where he could pick it up again without losing those he followed. There weren't all that many places a man could take a horse in the mountains, and Swede wasn't worried about their leaving the trail before the river crossing, where he would be waiting for them next.

He put the gray to the slope before her, feeling her shoulders bunch and heave to the effort, the needles slick beneath her shod hooves and making her scramble for footing. Pine boughs slapped at his face, loosening a shower of rain drops, and in twisting to dodge them he felt the sharp twinge of Hawk's old knife wound, still tender to the touch.

It all seemed a long time ago now, Hawk and Old Tom and the Jessups, though longer in thought than actual time, he supposed; it had been only a couple of weeks since he'd ridden from their camp and caught the road to Deadwood and his revolvers, less than that since coming back to Easy Street and nosing around like some down-on-his luck miner.

Still, in all that time—the two weeks since leaving the Jessups and the lost-track-of time before that, lying wounded and sick and out of his mind with fever, then the slow weeks of recovery—he had seldom thought of Sand Creek or his job with the Cattlemen's Association. Nor had he thought much of the men he considered his partners: Harper and Doc and Red and Sanchez and Howard. It was as if, after the one-armed man's bullet had cut him down behind O'Hanaran's, the whole business of the rustlers had become something personal, something to be handled alone.

He'd been surprised, seeing Harper and Red walk into the saloon, even more surprised when he felt their eyes pass over him without recognition, until he remembered how he looked now, the matted beard and greasy hair cocked out at odd angles from beneath the cloth cap he still wore, and the dirty face poking up from Hawk's old, grimy wool coat, so bulky it made him only a sizeless, shapeless bum; so much so that he was able to pass almost unnoticed through Easy

Street, his questions no more threatening than any other bum's, trying to pass the time of day.

Yet it was a puzzle, sure enough, and not only the unexpected way Harper and Red had showed up, but the way the one-armed man had suddenly appeared, too, as if expecting them, and the five strangers, then, all tired-looking and trail-worn.

Some of it he could guess, of course. Harper and Red wouldn't be in the Hills unless another herd had been taken, and that fit easily enough with the five worn riders. But there was still a bundle of unanswered questions, and Harper and Red riding like outlaws through the night was the one bothering him the most. Were they being forced, he wondered, or going on their own accord? Nothing much surprised him anymore, and discovering that Harper and Red were in cahoots with the rustlers wouldn't either. Yet it didn't mesh with their words and actions on the range, and he thought again that they were being forced to ride along, maybe for some purpose only the one-armed man knew the whole of.

Then he smiled, because one way or another it really didn't matter. There would be gunplay before the night was over, and that was what he was waiting for.

They paused for a time at the river, letting their horses drink some, and catching a last smoke; then they left the trail altogether and cut over a low, timbered ridge, pausing once more just before they started down the far side.

"Bottom of the hill," someone said, his voice, even whispered, sounding loud in the night.

"Let's go," the man in the poncho, Bishop, said.

Red gigged his sorrel on downslope with the others spread out behind him, everything silent now save for the dull thud of hooves against the soft earth and the occasional bark of a broken limb. It was almost pitch-dark in the close timber, and he gave the sorrel his head, trusting the animal's instinct on the steep slope. Finger-slim stubs of old limbs, long dead and brittle, reached out to pluck at his clothing, snapping easily against his shoulders. Below, the soft lowing of the cattle rose like a beacon on the breeze, drifting ghostlike through the forest, haunting in its way and enough to spook a man if he was given to spooking easily.

Yet to Red, the sound brought a stab of desperation, a sense of time running out. The rim of the valley wasn't more than ten or fifteen minutes away now, Howard and Sanchez not far beyond that. In his mind's eye he could see them now, standing wary but curious and back from the fire's light, wondering at the stealthy approach from the timber, but knew that if one of the rustlers made them call out . . .

The time to act was now, with everyone scattered through the timbers and shadows thick as ink. He cut a quick glance toward Harper, gliding easily through the black forest, the long legs of his bay tucked under him on the slope, then looked over his shoulder. The rider behind him had fallen back some, but the one on his left, the chubby-faced ex-puncher with the Smith and Wesson they called Ace-High, was almost close enough to touch.

Ace-High was riding a bald-faced black horse with a rough gait, young yet, clumsy and ill-mannered on the steep pitch of land and skittish at the shadows. Ace-High had been fighting the black all night, sawing back on the reins every time his horse tried to push ahead of another, until both rider and mount were locked in a private battle for control.

Watching him, Red saw that Ace-High still had his revolver drawn, but on this final slope, with the black buck-jumping over fallen logs and small upthrusts of granite rock and tossing its head like a spoiled child, the S&W looked more of a hindrance than a threat. It's now or never, Red thought, and pulled his hat off and slapped Ace-High's black across the face, loosening a wild Indian cry as he did.

The black squealed and reared, his hind legs sliding out from under him. Ace-High yelled and kicked free of his stirrups, twisting in midair to fall away from the black's flailing hooves. Red let his hat fall and drew his Peacemaker, firing into the timber behind him without aiming, the sorrel wanting to run now, spooked in the sudden flurry of action. There was a hurried volley of shots on his right, muzzle flashes popping like oversized fireflies. A bullet tore into a tree at his side, showering him with bark. The sorrel had his head now, running, twisting through the timber like an elk, his head thrown up and out. Dead branch stubs dug at Red's body, at his face, his eyes, until he finally just lowered his head and let the sorrel run.

The sorrel lost his footing at the base of the slope, his hooves gouging long, curving troughs in the dirt as he slid down the few final feet, coming up riderless in the deep meadow grass and hightailing it for the far side of the valley, kicking and squealing as he ran. Red grunted and swore, his face gone slack with pain as his leg was first pinned under the saddle, then roughly jerked free. He rolled to his belly, his face chalky though streaked with cuts that looked black in the moonlight, hearing the crash of a horse in the timber bearing down on him.

Red thrust the Peacemaker out and fired blindly, hearing a shrill yelp of pain and seeing in the shadows a horse with its rider slumped in the saddle. With the reins suddenly slack, the horse nickered frightfully and bolted, its hooves arching wickedly just over Red's head. The rider swayed in the saddle but clung to the horn as his horse ran out of control along the edge of the timber. Red twisted, following the rider with his revolver until he disappeared from sight. He turned back then, hearing from upslope the slow, rolling booms of Harper's big Colt. He heard Ace-High, horseless now, shouting and fearing desertion, and from time to time could see the quick, flitting shadows of riders in the forest, but he held his fire, unable yet to tell friend from foe.

He crawled to a log lying half in the forest and half in the meadow and put his back to it. Sweat clung to his upper lip, and he drew his breath in short, sucking draughts, the frosty night air like ice to his lungs. He tried wiggling a toe once but felt nothing save the dull throbbing that kept time to the beat of his heart.

For a while the gunfire slackened and threatened to die, then suddenly burst afresh. Red hitched around, bringing the Peacemaker up expectantly, but the fighting had pulled back to near the top of the ridge.

At his back, though still out of sight, he heard the restless milling and bawling of the cattle, choused but too worn out to stampede. Howard and Sanchez would be back there, too, with their weapons drawn and ready, though they weren't likely to nose into a fight without knowing who was involved.

A horse came out of the forest and he swung his revolver around, but it was only Harper, hunched in the saddle and favoring his side. Above them the firing continued, though sporadic now, and muted, as the rustlers dropped over the far side of the ridge.

Harper reined up beside Red, his face puzzled. "I thought maybe you was Luke or Pete," he said.

"They're probably still with the herd."

"Then . . . who?" He looked toward the timber. Only silence drifted from it now.

Red rose and hobbled over to Harper, hanging onto the saddle to ease the weight off his bad leg. A voice called softly from behind, questioning, and Harper answered. Howard appeared then, and Sanchez soon after, both with their pistols drawn. There was movement on the slope, the sounds of a horse approaching at a walk.

It was a stranger that came out of the timber maybe thirty yards away, a man lost in the bulky mass of an old wool coat, handling the reins of a well-put-together gray. He turned toward them and Red's grip tightened on his Peacemaker. "That'll be far enough," he called, and the stranger halted. "What's your business here?" he added, and thought he saw the trace of a mocking smile behind the stranger's beard.

The stranger said, "Is that any way to treat the man who likely saved your hides tonight?"

It was Howard who finally put a name to the voice, saying, "I'll be damned. It's Swede."

"You'll all be damned," Swede said, gigging his horse forward, "if you don't get out of my way."

They rode in at dawn, saddle-weary and drawn. Hollis heard them coming and rose from the narrow bunk nailed to the shack's rear wall and padded stocking-footed across the cold floor with his Colt in his hand. He spotted Bishop's poncho first, the colors loud in the rising sun. Dutchy came behind him, and when they rode closer he saw Ace-High riding behind Dutchy, his arm cradled in a makeshift sling. Frick brought up the rear, his face pale and his shoulder hunched, though from the shack Hollis could see nothing wrong with him. He already knew they had failed, of course, that Harper and Red had somehow double-crossed them and likely gotten away. That they were without the cattle told him that much.

Hollis dressed while the others rode behind the shack and took care of their horses, then waited with a growing anger until they trooped inside. They stopped when they saw the Colt in his hand, fanning out just inside the door with their heads coming up in surprise.

"You lost them," Hollis said harshly, the Colt unwavering.

"They tricked us in the timber," Ace-High said. His voice was tight with pain and there was a deep, angry patch of raw meat on his cheek, clotted with dried blood and bits of dirt and pine needles. His eyes were puffy, almost swollen shut, and his face was a mask of tiny, irritating scratches.

"Did they follow?" Hollis asked quietly.

Dutchy shook his head. "Mebbe dey go as far as Easy 'Treet, but no fodder, uh, uh. Too demn much traffic, you bet." Of the four, only Dutchy showed no concern over the

Colt in Hollis's hand, though Hollis noticed he hadn't yet set aside his shotgun.

Hollis nodded and holstered his Colt. "There's medicine in that canvas bag in the corner there. Whoever feels the need can doctor themselves."

Dutchy said, "Need water, by Gott." He looked at Ace-High and grinned. "Deuce-Low here, he not be leefting no bucket too demn quick, you bet." He picked up a canvas bucket and headed out, chuckling at his words.

"He won't be doing much of anything for a while," Hollis said grimly. He looked from Ace-High to Frick. "What about you, Arch? How bad are you hurt?"

Frick had taken a three-legged stool near the fireplace. He looked up sullenly and said, "Don't worry. By the time you're ready for the next raid I'll be fit."

Ace-High sat on the floor next to the back door, his legs crossed Indian fashion. His wrist, protruding from the ragged end of the sling, looked puffed and tight, the fingers like small, curved sausages. He didn't look up when Hollis's gaze touched him.

Bishop still stood, his Winchester in hand, and after a while, almost lazily, Hollis raised his eyes and cocked a brow. "You have something to say, Bishop?"

"I say that was a fool thing to try," he said flatly. "That was like trying to make a deal with the devil. Did you really think you could buy them?"

"Everyone has their price. Theirs was just a little higher than what I offered."

"Morris didn't come back, if you ain't noticed."

"Since Morris didn't come back, I assumed he was dead. If he's dead, then he's of no use to us, right?"

Ace-High finally looked up, his face bewildered. Bishop said, "You cold-eyed sonofabitch. Morris was our friend, our partner, and you're acting like he was dead weight. By God, you're the one who got him killed."

"I wasn't there," Hollis replied icily. "If any man is to blame, it's the one who let them get the jump on you."

Ace-High ducked his head and Hollis read his guilt in the gesture. He nodded, his lips sneering, and looked back at Bishop.

"You're never there," Bishop said, trying to pick up the train of his anger, but his accusation sounded flat on top of Ace-High's silent admission.

Hollis walked to the front window and pulled aside the thin cloth that served as a curtain. "We're almost through here," he said, as if speaking to himself and allowing the others only to eavesdrop. "They're already running honest cattle into the Hills. By next summer there will be ranches up here. We've got one more drive coming where we can hope to make a profit. With Harper and Red riding with us and the others out of the way we could have made it without any problems at all. But by God, we are going to make that drive. We're going to make it if we have to cart them the last hundred miles on a sled. It'll be the biggest herd we've run yet."

He turned, his eyes bright with the excitement of it. Frick looked doubtful, worried maybe, but Bishop was shaking his head thoughtfully. "There's something else you should know," Bishop said. "They had help, some stranger I've never seen before."

Hollis frowned, and his face turned ugly with it. "Say it," he demanded.

Bishop shrugged. "Didn't get a good look at him. He was like a damn ghost, coming out of nowhere with a pistol in each hand. Knew how to use them, too. He was the one who took Morris. He was putting his shots close to us all."

"What did he look like?" Hollis asked.

"Told you, like a damn ghost."

"It was that bum," Frick put in. "The one from O'Hanaran's yesterday afternoon."

"Arch thinks it was the bum in the back corner wearing

the big white coat. I ain't so sure about that, but whoever shot at us was wearing a light-colored coat and riding a gray horse. I saw that much. Goddamn. Like to spooked the living Jesus out of me."

Hollis turned his mind back to the day before, to O'Hanaran's and the press of customers, the white-coated figure Frick spoke of coming slowly to mind. A stranger, he had thought at the time, but focusing on him, he thought there was something familiar about him after all, something in the way he sat, perhaps, or the way those cold blue eyes followed him from the table to the bar after talking with Harper and Red; dead eyes, as expressionless and unblinking as a rattlesnake's.

A chill ran down his spine, like the frost slowly burning off outside under the sun's touch. He knew who the stranger reminded him of, all right, but knew also that it was impossible, that Swede was dead and buried and likely forgotten by any who had seen him in the saloon that long-ago late summer day.

Watching him, Bishop said, "You know who it is, don't you?"

Hollis shook himself back to the shack. "No, I don't. But I will." He turned back to the window, dismissing those behind him. This new threat worried him only slightly. What worried him more was the possibility those he trusted most in Sand Creek might be setting him up. Might be that they, too, were seeing that the end was near.

The weather held all week, the sky high and lazy blue, and the breeze gentle from the west, so that even at night, with the frost heavy along the creeks and the stars looking like bits of ice, they didn't really suffer from the cold. By midmorning they were shucking their coats and by late afternoon, like as not, a few of them were working up a sweat.

They made fair time, the cattle settling into the drive without complaint now that they weren't being pushed, and everyone willing to let them set the pace. By the end of the week the swelling in Red's leg had gone down enough that he was able to help with the drive, and Harper's side, gouged by a protruding stub of a pine, had scabbed over and was healing nicely. By the time they dropped the cattle off on the northern part of the Sand Creek range it hardly bothered him at all.

They rode into Sand Creek in the middle of the afternoon, weary and disappointed, thinking back, Howard knew, to those long days roaming the Hills. It beat hell, he thought, how the rustlers always disappeared.

He rode slumped a little, his eyes narrowed against a teasing wind; in the small of his back a knot of tightening muscles was forming, something he knew only rest would cure.

There wasn't much traffic along the street—a few women, housewives, he guessed, on the boardwalks, and a canvas-topped wagon at the far end of town, heading south. The black and red box of the Ogallala and Black Hills stage stood empty in front of the stage office, empty of driver or passenger, the harness rolled up and stored away for the night. The Ogallala and Black Hills line was a small outfit, its schedule haphazard at best. Could be they didn't have a full load and were waiting until morning in hopes of getting a few extra passengers.

There was a group clustered around the big front window of Borland's mortuary and cobbler's shop, some big, rough-looking miners and a man in an expensive suit with a new-looking short stovepipe hat. He was staring wide-eyed at something in the window, looking both pale and disgusted. The miners, Howard noted, were grinning.

Howard reined up next to the boardwalk and stared over the top of those before the window, feeling his breath catch in his throat. Behind him, Harper swore in a dry, choking voice, and Sanchez's *"Madre Dios"* came like a soft prayer.

Doc rested in the mortician's window, propped up in a

plain wooden casket with his arms folded across his chest and his face white and restful, smooth-skinned like a child's, but wasted, too, and shrunken in at the cheeks and eyes. He was dressed in his buckskin shirt, with his gunbelt buckled about his waist and pulled around until the holster was resting near his crotch. His hat lay next to his head, the crown carefully creased.

Howard dismounted slowly, barely hearing the others do the same. He let his reins trail and walked stiffly across the boardwalk, elbowing those before him aside and ignoring their angry objections. A little bell tinkled overhead as he entered, the sound deceptively cheerful. Harper, Swede, Red and Sanchez crowded in behind him, and Sanchez heeled the door shut.

Borland's front room was small and cluttered, smelling of fresh-planed wood, oiled leather and rawhide. There was a counter near the rear wall, spilling over with a disarray of half-finished boots and shoes, stiff pieces of rawhide, rags, oils, awls and spools of thread. In the corner, haloed by the bright glare of an overhead lamp, a woman's high-buttoned shoe rested on a low desk, the front part of the sole still unstitched and gapping. Along the near wall three lidless coffins were stacked one atop the other, separated with narrow strips of wood. There was a shelf above the top coffin, and this was also lined with boots and shoes, each with a little tag wired to it bearing the owner's name and a repair price.

There was a blanket over a door leading into a back room, and as Sanchez swung the front door shut, a wispy little man with white hair and a pallid complexion pushed it aside and entered, his mouth twisting up into a welcoming smile that faded, seeing Howard.

"You Borland?" Howard asked.

The old man nodded, his gaze swinging out, passing over Harper and Swede to Howard's right, and Red and Sanchez on his left, coming back then, quick and flighty. "I'm Borland, yes." He sounded scared already, and Howard wished he was a younger man, one without fear. He wanted to curl his fists and swing.

"You the one put Doc up in the window like that?" Howard asked. A foolish question, but all he could do. His rage was like a hot coal burning in his belly and his voice was shaky with it.

Borland backed up a step, looking quickly to the back of the coffin in the window, then away quicker. "You mean . . . that one?" he asked timidly.

Howard leaned forward, putting his knuckles on the counter. "Get him down," he breathed. "Get him down and buried proper, and get those goddamn gawkers out of the window."

"Jesus, mister, I didn't do nothing that ain't been done a hundred times before." He sounded scared yet, but confused, too. "That guy, he was a gunfighter, a celebrity. People just wanted a last look, is all."

"You got him propped up there like some damn thief, or outlaw," Harper said hoarsely.

Swede suddenly drew a revolver and cocked it. Borland cringed, his eyes going wide and coming back to Howard, pleading. Howard shook his head. "Get him down," he said, the rage strangely gone then, and in its place a weariness as he had never known before. It took all his strength to dredge the words up and out. With an effort, he pushed away from the counter, turning and heading for the door. He only dimly heard the others following, and Swede's warning: *"Get him down, like the man said. We'll bury him this afternoon."*

The crowd backed away as they came out, backed away and stood there muttering to one another, and now and again spitting or hitching at their trousers and showing they weren't afraid. The pale man was gone and only the miners and drifters were still around. Howard leaned against the front wall and fingered what was left of a cheroot from an inside pocket of his coat. He heard the old man inside,

lowering the coffin and pulling it away from the window, and
seeing in his mind Doc's face, his hand shook as he lit the
cigar.

The others waited with him, Harper and Red sitting on
the steps and Sanchez leaning against the hitching rail. Swede
had mounted his gray like a man determined to go on, then
suddenly and without explanation turned back, not dismounting but just waiting quietly, his eyes hooded and
turned elsewhere.

They smoked and waited, and now and again one would
speak and another answer and the conversation would die
then, the words hanging in the air for a long time after the
silence had settled. Traffic remained light, a few wagons, a
couple of Circle-R punchers who rode past with unabashed
stares, a youngster with a basket of eggs circling way around
the group in front of the mortuary and keeping his head
down. The town seemed silent, shut down and empty, with
the same air of desertion Howard had sensed at the Wagon
Wheel the evening he and Young had ridden there and
found the notice. Yet there were people, all right, and
sounds, too, the slamming of doors and the ring of hammer
against iron from the blacksmith shop. It was the cold, he
thought, keeping people indoors, and the wind; the wind
had a lonely sound, nosing down the street, into crooks and
crannies like an old hound sniffing news.

It was an hour before Borland finally came out, hatless
still, but bundled in a knee-length greatcoat that gave him
bulk. "We've got him in a wagon out back," he announced.
"The grave was dug yesterday and I made a cross this
morning, but I didn't know what to put on it. Does anybody
know his real name, or when he was born?"

Howard looked at the others and felt his embarrassment
growing. It seemed wrong somehow, their riding with a man,
yet not knowing his full name, nor much else. It seemed to
make a mockery of their feelings. Howard ducked his head
and shook it; the others already had.

"I've got to carve something on the cross," Borland said with a little tone of indignation.

"Call him Davis," Red said suddenly. "I remember him saying his father was stationed at Fort Davis when he cut his pin. And he must have been . . . what? Seventeen? Eighteen? Eighteen, say, so just figure out when he was born and put that and the date he died on it. It'll have to do."

"We'll get word to Fort Davis," Howard said. "Maybe his pa is still stationed there."

Borland nodded, then said, "We don't have a regular preacher here, just the circuit minister who comes around once a month. I generally say a few words over the deceased when we bury them, maybe quote something from the Bible, then have the proper send-off when the minister arrives. If that'll do?"

"That'll do fine," Howard said. He mounted with the others and waited in the street for Borland to bring the buckboard around, then fell in behind and followed him onto the prairie.

Sand Creek's cemetery lay on a small rise about a mile west of town. On the near side, surrounded by a picket fence and laid out in neat rows, was a small section of wooden and granite headstones, some covered with elaborate figures and pieces of religious verse. Beyond the fence, scattered haphazardly toward the crest of the rise, lay the pauper section. At best, simple wooden crosses rose like pieces of driftwood washed up after some long-forgotten flood, sun-bleached and tilting. A few, from hide town days, were marked only with a piece of stone, dug up with the grave, maybe, and stuck into the dirt at an odd angle to mark this as man's work, not nature's. Prickly pear grew here, and sage, and yonder a little mound of fresh dirt next to an open grave.

Borland halted his team and snapped a tether weight to the off mare. He had replaced the long greatcoat with a lighter black one more fitting to the occasion, and stood now at the head of the grave with a quiet dignity while they muscled Doc's coffin from the buckboard and lowered it with ropes. Howard was almost shocked at the seeming weightlessness of the coffin, and wondered briefly if Borland, for some insane reason, had switched coffins and had them burying an empty one. It was a foolish thought, he knew, yet one that stayed.

With the ropes pulled free and recoiled in the buckboard, Borland opened a worn, leather-bound Bible and stabbed at a page with a trembling finger. They all stood to one side with their hats off, listening with only half an ear, and maybe not remembering the way a man would with someone close, but thinking instead of the close calls they'd had and the people they'd put under, and wondering if maybe somewhere there was a coffin like this already built that they'd use. More foolish thoughts, and probably dangerous to boot, Howard thought, but it was something a man couldn't help, either, on his last gun job and with a bunch of brood mares waiting.

After, they walked to their horses and climbed on, and Red pulled the collar of his sheepskin jacket up, saying, "Damn, I think it's turning cold again."

CHAPTER 14

IT was coming on to dark as Howard lifted the bay into a shuffling jog, the sun already down and the night creeping and growing. With the sun gone the cold had a bite that had been lacking earlier, and the wind swung around and came down from the north again, and gusting stronger. Still the sky remained clear, without hint of anything more.

The steady clopping of the bay's hooves against the hard-packed road and the lulling creak of saddle leather were the only sounds to disturb the night. The lights of Sand Creek had blinked out behind a swell of land, and the Sand Creek crossing lay like a black scar across the prairie. He slowed as he approached, remembering the deep ruts cut in the sod there from all the wheeled traffic, the bay dropping to a walk without protest.

The orange-red flash of a muzzle blast lashed from the shadows along the bank, the report booming, startling, in the twilight. Howard grunted and jerked involuntarily at the bite of lead at his neck, then brought the bay around and raked his flanks with his spurs. The bay stretched out, running hard with Howard bent low over the horn. The second shot seemed muffled by wind and distance, but he saw a piece of sod kicked into the air a yard or so ahead of the bay, still climbing as they passed.

He pulled the bay down to a walk after a while, twisting in the saddle to listen for pursuit, then stopped altogether. He explored his wound with careful fingers, bringing them away sticky with warm blood. There was a ringing in his ears, and his head thumped; he felt light-headed with a throbbing that seemed to center not from this fresh wound, but from

Bronson's old scar etched above his ear. He touched the old wound, his fingers traveling its jagged, torn length, feeling the flap of scalp move freely under his thumb.

Howard took the bandanna from around his neck and pressed it lightly to the torn flesh of this new wound, looking back the way he had come and waiting. Full darkness had dropped sometime during the bay's run, but the moon—though not full—gave the prairie a silvery sheen; he could still see a fair piece with its light. It wasn't long then that the bay began pawing impatiently at the ground, and after a few more minutes, Howard gave him his head.

They'd hauled the big stoves into Goff's, and tied the batwing doors back so the heavy, solid double doors could be pulled shut. There was firewood stacked high along the back wall, and even more behind the saloon, Sanchez had noted; maybe a couple of big freight wagons' worth dumped there, and no telling where it all came from.

Sanchez stood next to one of the stoves, holding his hands out to its warmth. It popped and cracked and radiated its heat outward in little shimmering waves a man could see. He hated the cold's coming, hated everything about it, and wondered that some could complain of the heat in the summer. He had never complained of the heat, though he knew he would complain plenty of the cold. Of course he hadn't expected to still be here. Mostly gun jobs were quick work for good money, then drift on. He had hoped to winter in New Mexico this year, it being a spell since he had been back, but time seemed to stretch on and luck had turned her back, so he was here now and in his mind already cursing the cold.

There was a fair crowd of mostly drifters who stood in small groups here and there and talked in low tones, so that the occasional laughter seemed loud and out of place. Or maybe it was his mood, Sanchez thought. He hadn't felt this low in a long time, and knew it was a lot of things causing it, the job and the weather and Doc, *Madre Dios,* poor Doc, propped up in Borland's window like some curio, and his yearning to go south again, to go home. He missed his sons, and his wife, some.

The door swung open and a couple of men entered, letting in a gust of wind that swirled in smelling fresh like the prairie, and kicking up a skitter of sawdust before dying. The whore, Belle, passed him and did a double take with recognition widening her eyes, then passed on uncertainly with a curly-haired Bar-W puncher in tow. Funny, that, but he put it from his mind and went to the bar for a drink, feeling thawed now, if not yet warm. Whiskey would help that, he thought.

He ordered rye from Johnny and stared after him while he went to fetch a bottle, wondering at the question in his eyes. Belle first, and now Johnny.

A body came close and he smelled perfume before he turned, and turning, felt surprise.

Belle laughed. "No, but he was easy to put off. I wanted to talk to you, if you're Pete Sanchez."

"*Si, senorita.* At your service."

"I've got to talk to you. Privately. It's very important."

"Me? Surely you must mean someone else, *senorita.* We do not even know one another."

"You," she said, with a little note of desperation. "Please. I'm going out back toward the privies. Give me a couple of minutes, then follow." She took his arm and squeezed, leaving quickly before he could question her further.

Sanchez stood puzzled while Johnny brought him his rye, remembering her voice, the look in her eyes, and wondering what frightened her so much. He turned and casually studied the room but saw nothing that looked out of kilter or suspicious. It was a puzzle, all right, and only one way of solving it. He knocked off his whiskey in two quick swallows and set the glass on the bar. From down its length Johnny raised his head in question, but Sanchez shook his head and patted his stomach. He turned and made his way without hurry to the back door.

The wind was cold from the north, and he swore and pulled his coat tighter. It swept low and rattled the tall weeds next to the building, swung the lantern on its spike above the door. He paused and sensed movement off to his left and moved slowly in that direction, his hand on his revolver. Empty bottles rolled under his feet, and dented and crushed airtights skidded away. Before the wind closed his sinuses, he smelled the sour odor of discarded food thrown from the window of the small kitchen. In the weeds to his right, away from the building, he heard the soft pad of trotting feet and wondered if it was a dog or a coyote.

He paused, sensing movement again, and close this time; then he saw Belle's white face and shoulders take shape in the thin light from the lantern. She had come without a wrap and looked nearly frozen. Closer, he heard the rapid chatter of her teeth.

"*Senorita,* you should not be out in such a night without a shawl," he scolded. He pulled his coat off and slipped it around her shoulders.

Belle sniffed and pulled it tight, shivering violently. "God, that's warm," she said. "Working inside, you forget what the weather's doing sometimes."

Sanchez smiled, but he was cold now too, and said, "*Senorita.* It was important, you said. What could be so important that it brings you into this?"

"Luke Howard is your friend, right?"

Sanchez nodded, waiting.

"Isaac Goff just hired three men to kill him," she said bluntly. "The three Broken Axle hands let go last—Hogan, Tyson and Slaughter. Know them?"

Sanchez nodded again, his mind whirling at the news. "Why?" he asked.

Belle shook her head. "I'm not sure I can tell you that. But

I won't let him ride into trouble without helping, either. Can you get word to him?"

"*Si*, tonight. But why? Surely there is a reason?"

She shook her head again, saying, "I've told you all I can. If Goff knew this he'd probably kill me." She paused as if in thought, then added, "I'm not doing this for him, okay? I want you to know that, and I want him to know that, too."

That much would have been easy to guess, Sanchez thought, but he still felt confused. He wondered why Charity hadn't delivered the message herself. Belle suddenly shrugged out of his coat and gave it back, smiling again. "On a night like this, that coat's worth a hundred dollars."

She brushed past him and stepped into the circle of light from the lantern and hurried inside. Sanchez stood in the shadows a while longer, then slipped into his coat and went around the outside of the building to his horse and mounted.

In the waning light of the moon, the Broken Axle bunkhouse looked empty, squatting dark and lifeless at the lower end of the ranch yard. On its roof the tall grass swayed forlornly in the wind, down and up, the way a dog's hair sometimes did under a man's hand.

The main house was dark, too, its small windows shuttered and the chimney without smoke. The windmill was shut down, and even the horses in the corral stood unmoving, their tails to the wind and their heads down, hipshot and asleep. In the small corral next to the bunkhouse, Luke's bay lay stretched out on his side, dead to the world.

Little wonder, Sanchez thought, reining up close by and looking down at the slim withers of his own horse. They'd covered a sight of country over the past couple of weeks, covered it hard and fast for the most part. He dismounted and dropped the reins, letting the paint nuzzle the ground, looking for a bite of grass. She'd earned some time off herself, he thought, a few days of loafing with grain and hay and fresh water.

The bunkhouse door cracked open just as he reached it, the faint moonlight glinting dully off the oiled steel of Luke's Navy revolver. Out of habit, Sanchez smiled, but the humor was strained tonight. "Do not shoot, amigo. I will surrender peacefully."

Luke let the door open and Sanchez stepped inside. Low snores rose from the sleeping quarters, and Luke nodded toward the kitchen. He went in and found a match in the box nailed above the stove and scratched it alight and lit a lamp.

"You're up late for a man who's just come back from a long drive," Luke said.

"This is true," Sanchez admitted. "But it seems I do more than just recover wandering cattle. Tonight I deliver messages as well. I have word from a woman, Luke."

"Charity?"

He saw the hope flash quickly to Luke's face, and felt a strange reluctance to quench it. "From Belle," he said gently.

"Belle?" Howard looked puzzled. "What does she want?"

Sanchez shrugged. "She sends a message that is not good to hear." He told him then of Belle and the way she acted and the warning she sent, and saw the confusion deepen on Luke's face. He said, before Luke could ask, "I do not know why. But she did say this. She does not do it for you. She wanted me to tell you that."

"Then who? Not herself?"

Sanchez smiled. "Do you really wonder?" he asked.

"Charity?"

"Who else, my friend?"

Luke was at the window now, bent low with his hands on the sill, as if he could peer through the shutter. "Somebody took a pot shot at me tonight. Down on the Sand."

Sanchez snorted. "Ambushers. They have sunk low, amigo, those three. Like a calf in a bog, eh?"

Luke shrugged. "A man will sink no lower than what he already is, Pete. Hogan was the troublemaker, but if the other two have thrown in with him I'll feel no pity when I find them."

"You will go to them?"

"I don't have much choice. They know where I bunk, they know where I ride. It would be only a matter of time if I didn't."

"Then I think maybe I will ride with you, my friend. There is much that is unfinished on this job, and we are shorthanded now."

"No," Luke said, turning. "Pete, thanks, but this is my fight. It's something personal and I want to handle it alone."

He thought about that for a moment, then nodded doubtfully. "Okay, it is your fight, then. But if you do not come back, I think I will make it my fight, also."

Howard rode down into the crossing with the first light, the dun blowing and acting sassy, full of energy. He dismounted but kept the reins in his hands, not yet trusting her to stand ground-tied, and searched the sandy soil for tracks. There was a good bit of water in the main channel of the creek, though slowing some from what it had been right after the rains. Still, it left the ground moist and sign plain, even under a hoary coat of frost.

He found what he was looking for without trouble, maybe twenty yards above the crossing and under a tangle of choke cherry. The ground was scarred from long hours of waiting, and a score or more of cigarette butts littered the ground, some almost weathered away already. Another fifty yards or so upstream, hidden from the road by a high bank and sheltered some by the cottonwoods, he found the spot where the lone ambusher had picketed his horse. The grass was trampled, cropped close, and some of the droppings looked a week old. Hogan had been a patient man, Howard thought.

He mounted and followed the trail upstream, losing it finally where it left the creek and angled toward the northeast. He cut back and forth for an hour, gaining maybe a mile, and knew he couldn't continue this way. Yet he knew the direction Hogan had taken, and thought he knew where it would lead.

He rode at a slow jog, ignoring the cold in a way he hadn't been able to in its earlier days. The sky was high and wide, pale blue and cluttered with tiny puffs of clouds sailing south under a brisk breeze. There wasn't much frost away from the low ground along the creek, and the prairie grass lay like a weathered blanket over the hills. Cattle grazed the sunny sides of the hills, and here and there, far off and indistinct save for the white flash of their rumps, he saw antelope.

Howard reached the badlands late in the afternoon, coming in from the west with his rifle out and canted across the pommel. The barren thrusts of earth had a reddish tinge, flaming scarlet in the setting sun, with tiny bits of mica sparkling in the light. He rode at a walk, following a grassy finger into the heart of the badlands, the ridges rising steep on either side of him, flat-topped and crowned with a spattering of twisted cedar. The dun kept stretching her neck for the tall grass as they rode, and Howard kept pulling at the reins with irritation, his eyes scanning the hills near and far.

He had thought the grass was only a slim pinch, but it kept winding back, eventually funneling into a wide draw with sloping sides more than a mile into the badlands. The ground was soft and trackless here, save for the padded prints of a coyote, hugging the south bank and heading out. Still, the badlands covered a big sweep of country and the lack of sign meant little. He'd covered a big chunk of this country on earlier forays, and knew there was a lot of places a man, or even a group of men, could hide without leaving much sign. Places with wood for fires and enough grass to graze a few head of horses for a month or more. But there weren't that many with steady water, and most of those were toward the eastern rim of the badlands, so when he found a way out of the draw he turned the dun in that direction, keeping off the ridges and pausing often to listen and smell. In that tangle of twisting canyons and deep draws, he knew he was likely to hear them first, or catch the scent of their fire.

Dusk caught him on a rocky slope peppered with small cedar and sage. He rode to the bottom and stripped the saddle and his gear from the dun, then hobbled her. Taking up his rifle, he made his way back to the top of the slope on foot, finding a twisted cedar to put his back to.

There was already a star or two showing dim in the south, but behind him the dying rays of the sun still arched above the horizon, painting a ridge of clouds there pink and crimson. In the south, toward Sand Creek range, he heard the clamoring of a pack of coyotes on the hunt, and opposite, so faint it might have only been a trick of the wind, he thought he heard the lonesome, drawn out howl of a wolf. Yet other than the coyotes and the maybe-wolf he heard nothing, only the teasing of the breeze and the scratchy rustling of cedar.

He stayed there for an hour, waiting and listening, watching for the reflective glow of a campfire, and seeing nothing but steel gray shadows fading gradually into full darkness. He walked back to the dun and rolled into his blankets then, waiting well into the night for sleep.

They came down the slope in a shower of dust and pebbles, the dun stiff-legged and snorting, then cut into a twisting arroyo and followed it a mile or more before finding a way out. They skirted a crumbling section of sandstone cliffs, the ground below littered with fallen slabs, and found a game trail heading in the direction he wanted to go.

Howard brought the dun to a jog, the reckless flight behind them now. There was a twitch in his side, like the bits of tiny augers working at his ribs, and he pulled his coat aside to find his shirt freckled with nickel-size spots of blood. He took his bandanna off and folded it into a large square and slipped it inside his shirt, tight against his ribs, never slowing the dun.

Hogan's bullet had drawn the blood. Luke had found their camp a little after noon, hearing the bellow of a steer so close and out of place it had startled him into pulling the dun to a sliding stop. He hadn't seen Hogan slipping along just below a far rim, hadn't even known he was about until that first shot had slammed into stone at his side, smashing a fist-sized piece into a handful of miniature projectiles that stung both the dun and himself.

He'd had the Henry out, and at Hogan's shot he'd whipped it around and let fly. It was a wild shot, screaming off into the sky, but Hogan had ducked anyway, and when he came back up Howard figured the dun was only a flash of color to him, disappearing around a bend in an arroyo.

That had been at the eastern edge of the badlands, maybe five miles back, and he had kept the dun at a run or as close to it as the country would allow until the game trail. He wanted distance between them now, and time enough to take stock of the situation. He wanted to draw them away from their camp, too, and deeper into the badlands. He was counting on their not knowing the interior well.

The trail wound its way deeper, climbing and dropping and sometimes almost doubling back on itself, until it finally disappeared in a grassy basin. Howard rode to the far side, to a break in the wall of a cliff, and put the dun to a steep, scrambling climb. On top, he dismounted and loosened the cinch. The dun's sides were heaving, and she was lathered with sweat. He took the bridle off and with a hand on her jaw, led her to a patch of grass, hobbling her there, and climbing back to the edge of the cliff with his rifle and canteen.

He sat and studied the country before him for a while. There was no dust along his backtrail that he could see, no sign of riders at all.

He took his coat and shirt off and peeled the top of his

longhandles down off his chest, shivering suddenly in the breeze, and raising the white flesh across his torso. The wounds along his ribs were slight, little craters of torn flesh rimmed with blood already dried. He soaked a corner of his bandanna with water and dabbed at the tender flesh, flinching some at the water's touch. His ribs were more bruised than torn, painful only in an irritating sort of way, yet it marked the third time Hogan had drawn blood on him. He figured the time had come to quit his running.

He saw them then, a spot of movement coming around a bend and into sight, three of them coming along at a good clip, maybe a mile off. Tyson was in the lead, his light-colored chaps standing out against the dark horse he rode, and leaning from the saddle to read sign. Hogan and Slaughter followed, each carrying a rifle canted from their thighs. Howard slipped back from the rim and into his shirt and coat. Coming along like they were, he thought they'd be in the basin within twenty minutes or so, well within the Henry's range. But such an encounter could only lead to gunplay, and he didn't want that. He wanted the drop on them, wanted to know why Goff had put a price on his head. Time enough then to wonder what to do with them.

He readied the dun and rode down the far slope, dodging the slim-bladed yucca and the clumps of prickly pear, and at the bottom veered back toward the interior, following the winding path of an arroyo. The ground was hard here, leaving little sign, but there was enough to follow, which was all he asked for. The arroyo's sides rose after a while, becoming almost sheer in spots, and the bottom widened into canyon size, patched now with tall grass. He came to a small grove of trees—not the shallow-rooted cedar or piñon that did so well on the ridges, but oak and box elder and cottonwood, all of it young and slim-trunked, but still arching overhead and hanging onto a few yellow and scarlet leaves. Here and there he came to pockets of water, edged with soggy fallen leaves, though clean-looking, and inviting.

Howard rode with a simple pleasure, forgetting for a time the pressure from behind. The canyon was like a gem set in sandstone, and although it was too small to support more than a few head, he admired it as a cattleman would, for the richness of the grass and the water and the protection it offered from the wind. Yet when it ended in a small, round meadow and the walls rose boxlike around him, he felt betrayed, as if the canyon's beauty had been only an illusion, a lure before the trap—until he spotted the narrow shelf of a trail against the west wall.

The trail was steep, strewn with rock and loose dirt that kept the dun scrambling and grunting and now and then losing her footing and coming close to falling. Narrow at the base, it narrowed even more as they climbed, the cliff wall that had looked almost flat and smooth from below tilting outward now, above the path, so that Howard was finally forced to slide back over the dun's rump. He fell sprawling and crawled after the mare on his hands and knees.

On top, he kneeled and studied the canyon, empty still but for the flight of magpies. He wasn't surprised. Hogan and the others were probably an hour or more behind yet, and with the afternoon shadows growing long it struck him suddenly that they wouldn't follow beyond here tonight. They'd come as far as the meadow, maybe even to the base of the trial, but they wouldn't climb it. They'd stop here, or go back a ways where there was water and wood and sure grass for their horses. They'd make a camp and likely think themselves safe doing it.

Howard nodded, satisfied, and led the dun back from the rim. He removed the saddle and bridle and hobbled her, knowing she wouldn't stray far, worn as she was. Taking his canteen and some dried meat, and with the Henry cradled in his arm, he made his way back to the rim to wait.

CHAPTER 15

THE flames bit into the old wood and grew, nudging the night back some, and throwing their shadows high along the wall of the canyon. A horse nickered softly at the flare of light and they tensed, reaching for their rifles and stopping abruptly, laughing some at the simultaneous action. Tyson settled back against his bedroll, picking up the sack of Bull Durham and the little packet of rolling papers he had dropped. "We're turning spooky as old mossy-horns," he said, chuckling a little.

Hogan looked up from where he was grinding coffee beans under the butt of his revolver. "It's Howard, the bastard. Riding into camp like he had a goddamn map. Lucky I was up above, or he'd have caught us all flatfooted."

"It's spooky, all right," Tyson agreed.

Slaughter shook his head. "This is wrong. I knew it from the beginning. He's going to get us all if we ain't careful." He was hunkered down close to the fire, turning a green-wood spit slowly over the flames. From time to time a piece of fat would drip from the meat roasting there, popping and sizzling as it fell through the flames.

Hogan glowered. "You're not thinking of cutting your picket, are you, Charlie?"

"It was you who made the deal."

"You went for the beans and bread quick enough," Hogan replied. "I reckon that buys you a part of the deal."

"Ain't saying it doesn't," Slaughter said. "Just saying I don't like it."

"He's alone," Tyson said. "We can handle him alone. Might take some time, is all."

Hogan grunted as if he hurt. "He's a tricky bastard, though. I say we ought to move downstream a ways to spread our blankets. Be just like the sonofabitch to double back on us."

In the canyon's shadows, Howard smiled. He rested with his back to the wall, his arms crossed in front of him with the Henry caught there. From time to time the smell of meat would come strong to him and his mouth would water with anticipation. Food had been skimpy at best the last couple of days, and the jerky he had eaten at dusk had long since abandoned him.

Tyson had his cigarette rolled, and he lit it with a twig from the fire. Leaning back against his saddle, he said, "What are you going to do with your share of the money, Charlie?"

"I'll not be squatting over a smoky fire roasting antelope, by God," Slaughter replied.

"He'll be squatting over some high-priced Kansas city whore, likely," Hogan said, and Tyson laughed.

"Huh, likely," Slaughter said, looking up from the fire. "How far do you figure five hundred dollars will go, split between the three of us? Goff is giving us a grubstake and little else, by God. Enough to maybe get us through the winter if we don't let it run through our fingers like our last month's pay. We'll be punching cows by spring, if there's a ranch around that will hire bushwhackers."

That brought them up quiet for a while, then Tyson looked at Hogan and said, "He's right, goddamnit, we're risking a hangman's noose for damn little money."

"I want Howard," Hogan said flatly. "I want that sonofabitch dead."

"Hell, it ain't Howard that lost us our jobs," Slaughter said. "It's the rustling."

"You ain't turning yellow on us, are you, Charlie?" Hogan asked.

Slaughter's eyes flashed. "I'm in, and I'll hold up my share and likely more. But I ain't got Luke Howard in my craw the way you do. I ain't saying I like a damn gunny, just that I ain't got nothing personal against this one."

Hogan laughed, the sound flat and emotionless. "You do now. He won't stop until it's us or him."

"We'll have to leave the country," Tyson said. "They'll know it's us. Five hundred dollars doesn't seem like much to give up your home range for."

"Well, sheeit. You too?" Hogan looked disgusted. "I'll tell you how I feel," he said. "That dirt-roofed bunkhouse of Young's ain't home to me. Texas is home, and it's been a long damn time since I've set eyes on it, too."

"Texas sounds good," Slaughter said wistfully. "I'm tired of freezing my butt in a saddle all winter." He pulled the spit off and poked at the meat with his knife. It was dark, almost black on the outside, but when punctured it welled a thin, red juice that set a man's mouth to watering. "Almost there," he said.

Hogan nudged the pot closer to the flame. "Coffee'll be done when it is," he said. He looked at Slaughter, sitting so stiff, and then above him, his eyes going wide. He reached slowly for the Winchester propped against his saddle, but Howard shook his head.

Howard took the muzzle of the Henry away from Slaughter's neck and stepped back until he was only a flickering shadow in the fire's light. The Henry showed up well enough, though, the firelight dancing off the brass.

"That's the way, Hogan. Nice and easy and no sudden moves."

Tyson dropped his cigarette, reached for it, then froze. "That you, Howard?" he asked.

"You weren't expecting anyone else, were you?" He let the Henry swing toward Hogan. "You, Hogan, I want you to pull that hogleg of yours real slow and toss it over your shoulder. Then the rest of you can do the same."

Hogan gingerly lifted his revolver and flipped it into the darkness. Tyson and Slaughter followed suit.

"Now the rifles, poking out of the scabbard there, and you, Hogan, the one you were reaching for."

Hogan and Slaughter took the Winchesters Goff had sent them and tossed them after the revolvers. Tyson kept his seat, his eyes on the fire, and a film of perspiration spread across his forehead. Howard looked at him questioningly, and he shrugged. There was no scabbard on Tyson's saddle, and Howard nodded.

"Didn't you say that meat was about ready, Charlie?" Howard asked.

"Near about."

"Why don't you pull it off the fire and slice me a piece? And pour some coffee while you're at it. The smell of that meat cooking is about to cave my belly in."

Slaughter leaned forward and cut a chunk off, setting it aside while he poured coffee. Howard ate slowly, then ravenously, the fresh meat awakening a hunger that had lain dormant under jerky and hardtack. He finished a second piece the size of the first, and washed it all down with three cups of coffee. He let Slaughter pour each time.

Afterward, wiping his chin with the sleeve of the duster, Howard said, "You got the makings of a good cook, Charlie. Seems you picked the wrong line of work." He pulled a cheroot from his pocket and came into the light to take a glowing limb from the fire to light it. Standing back, he said, "Man had the right company, he'd be satisfied about now, wouldn't he? Course, with you three busting your butts all day trying to put lead into me, I don't guess you'd qualify."

"Say your piece, Howard, and get it over with," Hogan growled.

Howard put a bullet into the ground at Hogan's feet, spraying him with a shower of dirt. Hogan jerked back, tucking his legs up, his eyes going wide, but there was still anger in them, Howard saw. Anger and hate. Howard jerked another round into the chamber and said, "Okay let's hear your story."

Slaughter and Tyson exchanged glances, and Slaughter said, "Ain't much to tell. Isaac Goff wants you dead. Didn't say why."

"Shut up, Charlie!" Hogan said sharply.

Howard swung the Henry around and loosened another shot, this one digging into the dirt next to Hogan's thigh. "Don't talk unless I tell you to," he instructed, then looked back at Slaughter. "Too short. Try again."

"You already knew about Goff then?"

Howard nodded.

"Who told you?" Hogan asked.

"Don't push me, Hogan. Speak up, Charlie."

"He was paying us five hundred dollars. Told Hogan that if we backed out he'd put a price on our heads." He had been staring into the flames and now he looked up, his eyes searching out Howard's. "Been a hard fall, Luke. We was hungry, that's why we did what we did. There was nothing personal about it, far as I'm concerned. That ain't no excuse, mind you. Just an apology for what we tried to do. Still would, I reckon."

"You should have been a cook, Charlie," Howard said. He let the muzzle drop some, running through his mind what Slaughter had told him, putting it to what he already knew. Hogan was easy to understand. Hate had been his motivation, an unaimed rage until chance had put them both inside the Colorado Lady at the same time. Tyson and Slaughter were followers only. Maybe they felt as Hogan felt, as a lot of Sand Creek punchers felt, but it would have never led to this if not for hunger and Hogan's hate.

It was Goff that puzzled him most. There was no sense to his malice, no reason for it. His warning to stay away from Charity had been plain enough, but nowhere near enough for this, no matter that he hadn't seen her in weeks anyway. Yet Charity was his only connection with Goff, and he felt certain that she was somehow connected with it all. What had Belle told Sanchez? That it wasn't for him that she sent

the message. Then who but Charity? So why hadn't she sent
the message?

She's dead.

The thought hit him like a club and drained the color
from his face. It made sense now; it was the only thing that
did.

Through a haze, he saw Tyson lean back, saw him sit up
again and the rifle, an old Ballard with a saddle ring, come
around, Tyson clawing at the hammer, Hogan and Slaughter
frozen, watching. Only the solid, throaty roar of the Ballard
broke his trance, clearing the haze of Charity from his mind,
the sound and muzzle flash coming as one. He fired without
thought, the recoil slamming back against the crook of his
elbow. Tyson seemed to jerk up, then flop back over his
saddle. One leg kicked, then kicked again, and straightened
slowly and was still.

Hogan and Slaughter had come to their feet, their mouths
gaping. Howard slammed another round into the chamber
with a savage motion. "Who wants to be next?" he shouted.
"Who wants to goddamn push me now?"

Neither Hogan nor Slaughter moved. In the firelight he
saw terror stark on the white plate of their faces, the sheen
of sweat there, though the wind still blew cold through the
canyon. Howard's rage slackened, then disappeared altogether. He said, "All right, go get your partner and bring
him into the light."

For a second, they hesitated, and Howard spoke sharply.
"I said bring him in."

They dragged Tyson next to the fire and Slaughter knelt
at his side, then looked up, shaking his head. His face,
Howard noted, looked white still, though working, too, jerking and jumping as if with a tic. Howard stepped in close and
looked down. He had fired blind, caught in the jumble of his
emotions, but his aim had been true. His bullet had taken
Tyson just above the vee of his half-buttoned coat, making a
fair-sized hole and spilling a lot of blood. Slaughter was still

looking at him, his eyes wet and childlike in their accusations,
and he choked out, "Jesus," and looked away.

Howard felt a knot like ice settle in his chest and spread
until everything inside seemed frozen over, solid. He let the
muzzle drop, the rifle like lead in his arms, and said thickly,
"It's over. You've earned your money. It's between me and
Goff now."

He turned and walked into the darkness, feeling their eyes
on him yet, Slaughter's like a misunderstanding pup, but
Hogan's bright with hatred.

Sand Creek lay cold and colorless under the afternoon
sun, its once muddy streets dry again, but hard, not dusty;
here and there a mudhole still lingered. There was black
smoke coming from most of the chimneys, rising some, then
flattening off, and in the north and west the sky looked gray
and pregnant. There was a high-sided farm wagon with a
four-mule hitch in front of Clark's, and farther, a buckboard
stood parallel to the street in front of the Lone Oak, its team
tethered to the tree. There were only three horses standing
at the rail in front of Goff's, though Howard knew that most
men who planned to stay awhile would take their horses to
the livery in weather like this. Looking up and down the
street, he saw no people.

He reined in at the saloon and stepped down. The wind
came up from behind and rattled the big double doors, as if
seeking entrance, then hurried on to try somewhere else. He
put his back to it until it passed, then reluctantly pulled his
revolver and checked the loads, ramming them down a last
time and checking the caps, then eased it back in the holster
and tested its pull. It came out smoothly, without resistance.
He took the duster off and tied it behind the cantle, then
slowly climbed the steps to the saloon. There were six of
them; he hadn't known that before.

With the windows shuttered and only the lamps behind
the bar lit, the big room appeared gloomy, almost desolate,

and the voices of the dozen or so men standing around the stoves seemed to echo in the cavernous space. Except for Meg sitting alone at a table, and Johnny leaning over the bar and thumbing sleepily through a newspaper, Howard saw no one he knew.

They all looked around when he entered, their faces expectant, as if the day had grown stale and the conversation old. Only Meg, taking in the raw look of the flesh below his ear and the blood-spotted side of his shirt, showed more than curiosity. She straightened and shot a worried glance over her shoulder toward Goff's office. Howard smiled and held a finger to his lips in a shushing gesture. He took a place at the bar and Johnny brought a bottle and glass and poured. "You look like you been to hell and back," Johnny said.

Howard took the glass but didn't lift it. "Charity," he said. "Where is she?"

"Upstairs." Johnny nodded toward the ceiling. "Laid up."

"What happened?"

Johnny looked at Meg, then toward Goff's office. "She was hurt," he said finally. "Hasn't been down in two weeks."

"*Johnny!*" Meg hissed.

"It's okay, Meg. Howard was bound to find out sooner or later." Goff stepped into the main room and pulled the door shut behind him. He backed into it then, putting his palms flat against the wood. His face looked pale with a quiet kind of fear, but determined, too, and he wore a new-looking Colt .45 in a fast-draw holster at his waist. He said, "Hello, Howard. I guess I've been expecting you."

Howard set the drink aside and stepped away from the bar. He let himself relax, his right hand hanging loose above the Navy's grip, his fingers flexing slowly. "Your boys quit on you, Isaac. After they finished the burying."

"I suspected they would. They were willing but lacked the experience." He staightened and took a step away from the door, a dim target in the shadows of the rear of the room, except for the white linen shirt that caught and reflected the light. "Always said a man was better off tending his own affairs," Goff said in a high, wound voice. "Guess I'd . . ." he started his draw, his hand coming up without warning, and he was fast, faster than Howard would have thought . . . "be better off . . ." Howard pulled the Navy, slapping it out of the holster and cocking on the rise. He fired from the hip, his bullet taking Goff high in the stomach, driving him back against the door, driving the wind from his lungs with an audible *whoosh.*

Goff dropped to his knees, the Colt free of its holster, but dangling toward the floor. He blinked rapidly, his face pulled tight in a grimace, and chalky, then toppled forward, pushing his hands out before him in the sawdust and digging a little trough through it. The Colt stayed in his grip, cocked but unfired.

Howard rose from a half-crouch with the Navy, the gray cloud of powder smoke heavy before him, stinging his eyes and getting in his nose. He looked toward the bar, but Johnny was standing motionless with both hands on the bar. He saw that Meg had joined the miners and drifters who had stood at the stoves, and that they had crowded against the side wall as far away from the line of fire as they could get. He saw puzzlement on their faces but nothing more. Meg stood toward the front of the crowd, looking like she wanted to scream, or cry.

Howard holstered his revolver and looked again at Johnny, then at the drink on the bar, and of a sudden he took it and downed it in three long swallows. Johnny came up slowly and uncorked the bottle. "Another?" he asked.

Howard shook his head.

"He drew first," Johnny said. "You won't have any trouble from Bronson on that."

There was a note of admiration in Johnny's voice that sickened him, and he said, harsher than he had to, "You're damn agreeable for a man who's just lost his boss, aren't you?"

Johnny shrugged. "I could never abide a woman beater."

"Woman beater?" Howard digested that information slowly, the last pieces finally coming together. "What room is she in?"

"Her own. Top of the stairs, all the way back. Last door on the left."

Howard nodded and headed for the stairs, climbing them two at a time. He found Belle and Sue at the top, leaning over the railing to stare at Goff's body sprawled in the sawdust. Belle looked up as he approached, something like relief on her face, and a small, strained smile. She said, "She's okay, Luke. She's still hurting and her ribs are still tender, but she's going to be okay."

He paused, feeling all the old doubts come crowding back, but Belle smiled and shoved him lightly down the hall, saying, "Better go. I think she's been expecting that shot."

He paused again just outside the door, then pulled his hat off and twisted the knob. Charity sat in an overstuffed easy chair, wrapped in a flannel robe that buttoned tight against her neck, and with a shawl draped over her lap. She sat twisted a little as if to favor her side, and there was a trace of puffiness to her jaw that gave her face a lopsided appearance. The flesh under one eye was swirled with a sick yellow tone, though faint and fading.

Howard paused inside the door, his hat hanging carelessly in his hand, feeling suddenly big and awkward, afraid to move. He hadn't rehearsed anything to say, and now stood tongue-tied and uncertain.

Charity rose, having to push herself up and staightened slowly. "I heard a shot," she said shakily.

Goff, he wanted to say. Isaac Goff, shot and killed for what he had done, for what he had thought Goff had done, but the words wouldn't come. What came instead was, "I reckon we ought to get married. Seems like . . . seems like we been aiming in that direction all along. Seems like we ought to go ahead and do it." He thought maybe the words surprised him as much as they did her, but spoken, he had no urge to bring them back.

Charity looked confused, her eyes were swimming in it, and for a while, for a long while, she didn't say anything, just stood looking up at him, her face asking questions and maybe his own answering, but no words spoken. Finally, taking a deep breath, she said, "Luke." She tried another breath, shallower this time, and said, "I guess maybe you're right."

CHAPTER 16

WINTER came finally, and the snow lay in a thin cover over the prairie, glistening in the sun, broken occasionally by patches of prickly pear or clumps of sage that rose from the snow like hunched old men. The air was crisp, pressing against Young's cheeks like cold steel, but the wind was down so it was bearable. The sun was packing a punch, too, turning the snow soft under its touch, slushy in spots, so that his horse's hooves was throwing up little puddles of it as they jogged toward town.

The sun and the snow gave the country a different look, Young thought; more than just covering the dusty grass with a fresh layer of moisture, it was like giving it a new beginning. And maybe it was. They had enjoyed three weeks of peace now, since that bloody day at Goff's. Hogan and Slaughter had shown up later that night with Tyson across the saddle. And there'd been hell enough raised before that, with young Doc Davis giving in to the pneumonia and lying up in Borland's like some traveling exhibit from a prehistoric age, the way they did the big bones they were always finding. It seemed the whole summer and fall had been a thing he hadn't cottoned to, what with the hangings and the shooting down on the Grant. It all had the earmarks of an untamed frontier, something you'd expect up Montana way or in the Hills, but not in Nebraska in 1876, a state for nine years already.

Still, he supposed it couldn't be helped. State or no, a man had to protect his property any way he could, and a line on a map was no deterrent to crime. Sometimes he wasn't so sure he wouldn't rather see civilization, or what passed for it, remain in the East, and keep those who needed it there, too. It seemed like anything permanent or settled brought in the vultures, the grangers, or men like Jordache, all of them ready to latch onto anything not tied down and branded as their own, with all the laws—and loopholes, when the laws didn't work for them—and smooth arguments for their rights that didn't amount to an apronful of cow chips to those who had been there first and fought to make a place permanent and settled. Times like those, maybe it was best to administer a little old-fashioned range justice, just to see if they had enough backbone to hang onto what they claimed, as those before had had to do.

Wyatt had been right, not wanting the grangers to get a foothold on the Grant, though Young wasn't sure a couple of well-placed fires wouldn't have been more efficient, at least to start with. Not that he had any proof that Wyatt was the man behind the mob, but there were rumors a man could believe if he wanted to.

And damned if when a man didn't think that the range had all the trouble it could stand, along comes Jordache and his talk of fencing the range, free range, by God, with water holes they all used from time to time, as if any man had the right to fence off more than the few acres he needed for corrals and buildings. Times were changing, it seemed, and all for the worse. The rustling first, and not just a few head like any rancher might expect, but whole damn bunches. Then the grangers and Jordache, all nipping away like coyotes on the carcass of a dead steer, and now damn if there wasn't a U.S. Marshal up nosing into the shooting on the Grant, though he'd been shy enough about the rustling.

Maybe Wyatt was right, taking the bull by the horns. Get a few more like Jordache in, or the grangers, and maybe they'd start seeing a few strands of fencing going up here and there. Wouldn't take much, thinking about it. A man's range was no larger than the water holes he controlled. With free range there wasn't much trouble, but let a man, even a dandy like Jordache, start stringing wire, and an honest rancher like himself might find himself huddling down with only a section or two.

There had been a good feeling in his breast riding out that morning, but now with the buildings of Sand Creek flanking him, he found his thoughts as dark as the mud in the street, churned fetlock-deep under the rolling wheels and plodding hooves. For all the promise of a new start, he knew there was still plenty of old trouble hanging over the Sand Creek range.

Young scraped what mud he could from his boots against the hotel steps, then paused on the veranda to light his pipe. Down the street, hitched to the rails in front of Goff's, he spotted Red's sorrel and Sanchez's paint. Harper's big bay was hitched with its ugly head drooping in front of the Frontier House. He didn't see Howard's bay or the gray horse Swede rode, though he figured they were around somewhere. It had been Ben Wyatt's word that had brought them in, asking them to wait at Goff's until the Cattlemen's Association adjourned its monthly meeting.

Wyatt was there when he entered the Nebraska bar, sharing a drink at the bar with Plumb and Leonards. Robinson sat in a leather chair with his boots stretched out before him and a drink resting on the arm of the chair, staring moodily at a spot on the floor. Jeff McKinley sat alone at a poker table next to the glass-encased gun cabinet, idly shuffling a deck of cards. He was the only hired man in the room, outside of the bartender, Tom, and probably the only hired man on the Sand Creek range who could sit there with such a look of lazy indifference, Young thought. Jordache, he noted wryly, was conspicuously absent.

"Jim," Wyatt greeted expansively. "Come and have a drink. Tom, get Jim a brandy."

Young nodded to McKinley and spoke to Robinson, falling in beside Plumb. There was a certain stiltedness to the air, a sense of melancholy, for all Wyatt's attempt at lightness. Soon enough then, perhaps sensing the mood of the room, he said, "Why don't we sit down and get the business over with first?"

They took their drinks to a table, and Plumb brought along a bottle. There was a time, Young remembered, when they had saved their drinking for after the meeting. Seated, Robinson spoke before Wyatt officially brought the meeting to order.

"I've got something to say before we begin here," he said. "This is kind of difficult to say, since we've been neighbors and friends for a hell of a long time."

Robinson paused and looked down at his hands holding the glass. Tom removed his apron and came around the end of the bar and said, "Gentlemen, I'm going to leave you to your business. If you need anything just help yourself or give a shout. I'll be in the lobby."

Robinson waited for him to leave, appearing grateful for the diversion, then cleared his throat and began. "I guess I know now how Hutchinson must have felt, leaving the way he did. But I feel I owe you more, an explanation at least." He paused, looking up and letting his gaze circle the faces at the table, then dropping it again. In his hands, his glass began to slowly spin.

Leonards said, "Go on, Owen."

"Well, being blunt, the Circle-R went under. There was a mortgage with the Sand Creek Cattlemen's Bank that Jordache somehow got his hands on."

"Jordache!"

"Apparently we underestimated the power of the Dallas Land and Livestock Company. They own stock in the Cattlemen's, and forced its hand."

"Sonofabitch," Young said under his breath. That dirty little clammy-handed vulture had struck again. It made a man feel impotent, knowing there was a company out there that big and that powerful, just sitting, waiting and watching. It made him feel almost like a child again, though the fears were real now, and not just darkness or the pop of some joint

in an old house that might be a Comanche, or pirates come
to take him off. It made him want to cuss, which he did
some, under his breath, and take another drink, though he
didn't, since Robinson was talking again.

"I was caught with my tail under the rocker and only two
ways out that I could see," Robinson said. "One was to let
Jordache get control of the Circle-R, which I didn't want to
see, or sell out to one of our own. Boys, I sold out to Ben
here. He paid off the mortgage and upped the ante enough
that I'll be able to start fresh somewhere else." He stood, his
face tight, looking around the table. "Guess I'll leave the bar
to the landowners now, but I'd be damn pleased to buy you
all a drink over to Goff's once you finish your business here."

Robinson picked up his hat and coat and walked out,
pulling the door shut gently behind him. Young poured his
drink and threw it against the back of his throat, grimacing
at its fire. He said, "Boys, I'm afraid they hung the wrong
man when they hung that old rustler. I believe Jordache is
the bigger thief."

Young stood on the boardwalk outside Goff's and thrust
his hands into his pockets. Behind him, inside, the piano
thumped in a noisy celebration of reopening. Bronson had
shut it down after Goff's death, while Frosty Johnson drew
up some management papers for Johnny and tried to locate
some next of kin. Now the crowd was large and loud, it being
a Saturday afternoon, with a lot of the hands riding in early.
He could feel the boardwalk humming under his feet, and
remembered the press of the crowd and the air heavy with
smoke and the aroma of whiskey.

He'd stayed awhile himself, drinking one with Robinson
and a couple for himself, but the levity had been too much
to handle, feeling as he did, the crowd too suffocating. He
felt a need now to be alone, so he walked back to where his
horse stood hitched at the rail in front of the Nebraska Hotel.
He grunted as he mounted, the mud sucking at his boots,

then reined the animal away. He paused in the middle of the street to button his coat and pull on a pair of calfskin gloves, eyeing Goff's as he did, or Johnny's, as some of the punchers were already starting to call it. He'd promised himself a good time tonight, on the ride in, when everything looked fresh and clean, then talked himself out of it, thinking of Jordache and the grangers and discovering Robinson gone under— Robinson, who had come up the trail with them and fought Indians with them, and blizzards and diseased cattle and a dozen other potential calamities—gone under; wiped out.

It made a man feel old, seeing someone he liked and respected so much looking so defeated, so worn out.

Behind him, at the Feed and Grain, half a dozen or so blond kids scrambled around an old wagon, playing, with a little one, a girl, he thought, wrapped in a too-big heavy coat and a scarf over her head, sitting splay-legged on the broad back of the near wheel mule. Glancing over his shoulder at them, he grimaced—he seemed to be doing that a lot, lately—and felt half inclined to ride on down and maybe tell them they weren't really wanted here, that what had happened before could happen again, if a man didn't take heed of warnings directed toward him. He didn't, though, thinking the time wasn't right for open threats, not with a god- damned U.S. Marshal in town.

He spurred his horse, wanting suddenly to be free of Sand creek and back on the prairie, wanting to recapture, if possible, some of the good feelings he had felt coming in. Yet he hadn't ridden a dozen yards when he stopped again, pulling his horse up so short it half reared, snorting and blowing and throwing mud. He felt a kind of cold shock, a sense of disbelief mixed equally with horror—no different from the time he had opened his door three years before and seen in the yard his dog dead, quilled with a dozen Sioux war arrows, left as a warning, and in the corral, his remuda gone.

That was the way he felt, seeing in Clark's window not the

stiff coils of lariats, the bits and spurs and buckles to catch a cowboy's eye and entice him inside, but instead a yellow-and-green steel-bottomed John Deere plow, and beside it, mockingly, a roll of barbed wire.

He sat loosely with his fingers numb around the reins, the cold feel of shock draining slowly, and in its place a rage that boiled in his gut, turning his vision red and watery until the lettering on the plow began to blur. He remembered that he had felt the same back then, too, kneeling beside old Shep and cursing in a low, steady monotone.

He started to dismount, changed his mind, and settled back against the cantle, his face wooden. From down the street he could hear the granger kids laughing, talking loudly in German. He drew his revolver, cocking it as he pulled it and drawing down on a line between his mount's ears. When he fired, the powder smoke billowed in a thick white cloud before him, blinding him to what his bullet had done. His horse squealed at the unexpected roar, coming up to pitch and landing spraddle-legged in the mud, trembling.

His bullet had cracked the big window in Clark's, splintering out like a child's drawing of the sun's rays, the sun a thumb-sized hole in the glass. Behind the cracked glass, a chunk of green wood was torn from the main body of the plow. He fired again then, and now the glass shattered, falling in a rainbow of reflected light that caught the sun's glare, the sound of its falling musical, but faint. This time the upper part of the letter D diappeared, flipping up and back before dropping from sight.

Clark was on the boardwalk then, his eyes wide and blazing. He was shouting but his words were lost in the ringing in Young's ears. There was a crowd gathering, too, yet hanging back, and from behind him he heard the deep, bass roar of Sam Bronson's voice.

"God's sake, Young, you gone loco?" It was Clark shouting, the words coming strong, heated. "Are you trying to kill someone? I had customers in there, goddamnit!" He jumped down into the mud and came closer, stopping abruptly with his eyes going even wider as Young turned his revolver on him.

"Hold on, Young," Bronson said, coming abreast then. He put his hand over the pearl grip of a revolver. "Put that hogleg up," he warned.

Young could feel his anger sliding away, and shame now, if not actual regret. He uncocked his revolver and slid it back into the holster, though keeping his eyes on Clark and ignoring the marshal.

Bronson came around, putting a hand against his horse's withers, his eyes taking in at a glance the shattered glass and bullet-scarred plow in the window. Looking at Young, he spoke angrily. "What are you trying to do, Mr. Young? You can't shoot up the town like some drunken cowhand."

"I'm making a public statement, Sam," Young replied, still watching Clark.

"Goddamnit, you can't shoot a goddamn window out making a statement," Clark cried.

"You pull your horns in, Clark," Bronson said sharply. He looked at Young, his face twisted with debate, then said softly, "You go on home, Mr. Young. I'll take care of this."

"Go on home? After this!" Clark flung an arm toward the window. "By God, I guess you have to be a member of the Cattlemen's Association to shoot the town up legally!"

"I won't tell you again," Bronson threatened.

Young looked at Bronson, then nodded. He turned his horse away and lifted him into a jog, his back set to the curious stares following him.

"What about my goddamn window?" Clark howled after him. "Do you know what it costs to ship glass this far out?"

Faintly then, he heard Bronson say, "Who were you trying to bait, Clark? The farmers or the ranchers?"

Toward the edge of town the ground was firmer, the footing surer, and he put his horse into a lope.

Howard knocked, then entered at her call, smiling to find her up and dressed. He removed his hat and dropped it on a chair as he walked to her. She slid into his arms, cool and soft and yielding, feeling good there, and natural in a way that surprised him.

She was up quite a bit anymore, her ribs knitting and the bruises gone completely. It was as if, after his return, she had discovered a new strength, a power to heal she had lacked before. She was quick to laugh now, too, the hard varnish of her professional life falling away in bits and pieces, revealing a woman strange to him in many ways, but one he found himself liking. It was as if she was just now beginning to fully relax with him, letting him see her as she really was, strong and capable as ever, but tender and understanding, too, and more giving than she had ever been in the past. In doing so, he thought she brought out something different in him, something new and sort of foreign, but appealing just the same. It had been a long time since he had been able to relax so completely with another.

He pushed her back a little, tipping her chin up with a crooked finger and kissing her fully, tasting a freshness that reminded him of spring. It was he who finally broke the kiss, stepping back with a troubled face that brought a quick frown to hers.

"What is it?" Charity asked.

"I just got word from the Association," he replied. "They're pulling us off the range for a spell."

She looked puzzled, but hopeful, too. "The job is over?"

He paused, wondering how much to tell her, deciding she deserved it all. "They're still worried about the rustling, Hollis and his bunch. Hollis threatened one more big drive, and that would just about put an end to a couple of these outfits."

"I heard about Robinson."

He nodded. "They want to pull us off the range and let the Hollis bunch make their gather. We'll follow, but this time we won't make any attempt to take the herd back. We'll let them go on through. We know who's behind it now. This could be our chance to end it all for good."

She caught her breath. "You're talking about a showdown. You're talking about men being shot and killed. Maybe you."

"It had to come. At least this way we'll all be together, and not caught out alone, like Doc."

"Do you think it matters how many you have with you? It only takes one bullet, Luke. Just one." Her fear for him was strong, alive in her eyes, and it touched him hard for a moment. But he had this last job to do, and no way to back from it now. "Luke." He thought she was going to argue. That old, hard, calculating looked flashed briefly into her eyes, but then she said, "You'll be careful, won't you. You'll come back to me?"

"I'll be back," he said. "Maybe a month. Maybe sooner."

Howard led the bay from the stall and tied him to a ring stapled to the wall. From the racks against the office he brought his saddle and blanket, laying the latter over the bay's back, smoothing it with his palm, then settling the saddle over the blanket. Reaching for the cinch, he saw a pair of legs step into the square of light at the livery entrance and pause there before coming on slowly. Letting the cinch hang, Howard straightened and put his hand on the Navy Colt. He saw before him a tall, well-put-together man of forty or so, solid and strong-looking, with a full mustache and thick, wavy hair beneath a new-looking cream-colored Stetson. He wore a double-breasted bright red shirt and a knee-length corduroy coat with a fur collar turned up around his ears. On the coat was pinned a United States Marshal's badge.

"You'd be Luke Howard, I understand?" the marshal said.

Howard only nodded.

"My name is Eli Leeds. I was wondering if we could talk for a minute."

"I don't have anything to tell you, Leeds, if it's the Grant Creek business you're asking about."

"I understand that you were there, that it was you and one of the Broken Axle hands that scared them off the first soddy?"

"A mistake on my part," Howard said flatly.

Leeds frowned. "By the Lord, man, you saved someone's life that night."

Howard bent and grabbed the cinch, lifting it and threading the latigo through the cinch ring.

"The grangers have as much right to the range as the cattlemen, Howard."

"I hear the Cattlemen's Association wrote the U.S. Marshal's office in Lincoln last spring when the rustling started. Was it you they sent?"

The scowl came back to the marshal's face. "I did what I could. I couldn't stay in Sand Creek all summer."

"They wore sacks over their heads, Leeds. All I could identify would be the sacks."

"You didn't recognize any of the horses? Or their brands?"

"Man I talked to had a Winchester. I recognized that quick enough."

"Lot of Winchesters out here," Leeds replied shortly.

"Let it go, Leeds. It's past now."

"No. You're wrong there, Howard. It's just starting. The Washington woman is staying, figuring to make a go of it with the kids to help, and there's another settled on down creek a ways, a Missouri grayback with half a dozen kids."

Howard laughed cruelly. "If they could raise crops like they do kids they'd do all right. But they can't. The prairie can't be farmed."

"They're doing it."

"Won't last."

"Why do you hate them so, when you risked your life to help them?"

There was no hate involved, Howard thought. Just a lack

of respect. He had done what he had to do that night on the Grant, but that didn't change his feelings any. He led the bay around the marshal, onto the street. "Anything else, Leeds?"

"Your help, if you'd give it."

He looked down the wide street, hearing the kids down there swarming over the wagon, the girl still up on the mule but crying now, and wanting down. Nearer, he saw Clark on a small ladder, nailing a piece of canvas over his shattered window. "It wouldn't make any difference even if I did."

"You can't tell."

"That's just it. I can." He stepped into the saddle, reining the bay back, away from the marshal. "You'll get no help in Sand Creek, Leeds. This is a cow town."

"Think about it, Howard. I figure you could make a difference."

Howard reined away with a sudden anger, spurring the bay. It was a fool thing to say, he thought, that one man could ever make a difference. A damn fool thing.

CHAPTER 17

THE wind funneled knifelike through the canyon, flattened the fire into coals, then moved on. Like a thousand tiny fingers it played at their collars, slipping down their necks, numbing their ears. Overhead, past the canopy of bare cottonwood limbs clattering in the wind, above the rim of the canyon, the stars twinkled like tiny bits of frost sprinkled along the dark band of the sky.

They'd been there a week now, huddled among the cottonwood and box elder and oak along what they had come to call Slaughter's Canyon, ringed by the broken maze of the badlands, and beyond by an empty and snow-patched prairie. They'd strung a canvas shelter up against the canyon's wall, piling brush around it in an effort to cut some of the wind, and then put up a crude stone wall in front of the firepit to reflect some of the heat back into the shelter, for all the good it did.

Days, they'd take the horses out to hobble on grass, bringing them in at dusk to tether on a line strung between a pair of cottonwood. From time to time one of them would go out to hunt, keeping to the badlands mostly, and out of sight, like a man riding the owlhoot. Game was scarce where they hunted, though occasionally one of them would come back with something, an antelope maybe, or rabbit. For the most part they ate what McKinley had brought with the pack horse, which was fair enough for the way they were living, beans and bacon and tins of fruit. Still, they hunted, maybe needing to get out of the canyon and away from the others as much as anything.

It seemed a crazy notion, their holing up here hours from

the Sand Creek range. Crazier even then splitting the riders, and Red wasn't surprised to learn it had been Wyatt's idea. Though he seemed mostly a competent man, sometimes he was enough to make you wonder. Some, Red knew, like Howard and Sanchez, thought it made sense, but he thought they were too far away and Hollis too smart to take the bait. They were five hours from Sand Creek, maybe seven from the Bar-W. If a cowhand from some other spread discovered a bunch missing, it might take six or eight hours to get word to Wyatt, and that much again for McKinley to get word to them. A full day and then some, as early as it was getting dark anymore, and no telling how much time between the taking and its discovery. It was chancy, he thought, and all the more so because so few knew they were even out here.

Harper stepped in from the darkness, dumping a load of firewood on the pile already there and hunkered next to the fire, grabbing the coffeepot and swearing when it burned his hand, but keeping it anyway and pouring, as if the pain was some personal challenge to be conquered. He'd been that way since they'd found Doc propped up at Borland's, sullen and hard to get along with, touchy as a fresh wound on the subject of Hollis and the rustling. He took Doc's death personally, Red thought, and maybe blamed himself for it, though Red didn't know why.

Swede was another who was touchy about Hollis, though for reasons that were easier to understand. Hollis seemed to eat on him, making him quicker to flare than even of old. Swede stayed to himself most of the time now, ignoring those who spoke to him, or answering quickly and with an edge when he did reply. Red had been about half surprised Swede had stayed with them this long; he had expected him to cut his pin early and head on back to the Hills in search of Hollis and the others, letting the rustling take the hind teat.

Inside the shelter, Howard trumped Sanchez in euchre. Sanchez smiled, his teeth flashing white in the firelight, but there was little humor in it, nor in Howard's short bark of laughter as he raked in the cartridges they were using as stakes. They played with a grim determination, long past the point when the game had been fun. Watching them through slitted lids, seeing them dance and waver in the diffused light, Red was reminded of fuses, short and ready to blow.

They were all like that now, the waiting gnawing at them, fraying their nerves until all the past infractions, every slight offense laughed off or brushed off, came back like a dog to a bone, building now into something more than it ever was, until the very air seemed to crackle with the tension.

Harper looked at Red, then Swede, sitting hunched and brooding, then said, "This is loco, by God. We're stuck up here like we was forgot, like a bunch of damn Indians."

He lapsed into a silence, waiting for someone to take it on, and Red did, as he knew he would, it being something of a ritual by now. "The whole Sand Creek range could be cleared of cattle while we squat up here. We ought to be back on the Broken Axle, together." He looked expectantly toward Sanchez.

Sanchez stirred and folded his cards to his chest. "The fewer that know we are here, the fewer to let word slip to Hollis. Myself, I think Bronson—"

"Bronson!" Harper snorted. "You and Luke have got Bronson fixed in your craw tighter than a burr. He ain't nothing but a small-time marshal biting off more than he can chew."

"He's got a fair amount of money for a small-time marshal," Howard said. "More than he ought to, without some kind of explanation."

"Lots of ways for a man to earn money without setting up a rustling operation," Harper said, laughing. "Been more than one man come west from a rich family."

Harper argued for the sake of argument, Red knew, but after Easy Street he wasn't so sure himself; he didn't think Harper was either.

Sanchez shrugged. "So maybe we are wrong about Bronson, eh? Maybe his papa owns a steamboat company. But I think we are right about the help. I think this hombre, Hollis, he has some in Sand Creek. The others, we catch. The old man, the boys on the Niobrara, the others. But Hollis, he is like the coyote, eh? Always slipping in and out when we are not there to catch him, always knowing which herd to take and what range is being worked."

"Hollis is just crafty, like a coyote. But Bronson is a town boy, buckskins or no, and he doesn't get no farther from Sand Creek than it takes to practice with those fancy pistols of his."

"Maybe," Howard said. "But Hollis's luck is too steady to be just luck. He's got help somewhere."

"What's to keep Hollis from scouting his own range?" Red said. "Or sending riders down to do it for him. Lots of strangers through Sand Creek these days."

"To the Hills," Sanchez said. "To Ogallala, yes. But on the range, there strangers would be spotted."

"So would Sam Bronson," Harper added dryly.

"What about the grangers?" Red asked, and couldn't keep his gaze from sliding toward Howard, couldn't help the satisfaction he felt, seeing Howard stiffen and look up.

"Rustling started a long time before the grangers got here," Harper said, then laughed and added, "Besides, a granger's built to follow a plow, not scout range. Most of 'em sit a saddle like they're straddling a corn cob."

"A granger's easy to blame, though," Luke put in suddenly, and Red felt his face flushing. "Alone like they are, a mob could pretty well accuse them of anything," Howard added. He stared unblinkingly, and Red matched his stare and gave it more; he was sitting cross-legged before the fire and now he put his hands on his thighs, as if he had half a notion to rise.

Harper grunted. "A man comes out here, he'd better be ready to defend himself. Could have been a lot bloodier down there if it was the Sioux come a-knocking."

"The grangers come like the spring grass," Sanchez said,

puzzled, his eyes going from Red to Howard. "Already another family has settled on the Grant, or so they are saying in town. I am not so sure they can be pushed out now."

"They're getting a hold like the damn pox," Red said vehemently. "Be crowding the range until a man can't live like God meant for him to."

Howard laughed. "Seems that's what the Sioux were saying before they got pushed north."

Howard was baiting him, Red knew, but he couldn't slow the quick boil of his temper, nor still his tongue. Hating himself for it, he rose to the bait. "The goddamn Sioux didn't use the land the way it was meant to be used. They didn't get the full benefit from it."

"Seems like that's what the grangers are saying about the ranchers," Howard said quietly.

From the shadows Swede snorted. "I knew he was a damn farmer all along."

Harper looked puzzled. "You taking the grangers' side in this, Luke?"

"Nobody sides with the grangers," Sanchez interjected. "Nor do they side with the Indians." He folded his cards and stood up. "It is late, I think it is time for the blankets, eh?"

Harper was still studying Luke, though, his face puzzled yet, but with a slow rise of resentment building in it, and Red smiled to himself.

"I don't know," Harper prodded. "Sounds to me like he was siding with the grangers. Hell, I ain't faulting the man for what he did down there, but I didn't figure he'd side with them. If that's so, I ain't so sure I want to ride with him."

"A man doesn't have to side with someone to see his point of view," Howard said.

Swede's laugh was low, contemptuous, but Harper only looked more puzzled. "I ain't so sure I see your point," Harper said.

Swede stood and picked up his bedroll. "You aren't looking

low enough, Barney," he said, turning his tight smile and cold eyes on Howard.

Howard dropped his cards on the blanket and stood. "Maybe you'd better make yourself clear before you go trotting off," he said.

Swede laughed and turned his back, slinging his bedroll over his shoulder and heading for the darkness. Swede never shared the fire at night; he always claimed the sound of their snoring was enough to attract every Indian within half a mile.

Harper was standing, too, looking more puzzled than ever, but with the resentment gone from his face. Sanchez still knelt at his bedroll, his dark eyes looking worried.

"What the hell?" Harper wondered.

Sanchez ducked his head toward his bedroll. "Maybe Hollis will make his drive after all," he said softly, to no one in particular. "Maybe we will all kill ourselves up here before someone comes, eh?"

No one said anything but Red got the sudden image of McKinley riding into the canyon with news of the rustlers or maybe just with a packhorse loaded with fresh supplies, and finding them all dead and maybe frozen, or coyote-torn, turning on themselves in the end like a pack of wolves gone rabid.

A dust devil rose and whirled down the canyon, scattering leaves and twigs and weeds torn from the scanty soil at the canyon's wall, whipping through camp, stinging their eyes with dust and ashes from the fire so that they ducked their heads into their shoulders and swore in unison. Overhead, the flat, gray sheet that was the sky moved diagonally above the canyon's rim, carrying with it the threat of snow, even loosening some now and again, fine hard grains that tapped against their hats and slickers like pieces of sand.

Sanchez sat with his back to the wind, sipping at his coffee and now and then reaching out with his tongue to lick off the droplets that clung to the straggling tips of his mustache. He guessed he was some shaggier than he had been, but then, they all were.

Harper came from up-canyon, his bay snorting and wall-eyed at the white carcass of an antelope carried over its withers. There was blood on the meat and the bay had gotten a whiff of it—blood and death—and spooked close to blowing. It was like Harper, he thought, watching him force the bay on in. It was a test of wills, his anger versus the animal's fear.

Across the fire, Luke looked up from the piñon limb he was shaving for tinder. "He's going to ruin that horse someday, pulling that kind of crap."

"My mare will spook faster at blood than she does a bear," Sanchez said.

Out a ways, Red was chopping firewood from the dead stuff Howard had dragged in the day before. He had his coat and hat off, and even with the wind blowing cold through the canyon, Sanchez could see the dark stain of sweat under his arms. Red sunk his axe into a piece of wood and straightened slowly. His gaze slid over the camp, passing Howard and settling on Sanchez. "Ain't no law says you can't help," he called. "If you could pull yourself away from the fire."

Sanchez grinned into his coffee, his eyes twinkling over the rim of the cup. "Yesterday you said the wood I cut was too long for the fire. Today I watch an expert to learn how it is done."

"Crazy bastard," Red said, and wrenched the axe from the wood and drove it into a fresh piece.

Sanchez grinned at Howard, then let the grin fade. Howard had stopped what he was doing and was staring at Red with hard, flat eyes, and Sanchez wondered again at what had come between these two who had once been friends. Whatever it was, he thought it was still eating at the both of them, and he sighed softly, thinking of it. There was no humor in the canyon any more, save for his own, and that something he was afraid to show.

Harper had his bay unsaddled and hobbled now, and came into camp with the antelope held in one hand. A small one, Sanchez saw, the carcass no bigger than a dog's, though even full grown they wouldn't go a lot bigger. Harper took a piece of firewood and forced it between the tendon and bone on the back leg, then took it to a cottonwood and hung it with the other carcasses there, antelope and deer; enough meat to last them two weeks, Sanchez thought. Coming back to the fire, Harper squatted and held his hands toward the warmth, sniffing and now and again rubbing his nose. "I keep riding north, thinking there's bound to be some buffalo left somewhere close, but I ain't seen none yet. Not even old chips. Hell, it don't stand to reason they've been all shot out around here."

"Be too much meat anyway," Luke said, glancing up at the cottonwood limb where Harper's last antelope still swung.

"Wouldn't take it all," Harper said. "Just some hump meat and ribs."

"And tongue?" Sanchez asked.

Harper made a face. "Hell with tongue. I can't stand mushy meat."

"Tongue isn't so mushy dried," Howard said. "Only when you cook it too long. I ate a sight of tongue down on the buffalo range."

Sanchez remembered his first tongue, fresh from the cow, sliced and roasted over a fire. There had been hump meat, too, and marrow melted over fry bread and boudins fresh and warm. He had been a tyke then, no more than belly high to a horse, but it was something he remembered vividly. Even now he felt the stirring of pride that had blossomed full and strong then, staring up to where his brothers sat their buffalo horses, eagle feathers and scalp locks dangling from their lances. He didn't say anything now, though. Most people couldn't see the difference between a *cibolero* and a Comanchero, and he knew what most men thought about the Comanche traders.

"I don't like tongue," Harper repeated. "But I'm sure as hell getting tired of wild meat and bacon. Like to rustle a beef myself, something don't happen before long."

Out toward the middle of the canyon Howard's bay threw its head up and nickered, his nose quivering afterward. Howard came up in one smooth motion, spilling the shavings off his lap and belting his Bowie. Sanchez rose too, and Harper with him, and faced down-canyon where the bay was watching. Behind them the sound of Red's axe halted abruptly, the echoes fading. "Speak of the devil and then he comes, eh?" Sanchez said. From around the first bend he could hear the approach of horses through the crisp fallen leaves of a grove of box elder.

Jeff McKinley came into sight first, looking wind-whipped and cold, bunched into a red plaid coat. Behind by a few paces rode the Broken Axle *patron*, Jim Young, bundled up in a bulky coat and a heavy wool scarf and looking from a distance like a wooden keg perched atop his horse. They jogged into camp without slowing, stepping down and dropping their reins.

Howard motioned toward the fire. "Coffee's hot," he said.

Young hesitated at the offer, then nodded and squatted slowly, awkwardly, like a man plagued with age and stiffness. McKinley rummaged through his saddlebags for a moment, then came over with a pint of whiskey and hunkered next to Young. "Coffee might be hot, but it won't warm you like this will," he said.

They all took coffee, rounding their cups with a splash from McKinley's bottle. Young shivered and blew through his lips, the sound like a horse's nicker, though unintentional, Sanchez thought. "There's snow in the air, boys. More than the little dab we've been getting off and on all morning. I feel a real blizzard coming on in my bones."

"Warm here, though," McKinley said. "At least not like it is on the prairie. The wind ain't so bad."

"Wind cuts here, too," Red said. "When she's blowing right." Red had put his sheepskin back on and had the collar turned up and his hat pulled tight, and still he looked cold.

Young let his gaze wander, taking in the camp, the horses grazing nearby, and the meat hanging in the tree. "Where's Swede?" he asked.

"On a scout," Howard replied. "He'll be back soon enough."

Young nodded, letting his gaze drop then, and drawing in the dirt with a piece of firewood. "They struck, like they said they would. Here," he jabbed the dirt with his limb, "where Sand Creek bends sharp to the west. Crooked Arrow range, though it's likely they've got some Lazy-L stock, and maybe some of mine. A rough estimate is two hundred head, though it could easy go two hundred and fifty." He tossed the limb aside, looking up. "They were heading north. The trail was maybe two days old when it was found. I was with Wyatt when the word came, so I thought I'd ride up here with Jeff." His eyes traveled the circle of faces. "This is it, boys. Make or break."

Howard leaned forward in the saddle, both his hands resting on the wide horn, and his hat brim pushed back flat against the crown. In the wind his eyes were watering. Behind him, their backs to the wind, Barney and Red waited with their shoulders hunched, looking miserable and cold, their horse's tails fluttering between their legs. Swede sat his gray off a ways, a toothpick wedged unmoving in the corner of his mouth; he refused to put his back to the wind, yet showed no interest in the valley below either, where Sanchez rode along the base of the ridge, leaning with the easy grace of a *charro* over the paint's shoulder, his eyes on the ground.

Beyond Sanchez, to the north, the prairie stretched bare and brown, climbing in gentle swells toward the horizon, and patched here and there with old snow from a couple of weeks past. Against the barren landscape, Sanchez and his paint were a bright splash of color, riding east for a spell, then cutting back to the west at an angle, stopping finally maybe a mile out and pulling his sombrero off and waving them on.

"He's through," Howard said, gigging the bay over the ridge and riding down at a lope. The others followed, and they all crowded in close to where Sanchez waited.

"Three days old now," the Mexican said. "Many cattle. Too many to tell for sure, but I think maybe Young was right. Two hundred head, maybe a little more."

"How many men?" Harper asked. He wiped at his nose with the sleeve of his coat, wincing as the coarse material dug at the tender flesh. He'd been sniffing and wiping ever since they'd left the canyon, and now his nose was bright red, with little watery blisters rising around the nostrils.

Sanchez looked over his shoulder, into the wind, and frowned. "The ground, she is harder this time, and the sign is not so plain, but I think maybe six."

Harper grunted. "Six, huh? Looks like the bastard found a couple more hands after all."

They struck out, riding in a loose group with their faces tucked into the collars of their coats and their hats pulled low. It put Howard in mind of the last time they had ridden north. It had been cold then, too, with a slicing rain that made the world damp and miserable, and feeling all the worse for coming so hard on the final days of summer. But this was a different cold, a deeper, more penetrating cold that didn't just work its way past the buttons and flaps of a man's clothing, but came right on through everywhere, burrowing steadily deeper. This was the real thing, with the wind from the north and the sky low and gray and threatening.

The trail was harder to follow this time, too, with no rain to soften the earth, and everything freezing. Still, the sign was there, the flattened grass and chipped earth, the patties that still showed a little color. They held a fair pace all day and holed up that night in a wooded draw, starting again at first light.

The land passed as it had before, the rustlers swinging onto the old trail after a while, as though the routs had become established, the streams and crossings and shelters known. The snow on the ground became deeper and more frequent as they rode north, but still old and patchy. The cold held without letup, the sky gray with overcast, though occasionally it would break and allow a thin shaft of cold light to strike some distant ridge, turning the land there tawny and cheerful, if only for a moment. Sometimes it snowed, hard tiny flakes slanting on the wind, stinging and popping and never lasting long or sticking.

Night seemed to fall early that day, catching them in the middle of a wide basin with no wood handy and nothing around them but rolling hills. They swung down and picketed their horses, not trusting to hobbles with the wind as a quirt, and made a small, cheerless fire from old cow chips from earlier drives. Fuel was scanty, and by the time they'd heated water for coffee they were out.

Howard spread his bedroll away from the others, close to the bay, and stretched out with his saddle for a pillow, feeling stiff and old from the cold, and half angry for it. He felt his blankets shift at his feet and looked down to see the dark bulk of the bay nudging at the top blanket, grabbing it with his teeth and jerking it back. Howard laughed and pulled the blanket away from him, but the bay was persistent, and he let him have it this time. The bay backed off a step and shook the blanket in his teeth, like a dog.

Sanchez chuckled from the shadows close by. "The bay, he feels like the colt."

"Frisky, for a fact," Howard replied, keeping the chatter from his teeth with an effort. The wind sliding over him brought him to a shiver. The bay dropped the blanket at his feet and backed away, blowing softly. He'd likely be back,

Howard thought, reaching for the blanket and pulling it over the others. The bay had his moods and sometimes wouldn't let a thing rest unless Howard spoke sharp.

"They say that in Arabia, the Indians of that country bring their horses into the tent with them," Sanchez said. "They treat them as a man here would a dog."

"Maybe," Howard said. "But I think this horse has just stored up foolishness. Day or so on the trial will take it out of him."

The wind died during the night but the cold stayed, and the air grew thick and silent. Howard came awake to the muffled sound of Harper's cursing, his head covered with blankets and his arm creating a little pocket of warmth around his face. But he could feel the cold digging at his hips and shoulders, and worming deeper, too, seeming to curl around his spine like a vine around a fence post. Suddenly, the weight of cold seemed almost real, smothering, and the air thick to breath. He threw his blankets back in a panic, still half asleep, his hand groping for the Henry and the world leaping at him, white and startling and close.

It was only snow, after all, on his blankets, and still falling in big, wet flakes that melted against his face. Around him the world was so quiet he could hear the snow striking the ground with a soft hiss. Everything was white and dull, the horizon pulled down to a hundred yards.

"If this ain't hell on a platter," Harper grumbled, stomping into his boots and glaring at the low-hanging sky. Closer, an oblong hump of snow shifted and broke, and Red poked his head out turtlelike, wide-eyed and blinking. "Sonofabitch," he said hoarsely.

Howard kicked his blankets back and pulled his boots on, the leather stiff and cold. He dug his hat from under the snow, shook it out, then clamped it on. Somehow or another a bit of snow had worked its way down his collar, melting slowly against his shoulder. He swore to himself then, swore at the snow and the buried trail that shot their plans to hell and gone.

"Pete, come on, goddamnit, you're wasting daylight," Harper growled. Then, staring again at the sky, he added grimly, "Or what will pass for daylight this day."

"Go to hell," Sanchez replied, his voice muffled some by the blankets and snow. "It's snowing out there."

Red laughed, the sound loud and unnatural in the gloom of weather and mind, the unexpectedness of it catching them all by surprise. Red laughed again, and Howard, surprising himself, joined him, and finally even Harper laughed, the strain of the last few weeks breaking away like a shell. Sometimes, Howard thought, no matter how much a man planned ahead, everything got shot all to hell without a damn thing to do about it except buckle under or push on. "This weather can't last forever," he said. "And they won't be making much time in it, either. We can just push on slow until the snow stops, then spread out and hunt for sign. Ought to be easy to find."

They saddled their horses and rode on until they found a grove of trees bordering a black ribbon of creek, then stopped and built a fire and made coffee. Sanchez had brought bacon wrapped in waxed paper that he sliced into a skillet and fried.

They pushed on afterward, keeping generally to the north. The snow fell all day, piling up in the draws, leveling the land under its cover. It finally let up sometime during the night, and they awoke to find the clouds high and broken, scattered like cotton before a breeze. The snow was dazzling in its brightness, the early sun glaring off it with a power that made a man squint. Their breath hung frosty in the air and clung to their mustaches and froze there.

They rode slowly, not daring to push over ground they couldn't see, with the holes of prairie dogs and badgers waiting like unsprung traps for the horses' legs. They chafed at the delay, ate their meals in the saddle, and pushed on into the night. By sunup the Hills rose rounded and white on the horizon, the taller peaks standing sharp against the bright blue sky, slashed with the blue-black shadings of the forests.

They pulled up and dismounted, cold and stiff and pushing their endurance. Their eyes were red from the glare of yesterday's snow and the lack of sleep, their faces drawn. The horses stood with their heads down, too tired even to paw for grass.

"Reckon this is far enough," Harper said. "We'll split up and ride a long curve, maybe five miles out, then back." He paused, as if waiting for comment, then simply crawled back in the saddle and rode off to the northeast with Red trailing. After a moment's hesitation, Swede followed.

Howard watched them climb an easy ridge, pause at the top, then drop from sight. He dug into his saddlebags and brought out a couple of strips of jerked beef, tossing one to Sanchez and working a piece off the second for himself.

Sanchez held the jerky in the corner of his mouth like a flattened cigarette, sucking on it and letting it soften. "You and Red," he said quietly, looking toward the blue shadows of the Hills. "I remember a time when you and he were like one. Now you grunt and growl at one another like dogs, and he teams with Barney and Swede when there is a need to team." He held his reins laced through the fingers of his hand, and began to idly flip the ends with his thumb.

Howard thought of the first time he had ridden into Sand Creek and the little start of recognition on Red's face, and his own pleasure. He remembered the buffalo range along the Canadian and the Cimarron, and the good times they had shared at the hide towns, and later, at the end of the season, in Dodge. There had been some wild times back then when they were both a little younger, a little wilder. Yet even now, with everything far in the past, the torchlight still flickered in his mind. It was funny in a way, but when he thought of that night anymore, it wasn't George Shatner that he thought of, nor Simon Washington. It was Red he saw in his mind's eye, sitting among the nightriders with the sack over his head as white as any sun-bleached skull.

He shook himself back to the Dakotas then, shook away the lethargy of his mind, and stepped into the saddle. "Times change," was all he said.

Sanchez nodded, willing to let it drop, Howard thought, and maybe wishing he had never brought it up. He swung onto the paint and they turned toward the southwest, following the curving lip of a draw.

They rode silently, feeling the land rise and fall beneath the horses, and the crunch of new snow and the cold creak of saddle leather. They spotted a coyote once, trotting along a far ridge with his nose to the surface of the snow, and around them the tiny prints of mice and birds. The sky was a wide, blue bowl empty of clouds.

They rode for an hour or more, stopping finally on a low rise and scanning the country around them. "I don't see a damn thing," Howard said. "Guess we may as well start back and see what the others have found."

Sanchez leaned forward, his gaze to the northwest, where a grove of bare-limbed cottonwoods stood guard at the mouth of a small valley.

"See something?" Howard asked.

"Broken snow," Sanchez replied, sitting back. "One trail leaving. I think maybe someone camped there, then left after the snow quit."

Howard looked again, but saw only the glare of sun and snow. "Cattle?" he asked, but Sanchez only shrugged.

They rode down with their rifles out, coming into the grove at a walk, their eyes sharp on the hills around them. The black ashes of a cold fire stared unwinkingly at the sky, and peeled cottonwood limbs laid where a dozen or so horses had stood tethered. The snow around the grove was trampled, and there was a pile of unused firewood close to the ashes. Howard rode to the northern edge of the trees and sat with his rifle across his saddle, staring at the single line of tracks that disappeared around the nearest bend. Sanchez dismounted close to the old fire and dropped his reins, wandering slowly through the camp. When he had finished he joined Howard, his face tight, worried.

"Those tracks lead out single file, Injun style," Howard said, nodding toward the trail.

"*Si,*" Sanchez replied, sounding tired now. "Maybe a dozen. Maybe fifteen."

"Sioux?"

"This I cannot say. They travel light and leave little except their tracks." He looked at Howard. "But there were no women, no lodges."

"How old?"

Sanchez seemed puzzled. "The fire, this has not burned since last night, but the tracks, the water marks, the cottonwood bark they fed their horses, these are not so old. This morning, maybe."

"Couple of hours?" Howard's grip tightened on the Henry. "They wouldn't sit the night without a fire without reason." He paused, shook his head, and said, "Damn, we've got to follow."

"Follow?" Sanchez suddenly looked scared. "We do not come to fight the Indian, Luke. We come to fight the rustler, the man called Hollis." His nostrils flared a little. "You do not fight the Indian," he said quietly. "You just die, slow, with your eyes burned out and the red ants crawling in your ears before you are dead."

The fear in Sanchez was big and close to unmanageable. He came from Apache country, Howard knew, and had likely seen their work, or what was left of it. He said, "Pete, they're after someone. That's the only reason that makes sense for putting a fire out so early. If it's Hollis's boys and the cattle, they've likely got a spot already picked out to hit them."

"If they have attacked already, we are too late."

"We'd have heard gunfire, the weather like it is. More than

likely they're waiting in ambush now. We get there first, maybe we can do something about it."

"Two guns against twelve?"

"They're white men, damnit."

"They are rustlers. Likely we kill them anyway."

Howard stared at the trail, torn between Sanchez's arguments and the thought of the rustlers, outlaws or not, riding into a trap.

He thought too, strangely, of the ranchers trying to hold their land against the grangers, and the Indians trying to hold theirs against everyone, ranchers and grangers and miners and hide hunters and the railroads, all of them pushing deeper, taking more, and being pushed in turn by those who came later.

Yet it was different with the Indians, or so he argued with himself. Not that the land would be put to better use, but that it seemed there should be enough for all. He knew that wasn't true either; knew that, eventually, there would never be enough. The buffalo were already gone from Nebraska, or close enough to it that the few left really didn't matter, and those up Montana way, or in Wyoming or the Dakotas, were thinning before a man's eyes. And the ranchers were crowding in almost before they were gone, with towns following, and surely the grangers not far behind.

He wouldn't blame the Indians, in a way, though it wasn't a sympathy he'd want to voice where too many could hear him. Maybe someone who'd lost his wife and children to a raid, or come back to camp to find his partners scalped and butchered and everything he owned either carted off or destroyed. Yet in the same breath, how could he blame the ranchers for wanting to hold onto what they had against the grangers, with no more real claim to the land than the Indians had, and maybe less, for all the buildings they had put up, or the windmills they raised?

It was an enigma, all right, and enough to leave a thinking man confused, the right and wrong of it all, until you just had to push the whole thing from your mind and concentrate solely on what was before your nose. It didn't matter why the ranchers wanted the grangers pushed on to become someone else's worry, or, really, why they trailed the rustlers. There was a basic right or wrong to every situation, and for him, enough troubled conscience to make him meddle where he knew he had no rightful place to be.

He glanced quickly toward Sanchez, wondering if he ever felt regret, or guilt. Did the old man, or the boys on the Niobrara, ever come back to haunt his dreams, to wake him in a shivering sweat with the image so vivid, so real, it took a minute to realize it was all only a dream after all?

"I'm going on, Pete. I've got to try." He gigged the bay into a walk, and kept the Henry unbooted. After a while, he heard the crunch of Sanchez's mare coming through the snow, and breathed easier for it. Sanchez was a steady hand, but the Indian fear in him was strong, that generations-old fear of the Apache's hatred toward the Mexican. Seeing it so plain in Sanchez's face back at the cottonwoods, Howard wondered if maybe it would be strong enough to turn him back.

They followed a narrow valley for a good bit, then crossed a low hump with a ridge climbing from it, leading off to the west and cut with deep coulees that trailed to the north, petering out at the edge of a wide basin. The Indian trail led down below the southern rim of the ridge, toward the Hills that rose high before them now, only a few hours away. They rode slowly, the horses kicking up a white powder that glistened in the midday sun and rolled back in their tracks afterward. A hundred yards farther, the trail branched, with maybe three or four riders veering off to the north, into the first of the coulees. Howard pulled the bay to a stop and let Sanchez come up beside him. The cold air felt suddenly thick in his lungs, the fear alive in him too, and clawing to break out.

Sanchez's eyes were darting like a rabbit's under the

shadow of the hawk. "Luke, *Madre Dios*. The basin, she is empty. I look for the tracks as we came over the hump and there was none!"

Ahead by some fifty yards a second set of tracks branched off and passed over the ridge. Faintly then, but clear in the cold air, he heard the distant pop of a whip and the angry bellow of a steer.

Madre Dios," Sanchez repeated, and made the sign of the cross. "We are too late, Luke. Too late!"

"Maybe not," Howard replied grimly. He slid from the saddle and tossed his reins to Sanchez. He plowed up the slope as quickly as possible, sinking almost to his knees in the soft powder, dropping to crawl the last few feet on his belly, and feeling his breath catch in his throat at the sight spread below him.

The cattle were coming in from the east, curving across the basin like a short, blunt snake, black and rippling against the snow and distance. There were only a handful of men with them, a pair of point men, a pair of flankers, and two riding drag, all with their hands full. They were still a mile or more away and intent on their work, but bearing toward the ridge with its deadly coulees. Their cries came faintly on the breeze now, mixed with the lowing of cattle pushed and the sharp crack and pop of whips and quirts.

Closer, no more than a quarter of a mile away and hidden deep within the coulee, the Indians waited silently. There were four in this group, Sioux from their looks, riding a pair of bays and a couple of paints, the horses shaggy with their winter coats, hammerheaded and thin, but iron-tough likely, small and fleet. The warriors were all young, eager, from the way they sat their horses, but looking somehow old and time-worn, too, like men too long on the run. One last flicker of the flame, Howard thought, before the fire went out.

Their bare skin gleamed like copper in the sun, layered with a sort of film that might have been bear grease, and streaked with yellow and black paints across their faces and chests. They wore leggings and breechcloths, and one of the riders on a bay had on a yellow war shirt. They all carried rifles, and the one in the shirt had a short bow and quiver of arrows slung across his back.

To the west, Howard could see the bunched movement in the second coulee, though he couldn't make out their horses or the number of warriors that waited there.

The cattle came on, the rustlers taking a false security in the Hills looming so close now, pushing straight into the trap. Behind him, he heard the soft nicker of Sanchez's mare, and the quick snap of the bit as Sanchez jerked at her mouth. The cattle surged closer. Time slipped quickly through his fingers as he discarded ideas. Sanchez's words came back to haunt him. *"Two against twelve?"*

Below him, the warrior in the hide shirt suddenly looked over his shoulder, his gaze climbing the draw until it met Howard's. It was as if he sensed Howard's presence, the danger behind him. There was no time to think then, no time to sort through the tangle of his thoughts for a plan that sounded best. The warrior's eyes were already widening, his mouth opening in warning, when Howard raised his Henry and fired, the sharp bark of the rifle cracking flatly over the frozen world. The warrior in the hide shirt yelled, the yell breaking off into a series of short yips. Howard fired again, saw the spurt of snow kicked up twenty feet short of the grouped Sioux, saw the milling cattle and the rustlers drawing their weapons and staring uncertainly toward the ridge, and took time for no more.

He whirled and came barreling down the southern slope, the snow clutching at his chaps, hampering his movements. Sanchez's paint reared and lunged as Howard raced up, and Sanchez dropped the bay's reins, fighting his horse around. Howard grabbed the reins on the run and swung into the saddle without touching the stirrups, wheeling after Sanchez and spurring for the hump, and the valley beyond. From over the ridge, though out of sight now, he could hear the shrill echo of war cries and an answering volley of gunfire.

Howard turned in the saddle as they crossed the hump, not slowing any but wanting a look nevertheless. All he saw was the first bunch of warriors, whipping their horses through the wind-thinned snow along the top of the ridge, their faces twisted with cries of rage for the two men who had spoiled their ambush.

CHAPTER 18

THE fire was a tiny spark of orange among the blue shadows, flickering in the breeze. The snow was deeper here in the foothills, drifting almost stirrup-deep in places, though soft and powdery yet.

Above and to the west the Hills rose abruptly, topped with a reddish golden crown of fading sunlight, and black along the eastern slopes; black out on the prairie, too, with their trail lost in the shadows.

"They're gone," Howard said hoarsely. "Probably quit hours ago."

Sanchez grunted a reply, looking toward the fire and the hulking shape of the man standing before it, peering toward them, seeing them, but not recognizing them yet. "I think maybe a man would be foolish to camp by a fire this night," Sanchez said. "Maybe foolish to camp at all."

"Maybe," Howard agreed, although he wasn't so sure he could push through another night without letup. They had already been in the saddle for thirty-six hours, with not much rest before that. The bay was beginning to stagger some on the grades, sapped by the snow and the cold as much as any lack of rest. Still, pushing on for a ways wouldn't be a bad idea, he thought. No telling how determined an angry redskin could be, or how far a man could see a fire after dark.

They rode on into the trees, calling out as they approached, and reining up just inside the pulsating circle of light. Harper grunted wearily and said, "Fall off and have some coffee—before you fall off, period."

They dismounted and loosened their cinches but kept the

saddles in place. Howard rummaged through his saddlebags for his cup, then squatted stiffly before the fire.

Swede laughed a short, humorless laugh and said, "You two look like hell. Did you get lost?"

"Sioux," Howard said, and let the single word settle over the camp.

Red sat up in his bedroll, and Harper walked to the edge of the firelight, staring along their backtrail. "How many?" he asked, his voice edged.

"Twelve, maybe, or more," Sanchez said. "But only a few followed us. Their ponies were thin and tired, and they are far behind us now, but who knows if they come on." He paused, sipped at his coffee, and added, "Who knows what the Indian ever does."

"We covered a sight of country today," Howard said. "Wanted to throw them off our trail without letting them know where we were headed, though I guess they'll figure the Hills, at one point or another."

"Son of a goddamn bitch," Harper said, spacing the words for emphasis. "Just when things were starting to look up again."

"We found the trail this afternoon," Red said. He was up now, and dressed. "About a mile south of here, and moving like hell."

Sanchez said, "It is good to know they made it." He looked at Howard, nodding. "Good to know you did not risk your scalp for nothing, eh?"

The others waited expectantly, but Sanchez said no more. Harper came back to the fire carrying what was left of the bacon they had fried the morning of the snow. "Reckon we can hear your story later," he said. "Why don't you two finish this while the rest of us saddle our horses. I figure there's been more men to go under by arrow than lack of sleep."

They rode until midnight, pushed ever deeper into the Hills, stopping finally with the trail still clear before them, and fresh too, but with the long hours in the saddle finally taking their toll. "We'll rest a spell here," Harper said, halting next to a fast creek that wound out of an aspen grove. "My horse is about done in."

"Looks like Hollis's bunch pushed on," Red said.

"They ain't been pushing like we have," Harper snapped. He swung down and led his gelding into the trees. The others followed slowly, pulling their saddles off and hobbling their horses. They rolled into their blankets, too tired to feel the cold, and rolled out again at dawn, clumsy with chill, feeling as tired as they had at midnight. They made a fire and fixed coffee for its warmth, and ate lightly of trail food, jerky and hardtack, and afterward climbed reluctantly into their saddles.

There was a slim crust on the snow now, nothing to bother the horses, but loud and advertising. They came, after a while, to the Ogallala and Black Hills road, and turned north on it, the trail old again but still clear.

Traffic was light after the fall's exodus, and in an hour they passed only two freight outfits, traveling together and heading south. When the trail branched off to follow the Easy Street fork, they took it without surprise. It was only when the trail left the road and cut back sharply to the north that they finally halted.

"Reckon they won't be much farther," Harper said, loosening the thong over the hammer of his Colt.

Luke pulled his Henry and levered a shell into the chamber, taking a kind of comfort in the quick, metallic sound of it. He felt the old, familiar tightening of his muscles, the keen edge of anticipation.

The trail drove straight into the timber, spreading some as it did, the cattle probably balking and having to be pushed through. The ground climbed for a ways, up and to both sides. They came to a little notch like the rear sight of a rifle, with the trail dropping down the far side and the timber opening ahead. It revealed a long, wide valley flanked with timber, a tilted shack on the near side with a small corral behind it, and the cattle beyond that, spread out and bedded down. A pair of riders sat their horses close to the herd.

They fanned out just beyond the forest, halting again to study the shack. There was a creek beside it, narrow but fast, coming out of the mountains somewhere on their left, and a lone pine towering over it maybe fifty feet from the front of the shack, with a pile of firewood against its trunk. A thin curl of smoke drifted from the mud-chinked stone chimney, and there were horses standing quietly in the corner of the corral.

Howard's palm was damp with sweat, even in the cold, and he kept wiping it against his coat, feeling the tension building. Their horses shifted impatiently, nervously, stamping their feet, and finally Sanchez's mare nickered, as one of them had to do before too long, the sound creating a sudden flurry of movement behind the thin cloth that served as a curtain.

The door cracked after a while, then opened fully, and Hollis stepped out, his coat open, with Bishop following. There was a Winchester in Bishop's hand, but he had replaced the poncho with a knee-length coat made of buffalo. He sauntered to the far end of the porch and put a foot up on a chopping block there, balancing the Winchester across his knee. At the edge of the porch Hollis raised his hand in a greeting of sorts, and motioned them in.

"Couple of you stay back," Harper ordered, lifting his reins.

"Hold it," Swede said sharply, and Harper halted, surprised. "Hollis is mine," Swede said, letting his gaze rake them all. "Anyone tries to cut in on me, and I'll kill them."

Harper's face turned red. "Damnit, this isn't the time for a personal vendetta."

"Hollis is mine," Swede repeated, and lifted his gray to a jog, brushing past Harper, forcing the bay aside.

Harper swore and followed, with Howard close behind.

Swede rode to a spot maybe halfway between the lone pine and the shack and halted; Harper and Howard flanked him.

Hollis brushed his coat back, behind the butt of his revolver, and left his hand there. "Truth to tell, I kind of figured you'd show up," Hollis said to Harper. "The snow was bad luck." He looked at Swede then, and smiled. "You're a hard man to kill, Swede. I'll do better next time."

Swede didn't reply. He let his reins drop over the gray's neck and sat loosely in his saddle, his hands on his thighs and close to his revolvers. His stare was cold and unyielding, and in time, began to have its effect.

Hollis licked his lips and turned back to Harper. "Too bad you didn't throw in with me. Winter being what it is, I look to make a small fortune off this herd."

"Who killed Doc?" Harper asked.

"Doc?"

"The kid. Who killed him, Hollis? You?"

Hollis shrugged. "It's a rough land, Harper. Lots of people turn up dead for one reason or another. Maybe your friend Doc got in someone's way. Who knows?"

"You do, I'd guess," Harper said flatly. "You want to come in peaceable? Take your chances with a jury trial?"

Hollis smiled and shook his head. "I don't think so."

"Didn't figure you would, but the Cattlemen's Association wanted me to ask, polite-like, before we started shooting."

There was a stirring behind the cloth over the window, and small parting, and the double-barreled muzzle of a shotgun slid into view—just the tip of it, like a nubbin.

Howard looked at the others, then sidepassed the bay to the right, coming even with the edge of the shack. Harper moved an equal distance to the left. Bishop straightened at their moves, his rifle coming around toward Howard, though he kept his boot on the block and the rifle on his knee. Howard tipped the muzzle of the Henry up toward Bishop, though the move seemed innocent enough, an accident of his shifting horse. Only Swede remained unchanged, his gaze still working on Hollis, and now Hollis kept sliding a look toward Swede, then quickly away.

"Why don't you all just hold steady there," Hollis commanded, but there was a strain in his voice, a crack in his confidence.

"How many have you got holed up in that shack?" Harper asked.

"No one. Just me and Bishop here, and a couple of the new boys with the herd. Rest are in town."

"That shotgun ain't hanging by a thread, goddamnit," Harper said.

Hollis looked over his shoulder, then chuckled. "Might've missed one or two at that," he said, and then his voice hardened. "Why the hell didn't you stay in the badlands, where you belonged?"

Harper smiled thinly. "Like you said, ol' hoss, just plain bad luck."

Hollis took a swift, unexpected step backward, lifting his revolver. The shotgun roared before anyone cleared leather, and Harper's bay shuddered and seemed to draw into itself, the front legs giving as though turned to water. Luke swung the Henry on Bishop while Bishop lifted the Winchester, and they both fired at the same time. Bishop cried out and twisted away, dropping the Winchester and clutching at his thigh. Howard's bay squealed and reared at the bite of Bishop's bullet across his withers, lunging against the reins so that Howard's next shot went wide.

He wasn't really sure what happened after that. Separate incidents seemed frozen in his mind, but there was no order to them, nor coherence; afterward, he wasn't absolutely sure he had even seen all that he remembered. He remembered Hollis lunging for the door, the wood around him splintering under the impact of bullets, and Harper crouched behind the wood pile under the lone pine with his Colt leveled on the shack. Swede was there, too, crouched low and firing methodically with both revolvers, and Bishop on the porch, lurching unsteadily toward the door; then in the next instant, sprawled across the porch with one arm curled around the door's frame.

Then the bay, lunging yet, took Howard past the edge of the shack, almost to the corral before he could turn him. He levered another round into the Henry and set his spurs into the bay's flank just as another flurry of shots exploded from the front of the shack. He heard a scream, the sound of splintering furniture, and the squeal of a horse from the timber, Red's maybe, or Pete's. Then the rear door flew open and Hollis stumbled out, his shirt bloody under the flapping coat. Howard pulled the bay up, bringing him around as Hollis lifted his revolver, and fired from the hip, the Henry bucking back against Luke's thigh.

Hollis fell backward, his feet kicking up high, and he landed sitting, spraddle-legged, with his chin resting on his chest. Howard jacked another round into the chamber. Hollis looked up slowly, his eyes starting to glaze, then looked down at his revolver, half-buried in the snow next to his knees. He leaned for it, fumbled with the butt, then swayed back, bringing it out of the snow.

"Hollis, don't," Howard said tightly. Behind him, from the far end of the valley, he could hear the pounding of hooves, and knew it was the men left to watch the cattle coming on at a run.

Hollis brought the revolver up, the muzzle wavering, his thumb straining at the hammer. His face was twisted with the effort. The hammer came all the way back with a series of cold clicks, the sounds loud in Howard's ears. Howard's finger tightened on the Henry's trigger.

"*Hollis!*"

It was Swede, standing at the corner of the shack with his revolvers holstered. "On me, Hollis. Turn it on me."

Hollis's lips peeled back and a sound almost animal-like broke from his lips. He brought the revolver around slowly, the muzzle steadying some, swinging to a line on Swede's chest. Close now, Howard could hear the drumming of hooves, but he couldn't turn away from the scene before him; he seemed caught there, as helpless as a fly caught in a spider's web. When Hollis's revolver finally stopped, Swede drew, pulling his right-hand gun and snapping a shot from the hip.

Hollis flopped back, his revolver dipping toward the snow. When he fired it was the result of a spasm, the bullet kicking up a small white geyser close to his boot.

Howard swung from the saddle and dropped to one knee, leveling the Henry and firing rapidly at the approaching rustlers. Under the Henry's fire, they swung in a tight hook and spurred toward the far end of the valley without having fired a shot.

Howard rose and turned, finding Swede watching him as he punched the spent shells from his revolver and reloaded. "Piss-poor shooting," Swede said, and mocked a smile. "They were easy targets."

Howard looked at Hollis and felt his stomach tighten. Hollis's legs were still twitching in the snow, but slowing some as death took over. The snow around his chest was splashed with blood, an obscene crimson against virginal white.

Swede holstered his right-hand gun and drew the left, repeating the loading procedure. "Could have been you, you know," he said, nodding at Hollis. "I meant what I said when I said I'd kill the man who interfered with my killing Hollis. That bastard was mine."

"You're a hard-core sonofabitch, aren't you, Swede?"

Swede stopped what he was doing and for a moment just stared, debating, maybe, whether to let the words slide on past or push them. In the end, though, he just turned away.

Howard took the bay's reins and led him around the front of the shack, keeping the rifle handy just in case, but not expecting to use it.

Red was on the porch, his big Peacemaker already holstered, and Swede was mounting his gray. In the saddle,

Swede turned toward the end of the valley, and Red called, "Whoa, Swede, where you headed?"

Swede paused, looking at Howard. "Ol' Deadeye there let a couple get away," he said. "I'm going after them."

"Hell, let them go," Red said. "We got the main bunch. It's over now."

Swede looked at Red with obvious contempt. "Two got away. It won't be over until they're dead."

"You could bring them in," Howard suggested.

Swede just looked at him, then lifted the gray into a trot, skirting the corral and riding toward the far end of the valley.

Howard watched him go. The Henry felt clumsy in his hands, so heavy he didn't think he could boot it, and Red's words seemed muffled through the ringing in his ears, so that it took him a moment to catch their meaning. "We'd better get out there. Barney and Pete are hit."

Howard swore, letting the reins drop, and the Henry, running awkwardly through the snow with Red coming up behind. They got to Barney first, still crouched over the wood pile with his Colt gripped loosely in his hand. Red pulled at his shoulder and he fell back, sprawling in the snow. There was a neat, round hole in his forehead, just above the vee of his brows, puckered red and still oozing. The skull around the wound was concaved. Red took the Colt and uncocked it and laid it on Harper's chest, while Howard rushed on to Sanchez.

Sanchez lay on his back at the edge of the timber with one arm thrown out and the other plucking listlessly at the front of his shirt, his fingers red and slick. His sombrero rested on its crown some distance away.

Howard knelt beside him, nudging his coat back and working quickly, if gently, at the buttons of his shirt. There was a rattling in Sanchez's chest, and a pinkish froth bubbling at the corner of his mouth. Howard said, "Pete, are you okay? Can you hear me?"

Sanchez's eyes fluttered, then opened, glazed some, and rolling. It was with obvious effort that he brought them to focus on Howard. "Amigo," he greeted weakly, his smile as fleeting as the turning of a leaf in a passing breeze. "We did it, eh? We stopped the rustling for good this time?"

"Seems like it," Howard replied.

"Bueno," he whispered. "That is good. Now it is over." He coughed suddenly, the rattling in his chest increasing, becoming loud, then tapering off with the cough. "Whewee," he grinned, and closed his eyes against the pain. "That hurts down to a man's *cojones.*"

Howard pulled the shirt back from the brown flesh of Sanchez's chest, wincing at the sight. There was a single hole, low in the chest and just to the side of the breastbone, though high enough to nick a lung. There wasn't a lot of blood, just a splotch above the wound and smeared some by his fingers, but his belly was already distended, the bleeding all on the inside.

Red came up, and Luke spoke without turning. "We need bandages, medicine, whatever you can find," Red took off without comment, leaving them alone again.

Sanchez said, "Luke, what do you do with the bandages, eh? Are you hurt?"

"Shut up, you goddam bean-eater."

Sanchez chuckled, but gently, not wanting to bring on another coughing fit. "We did good here this day, I am thinking, but maybe we would not have done so well without Swede. He is a little crazy, I think, but he is very good with the pistol."

"Forget Swede. He's gone."

"Gone up here, eh?" He tried to touch his forehead but couldn't seem to find the strength. He rested for a while, his eyes closed, then said, "The filly at Sand Creek. Have you put your brand on her yet?"

"Save your strength, Pete."

Sanchez smile, then choked and coughed, the froth coming thicker now, and with it a thin stream of blood that ran down the side of his face and into his hair. "Wheweeoo." He let it out like a long sigh, panting afterward, until he caught his breath. "It is funny, the things a man thinks of, is it not," he said then. "Remember the aspen, so pretty and gold in the fall, and the way the buffalo ran once, when I was young and full of piss and vinegar." He looked at Howard, his face puzzled. "Why is it, my friend, that a man forgets how blue the sky can be, or that there are strange animals in the clouds? How is it that a man looks, and often does not see?"

Howard pulled his shirt together, the coat over the shirt. His face felt tight, and there was a hard ball of something unfamiliar caught in his throat, so that for a moment, he didn't trust himself to speak. He looked up to where a camp robber jay flitted along the edge of the forest, lighting now and again on boughs heavy with snow, his sharp trill driving deep in a man if he'd just let it. It was true enough, what Sanchez said, but nothing to be done about it. That was life, and after life came death, and who knew what beyond.

He heard Red coming, the crunch of his boots in the snow, and the sudden silence that filled the spot of Sanchez's breathing. Howard looked down and blinked. Sanchez's eyes were closed, his face relaxed and peaceful, the smile staying naturally to his lips.

CHAPTER 19

IT took a while to chop shallow graves in the half-frozen earth and haul the rocks up from the creek to top them with. It was just dark when they finished, the stars winking into place and the moon coming up bright through the shifting pines. They stood between the graves of Harper and Sanchez afterward, while the wind plucked at their faces and dried the film of perspiration there. For a while, Red fumbled with putting some words together, something remembered from Doc's service, but it seemed out of place here, unnatural and unneeded, and after a bit he gave it up.

Later, while Red brought the cattle in closer to the shack and saw to the horses, Luke knocked the ashes down in the fireplace and built a fresh blaze. There were quite a few supplies in the shack, flour and coffee and a burlap bag of wrinkled potatoes, and even some airtights of tomatoes and peaches and such. There was a side of fresh beef hanging from an outside rafter behind the shack, and Howard fried some of that, and some potatoes and biscuits. Afterward, with the fire banked and a lamp casting its warm, yellow light, they sat with their backs against the wall and smoked and drank coffee while their muscles relaxed and settled and the cold crept out. The cattle kept up a restless lowing, too tired to bed down.

"Barney was a good man," Red said suddenly, and Howard thought his voice sounded small in the long silence that had drifted over the cabin. "Quick to prod sometimes, but steady. Rode for the brand, too, by God."

Howard didn't reply. He felt sleepy now, lethargic, the way he always did after a fight, and only wanted to finish his

286

cheroot and coffee and roll up in his blankets. Yet Red
wanted to talk, perhaps needed to talk, to clear his conscience
of the men they had killed here today. There was none of
the old animosity in his words, and thinking about that,
Howard discovered that his own anger had disappeared. It
was as if that night on the Grant had been pushed aside in
the wake of all that had happened.

"Barney was an orphan," Red said then. "No family that
he knew of. What about Pete?"

After a pause, Howard shook his head. "None that he
spoke of."

"We've got a lot of gear stacked up here. Too much to haul
back to Sand Creek. How about if I take what we don't want
into Easy Street tomorrow and sell it? We can split the money
between us."

"Fair enough," Howard agreed, then added, "But I want
to keep Pete's little paint. He was fond of that horse, and I
thought I'd make her a brood mare."

"Sure," Red said. "Pete would like that."

Likely he would, Howard thought, and rose suddenly, with
his bedroll. "Reckon I'll sleep outside," he said, knowing Red
could see through him, but not caring anymore. "It seems
hot in here," he finished lamely.

"Sure," Red said. "Sure." But if he said any more, Howard
closed the door on his words.

They left the day after, forcing the cattle back through the
notch and following the road after that, down out of the
Hills and across the white, rolling prairie, pulling off now
and again to let a freight outfit roll past, or a stage.

The cattle settled into the drive readily enough, taking
their places in the herd in the morning and keeping it all
day, while Howard and Red rode at the fringes and nudged
them toward their home range. The horses, Sanchez's paint
and a gray mare Dutchy had ridden, and Hollis's black that
Red had taken a shine to, followed on their own, maybe

preferring the company of men and cattle to the loneliness of the plains.

The weather held for them, the sky deep and blue and ragged with clouds, and the snow crusting at night, but melting a little more each day, until by the end of the week there were pieces of brown earth peeking through on the southern slopes.

It took a while, though, with the snow hampering and the herd large for just two men, but on the eighth day after leaving the valley in the Hills, they pushed the cattle off the road and into a herd of Bar-W beef grazing on the ridges where the snow had blown clear. They pulled up together, Howard and Red, and watched the cattle mix and spread, the extra horses stopping nearby, nipping playfully at each other and kicking up their heels, maybe knowing that they were almost there.

"Close enough," Red said wearily. "They can cut their own brands out at spring roundup."

Red turned his sorrel away, but Howard remained where he was, staring at the cattle while everything fell into place. It was all so simple, so clear and easy to see, that for a second he wasn't sure he really believed it himself.

Red pulled up and looked over his shoulder. "You coming?" he called.

"I'll be damned," Howard said softly. "Under our noses all along, but too damn close to rope."

Red came back, his face puzzled. "What the hell are you talking about?"

"The cattle, damnit. Look at them and tell me the difference between the two herds, the one we brought back and the one already here."

Red looked without seeing, and Howard pushed on, an edge of excitement to his words now. "Crooked Arrow and Lazy-L stock. The last bunch, too. Crooked Arrow and Lazy-L and some Broken Axle and Circle-R stock."

"So? Cattle mix on the range."

"Damnit, Red, can't you see it? The Bar-W and Lazy-L lie closest to the Hills. The Broken Axle and Circle-R are way the hell and gone on the far side of the range. So why isn't there any Bar-W beef in the bunches we've brought back?"

"Hell, rustlers ain't choosy. They'll take what they find and push like hell. Besides, the old man had Bar-W stock. So did those boys on the Niobrara."

"The old man and the boys weren't working for Hollis. The old man wasn't even pushing for the Hills. They were just Johnny-come-latelies." He looked at the cattle and shook his head. "Hell, it wasn't Bronson we were after. It was Ben Wyatt."

"Whoa, there, Luke. You're accusing the man who hired us."

"I'm accusing the only man who hasn't suffered from the rustling this summer," Howard answered. "I'm accusing the man who split us up to where we almost lost that last bunch, then put us way the hell up in the badlands while this bunch was taken. Damnit, Red, Wyatt should have suffered worse than anyone. His is the largest herd on Sand Creek range, and closest to the Hills."

"It was McKinley brought us word this last time," Red said, but uncertainly. He was studying the cattle again, and seeing them in a different light.

"Young was there, too, remember? And you heard what Hollis said. Asking us why we didn't stay in the badlands. Hell, Bronson didn't even know where we were that last time, but Ben Wyatt did. Him and only a few others."

"Wyatt," Red said quietly.

Wyatt, Howard repeated in his mind. It was like throwing a broken bottle into the air and having it all come down in one piece. His mind went back over the bunches they'd trailed, bunches lost and others recovered, and Hollis's words ringing sharp in the cold air, *"Why didn't you stay in the badlands, where you belonged?"* and none of it making much sense until you remembered that Wyatt had bought out the Circle-R.

It was dusk when they rode under the Bar-W cross bar, with only a little band of fading light across the western horizon. There was a soft, orange glow of lamplight from the front window of the main house, and the smell of food cooking. The windmill turned lazily under a gentle breeze, and in the big corral the hundred-plus head of the remuda settled for the night. North of the main house, chained to a big cottonwood, a pair of hounds set up a wild baying, a lonesome sound, Howard thought, but warning, too, and turning almost frenzied as they came into the yard.

They spread out in front of the house, crowding the porch. Young sat in the center of the rough-shaped crescent, with Howard and Red on his left, and Jess and Jory next to them. Bronson sat on the far side of Young, bundled in a bearhide coat that added dimension to his already large frame, with Frosty Johnson beyond, looking cold and pathetic on a hammerheaded little buckskin with a knocked-down hip, and Roscoe Plumb on the far side of Johnson, drawn down into a sheepskin coat, his face stolid. The truth had hit him and Young hardest, Howard thought.

Smoke curled from the chimney and disappeared into the sky, and from the bunkhouse a guitar and harmonica beat out a fast tune.

The front door opened without any of them having called out, and Wyatt stepped outside, shrugging into a heavy coat. He pulled the door shut behind him, but not before Howard caught a glimpse of Wyatt's wife standing on the far side of the room and looking worried. Stepping to the edge of the porch, Wyatt let his gaze circle the men, then settle on Young. "What is this, Jim? You look like a vigilance committee."

"I guess maybe we are, Ben," Young said, looking like he was hurting somewhere, but couldn't understand why. "We've come to take you in. You'll have to stand trial in

Ogallala for conspiracy in rustling and murder, plus possibly fraud."

Wyatt looked almost amused. "Rustling? Murder? Fraud? What in God's name are you talking about?"

"It's all over, Ben. Jordache spilled everything."

Wyatt hitched himself straighter, hooking his thumbs in his belt, and looked again at the men before his porch, as if fixing them all in his mind. But when he spoke again, it was still to Young. "I think you'd better tell me what you're talking about, Jim. And what Jordache has to do with it. Those are some pretty strong accusations."

"My God, Ben, don't do this to yourself," Young cried, and the pain was there in his voice now, Howard thought. He looked at him. Young was bent over the horn, and his face was twisted with what might have been grief. "Hollis and the rustling, and your owning forty percent of the Dallas Land and Livestock Company. Jordache told it all, and it's over— the rustling, the land grabbing, the damn *killing*."

Wyatt stared at Young for a long time, the silence stretching while the band of light in the west faded and grew dark. When Wyatt finally nodded, all Howard could see was the dark bob of his head among the deeper shadows of the porch. Stepping into the yard, Wyatt looked toward the trees where the hounds still bayed, and said, "Put the rifle up, Jeff, and saddle my horse."

McKinley stepped from behind the tree with a rifle, and Bronson swore. McKinley headed for the barn without speaking, and Wyatt looked at Young. "I'll see my wife and children for a minute."

"You'll stay right here," Bronson warned. He brushed his coat back until his revolvers were handy to grab.

Wyatt looked coldly at Bronson. "You're a little beyond your jurisdiction, aren't you, Marshal?"

"Sam is here at my request," Young interrupted quickly. "He and Frosty are acting as advisers only. You'll be turned over to Leeds, as soon as we find him."

Wyatt snorted and turned, starting toward the house, but Young's voice stopped him again. "Why, Ben?" Young asked. "You already own the biggest ranch on the Sand Creek range."

Wyatt's smile was sad. "Haven't you seen what's happening out there, Jim? Free range is dying, and we will too, if we don't dig in. The grangers will move in faster than we can keep them out. For every boxcar of beef that we ship East, the railroad brings back a car full of immigrants. They'll be a worse plague than the grasshoppers before it's over."

"Homesteaders have as much legal claim to the land as anyone," Johnson said.

"Shut up, Johnson," Plumb growled.

Wyatt continued as if there hadn't been any interruption. "I guess I travel more than you, Jim. I get back East more, and I've seen this coming for a long time now. The East is creeping West, and it won't stop until it reaches the Rockies. Sometimes I wonder if it'll stop there anymore.

"When we came out here there wasn't much except Indians and buffalo. They're all gone now, and we will be too, if we don't fight it."

"Who are you fighting, Ben? Your neighbors?"

"I'm fighting for survival," Wyatt said harshly. "The barbed wire at Clark's is mine, and I've got more ordered. That's what it's coming to, Jim, and nobody can stop it."

Young sat back, looking rigid and maybe angry, though he didn't let his anger slip into his voice. "I'll fight for my range, Ben, but I'm not sure I'd be able to turn on my neighbors, my friends, if it came to that."

"If you don't, the Broken Axle won't have a thousand acres in ten years," Wyatt said flatly.

"I don't guess there's anymore to say," Young said quietly.

"We came here to do a job," Plumb added.

"You're under arrest, Ben," Bronson said. "You'll have to come with us."

Wyatt looked at Plumb, then back to Young. He started to

speak, then shut up and nodded. "I'll still need to speak with my family," he said. He turned to the porch.

Bronson drew his revolver, but Young reached out suddenly to still his hand. "Let him be, Sam. He has too much pride to run."

Well, Red thought, it was all winding down, all right. Doc and Pete and Barney dead, and Swede off who knew where, and Howard serious, after all, about hanging up his gun, and likely marrying to boot, and starting a ranch somewhere. Only himself left now to worry about. Only himself, with nowhere to ride, nowhere to go. No job now, either, and winter on the land for sure, with summer after that, and then another winter. He had thought of settling down, of course—what drifter didn't—but knew he wouldn't, or couldn't. He figured he was born to drift, like a tumbleweed, but a man still wondered about the future some. Could be that of the six, only Howard would be escaping, unless you called what Doc and Pete and Barney had found escape.

He and Howard stood alone on the boardwalk outside the marshal's office. Sand Creek lay quiet and cold, the street deserted this late, save for the horses tied up at the rail, and the surrey waiting at the livery. The night was like a gentle hand upon the town, pocked here and there with the yellow glow of lamplight outside a business, or shining from some window.

The street, rutted and torn and muddy through the day, was frozen hard, and the snow, drifted in the alleys and under the boardwalk, looked gray in the shadows, broken and littered and coated with a layer of soot that had settled from the chimneys. Off to the west, beyond Doc's grave, where the prairie turned wild and lonely, a coyote howled, breaking off into short yips that hung thin and wavering in the night. From the residential part of town a dog answered, his cries fading when he received no reply.

The sorrel stamped his hoof impatiently and blew a frosty

cloud into the air. Red loosened the reins and stepped into the saddle, holding the lead rope to Hollis's black in a gloved hand. He studied Howard for a moment, wondering if, now that the time had come to part, he would speak. He thought that with Howard it could go either way; his conscience was like sharp Mexican rowels that kept up a constant tickling.

Looking up then, Howard said, "You're riding on?"

"Maybe," Red said, and looked away so that Luke wouldn't see the relief on his face. "Kate sent word that she wants to see me at the Colorado Lady."

"She'll offer you a job."

"Yeah, I know. Might take it, too." He looked at Howard then, and smiled and nodded, embarrassed suddenly. "Well, watch yourself, Luke. And the lady."

He turned and rode away fast, rode away before Howard could reply, thinking that it was best that way.

There was still a light on inside the Colorado Lady, although the hitch rails were empty. He swung down and tied the sorrel and the black to the rail, and ducked under it, thinking he would go in for a quick drink and hear what Kate had to say, and if it sounded good, maybe take it for the winter. But if not, he would ride on. To the Hills, likely, and see what he could turn up. He figured there'd be plenty of opportunities for a man with a gun in the Hills come spring.

There were still a few customers inside despite the late hour, and Kate, sitting at her table with a bottle and a couple of glasses already there. She smiled and inclined her head and he started across to her, but a stranger suddenly stepped into his path, wearing a good corduroy coat and a damn serious expression.

"Tom Wheatherford?" the stranger asked.

For a moment, the first name threw him, then he laughed and said, "Yeah, I'm Tom Wheatherford."

"Mr. Wheatherford, I'm Eli Leeds, a United States Marshal

from Lincoln. I have a warrant for your arrest for the murder of Simon Washington."

For a moment, Leeds' words puzzled him, and he just waited with a smile still on his face. Then the meaning came and he reared back some, looking down and seeing for the first time the badge almost hidden behind the fur collar on Leeds' coat, and the revolver below that, drawn and cocked.

"I'm sorry, Mr. Wheatherford," Leeds said, indicating the revolver. "But you have something of a reputation, and I know my own abilities. I'm afraid they're not up to your standards. Please turn around and walk outside." He reached down and pulled the revolver from Red's holster.

Over Leeds' shoulder, Red saw Kate, her shoulders lifted in a shrug, and a tough-luck arch to her brows. Raising her glass of whiskey, she offered a silent salute as Leeds took his arm and escorted him from the room.

Howard stood in the thin light on the boardwalk in front of the marshal's office with his coat buttoned to the neck, his breath puffing out in small clouds around his face. Frost made little lace-edged designs on the window behind him that looked as fragile as the silence. Listening, he couldn't even hear the clop of Red's horses on the street anymore.

The door swung open behind him and Young stepped out, glancing toward the sky from habit. "Cold enough," he commented, pulling a pair of lined calfskin gloves from the pocket of his coat.

"Winter will pass. It always does."

Young nodded and busied himself with his gloves. "I was wondering," he said, without looking up, "if you had ever considered settling around Sand Creek? Robinson will be coming back to the Circle-R now that the bank doesn't have Jordache breathing down its neck, but the Wagon Wheel will go on public auction pretty soon now. I think if you wanted to bid on it, nobody around here would stand in your way."

The offer was sincere, Howard knew, but Sand Creek had

soured for him; he would never be satisfied living here, he needed a clean break from the past. "I'm obliged just the same," he replied. "But I was thinking of southern Colorado. There's land down there free for the taking yet."

"Not to hear some talk," Young said, then sighed. His next question caught Howard by surprise. "What do you know about the grangers down on the Grant, Luke?"

"Not too much." He remembered his conversation with Leeds. "The Washingtons are staying on, and they say there's another family moved in."

"And the Shatners?"

Howard shrugged. "They'll hang and rattle, I figure."

Young nodded thoughtfully. "I remember our first winter here. We lived in a tent right down on the creek, and even with a log windbreak and a good stove we like to froze. The first year is always the roughest."

Howard waited expectantly while Young stared south, though looking inward, Howard thought, to the past. After a spell, he said, "Reckon it wouldn't hurt to send one of the boys down to the Grant with a few extra head of beeves. Just enough to get them through the rough weather."

"Make it all the harder to move them out in the spring."

"Well, I never did use the Grant Creek range, even with a full herd." He looked at Howard and thrust a hand out awkwardly. "I'll see to your mares, then, Luke. Get yourself set up wherever you've a mind and come back and get them when you're ready."

"I'm obliged to you for that, too. I'll be back in early summer, at the latest." He dropped the rancher's hand, watching him mount and pull his horse into the middle of the street.

"Luck to you, then, Luke."

Howard nodded and waited until the rancher had disappeared down the street before mounting the bay and riding down to the livery. He dismounted behind the surrey and slipped a halter over the bay's head, tossing the bridle among the trunks and camping gear stowed in the surrey's rear box. He loosened the cinch, then came around the canvas hood and paused with his hands on the seat railing. Charity waited inside, wearing a heavy wool dress and a scarf over her head. She had a buffalo robe on her lap and pulled up around her shoulders, and her cheeks were flushed and spotted from the cold.

"Ogallala first?" he asked. "Find a minister, then on to Colorado?"

She smiled her reply and held the robe up for him to enter. He brought his boot to the carriage step, but she stopped him with a word. "Luke." Her eyes went to his gunbelt.

He stood back and looked at the heavy belt wrapped around the outside of his coat, so much a part of him for so long. Then he unbuckled it and wedged it under the seat, next to the Henry. He felt strange without it, naked almost, but free, too, free in a way he hadn't felt in a long time.